MW00639575

"Ava's story is witty and charming."

BARBARA FREETHY #1 *NYT* BESTSELLING
AUTHOR

"If you like Nora Roberts type books, this is a must-read."

READERS' FAVORITE

"If ever there was a contemporary romance that rated a 10 on a scale of 1 to 5 for me, this one is it!"

THE ROMANCE REVIEWS

"I could not stop flipping the pages. I can't wait to read the next book in this series."

FRESH FICTION

"I've read Susan Mallery and Debbie Macomber... but never have I been so moved as by the books Ava Miles writes."

BOOKTALK WITH EILEEN

OTHER AVA TITLES TO BINGE

The Paris Roommates

Your dreams are around the corner...

The Paris Roommates: Thea

The Unexpected Prince Charming Series

Love with a kiss of the Irish...

Beside Golden Irish Fields

Beneath Pearly Irish Skies

Through Crimson Irish Light

After Indigo Irish Nights

Beyond Rosy Irish Twilight

Over Verdant Irish Hills

Against Ebony Irish Seas

The Merriams Series

Chock full of family and happily ever afters...

Wild Irish Rose

Love Among Lavender

Valley of Stars

Sunflower Alley

A Forever of Orange Blossoms

A Breath of Jasmine

The Love Letter Series

The Merriams grandparents' epic love affair...

Letters Across An Open Sea

Along Waters of Sunshine and Shadow

The Friends & Neighbors Novels

A feast for all the senses...

The House of Hope & Chocolate

The Dreamer's Flower Shoppe

The Dare River Series

Filled with down-home charm...

Country Heaven

The Chocolate Garden

Fireflies and Magnolias

The Promise of Rainbows

The Fountain Of Infinite Wishes

The Patchwork Quilt Of Happiness

Country Heaven Cookbook

The Chocolate Garden: A Magical Tale (Children's Book)

The Dare Valley Series

Awash in small town fabulousness...

Nora Roberts Land

French Roast

The Grand Opening

The Holiday Serenade

The Town Square

The Park of Sunset Dreams

The Perfect Ingredient

The Bridge to a Better Life

The Calendar of New Beginnings

Home Sweet Love

The Moonlight Serenade

The Sky of Endless Blue

Daring Brides

Daring Declarations

AGAINST EBONY IRISH SEAS

THE UNEXPECTED PRINCE CHARMING BOOK 7

AVA MILES

www.avamiles.com
Ava Miles

As this book is the final in this series, I would like to dedicate it to the following:

To women of vision and grit like Bets;

To communities like Caisleán;

To reporters like Arthur Hale and my great-great grandfather Miles;

And to the wonderful man who inspired Liam and the unexpected Prince Charmings.

It's said Ireland is a land where you have to fight for everything.
Love most of all.

For generations, pirates ruled the Irish seas and often fought against those who would curtail people's freedoms and take what was not rightfully theirs. Times change, but like the seasons, those turbulent waters flow yet again onto Ireland's rocky shores. Those who stand for love and all that is good in the world face great odds.

As in legends, the seas have once again turned black, and those who would save all we hold so dear—those we love, the land on which we build, the very lives we choose, and the freedom to be—must stand against those ebony Irish seas.

For love and the preservation of all that is good restores the water's brilliant turquoise magic and makes those very shores the kind where couples and families desire to stroll.

Love must triumph.
And it is through love that the fight will be won.

CHAPTER ONE

S he was being paranoid.
    Taylor McGowan wanted to be swept away by the Irish countryside as she drove to her new job in charming Caisleán. The artist in her wanted to swoon at the endless verdant green fields, the wild yellow gorse blooming along the road, and the cerulean sky filled with puffy, dragon-shaped clouds.

Only...she was sure she was being followed.

"Didn't I tell you not to drive alone?"

She cried out sharply as the bane of her existence materialized in the passenger seat. Since being offered this job, she'd been stalked by the ghost of the woman whose name graced the new arts center where she'd be working as the media director.

The legends had gotten at least one thing right. Ireland *did* have ghosts, and somehow she'd been assigned one. Lucky her.

"Dammit, Sorcha!" She glanced over sharply at the "woman" decked out in a flowy white summer dress and bare feet. Her beautiful oval face was creased with a potent frown, a constant since Taylor had done her best to ignore her since she'd shown up in her Manhattan studio apartment. She'd had a harder time ignoring what Sorcha had told her: her soulmate was waiting for her in Ireland in the person of Liam O'Hanlon, the son of the arts center's founder.

Drop. The. Mike.

"Excited to meet Liam, aren't you?" Sorcha asked in her melodious lilt, flicking her flowing brown hair over her shoulder.

Know-it-all. For a month, this ghost had been popping up in Taylor's apartment, making smug comments as she researched everything she could on Liam O'Hanlon—because hey, she *was* a journalist. Considering the number of unexpected visits she'd gotten, they should have stopped surprising her, but when Sorcha popped up next to her while she was packing her last suitcase, preparing for the move, she'd nearly fainted.

"I'm so not talking to you," she ground out, clenching her hands on the wheel to keep herself grounded as she braked for another wild turn in the narrow road.

"You *are* being followed." Sorcha jerked her thumb toward the white truck keeping a fair distance behind her. "Since you left Dublin airport. Everyone knew you were coming today, so it wouldn't take much to put two and two together. JFK to Dublin flight. Your picture is online with your art and culture articles as well as your social media accounts. You should have let Bets and Linc pick you up."

Except Betsy O'Hanlon was Liam's mother!

She wasn't admitting this ghost knew anything about soulmates. Okay, sure, he looked like a hot pirate. Taylor's friend Sophie had sent her his picture from Caisleán. But he also unnerved her. According to Sophie, he had "the gift," and apparently he'd gotten a super psychic message with Taylor's name from the beyond while he was meditating. It had freaked Sophie out a little, and Taylor twice as much.

She didn't have a clue what to do with all of that, so she figured she'd prefer not to spend several hours in a car with his mother. That's why she'd told the founder of the Sorcha Fitzgerald Arts Center, Bets O'Hanlon, and her now partner in everything, billionaire Linc Buchanan, that she preferred to drive alone from Dublin and settle before meeting with them tomorrow.

Taylor looked in the rearview mirror again. Same white Berlingo. Same shrouded man with dark shades in the front seat. "Why would someone be following me?"

"*Seriously?* After everything you know about what my arts center has faced and who our enemies are?" Sorcha gestured in the air dramatically, which was really weird since she didn't technically have a body. To Taylor, she looked a little like the woman called the Blue Fairy in Walt Disney's *Pinocchio*. Her body glowed. Somehow. In a painting, Taylor would find it charmingly Madonna-like and beautiful. Only this ghost was no Madonna.

She was a soulmate-pushing pest.

But she had a point. Sophie had told her about all of the arts center's troubles, and so had Sorcha for that matter.

"So you're saying Malcolm Coveney, the corrupt politician from Watertown, sent one of his goons to follow me?" she asked.

"Intimidate you, more like." She pointed to Taylor's phone resting on the console so she could follow the online directions. "Call Linc. He has a new security officer for just such things. You can pull over at the next pub, have a pint, and wait for them to accompany you the rest of the way to Caisleán."

And look like some chump girl who couldn't handle herself on her first day? She was starting an important new job. She was not going to be a problem they needed to solve on a Saturday. "I'm here to handle things like this—"

"In the media," Sorcha broke in. "This is different. I respect independence in a woman, but you need help this time."

"I'll be fine." Taylor waved her off. "You don't know some of the spots I've been in doing my work."

Sure, the work she was referring to was hardly official—more of a Fort Knox secret she kept to herself—but that didn't mean she hadn't learned skills along the way to keep herself safe in dangerous situations.

Sorcha uttered a heartfelt shriek. "You leave me no choice."

With that eerie statement, she vanished.

Taylor took a deep breath and reviewed her plan. She would keep driving, obeying every traffic law in sight, and head straight to Caisleán. She eyed her navigation app. She only had another hour to go. The guy following her hadn't done anything for the past two hours. If he worked for the corrupt bully she'd researched, Malcolm Coveney, then they'd want her to be intimidated. Well, good luck with that. She'd been dealing with intimidation tactics since high school.

Cranking up her music seemed a good plan, so she flipped to her Jay-Z playlist and sang her heart out when "99 Problems" came on. She didn't even have close to that many problems. And some jerk in an ugly truck didn't warrant a place on the list.

Thirty minutes out of Caisleán she was feeling juiced.

Minion Jerk was keeping his distance. Her voice was getting stronger with her singing. And damn if the countryside wasn't getting more beautiful. There were mountains not far from her new home. Low ones, yeah, but they were gorgeous sweeping peaks with curves covered with trees and brush in earth tones that would have enticed Bob Ross, her personal hero.

The narrow roads weren't fun, especially since she wasn't used to driving on the left side, but she was almost there.

Then she spotted a portable red STOP sign in front of two black Mercedes parked in the middle of the road. There was no way around them. Taylor's pulse picked up. The only other cars on the road were hers and the truck behind her. Sorcha's concern blared an earsplitting alarm in her head.

She slowed down as she neared the roadblock, giving herself time to think. Three men in black leather jackets exited the first car, followed by another man in a long British formal coat from the second vehicle. She instantly recognized Malcolm Coveney. He was short with a large girth, gray hair, and overbleached teeth. She couldn't see the ten gold rings shot with diamonds he was known for wearing nor the curve of his sagging jowls, but she soon would. From the looks of it, he wanted to have a talk with her, and he'd brought a few of his minions to intimidate her as much as show her what a big man he was.

She hated men like Malcolm Coveney.

Pretending to be scared of him would only play into his whole predator/victim show, and if there was one thing Taylor McGowan wasn't, it was a victim.

She put her Audi in park but purposely left the car running. The truck stopped behind her, boxing her in, but the driver stayed in his car. Pulse hammering, she swung out her phone, tapping the Live video option on her professional Facebook page to start a transmission.

"Malcolm Coveney!" she called out as she started walking at a good clip toward him, making sure her boots pounded on the road. "I'd planned on asking for an interview when I got more settled into my new job at the Sorcha Fitzgerald Arts Center, but seeing as you're here on this quiet country road blocking the way for a reason I'm sure is legit, I'd love to ask you some questions."

Shock rippled over his moon-shaped face as she held up her phone and pointed the camera at him. His minion with the square head and beefy chest started toward her.

"My video is streaming live on Facebook, FYI," she told the jerk.

That didn't stop him, which had her planting her feet. "That means anything you do to me will be seen by my thousands of followers and can be used as police evidence. I understand there's a new head of the Garda—"

"Only in Caisleán," Malcolm called out in an arrogant tone. "That's thirty minutes away. Isn't it a coincidence that me and my employees both had a vehicle breakdown right as you were coming down this road?"

She knew all about lies and the men who wielded them to do bad things. After all, those seeds had given a start to her secret life when she was a teenager. "I'd say the odds are about like us flying off to Jupiter today, wouldn't you?"

His smile was now eerily wide over his overbleached teeth. "Not at all. That's Ireland for you. It's a small world where everyone knows everyone else and their business. I'm glad you seem to know mine, Ms. McGowan. I look forward to our next meeting. Call my office anytime for an interview."

Her smile was as fake as his. "Thank you. I wasn't sure if you wanted anyone asking you questions about what it feels like to have such international support for an arts center you tried to move to your own hometown of Watertown through tactics that could be perceived by some as outright corrupt and coercive."

His mouth took a severe line. "I don't know what you mean. You're a media director now, Ms. McGowan. Not a journalist. Your time in Ireland will be much happier if you remember that."

She gave him unflinching stare. "Is that a threat, Malcolm?"

His chuckle raised goose bumps on her skin under her green sweater. "Not at all, Taylor. Haven't you heard about Irish hospitality? I was only giving you some advice on how to make your stay a magical one."

There wasn't a shovel big enough for his bullshit. "You're a sweetheart, aren't you? But just so you know...I'm not a fan of roses. I'd heard you sent one to Linc Buchanan and Betsy O'Hanlon recently, but it was already dead."

His smile turned wolfish. "Perhaps the florist made an error."

"Care to tell me which florist?" she volleyed back. "I want to make sure I don't use them, of course, being new and all."

His mouth curved. "I send so many gifts—"

"Being the generous man you are," she interrupted, knowing powerful men despised that.

"Indeed, which is why I'm afraid I don't recall." He crossed his arms and regarded her silently.

The chill of the October afternoon seemed to invade her bones, and she fought a full body shiver as he swept his eyes over her. God, he was a creep—and a dangerous one.

He'd back his words up with action, and boy, did he like intimidating women. She recognized his type. God knew, she'd faced plenty of them before.

Maybe it was the hint of danger in the air, but everything crystalized for her. She'd come to Ireland for a meaningful new job. And sure, she was curious about this guy an Irish ghost insisted was her soulmate. But now she had a new reason for being here, one that made her blood race.

She was going to take Malcolm Coveney down if it was the last thing she did, and she knew just how to do it.

"Men like you often don't recall," she shot back, "but I don't think it's because of your age. What about you?"

"Insulting me will only make our time together on the road more unpleasant as we wait for my cars to be fixed."

She fought another chill. "Then I guess I'll have to back up and find another way to Caisleán."

The engine of the truck behind her car went silent. Malcolm shook his head. "Seems he has engine trouble too. Maybe we all were the unfortunate purveyors of bad diesel. It happens in Ireland."

That was some story...and this showdown was going nowhere fast.

The roar of a fast-approaching motorcycle reached her ears. Malcolm and his minions whipped their heads around and then darted out of its way as it carved a path between the two parked cars. The rider swung the bike in a circle between Taylor and the roadblock and cut the engine. Then he slammed the kickstand down and threw his leg over the bike, walking toward her, a long line of male attitude in a black motorcycle jacket and dark jeans.

The energy around him was palpable, the electricity in the air before a thunderstorm. His black boots slapped against the pavement in time with her heartbeat. And then he stopped right in front of her, pulling off his helmet. All she could focus on was the brilliant light in his intense leaf-green eyes before his features registered and her heart tripped into a new gear.

Liam!

"I'm Bets' son, Liam O'Hanlon," he announced in a deep baritone voice, his gaze sweeping over her face. "I heard you might need a friend. Are you all right, *a stór?*"

She smelled oranges—the scent which often surrounded Sorcha—and imagined the ghost wasn't very far away. So this was where she'd gone off to.

Suddenly breathless, Taylor tried to smile to reassure him. But she was aware of their audience. "I'm fine." Her gaze tracked to the beefy minion heading toward Liam.

A surge of wild protectiveness shot through her. "Hey, you! You're basically on TV, remember? Malcolm, call off your goon. Right now."

Liam was already setting his weight. "I can—"

"Clodagh was just coming over to greet Mr. O'Hanlon appropriately," Malcolm lied with a nefarious smile.

She snorted. "And you and I were just having a pleasant chat on an empty road with your four goons ready to bring us tea and biscuits after everyone's cars simultaneously broke down. Right, Malcolm?"

Liam took up a position beside her, nearly shoulder to shoulder, as Malcolm opened the back door of his sedan. One of his minions got in and started the car after his signal. "Isn't that a bit of Irish luck? The car starting like that. But don't worry, I'll have my mechanic look into the issue. Next time we *must* have tea and biscuits. Liam, give my best to your mother and Linc. And all the residents of Caisleán. I can't wait for our next encounter. Taylor... It was most enlightening."

AVA MILES

Car doors slammed as they left, nearly making her flinch. Then she walked to the STOP sign and hefted it to the side of the road, kicking it down for good measure with her boot.

Aware of Liam eyeing her every move, she walked back to him with a smile. "Give me a moment."

The truck driver must have understood her intent as she angled her camera down to document his license plate. He started his engine again and honked at her, but she only grinned as she zoomed in on his face before heading for his door. She motioned for him to roll down his window. He shook his round head briskly before she rapped on the window. When he finally did as she'd asked, she held up the camera and said, "Care to tell me why you followed me all the way from the Dublin airport?"

His smug expression told her she'd get nowhere. "Miss, you're mistaken."

"I can pull the video feed from the airport and place you there," she told him in a hard tone. "Do you want to admit Malcolm Coveney asked you to follow me so he'd know where to set up a roadblock?"

"Yeah, Denis," Liam called out. "Tell Taylor why a recently fired Garda officer from Caisleán would be following a new employee at the arts center you tried to shut down."

Ah, she'd heard about this guy. "Got a new employer, Denis? Or simply coming out of the closet about working for Malcolm all along?"

"I don't know what you're talking about," he protested angrily. "I was picking something up."

Bullshit.

"Then you wouldn't mind opening your truck and showing me, would you?"

"Miss, I need to get home to the wife and kids."

Sure he did. "Denis, I'll have the new Garda officer question you—"

He suddenly reversed his truck, grinding the gears in his haste, and then he was heading off in the other direction like the hounds of hell were after him.

"Guess he didn't like your questions, Taylor."

She turned around and clicked her camera off, her now tired arms falling to her sides. She gazed at Liam—the man Sorcha had told her was her soulmate. Her soulmate! It was all too weird. But she suddenly wanted to walk over and hug him—for coming as much as to calm herself down. Thinking Malcolm's beefy goon was going to hurt him had scared her out of her wits.

"Thanks for coming. I've never had a Prince Charming show up unexpectedly."

And what a Prince Charming, although in truth, he looked more like a rakish pirate, standing in that sexy wide-legged male stance with a gold earring winking in his left ear. His sandy blond hair was long enough to tangle her fingers in and so thick she could already feel it brushing against her hot skin. He was tall and lean and all muscle, but it was those green eyes that held her spellbound. They were warm, interested, and filled with a dancing light she could only describe as delight. Like he was happy to see her.

His mouth curved, driving home the attraction she'd felt for him every time she'd looked at a photo of him. Only this time, he was here in the flesh—and all man. Powerful. Potent. And so heart-stoppingly gorgeous every molecule inside her grew supercharged. If he was her soulmate, she had won the jackpot because everything in her wanted to jump him and not let go.

"You looked like you were handling things just fine." He

walked closer, steady as a rock. "Still, it's good to have friends. Especially with the likes of Malcolm around. Denis too. Smart of you to video the encounter."

"Actually, I live streamed it on Facebook. I figured one of his goons might try and take the phone out of my hands and delete the video otherwise."

His mouth went downright grim. "So your wits saved you from some roughhousing. That doesn't please me at all. It certainly won't please the others at the arts center. I'm sorry I wasn't here sooner."

Was she supposed to ask how he'd known?

Then she smelled oranges again. Oh, to hell with it. "Let's start over. I'm Taylor, and you're Liam, and Sorcha—whom I'm sure you know—tells me we're soulmates. Any comment?" she asked, holding her hand out like she was interviewing him for live TV.

His gorgeous mouth transformed into a rich smile before he threw back his head and laughed, the sound a glorious rumble of masculinity that ignited something in her belly. "I'd scare you a bit if I told you all the comments I have swirling inside my head right now. So perhaps you'll let me buy you a drink instead?"

That was a start she could handle. "I'd love that, Liam. But I'm letting you know now: I might need two. It's been a day."

"For me too." Then he held out his hand.

She didn't know what to do with it. Shake it? Only when she extended her hand, he took it in a gentle clasp. The electricity around him jumped up her arm and stilled everything inside her. All she could see was the warmth in his fathomless green eyes. A breezy calm pervaded her, like the kind on a beach vacation. Suddenly she was happy—for no reason at all.

Then he started to let her go, so achingly slow. She almost tightened her grip on his fingertips. His touch was as powerful as he was, and she wanted to dive into these feelings. A rarity for her normally cautious self.

"Welcome home, Taylor."

The scent of oranges surrounded her, and she felt a presence behind her. She looked over her shoulder at Sorcha.

And for the first time ever, she could only smile at the pesky ghost.

CHAPTER TWO

Taylor didn't know it, but he'd already started their life together.

After meditating in the early morning, he'd signed his new long-term job contract with the arts center as its construction director. He'd been building sheds and doing various odd jobs as needed, but now they were moving into bigger projects like the museum and hotel. The board had wanted someone they knew and trusted at the helm, someone who had supported the center from the beginning. Someone they knew would fight to keep the arts center open at all costs like the rest of them.

He'd been thrilled to accept the offer, one perfectly aligned with Taylor's arrival. He wanted to be a complete partner, emotionally and financially. This job wasn't simply about providing, although at some point they would need a home. It was about being an equal.

He'd waited to sign the agreement until the day she was arriving, believing it was good energy to do so. She had come to Ireland for her job, and now his job supported hers, further weaving their lives together.

He'd marked this day as one of the most incredible in their lives already in his mind.

And then Sorcha had appeared to him and scared him to his very bones. Taylor was in danger. He needed to get to her immediately. He'd dropped everything, asking the wind to propel him as fast as he could and keep other cars out of his way. And when he'd reached her, the sight of Malcolm Coveney and four goons stalking her, blocking her way—on a public road for God's sake—planning on doing God knows what, had unleashed an anger he'd never known.

Liam let the wind rush over him, breaking up the remaining anger and fear inside him. They were lucky Taylor was so quick on her feet. He'd never have thought to start a live video stream.

She was brilliant, with a sound and canny mind. And beautiful, what with her auburn hair, creamy skin, and big brown eyes. The way she carried herself marked her as a confident, no-nonsense person, which only heightened the appeal of her enticing slender form, marked by curves he couldn't wait to appreciate. He had sealed with their touch what he'd already sealed in his heart when he'd first sensed she was coming months ago.

She was his.

Yet by the time they'd reached the pub he'd settled upon, he was fighting with the urge to text his mother and Linc about what had happened. He would have to, he knew. But now that she was here, he really wanted this moment alone with her. He'd sensed she needed to relax after what had happened, which was why he'd chosen a nearby pub instead of the Brazen Donkey in Caisleán, where the whole village would pounce. Not only to welcome her but because of what had happened on the road.

Everyone had been surprised—Sophie especially—

when Taylor had insisted on driving herself from Dublin to Caisleán and calling it an early night. Only he understood, sensing her moods and emotions already, since her energy was open to him in meditation. It had been since he'd first felt a glimmer of something, when he'd been feeling called to Paris, not knowing exactly why.

Now he knew Taylor had been there at the time before briefly returning to Manhattan to regroup. But more signs hadn't arrived until Sophie had reached out to Taylor to ask for a feature after she'd arrived at the arts center and unveiled her plans to do a pregnant goddess glass figure, who also happened to be nude, causing a backlash from their adversaries, his aunt Mary especially.

Then he'd felt her being—even heard her name in meditation—something that still freaked out some of his American friends. His Irish friends were long accustomed to his gifts, but then again, in Ireland the language of gifts was as normal as the language of Gaelic, although both were facing the impact of modern progress with all its cynicism. Still, he was grateful for his connection to the other side. Never more than today.

He parked his bike and stowed his helmet as she pulled into the space next to him in the parking lot.

"Cows and Cocks?" She gestured to the pub sign after exiting the car. "I fear this isn't a very farm-friendly bar given it's depicting an Orwellian farm scene. I admit to being surprised given what I've read about the primacy of agriculture in this part of Ireland."

Brilliant, hadn't he said? He would be able to share books with her. Bandy around ideas. The Universe knew what he needed, and for that he gave a moment of thanks before saying, "We Irish love satire. Especially with animals. Ask any farmer who runs the roost. When you watch a sheep farmer give one a merry chase, you'll see why."

"Speaking of sheep... You guys might have the best ones around. I can't wait to see the now internationally famous Kindness Sheep by Keegan O'Malley. Who would have thought to spray positive words on sheep?" She slung an oversized leather purse higher over her shoulder. "The world needs that kind of positivity. Now more than ever."

"On that we agree." He reached his hand out again, wanting to strengthen their connection. "Come on. Let me buy you that drink."

She eyed his hand before taking it, the electricity between them making her jerk at first in surprise. He felt it too, of course. Their chemistry was off the charts, as it should be.

This time he didn't let it go. They walked into the pub like that, hand in hand. The regulars he knew looked up and shouted out a greeting, which he returned. But wanting to chat with Taylor, he led her quickly to a booth in the corner.

"You didn't take me to the Brazen Donkey," she commented as she glanced around at the nicked mahogany bar and tables, the red-backed chairs, and the kitschy Irish beer and whiskey signs on the walls. "Not that I mind. I mean, all over the world Irish bars tend to look and feel the same. It's a comfort somehow. There's one in Manhattan I'm especially fond of. Best car bombs ever."

Being the son of two former bartenders, he knew the bubbling drink that came of a shot glass of whiskey being dropped into a pint of beer. "Best not order that in Ireland though, as it brings up bad memories of the past."

Her brown eyes widened. "Right. Sorry. Shit. Whiskey neat shouldn't get me into trouble."

"Not at all." He stood. "I'll grab our drinks, but first I need your thoughts on something."

Unease filtered into her eyes. "Yes?"

"I'm going to need to text my mom and Linc about what happened on the road. Especially with the live streaming."

"Yeah, someone might have seen that. Sophie follows me."

Liam did too, but he remained silent on that matter. Later he would watch the full exchange.

"Go on and text them, but could I ask a favor?" She winced. "First, I should say that I should have listened to Sorcha when she told me not to be stubborn about driving up on my own. I did it because... Oh, shit, I can't believe I'm admitting this, but all the cats seem to be out of the bag now. Can you please tell your mother not to treat me all weird if she happens to think I'm your soulmate?"

He bit the inside of his cheek. "She knows, but she hasn't said anything to me outright. Yet. But I'll talk to her and give her the business if I need to. We all want you to be comfortable. Me most of all."

She blew out a breath and gave him a wry smile. "Thank you. It's weird, talking about this. But it would feel even weirder not to talk about it."

He laughed softly. "I agree, and I'm glad it's on the table. Besides, I know Sorcha—who she was and who she is now. She's strong-minded, but her heart is in the right place."

"Is it true she helped bring Sophie and Jamie together?" She covered her eyes for a moment like she was hiding. "After Sorcha appeared in my studio apartment in Manhattan and said she was there on Sophie's advice, the first thing I did—after freaking out—was call Sophie and ask about it. She seems to believe Sorcha has special powers in matchmaking."

Clearing his throat, he sat back down. "I'd say it's more a mission. She wanted to thank us all for helping Carrick, her husband, after she died. It was a hard time—for all of us. He was the one who started putting words on his sheep, actually. In the beginning, the words were from her poems. It was his way of keeping her around him. Keegan took over when Carrick finally let her go and found love again."

"That's an incredible story." She touched his arm briefly. "I can't imagine, losing someone so young and vibrant. I've read her poetry—not that I plan to tell her—and it shows a big, bold heart in beautiful prose. But you're right. She's downright pushy about you and me. I have to ask: do you really believe we're soulmates?"

He met her gaze straight on. "I have my own gifts. I knew before Sorcha said anything. In fact, today was the first time she'd appeared to me about you, although I had a feeling something was off before she showed up."

Her brows shot straight to her hairline. "What did she tell you?"

"That you were in trouble and to jump on my bike straightaway." He imagined he would still have some bad moments, thinking about Sorcha's urgent call. He'd been angry, yes, but it was the fear that would haunt him.

"I'm glad you came. Now, I really need that drink."

"Coming right up."

He walked to the end of the bar away from the regulars and ordered, pulling out his phone to text his mother and Linc. He phrased the message carefully.

I'm with Taylor after a surprise visit from Sorcha.
Malcolm stopped her on the road thirty minutes out of

Caisleán. She handled it with aplomb. You can watch it on her Facebook page. PLEASE let her settle tonight. Plenty of time to discuss it tomorrow. Now I'm getting us a drink and turning my phone off. I've got her, okay?

Their drinks arrived as he stowed his phone. He could all but hear his mother's shriek as she read the message. News would travel fast. Linc had known Malcolm was readying his next attack. No one had imagined it would be this bold. He shut the thought down. Worrying wouldn't do any good, and he wanted his first moments with Taylor to be special.

"Your drink," he said, placing it in front of her with a flourish as he took in her casual beauty of no makeup, a loose green sweater, and jeans. "*Sláinte.*"

"Cheers," she said before taking a sip. "Downing it seems irresponsible, especially with the drive."

"I can take you home if need be," he told her, sipping his drink as well.

"No, I need my suitcase. After a transatlantic flight, all I want is a shower."

He nodded, making sure to keep his thoughts clean. "Are you hungry? They serve some decent bites here."

"My stomach isn't flip-flopping anymore, so that would be great. I hadn't thought about food tonight."

"We did a little shopping for you. I should warn you. There are a few welcome gifts too." His included. Not that he was going to say a word more. He wondered if she would. The idea had come to him in meditation, and it wasn't what he'd call a normal welcome gift. It had surprised him, but he knew she wanted it. Would love it, in fact. He couldn't wait to discover more about why. There was nothing about it on her social media pages.

The bartender came over when he beckoned him, and after securing menus, they ordered some food. She *was* hungry given her order, which was encouraging. Of course, he'd done his best to calm her energy down when she'd taken his hand on the road. He'd always had that gift as well as his others.

"So..." She traced a long scratch on the table's surface like she would a river on a map. "You have gifts. What's that like?"

He kicked back and sipped his whiskey, soaking in her presence. She leaned forward as she waited for his response, so active and alive she was like the first punch of spring. He could see why she was a good journalist. "In Ireland, it's not as strange as in the United States. I'm half-American, so I know how my mother's family views it. Pretty weird."

She nodded. "What do these gifts entail exactly?"

"I can see spirits like Sorcha and sense things. Like where someone died and how."

"Trippy," she said choppily. "That doesn't scare you?"

He shrugged. "When I was a kid, it was a little weird to wake up at night and see someone in my room. My dad had the gift, so he helped me see there was nothing to be afraid of. And he told me if a spirit ever did seem threatening, I could stomp my foot and tell him or her to leave. Now I don't need to. I have a better way of getting out spirits and negative energy. The place where I live—Summercrest Manor—used to be haunted. It isn't now." He waggled his brows, hoping to make her laugh.

She only continued to stare at him. "Incredible. I visited the cemetery in Sleepy Hollow, New York, one time and flipped out when I felt something touch my arm. I almost ran out screaming."

An interesting experience, he thought, and not one

every person had. "What did you do when you first saw Sorcha?"

She laughed. "I grabbed a knife and told her to get the hell out. Later, I fainted like a wuss."

"After she told you we were soulmates." His lips twitched.

She made a cute face. "Yep. Fainted dead away. In shock."

"I'm glad you aren't scared anymore, Taylor." He looked up as the bartender brought their food. "Smells good."

She sniffed the air after thanking the bartender, who gratefully didn't use the opportunity to chat Taylor up about who she was. Ireland was Ireland, after all. Liam imagined the news would get around soon enough. It always did.

"All I can smell now is oranges," she said, picking up a slider and taking a bite. "Sorcha's way of telling us she's around. Good thing the smell has a good memory attached to it for me. It reminds me of orange Life Savers candy that our doorman used to sneak me."

Taylor's story had him smiling. He could suddenly see her as a kid, adorable, of course, and kind and connected even then. "Like I said, she's strong-minded. Not one to back down."

"Has she ever been wrong?" she asked as she picked up a fry.

He was learning she didn't always appear to be watching when she asked a very direct question. She feigned disinterest at the answer, but she was actually intensely interested. "No."

She tried to disguise the audible release of her breath as she tapped a French fry against her lips. He was trying hard not to look at her lips, especially at her full and luscious bottom lip. Keeping things light at first seemed prudent. He hadn't expected her to call out what Sorcha had told her, but taking a direct approach clearly helped her feel in control. She liked calling the shots. And she didn't beat around the bush. He rather liked that.

"So what does that mean then?" She tapped her fry on her plate—this time until it broke in two. "I'm going to just fall in love with you instantly and want to be with you forever? Come on... You have to admit that's pretty crazy."

Since directness was something they both favored, he asked, "Are you really telling me you don't feel anything for me? Not even attraction?"

She gave his shoulder a gentle shove. "Of course I do. I mean, look at you. Hot pirate meets yoga dude. Gold earring. Sandy hair. Body like a Greek god. Totally chill. Who wouldn't want you?"

He bit the inside of his lip to keep from laughing. He hated to admit she had him pegged. "Then that's where we start. If you want. It's your choice, Taylor. Mine too. Even when a ghost says something."

"It's important to choose," she said quietly. "It's not that I don't want to believe her. But it has to be my idea. And yours, of course. Otherwise, it's never going to work. I'll start feeling resentful and push back and..."

When she trailed off, he leaned forward. "And what?"

She looked off for a moment, visibly emotional, before she met his eyes straight on. "Walk away. I do when I have to. Always."

He could hear all the pain behind those words. The hurt was so tangible, he could feel the breaks in her heart. "Walking away has made you happier even though it caused you great pain. But it opened up another whole life for you, didn't it? One where you got to do what you truly wanted.

Including being here. Because Taylor, everything you've done—every choice you've made—has led you to Ireland."

To me.

"Jeez!" She threw down the mangled fry. "What's it like reading minds?"

"I don't read minds, per se," he answered carefully. "I sense things. Strongly."

That wary look returned. "*Everything* about me?"

He reached for her hand. "No. I want you to tell me about yourself, although there are times when information comes through. Visions. Emotions. Messages."

She let go of his hand, a clear withdrawal. "I'm not sure I completely like that answer, although I appreciate the sentiment. I'm usually the one interviewing people and analyzing what I hear for the world to read. It's strange to be on the other end. Uncomfortably so."

Trust would have to built, but he didn't want her to fear his gifts. "It's just who I am. Although, yeah, some of my friends call me Yoda because of it."

"*Yoda?*" Her laughter was like Christmas bells. "You're way too hot for Yoda."

"Thank you. And Taylor... You can ask me anything you want. Anytime."

"Noted." She plucked up another fry and popped it in her mouth. "I'll start compiling my questions."

"Good." He pointed to her empty glass. "Something else?"

She shook her head. "Nah. Better not. Makes the jet lag worse after being so dehydrated from the plane."

Since her water glass was also empty, he pushed his toward her. "Drink mine. It's getting busier, so our bartender might not top us up quickly. And then we'd better get you to your new home."

"My mobile home palace fortified like a compound." She stretched her arms overhead, the sight making his mouth go dry with want. "I can't wait for the space. In my Manhattan studio, I could lean over and brush my teeth in the sink. I'm imagining doing yoga without hitting my elbows on any of the furniture."

"Need a yoga mat?" he asked, which made her smile.

"Got one you can offer me, huh?" she replied, downright flirty.

The energy arced between them. "Uh-huh."

"Ever teach it?" She reached over to touch his bicep and squeezed. "I wasn't joking about you looking like a yogi. Lean *and* ripped. Very hot."

"Glad you think so. Also, you can join me anytime for yoga." Joy shot through him at the thought. Yoga was something special to him, something few around Caisleán really understood.

"Maybe." Her smile was that of a minx. "I have to get up to speed with my new job, which hopefully won't be overshadowed by my earlier chat with Malcolm. Just how upset were Linc and your mother when you texted them?"

"I don't know." He grimaced. "I told her I had you and was turning my phone off. I might have also included a plea to let you settle in. Of course, she and Linc will be upset. Everyone will be. We take these kinds of threats very seriously. It's been incredible to see the kind of jealousy, hate, and avarice an arts center could bring out in some folks. My aunt included."

"Yeah, I've been briefed on her." She started counting on her fingers. "Fixed rose competitions. Harassment at people's homes. County interference. And hateful signs and calls for censorship. How are you related to a woman like that?"

27

He still didn't know what had broken Aunt Mary, and he truthfully didn't care anymore. She'd gone too far. "She's my father's sister. As to the other, I don't know. Only she's been that way as long as my mother has been in Ireland. Clearly you can handle yourself, but you aren't going to want to underestimate her. Start live streaming if you see her coming. And don't let her in through your gates."

"That was my plan." She touched his sleeve, fingering the hem, all the while gazing at him with her big brown eyes. "You worried about me, Liam?"

His heart sped up a little, answering for him. "Yeah. I know we've only just met, but I care about you. I want you to be safe, Taylor. More, I want you to be happy. And if I thought it would help, I'd camp outside the gate to your compound tonight just to make sure."

"That's really sweet, and again, unexpected." She took a sharp breath. "Although if I were open to having you around, I'd suggest the couch. I knew how cold October would be here, but experiencing it is different. It's the kind of cold that chills the bones, isn't it?"

The couch comment was progress enough. "I'm used to it, but the Yanks say it's winter cold. Do you have your phone? You should have my number. In case you need anything."

She dug it out, biting back a smile. "Not because you want to ask me out?"

"I *was* planning on asking you to let me take you around tomorrow and show you some sights, perhaps followed by ice cream or dinner. Your choice."

"Can we take your bike?" She leaned in conspiratorially. "I have to admit my heart sighed a little seeing your Triumph. Liam O'Hanlon, you have good taste in bikes."

He wanted to rub his hands together at yet another boon. "Do you ride?"

"I do on vacation sometimes. Italy. France—"

"Bali too, right?" Suddenly he could see her in the turquoise water with her arms raised to the sky.

She closed her mouth smartly before replying, "Yeah. Bali. I'm really going to have to get used to that. You strike me as a Bali kind of guy. Ever been?"

"Eight years ago. It's where I learned pottery."

Her laughter was belly deep and all the richer for it. "Of course you did. I'll bet she was hot and also dabbled in yoga and ate hemp burgers."

"My preference for steak was the straw that broke us apart, alas." He pressed a hand to his heart dramatically. "But truly, Taylor, it ended because she wasn't my soulmate. Every woman up until now, I've known she wasn't it."

She nudged him gently in the shoulder again. "Well, jeez, Liam, never say Sorcha upstages you in dropping the proverbial mike. Shall we go? I'm running out of witty ripostes."

He rose to go and pay the check. "You don't need any ripostes with me, Taylor. All I want is who you are. *All* of who you are."

That guarded look entered her eyes again before he headed for the bar. When they left the pub, the sun had set. The sole halogen light in the lot illuminated two tickets tucked against their windshields. He plucked his as she snatched hers.

"A parking ticket!" She waved it in the air after holding it in the light. "Malcolm said we were far from Caisleán and its new Garda. I guess he had to drill the point home."

Liam grew more concerned. Malcolm had arranged for an officer of the law to harass them in a public parking lot without just cause. "Let's take some pictures. It might not help matters, but we'll want to keep a record of his behavior."

She dug out her phone and started taking photos while he took out his and beamed his torch in her direction.

"You know..." he said as she tucked her phone back in her purse. "Your couch is looking better than ever now."

Her body stilled. "That's too fast for me. I can't let that happen, Liam. Not even to make you feel better."

He took a moment to answer. "I understand not wanting to let fear—or any other negative emotion—control you. But perhaps look at it the way I do. It's another good reason to be around a friend."

She walked over until she was standing in front of him. "But we both know you aren't only my friend."

The words hovered between them, shot through with sparks of attraction.

"I'm not ready for that yet." She rested her hand on his chest briefly. "But I promise to text you if I need anything. Besides, we have Sorcha to run back and forth between us. That's gotta be worth something."

It would be, but when he dropped her off later in front of her house, he was reluctant to leave.

She thanked him for taking her luggage inside the foyer but didn't invite him to linger, so he stepped out again. "We'll do a movie night some other time," she said, almost as if to soften her need for space.

"You like movies?"

"Love them!" Her face seemed to light up. "I like a good story. I won't just watch garbage."

She was full of craic. "What about *Jaws*?"

"Who doesn't like a man versus nature classic? It's one

of the best. Although *Moby Dick* with Gregory Peck is pretty damn satisfying."

"I haven't seen that one." He couldn't help but grin at the prospect of the endless number of dates before him with Taylor. "It's going to be fun. *This*. Getting to know each other. Are you sure you don't need anything? I find I'm having trouble stepping away from you."

She swallowed thickly. "You look all manly, and then you go for complete vulnerability. It's a killer combo, Liam. One I really like. Honesty means a lot to me."

No, it was stronger than that. The word *truth* came to mind. But a truth that came out of the darkness. He stopped the vision, sensing she was waiting for him to reply. "I'm an open book. Ask anyone."

Her flinch made him want to reach out to her, but she'd communicated her need for space.

"That's good." She opened her arms as if trying to explain something. "I'm not perfect. Ask anyone."

A confusing reply. "I don't want perfect, *a stór*. I'll leave you now. Get some rest."

"Do I need to make sure you aren't going to sleep in front of my gate?" she called out as he walked to the motorcycle.

"No, but I'll feel better once you set the house alarm."

"First thing," she told him. "The instructions are in my briefing package."

He knew. He'd helped put it together, just as he'd overseen the installation of the alarm itself. "I'm glad you're here, Taylor."

Their eyes met and held. He could almost feel the strong pulse of her heart across the short distance between them. Emotion rippled over her throat yet again. Yes, she felt the pull between them as much as he did.

"I'm happy to be here too, Liam. I'll see you tomorrow. Good night."

"Good night, Taylor."

She paused before heading inside.

Leaving her alone was one of the hardest things he'd ever had to do. Yet as he left, he used one of his other gifts. He called in extra protection for her and her home from every fairy, leprechaun, god and goddess, and angel he could think of.

But seeing Sorcha visible in the dark beside the gates as they closed gripped him hard as he thundered away.

CHAPTER THREE

B ets was out Summercrest Manor's front door the moment she heard the growl of Liam's motorcycle.

Linc was right behind her, probably along with everyone else who'd been holding vigil. If she wasn't so angry, her knees might have given out in relief at seeing him safe and sound. His text had scared the shit out of her, and it hadn't mattered that the incident was over before he'd sent it. She'd flipped out.

"Taylor's not with you?" she asked after he killed the engine in the driveway, a tall line of black in the shadow of the outside lights.

"Mom, I told you," he said as he secured the bike and took off his helmet, "I had her, and now she's at home."

"But Malcolm Coveney went after her today!" Bets gripped his arm and scanned his dear face, knowing he'd be as upset as she was, with Taylor being his soulmate and all. "Liam—"

He pulled her to him and simply rocked her. "I know you're scared, but she handled it like a pro. I didn't want to leave her, but she needed some time to herself. She's in the house with the alarm armed, and she has my cell—"

"I still think we should go over there." She dug her forehead into his chest. "Liam, she could have gotten hurt. So could you. When I saw that one jerk go for you... Malcolm had *four* guys with him, Denis included."

"Yeah, seems Denis is on the payroll officially full-time now," Linc said, finally making his large presence known with his Southern drawl.

Liam turned Bets until she fit into the comforting curve of his arm. "Linc, I told Taylor we'd talk about all this tomorrow. I figured you'd do what you can in the meantime."

"Already being looked into." Linc rubbed the back of his neck. "Our new Garda officer has the link to Taylor's live feed. I imagine he'll want to follow up with both of you."

Bets looked over her shoulder when she heard a baby cry. Angie had come out of the house with Emeline, followed by the others. Everyone connected to the arts center had responded to the call, worried about the newest sign of aggression. They'd all gathered at Summercrest to wait for Liam—Angie and Carrick, Donal and Ghislaine, Eoghan and Sandrine, Sophie and Jamie, and of course the two couples who lived here with Liam—Brady and Ellie and Declan and Kathleen. Sophie, as a longtime friend of Taylor's, was particularly concerned.

"You guys here for a party?" Liam called out in a bad joke. "Seriously, Taylor is fine."

"Yeah, she just texted me," Sophie said, rushing across the lawn. "I was sick with worry the moment Bets contacted everyone. I mean, I know Taylor is a strong woman—"

"She was as cool as a cucumber," Eoghan said with a pronounced lilt, coming forward with an agility Bets hoped she had at the ripe age of ninety-four. "Malcolm didn't expect her to go on the offensive. We're lucky she was quick on her feet."

"That's why you hired her as the media director," Ghislaine added, holding Donal's hand as everyone circled them, worry etched on their faces.

"We've seen a lot of lows in people's attempts to shut the arts center down, but this is a new one," Donal said gravely. "God knows what might have happened if Taylor hadn't handled herself."

Bets' mind had been spinning with terrifying visions of a woman alone on an empty road with five dangerous men. She'd wanted to punch something after watching the broadcast, and Linc's jaw had cracked more than once as they'd waited for Liam to arrive. Malcolm had promised he'd strike again, but Bets hadn't imagined he would orchestrate a scenario straight out of a Hollywood film.

"She's street savvy." Kathleen stomped forward, her strong Boston accent more evident in her anger. "We should applaud her, not pat her on the back and bemoan what might have happened. She clearly doesn't want that."

"I agree," Liam said, squeezing Bets a little harder this time. "She's just arrived, and she had her reasons for driving here alone, ones we've put in the past. Sorcha had her back and reached out to me. I was out the door in a flash."

"We would have gone with you," Declan ground out. "Dammit, Liam—"

"I didn't think," Liam shot back. "I just raced there as fast as I could. Plus, she's mine—something Sorcha has already told her."

A ripple of shock went through the crowd. Well, there it was. Bets had known—it was basic math being that Liam was the last of the men Sorcha had pledged to matchmake.

It had *killed* her not to say anything, even if Linc had to keep reminding her, insisting she should let them figure things out themselves. Still, hearing her son talk like this... It was like seeing him grow into being a man the rest of the way.

Someone coughed loudly before Sophie said, "Which I suggested to Sorcha. I thought it might be more effective for her to tell the woman first."

"She's saying men are thick in the head," Declan grumbled.

"If the shoe fits, Ace," his wife shot back.

"Not that Taylor wants any of you to talk to her about it," Liam continued, looking across the group to ensure he was heard and confirming Bets' gut. "Seeing Sorcha has freaked her out. Understandably so."

Brady put his hand on her son's shoulder. "We'd wondered, Liam, but we weren't sure we should say anything. Right, Jamie?"

"Sophie was the one who told us," Jamie corrected, "since Taylor talked to her about seeing Sorcha. She was rattled by it all, and no wonder. But we're getting off track. Malcolm obviously plans to continue his harassment of our people. What are we going to do about that?"

"We're going to hire more security guards," Linc said, tucking his hands in his pockets and rocking on the heels of his cowboy boots. "No one is going to go anywhere alone for a good long while."

"Nowhere?" Liam asked, his brow knit. "Linc, I'm the first one to support our need for increased vigilance and security, but curtailing our every freedom gives Malcolm all the power."

"And yet, he managed to block a public road today after having Taylor followed from Dublin airport three hours away." Bets took her son by the shoulders. "Malcolm will be ready for the live streaming next time, won't he? Aren't there electronic jammers or something to stop technology?"

Linc put his hand to her back and likely felt it trembling, but then again, he always knew when she was upset and did his best to comfort her or talk her down. "Sugar, we're going to find a way to make sure our people are always safe and connected. I'll be working with our security officer along with Donal and Carrick and a few others—"

"I want in," Declan said, his face as stony and determined as when he used to box in the ring.

"Me too," Eoghan said, taking his wife's hand. Sandrine had been Sophie's longtime helper since childhood. She and Eoghan met through her and married just weeks ago. "We can't just muscle up. We need to find a way to outfox Malcolm."

"*And* Mary Kincaid," Sophie added, twisting her hands. "Don't forget about Mary."

No, no one could forget about Mary Kincaid, and for that Bets felt a huge weight of responsibility. Mary's hatred was for her, but it had become her mission in life to stop the arts center. Now she had more friends, powerful friends. "We shouldn't have announced the day Taylor was arriving. We made it so easy for Malcolm. I want to kick myself."

Liam kissed her cheek. "Don't kick yourself, Mum. Eoghan's right. We need to focus on being smarter."

Donal shook his head, glancing over at his wife Ghislaine, a publicist who had helped the arts center after Sophie had called her in. They'd married at the same time as Eoghan, Donal's father, in a ceremony that would be remembered in town for years to come. "It's not like this village is known for discretion. You can't tell anyone anything without it being passed around. We're going to have to go back to some of our old ways and keep things to ourselves. Too many ears."

"Yes," Eoghan said, his angular face lined with tension. "We have enemies in our camp. We must act accordingly."

Bets shook her fist in the air as anger surged up again. "I'm having another moment where I'm questioning whether this is all worth it."

Linc took her aside and bored his beautiful blue eyes into hers. "Let me recount this argument. Mary was picking at you and undermining you even before you conceived of the arts center."

"Remember your prized roses, Bets?" Donal asked. "She cut them to pieces out of spite. She's been a viper in this village her whole life, and she's been gaining friends and flexing her muscles."

"Yeah, and now Malcolm is hanging around her cauldron," Bets cried out. "Dammit, we need to shut them down. What are the chances the new Garda officer will press charges on Malcolm, Denis, and the rest of his muscle?"

"We'll soon find out," Linc told her, holding up his hands for a peace she didn't feel capable of just now. "I know everybody is worked up. But nothing more can be done tonight. We should all go home and get some rest. For those who want to join, we'll hold a meeting tomorrow with the security officer at two o'clock. That should give our new Garda officer enough time to decide what he's going to do."

She hated waiting on other people. "He'd better do something," she said harshly.

"I think he wants to if the law allows." Linc massaged her shoulder, making her feel like a total shrimp next to his large frame. "He was genuinely upset about the news and pledged his full support."

"Except the incident wasn't in Caisleán, which Malcolm planned," Liam broke in, fishing something out of his black motorcycle jacket. "He made that point very clear to me and Taylor. We had parking tickets on our vehicles when we left Cows and Cocks—"

"You brought her to a different pub?" Brady asked, his face falling.

"I was trying to spare Taylor all of this." Liam gestured to the crowd. "No offense."

"None taken," Ellie assured him, nudging her husband in the side. "Brady is just being Mr. Hospitality like usual. We know she didn't need to be thrown into our proverbial zoo after what just happened. I mean, look at us. You'd think we were having an Irish BBQ in the front yard."

That made some people laugh a little, but Bets couldn't find it in her to join them. Not tonight. "All right. We could keep hashing this out or go home and get some rest like Linc said."

Not that she expected to sleep tonight. Like she had on other nights when the center and the people she cared about were under fire, she'd pace her worn hardwood floors before retiring to toss and turn in bed.

People started to say good night to each other. The embraces were a little longer, she noted, and the meaningful looks a little more intense. Despite feeling beside herself with worry, she did her best to comfort those who were out of sorts. And when she faced Liam in the dark night, she gave in to the urge to hug him again.

"I was so worried," she whispered fiercely. "Not only for Taylor. You might be an adult, but you're still my kid."

"I know, Mum." His embrace calmed her, a power he'd had since he was a child. "I also have to ask something of you. I need you to not treat Taylor like my soulmate."

Linc's snort carried to her ears, and she narrowed her eyes at him when she looked over her shoulder like he did every time this topic came up. "Some people should mind their own business."

"You are my business, sugar," he answered before strolling away. "I'll be in the car."

"Mum." Liam touched her face to turn her attention back to him. "One of the reasons Taylor didn't let us pick her up from the airport was because she was worried you'd know what Sorcha had said."

She sucked in her breath. Dammit, she was thrilled, like *over the moon* thrilled that her baby boy's soulmate had shown up. What mother wouldn't be? Hadn't she given herself this talk already? She'd told Linc to warn her whenever she got that "grandchildren dreaming" look on her face. "I hear you, Liam. I'll do my best, I promise."

"Don't go there, Mum," Liam cautioned, tapping her on the nose.

She moved his hand away. "What? Thinking is still free in this country, isn't it?"

"Not if Malcolm or Mary have anything to do with it," he said harshly, not his usual. "Mum, let's focus on making Taylor's first days easy. She's a strong woman like you and the others, and she wants to do a good job. Look at it from her perspective. She was offered an incredible job in a small town in Ireland, where she knows one person—Sophie. Then Sorcha appears and tells her about me. After which she realizes the founder of the arts center where she'll be working is her soulmate's mother."

She kicked at the ground and tried not to wince. "Dammit, it's like being put in a pressure cooker on high heat. I've already told myself this. No grandkids thoughts."

"*Grandkids?* Oh, Mum... That's way off."

"It is?" She caught his bland stare. "Fine. I'll stop them in their tracks. Like you've tried to teach me."

He tilted his head up to the sky as if imploring the heavens. "*Tried* being the operative word. Go on home and do your best not to fret too much. I'd suggest some meditative breathing, but I know it only winds you up."

"You're right about that. But I know I won't be calming down anytime soon."

"Mum, despite everything that's happened, we've gotten this far, light years ahead of where we were when Aunt Mary first shut us down when Angie and Megan arrived and started teaching. Hey, is Kade home with Megan and the kids?"

"Yeah, Sophie left her daughter with them for the evening," Bets told him. "We wanted to make sure the children were—"

"Safe," he finished. "Understandable."

Neither one of them wanted to discuss how Sophie had sent Greta away for a few weeks after the last harassment and vandalism incident at their home. The little girl was back because the new Garda officer had taken over for Denis, signaling the return of law and order in town.

Which is why Malcolm had struck outside Caisleán. Dammit, Bets hated what a clever bastard he was.

"Go inside." She zipped his jacket up the couple inches to his throat like she used to when he was a little boy going to school. "It's getting cold."

"Did that little bit of mothering make you feel better?" He took her hands gently.

"It's better than breathing exercises..."

He gave her a stern look before smiling. "Maybe you should ask Linc to watch a movie with you tonight to shut your mind off."

A movie wasn't going to cut it. Not even close. Especially hearing she'd have to wait for grandkids. "That's a great idea," she said brightly to assure him. "Okay, I love you and will talk to you tomorrow."

She was a few steps away when he called, "Hey, Mum."

She turned around. He stood in the porch light, looking very much like the man he was. Some Bruce. Some her. Mostly himself. "By the way, Taylor loves *Jaws*. She's really big on movies."

Of course she is, Bets thought, because she'd learned that was how it worked with soulmates.

She found her steps lighter as she walked to her car and *her* soulmate to go home.

CHAPTER FOUR

A good reporter wasn't supposed to be part of the story or the center of attention.

And yet, Taylor was. The barrel-chested new Garda officer, John Hart, had just finished interviewing her. With Linc and Ghislaine's husband, Donal O'Dwyer, in the room along with Linc's new security officer, Wilt Mather, a former Marine with a long history of corporate security.

She'd felt like Thumbelina around all those giants. Sure, it had happened in her new living room decked out with a beautiful Italian leather sectional in caramel tones, but the setting hadn't made her any less nervous.

She hated being interviewed by cops.

Of course, it hadn't happened for fourteen years...

She'd done everything possible to avoid a reoccurrence, learning new skills, researching everything she could to become more elusive and avoid being arrested. Again.

Since Donal and Linc were shooting the shit with the new guy, she walked over to Wilt to run through some of her thoughts. "Can I talk to you for a minute?"

He nodded his bald head, which was attached to a tree-trunk neck, and followed her over to the corner of her living room. "What can I do for you, Ms. McGowan?"

"First, please call me Taylor." She made sure to smile. "Second, I was troubled to read last night that pepper spray, cat eye key chains, and tasers are illegal in Ireland. I didn't bring mine as you can't travel with them. After yesterday, I'd like to have more than just my phone handy in case it's not enough of a deterrent, especially if four big guys decide to confront me again. What would you recommend that I and the other women artists carry?"

His already serious face somehow turned more grim. "That's a very good question. I'd planned to talk to Linc about some additional safety measures for female staff after the incident yesterday. We need to obey the laws in Ireland, but we also want everyone to feel safe. I would recommend over-the-counter hair spray as it's something you can easily put in your purse—"

"And something we can deny having bought for protection because we're chicks. Got it."

That made his mouth lift a little. "Between us, I think it's terrible you can't carry some basic self-defense tools."

She wanted to give him a high five for understanding something so many men were clueless about. "Right. But laws are made by men and yada yada. If it had been a man faced with four scary women yesterday on the road, those tools being legal for protection would be inked into the Irish constitution like that." She snapped her fingers.

"Exactly." He reached into his pocket and pulled out a couple of dongles the size of a half-dollar. "I'm checking out the possibility of issuing personal panic buttons. The problem in this area—"

"Is cell service," she finished. "No steady signal in the boonies. I was lucky to have cell reception yesterday, or I could never have streamed live. I realized that last night when I got home. And then I almost threw up."

He nodded crisply. "I can imagine. Linc said there's resistance to my idea of having each arts center employee assigned their own security guard."

Good. That kind of constant surveillance would cramp her style, especially given the way she was planning to take Malcolm down. "People huddled after the incident, huh?"

"Everyone takes security at the center and with its personnel very seriously," he answered like the professional he was.

"Anything else you can suggest, Mr. Mather? Because I've taken self-defense classes, and I know there are limits."

"It's Wilt, and yes, I have others. We're having a meeting on this topic later with the board and other interested parties."

"Do I need to attend that?" She'd been looking forward to going sightseeing with Liam, as she'd told Sophie when she'd called her this morning. First, she couldn't imagine a better diversion, and second, Liam was really great to be around. And that was all she would allow herself to think right now, something she'd *also* made clear to Sophie, who had practically sung out her goodbye after telling her to have a fabulous time. Funny, her friend.

"I can give you a preview, and you'll be receiving a supplement to our existing security manual—"

"Which I read again last night," she told him. "This time with a highlighter. Sorry for interrupting again. I get excited about things I feel passionate about. Security is one of them."

He met her eyes. "We're on the same page. It's important to be conversant in our security plans and to sign on to them. After yesterday, we'd like to put trackers on everyone's cars and have twenty-four seven monitoring. So if your car stops randomly on a road for no reason—"

"You'll know something is wrong." God, this was making her shoulders tight. She was going to have to act before the precaution went into effect; otherwise, they'd find her out because it wasn't like she could refuse the extra security when she'd gone in and asked him for it. "Unless we have to pee along the side of the road."

"That's what the sat phones are for, which we want everyone to carry after this," Wilt told her.

She'd already thought of buying herself one. "Yeah, because CBs won't communicate far enough, right?"

He regarded her with amusement. "Aren't you an arts and culture reporter?"

"What can I say? I'm a Gemini. I live for random info. Plus, CB radios are in plenty of older movies. Hello, *Breaker! Breaker!* I used to wish I could have one of those as a kid."

Which had displeased her snobby rich parents, who'd told her not to fantasize about the lives of "uneducated truck drivers." God, how she hated Bitsy Hartman-McGowan and Theodore McGowan III. Liam had called it last night—walking away from her parents had been the best decision of her life. Fuck her trust fund and their money. She'd done more than fine on her own and been a whole hell of a lot happier.

"I'll see what I can do about the CB radio—but only for fun. Can't be easy arriving as you did. Everyone is dedicated to making your first days smoother and more pleasant in the coming weeks. Me included."

She wanted to punch him in the shoulder and buy him a beer after that comment. "Thank you. You're a good egg, Wilt. I can see why Linc hired you."

"He listens, and when he gives his word, it's golden." He got a shuttered look in his eyes, as if he were reliving bad memories. "That's the kind of person you want to work with."

"I hear you. There are a lot of assholes out there."

She almost got a full smile out of him, but she imagined it would be bad for his image as a fifty-some-year-old security officer hardened by life. Oh, she was such a reporter sometimes.

"We plan to spread the word about the increase in security," he continued, "with the intention of getting Malcolm and those associated with him to back off. While Officer Hart didn't say, I think he's going to pay a call to Malcolm personally, and if he can get Denis Walsh on stalking you from the airport, I think he'll charge him. Denis does still live within this jurisdiction."

But would Malcolm find a way to get Denis out? Or had part of his motivation for orchestrating the showdown been to see what the new Garda guy was going to do? "Let's hope so. We're dealing with some pretty pugnacious pricks. If you'll forgive my French."

Smile achieved. "Forgiven. That sums up my unofficial take. I'm glad you're on board, Taylor. And I agree with everyone. You handled yourself with incredible toughness and smarts yesterday. Now it's my job to make sure it doesn't happen again. Excuse me. Linc is motioning me over."

Part of her wanted to sidle closer and listen to their conversation. But police officers didn't like to talk shop in front of victims, and to the new Garda guy, John, that's what she was. Disgusting really. She headed into her new kitchen instead, picking up her phone on the side table on the way. Liam's text shone like a spotlight at the top of the screen. Excitement raced through her. He'd been her happy thought last night and this morning.

Good morning! I hear you're talking with the Garda now. I thought I'd see if you wanted to go for a ride after to blow off some steam. Why don't you text me when you're ready and I'll pop by?

She reread the text. Easy. Casual. So like him. Save that insane chemistry between them, which had made her skin sizzle. She fired one right back at him.

Wrapping up now. Come on over.

He simply sent a thumbs-up emoji. Yeah, he was being good about taking things slow even though he believed they were soulmates. She was a little more open to the idea this morning. She'd watched the video of the incident herself—an out-of-body experience in some ways—so she'd seen the way her expression had changed when Liam pulled up. First, her shock and delight after he took off his helmet and then the fear and anger in her tight mouth as she'd stepped forward to protect him.

But maybe she would have felt that way about anyone who'd shown up to help? Hard to know, and she wasn't going for another roadblock meeting to find out.

Thankfully, Sorcha had left her alone last night. But she did need to thank the ghost at some point. She *had* been handling the situation, but she couldn't deny having Liam arrive had been a relief. What did a thank you gift look like for a ghost? Some cultures made offerings of fruits and nuts, but wouldn't that be cruel since they couldn't eat them?

Maybe Liam would know—since he knew so much about spirits and woo-woo.

When was she going to get used to that? And his mind reading? Although maybe that could be a plus. Communicating her feelings could be a problem for her. Sometimes it felt like she was still talking to her parents, explaining until she was blue in the face but not getting anything across.

Then again...

Maybe his mind reading was going to be a problem. She had her secrets, ones she'd promised herself to never reveal after being burned in the past right around her first encounter with the cops. And yet, Liam had told her he wanted to learn about her *from* her—not through his gifts.

Gifts!

He'd mentioned welcome gifts, and sure enough, her kitchen table was full of them. She'd noticed them last night when she was scanning the space—flowers in cut vases, a cute stuffed Kindness sheep with the word "welcome" on its fluffy belly (apparently they had memorabilia now), and some Irish green candles—but she hadn't taken inventory.

Her energy had crashed after she'd armed the house, her adrenaline giving out, and all she'd wanted to do was take a shower and start researching ways to protect herself better in Ireland.

She walked over to the gifts and, taking a huge breath to relieve the pressure in her sternum, sifted through them. She unwrapped a green blanket with an Irish wool sticker on it. It was from Sophie, the card said. Okay, her family too —but she knew who'd selected it. It was lovely, and she ran her fingers over it before setting it aside, her attention drawn to a large hand-carved box made of some kind of light wood with her initials carved into it that had her heart racing. She knew Liam had worked as a handyman, and maybe it was his influence, but she could almost feel his energy in the wood. She pulled out the card wedged inside the box.

Hi Taylor,
Look forward to meeting you. I heard you needed these. Welcome to our town.
Liam O'Hanlon

That was it? No *Your Soulmate* in parenthesis or *In Cahoots with Sorcha the Ghost.* He hadn't expected to meet her yesterday, so his chill approach made sense.

She unlatched the box and lifted the lid.

Three cans of spray paint were tucked into the box—all in her brand of choice. Her heart soared with delight as she touched them reverently before raw terror ravaged her. She pulled out a chair as her knees gave out. He knew! OMG! *He knew!*

Rage kicked in. So much for him not doing his woo-woo thing to learn more about her. That liar! Only two other people knew her secret, and she'd only shared it after researching their trustworthiness and hearing from others that they never betrayed a confidence.

"Liam is more than trustworthy," a familiar voice said from behind her. "Believe me."

She spun in her chair and stared at Sorcha, who was standing in her kitchen. "And to think I was going to thank you for sending him my way yesterday. Dammit, Sorcha, stop interfering in my life."

"You're only fighting with—"

"I don't care." She stood up and shoved the chair out of the way hard. "Liam said his dad told him he could banish ghosts by stomping his foot. Well, this is me telling you to go. Now."

She slapped her boot to the ground, the sound echoing in the kitchen. Sorcha only crossed her arms, her gaze thoughtful.

"I know you feel exposed right now, but I hope you'll settle down after you talk to Liam. You can trust him, Taylor. For the same reason everyone does. Not only because he's your soulmate."

She picked up the blanket and hurled it at the ghost. Sorcha vanished in a blur, but her disappearance didn't do anything to calm Taylor down. Air. She needed air. Pressing a hand to her heart, her chest heaving, she closed her eyes and forced herself to calm down. Losing her mind wasn't going to help anything. The sound of boots on hardwood snapped her into focus and she spun into action. Picking up the blanket, she laid it over the box, concealing the spray paint from view. Wilt's job was to see everything, and wouldn't he wonder why Liam had given her such a gift?

"You okay in here?" Wilt asked as he came into the kitchen.

"I was just killing a really nasty spider and giving him the business," she lied, breathing shallowly.

"It's the damp, I'm told," Wilt answered. "Why spiders are so common here. Funny how you can handle Malcolm and his detail, but a spider—"

"It was hairy!" She gave a playful shudder as Linc walked in. "I'm adding protection from spiders to Wilt's job description."

"Is that what all the ruckus was?" Linc asked, carefully looking around. "I hate them too. Sugar, can we make you some calming tea? Bug spray?"

There was no mistaking Linc's syrupy drawl. "I just need a minute. Are you finished?"

"I can't imagine how stressful this whole matter has been for you," Linc continued, his boots echoing in the kitchen. "Is there anything more we can do besides extermination services?"

She heard a motorcycle then and bit the inside of her cheek. "No. I just need some space. If there isn't anything more…"

Linc tucked his hands in his pockets. "Of course. Wilt and I can see Officer Hart out. Wilt mentioned you two had talked about added security. I'll check in with you later if that's okay."

"That's fine." He was a nice man, thinking she was in the grips of a delayed reaction to yesterday's showdown. "Thank you."

"Don't thank us yet," Linc said, inclining his head to Wilt, who murmured a farewell.

They left the kitchen in tandem, and moments later, she heard them talking with Liam in the front yard, Officer Hart's voice among them.

She took a few more cleansing breaths before setting the blanket aside and picking up the box Liam had probably made for her. Her fingers itched with the need to look at the spray cans again. She'd seen the colors in a flash, but she wanted to confirm it. Had he really chosen her favorite spray paint brand *and* her favorite colors of tangerine orange, white, and ultramarine blue? *Welcome to woo-woo central*, she thought, setting it on the kitchen counter. There was no way she wasn't going to confront him about blindsiding her.

She heard cars driving off. A polite knock sounded on the door. Nice of him, that, since Sophie had told her the Irish didn't knock—they just walked in. Unannounced visits were not her style. But he'd know that, wouldn't he?

"Come in," she called because her legs were still trembling. "I'm in the kitchen."

She crossed her arms over her chest and locked her muscles in place. When he appeared in the doorway, the punch of attraction and an insane joy rocked through her before her other emotions won out. The smile on his face instantly faded, and he closed the distance between them in a heartbeat.

"What happened?"

When he cupped her arm, she wanted to jerk it free, but the warmth in his damn green eyes held her. She remembered what Sorcha had said. That she could trust him. And in that moment, she wanted to. Which was crazy. There must be some uncanny power in his eyes because she couldn't look away.

"I got your present," she said, hearing how hoarse her own voice had become.

His grip turned more urgent. "And it made you lose all color and tremble? Taylor...I would never have gotten them if I'd known they would upset you. It was only that I heard you needed them. I thought it would make you happy. Nothing like this."

She hated to ask outright so she tried to hedge as she asked, "You don't know why spray cans would be a good present for me?"

"Not at all, *a stór*. They were a complete surprise, but I always trust my guidance. I would never willingly buy you a present that would upset you like this. I'm sorry I didn't sense that."

She searched his face. She knew the difference between earnest and devious, and he wasn't the latter. Letting herself sink back against the counter, she bit her lip to fight off the emotion attached to this realization. He didn't know her secret, but he knew the way to her heart.

Suddenly, she wanted nothing more than to trust someone this special with her secret. With the truth that lived at her core. Oh, what a heady thing it would be. But hadn't she learned her lesson? The last time she'd trusted a guy she loved, it had bitten her in the ass and broken her heart. Besides, her secret life did a lot of good, and being revealed could change all that. How could she take that risk?

She stared at him, teetering between her past experience and the present Liam was offering. In the end, she decided she needed more time. "It's okay, Liam. I got a little freaked out, thinking you'd used your woo-woo skills and invaded my privacy too far."

"I would never do that." He cupped her elbows, his eyes scanning her face. "Let's sit down and you can tell me—"

She looked off, trying not to gaze at the box again and the intention he'd put into making the present for her. "Please, Liam. Don't push me on this."

He let go of her and stepped back, and somehow that made her fortress start to crumble more. "That's fine then, Taylor. I had no idea my gift would upset you like this. I know we've just met, but I hope you believe that."

She sucked in another breath. "I do. This is me freaking out. I seem to be doing a lot of that lately. God, I didn't expect this. I just came here for a job I thought would let me do something meaningful, something I could—"

She stopped herself from saying, *something I could be public about.*

Because being a notoriously anonymous street artist who bounced around the world painting social messages was her secret and had to remain so. No one knew Taylor

McGowan was *Veritas* except the hacker who covered her tracks and the lawyer who advised her. Millions of her followers waited for her next street mural detailing everything from sexual abuse to domestic violence to human rights.

Only this time it would be about the harassment of a woman on a public road—her. And only she would know it was a self-portrait. The idea had started coming to her last night, and Liam's gift felt like a crazy confirmation of it.

Was it risky? Sure. Her first shot across the bow at Malcolm. But that was what she did. Had since she'd first used graffiti to right a horrible wrong in her high school after no one had listened to her and the other girls about another bad man who'd misused his power.

"Whatever you're thinking right now, it's really powerful." He touched her arm as if she were a skittish animal. "I know we don't know each other well, but I still want to remind you that I'm here for you. I have your back. Like I did yesterday. All the way."

Her eyes flew to him. He was watching her so intently she feared he'd read her every thought. "I don't know how we're going to do this. Get to know each other like normal people when you can sense everything I think and feel. Liam, it's too much, too soon."

His hand fell from her, and he took a slow breath. Then he tapped his thigh with his finger, the sound as stark as the ticking of a clock in a silent room. "I'm struggling a little with what to say here. Taylor, from the minute you've arrived, things have been at a fever pitch. I wanted to help you relax, but it seems I'm now doing the opposite. It's also really hard for me to turn off who I am. Because I *do* sense things, and I listen to what I hear. If I hadn't, I wouldn't have shown up for you yesterday."

Point one for him.

"More...I don't know how to act differently, and I wouldn't in any case. I love who I am, and that's the man I want to be with you. Not some half version of the truth."

The use of that word struck her hard. It couldn't be a coincidence. She lifted her head, shocked at how much hurt she felt at their discord. She didn't know him, and yet part of her was breaking over this confrontation for him as much as for herself.

"I don't know why I was supposed to drive all the way to Castlebar to an art store to buy you that spray paint in those particular colors," he continued, "but I did as I'd heard to. I have to keep trusting my intuition. If I don't, I won't be true to myself. I'll be lost. Taylor, I don't like that it makes you feel exposed and vulnerable, but I also don't want to back away. You're..."

For the second time, she watched his face tense and listened to him tap his thigh. "I feel something with you—something stronger than I've ever felt for another woman. That might freak you out even more, but I have to say it all the same. Taylor, I'm so happy you're here. After I finally calmed myself down last night, I could reconnect with the joy of you. How beautiful you are. How strong. How canny. And how you're so very direct and honest about everything."

His emotion ripped through her, and she could feel the rare burn of tears in her eyes. How was it this intense between them?

"I can't be any other way either, Liam, but I do have secrets," she confessed. "Important ones. For important reasons. Ones I don't share with anyone. Ones...I don't know if I ever will."

The tapping on his thigh resumed. "Trust takes time,

and I'm not asking for more than you can give right now. So... Can we simply go on a bike ride and maybe have some ice cream? Because I woke up smiling thinking about being with you today."

She sucked in a breath to control the crazy emotional storm inside her. "I woke thinking about you too. Liam, last night and this morning—you were my happy thought."

His throat moved with a feeling she recognized because she was filled with it herself. "I'm glad for that. Thank you for sharing it. I'd feared... Never mind, we've beaten that horse. Will you come for a ride then? If you have your license, I'll even let you drive for a bit on an easy road. That's something I've never done before."

Because it was an act of trust. Which he was offering her. She stared at him across the short distance between them. Every line of his body was tight with emotion, yet the warmth in his eyes was still there. "That's a pretty big deal for a guy. Letting a girl drive his ride."

His mouth broke into a short smile, one she knew cost him. "As you say. But it's your choice."

He was circling back to their conversation in the pub yesterday. She'd insisted they needed to choose to be together, not be corralled into it. He was honoring that, which was what sealed it for her. "All right. We'll do that. Maybe you can take me to the Brazen Donkey for a drink afterward. I thought it might be easier to meet everyone there for the first time. Keep it light. I'm going to explode if I keep having these intense conversations, first with the cops and now with you."

A burst of laughter shot through the room, making him look like the handsome man she remembered flirting with yesterday. "I hear you, *a stór*. I really do."

Then he held out his hand. Pushing past the part of her

that wanted to clam up and turn away, she took it, her chest as rigid as the metal spray cans in the box he'd given her.

"Thank you for not armoring up." He squeezed her hand with delicate pressure. "I know that was hard for you."

You think? "No mind reading there, huh?"

His green eyes were steady as he said, "No, and I'll do my best not to. Until you're more comfortable. But I can't go back on who I am any more than you can share the secret you hold so closely inside yourself."

The message between the lines was as clear as a bell: *until we both have to choose to simply be ourselves with each other.*

She glanced back at the box.

Could she trust Liam with her deepest secret?

Because damn it all, she really, really wanted to.

CHAPTER FIVE

Somehow Liam hadn't expected dating Taylor to be a challenge. He'd always thought he knew how to date, and in the past his gifts had been welcomed. The one he'd given her had been as spontaneous as it was heartfelt. But contained in those combustible spray cans was the secret to unlocking the heart of the woman he was already thinking of as his.

He was going to need to rachet it back a notch. Thankfully, she was growing less tense as they sped up the coast and the wind thundered over them. He'd headed straight for the water, needing the sea breeze with its clearing salt content to transform the negative energy around them. As they climbed a narrow steep road boasting a killer view of the dark water crashing against the craggy rocks below, he felt her body shift from tension to awe. Somehow, he knew she loved the water and the beach as much as he did. Not that he was going to mention that for a while.

Since he was a boy, he'd been able to put himself in other people's shoes. Understanding them was as simple as breathing. Over time, he'd come to learn the term empath.

So he could understand her fears—to be so known by someone without making the conscious choice to share such personal knowledge would be scary. He was well aware it bypassed the whole *getting to know you* part of dating. He would have to trust they would be able to navigate their journey together, that was all.

They coasted down the incline on the other side of the mountain, past goats and sheep grazing in the green and brown hills. Her arms tightened around him as they leaned into a curve. He could feel her heart racing as she pressed herself to his back and let out a cry of awe at the postcard scene before them, and he did his best to ignore the rush of pleasure at how her hips and thighs curved around his own. There was plenty of time for that.

Only locals knew the shrouded road he took at the end of the incline off to the right. Sure, the ground was a little muddy and bumpy, but it was worth the view from the private beach. He did his best to maneuver around the ruts, but when he heard her laugh as they hit one that was unavoidable, he could feel her joy. This outing was doing exactly what he'd hoped it might—bringing them back in balance.

At the end of the unpaved road, he guided the bike as close to the sand dunes as possible and then parked. She was off the bike in a heartbeat, lifting her helmet and then holding it out to him with a wide smile. The sunlight caught the reds of her hair, making it appear as though fire was dancing around her. He took the helmet with an answering smile and stowed both of them as she started off toward the path between the sand dunes, her arms flung overhead. The desire for her, which he was also trying to hold at bay, surged through him. She liked to stretch her arms like that, he'd noticed, and he wondered if she knew it was because she was opening her heart to all that was around her. Another thing he knew better than to say now.

He followed her, watching as she stopped to roll up her jeans and peel off her boots and then her socks. Did she know how cold the October water was? When she gave a yelp moments later from along the shore, he fought a laugh. She'd been skeptical when he'd advised her to wear a heavier coat. It was usually colder by the sea, and while he ran warm, he had on a waterproof coat lined with fleece.

"It's beautiful," she called out, braving the water again as the tide shifted the sand under her feet. "But freezing. Is it ever warm enough to swim?"

He walked closer after peeling off his boots and socks as well. "It takes a certain constitution. I've swum in it since I was a boy, so it's normal to me. I thought swimming in Bali was like swimming in a warm bath."

She raised her arms again, making his mouth water. The lines of her body were made for his hands, he knew.

"I like both. Bali lulls you into relaxation. The water here makes you feel so alive it's like your skin is charged with something powerful. I'm so glad this place is as I imagined it. Sometimes you visit a place and it's all hype, you know. Ireland has such a pull for some people—me included. Maybe it's my Irish ancestry from way back, but this is exactly how I thought it would look and feel."

His heart energy was gaining ground as she met his eyes, all soft and vulnerable.

"Thank you for bringing me here, Liam."

He gave her a smile, wishing he could cross to her and simply wrap her in his arms. *Soon.* "You're welcome, Taylor. Do you want to walk a bit?"

"I'd love that," she said and strode over until she was by his side.

Then she brushed her hand against his, and he took it as a sign and let their hands clasp together. When she threaded their fingers together, he sent up more thanks.

"I was hard on you earlier," she confessed, looking over at him with that intense directness of hers. "I'm sorry. You've been nothing but kind—and I freaked out on you. Not cool."

He hadn't expected an apology. "It's all right. We're figuring things out. Learning each other. There will be bumps along the way, but nothing insurmountable."

"Do you really believe that?" She shook her head. "I wasn't raised in a very happy family, and I haven't seen too many happy relationships."

"Everyone chooses the kind of relationship they have—whether they know it or not. Also, other people's experiences aren't ours. My parents, for example, were a good team. My mom had her part, and my dad had his."

He tightened his grip as the tide came in stronger on the next wave. "They both did their share well. But they didn't always support each other's inner dreams. My mom's especially—not that she ever spoke of them. Hence her decision to open the arts center after my dad passed away."

"How long ago did he die?" she asked softly as the seagulls screeched overhead.

"Six years now. In the fields, where he was the happiest." He drew in a deep breath, glad to feel peace in his heart as he thought about that time. "It was the hardest thing I'd ever faced. My brothers left shortly afterward because they simply couldn't take being here when he wasn't. Suddenly it was just my mom and me, and we were lost. That's when I started asking bigger questions, and when I look back, I can be grateful for it."

She gave his hand a comforting caress before saying,

"Meaning of life stuff, huh? I hear you. I had something kick that off for me when I was in high school. Don't look, okay? I mean... Can you control it?"

He locked his mind down to make sure nothing came through before he answered. "Sometimes a mere mention by someone triggers an image or a feeling—or a place does. Other times a feeling or vision comes to me out of the blue. Like I'm standing with a paintbrush in my hand, and suddenly I know a friend needs me to call them or there's trouble."

"That must be overwhelming," she said unevenly.

"Not always. When it works well, it confirms for me why they're called gifts. Like me hearing you were on the road and needed support."

She went for a comic face as she leaned down and picked up a rock. "Yeah, that was a good moment for me. I might have had to start fighting dirty if things had continued. Throw rocks like a kid on a playground."

Her attempt for humor and understanding made him want to enfold her in his arms to quell the last bit of wariness lurking in her eyes. "As for the other, I've worked hard to train myself to clear my mind. It's helped. Controlling one's gifts is an illusion, I've learned. Working with them is a better term. I promise to use all I've learned to respect your privacy, Taylor. But I'd like nothing better than to listen if you want to tell me about your experiences from your own lips."

She tossed the rock into the sea as the tide rolled in with a decisiveness he didn't fully understand but knew was significant. "Thank you for explaining all that. Honestly, I feel kinda guilty for asking you not to use your gifts only when it suits me. Because you're right. They're a core part of you. It's not right to ask anyone not to be themselves. My parents wanted that from me, and I hated it. Liam, I'm really conflicted about this whole thing."

He paused and turned, needing to face her. "We'll muddle through it until you're ready to trust me."

"No pressure, huh?" She stepped closer to him, laying a hesitant hand on his heart. "Well, that's sexy. Does it make you feel better to know I haven't told Sophie my secret?"

He wasn't sure whether he should laugh or not. "Not really. I'm not Sophie."

She huffed out a laugh. "No, you so clearly aren't."

When she started walking again, he matched her with an equal pace and waited for her to continue talking. She cast another searching glance toward him. He could almost feel her trying to read deeper into him. His character. His feelings. His intentions.

She stopped and picked up another rock, throwing it up and down meditatively. "Sorcha told me everyone trusts you, and from the moment I arrived, you've proven you're good to the core. I won't talk about the whole soulmate thing, and while I'm still learning to be comfortable with you and your gifts, I can't ignore the fact that they have helped me."

He walked over to her and planted himself in front of her. "Helping you is my soul calling, Taylor. In every way you need."

The rock fell to the ground when she missed catching it. "Your soul calling, huh? Wow! That's like...really intense and really great, because I haven't allowed anyone to support me with this thing I'm dancing around. Oh, to hell with it."

He watched as she fisted her hands at her sides and clenched her eyes shut.

A seagull called overhead as the sea crashed around

them. He could feel a change in the air, one radiating out from her. When she opened her eyes again, her breath rushed out and she nodded, as if to herself.

"I'm not indecisive as a rule," she told him in a serious tone. "I weigh facts and impressions and act accordingly. From the very beginning, my first instinct has been to trust you. But I didn't expect it would involve my secret. Shit. Then you go and get me the one welcome gift capable of both slaying me and freaking me out. Dammit, Liam, you'd better not crush me."

The love he already felt for her was as constant as the sea, but he didn't think that answer was what she needed right now. "Why would I crush you when all I want to do is help you and make you happy?"

She slapped a hand to her forehead. "How can I argue with that? All right, here goes. It's a long, ugly story, so you'll have to hang with me. It started in high school, after Sophie graduated. There was this teacher—"

His mind flashed an image of an older thickset man putting his hands on her waist from behind in an empty classroom, and his anger immediately surged. "Keep going," he managed, tamping back what he'd already seen.

She bent over and grabbed another rock, clenching her fist around it. "He wasn't just any teacher. He was from one of New York's power families going back to the Rockefeller days and he'd won a ton of national awards. We were all going to turn into Isaac Newton because of the math god and his stupid class. He was such a pompous jerk, but I did the work."

He calmly walked toward her until he was standing in front of her, wanting to lend her some of his strength. "I expect you were a good student."

She rolled her eyes. "I was, but me and trigonometry

weren't the best of friends. Three months into the term, he asked me to meet him after school about one of my tests, and he came on to me. I was sixteen. At first, I thought it was a mistake that his hands were on my hips from behind. But then he leaned in and whispered in my ear that I could get a better grade on my paper. I didn't understand, but then I felt him lifting my skirt, and I freaked. I do that a lot."

"Thank God you did," he managed, fury swirling through him like angry tidepools.

"I ran out of the classroom and headed straight to the bathroom. I had a meltdown the moment I locked myself in the stall. Some older girl came in—one I didn't know—and she said the teacher was looking for me."

That bastard, Liam thought, as she began to shiver. He shrugged out of his coat and wrapped it around her, despite her having a coat.

"Thanks," she said, forcing a smile. "The girl said she'd told him I was sick. Because she knew what he wanted to do to me. Turns out, he'd done the same thing to her. She freaked out too, when it happened, only she didn't run like I did. She froze. He...did some things to her. Things no one should ever get to do to another person without permission."

"He was forcing himself on his students," Liam said, pausing as she hurled the rock into the sea. "It's unspeakable."

"Yes, it was." She sniffed then, breaking his heart in two as he reached for her hand, which she gripped hard. "The girl told me he'd been doing it for years. Her parents had gone to the school's principal, but nothing had been done. They'd accused her of lying or misinterpreting what had happened. That kind of thing would never go down at our school. They suggested counseling even. She told me I was going to need to be careful because when he picked a girl he wanted, he usually found a way to get her. I was terrified after that, scared to go to school. I pretended to be sick, like really sick."

She'd been smart even then, and he knew telling her would keep her strong enough to face down this horrible experience. After, he would hold her. "Figuring out how to stay away was good, Taylor. Really good."

She gave a rueful chuckle. "Yeah, I thought so. Only my grades tanked from missing so much school and being too worked up to focus, and my parents, who never noticed anything, noticed a note another teacher sent home about my unusual drop in 'academic performance.' I still remember the stale smell of my dad's Cuban cigars in his office when he summoned me to demand I tell him what was wrong. My mother was clutching her little Pomeranian as she sat in the chair beside me. They thought I was pregnant, you see, and were ready to suggest I get an abortion."

His mouth gaped. "That must have been a shock."

"Yeah," she said shakily, gripping his hand again, "and maybe it's what made me tell them the actual truth. We weren't close, and I didn't think they'd have my back. But my dad said there was no way he was going to let some teacher get his little girl pregnant, so he went to the principal. It ended up being the same conversation the girl in the bathroom had told me about."

He fought the urge to take her in his arms, but her eyes were glassy and the need to offer her comfort was hard to deny. So he rubbed her arms briskly. "Keep talking."

"The administration thought I was crazy—clearly something was wrong given all my absences and my grades tanking. Maybe something at home? That enraged my father. He was going to pull me from the school, which I was fine with, only... That teacher was still going to hurt other girls."

In that moment, he fell in love with her all the way. The goodness of her. The warrior in her. Now he could understand how she'd known how to handle a bully like Malcolm —he was far from the first she'd faced. "You had to do something, didn't you?"

She nodded, her face pale. "Yes. Except I didn't know what I could do. I was sixteen. A kid. My dad, who was a big booster at the school, and the other girl's parents hadn't been able to bring a stop to the abuse. The school wasn't going to admit they had an issue. I changed schools, but I couldn't let it go. I kept hoping for an idea. *Something.* Then I was walking one day, and I ended up at the Bowery Graffiti Wall. It captured my imagination with its incredible wall mural. That day it depicted a woman fighting for her human rights. She had on a multicolored dress and huge tears were running down her arms and legs, almost like she was crying a river of tears from her skin. I just stopped. All I could do was stare."

In that instant he knew why she loved spray-paint. But he waited, watching as she gathered herself, standing taller now as the tide touched their bare feet.

"I thought...I can paint the scene with the teacher for everyone to see. Our school uniforms with our cute little preppy decals will give it away. Then I scoped out a place I'd researched in a neighborhood far from mine—one that street artists were known to use—and made a plan. I was terrified I'd get arrested. Or busted by my parents, who might figure out I wasn't at my friend Patty's house for a sleepover. I didn't know there was a territory thing back then with street artists, but I got lucky. When one of the guys showed up, I told him what had happened, and he offered to help me."

And you fell in love with him for it, Liam thought, as the next wave cresting on the shore sent her against him. He led her away from the shoreline but kept her walking. She was deep in the past now, and he knew she needed to keep going. With all of it.

"I painted what I'd drawn up in my design, and when I ran out of spray paint, which I'd never used before, the guy —his name was Darren—went to his place and brought me some of his cans. I had to improvise on the color scheme, but I finally got it done with his help. God, it took forever. My heart was pounding so loud, and my hand was shaking so it was hard to keep within my lines. It was crazy and terrifying and thrilling."

He could almost feel her heart pounding as she spoke, and he saw a flash of her on a ladder, stretching up as she sprayed.

"Turns out that I was really good at it." She laughed without humor. "My art teachers had always said I was mediocre, which was crushing at the time. But this... The teacher's face was portraiture perfect, as was the schoolroom and the uniform's decal. Even I knew I'd rocked it in a way I couldn't with a still life or a landscape."

She'd found her justice, he understood, and it had taken her art to a new level.

"When I got home later, after changing in a Starbucks' bathroom downtown and throwing away my filthy clothes, I was exhausted but happy." This time she gave a tight smile despite being pale. "I had a date with the guy who'd helped me *and* my revenge, so to speak. And then the media got ahold of the mural, and it all went crazy. Bad crazy. The kind you wish you could wake up from."

His impulse to comfort her couldn't be ignored any longer. He pulled her to his chest, and she melted against him, breathing hard. She gave herself a long moment, clutching his back as he wrapped his arms around her.

Then she pressed back and exhaled audibly, shivering again. "The school I'd left thought of itself as elite, and the alumni list was like a *Who's Who* of important people. Seeing a mural of this teacher—Mr. Big Shit and Teacher of the Year—doing that to a girl was akin to lighting a gasoline station on fire. The teacher and the school demanded that the 'prankster' be arrested for defamation and a whole host of other stuff. I was terrified. It hadn't gone down the way I'd thought. I mean, the school was still denying everything."

Except there was more. He could feel the crescendo bursting up inside her as he rubbed her arms to keep her warm.

"They suspected an art student." She gave a shaky laugh. "Since my father had gone to the principal and I'd changed schools, the administration gave the police my name. I was questioned in our home. I still remember the sugar on the lead officer's shirt from the donut he'd had that morning. I lied about doing it, of course, since the officer was very clear about the severity of the crime. The perpetrator could go to jail."

He couldn't believe they would have put a sixteen-year-old in jail. And yet, who knew how far people with power would go to protect themselves?

"I did tell them what the teacher had done." She reached down to pick up another rock and hurled it into the sea with an audible burst of emotion from her throat. "We'd already told the principal. Apparently, other parents had come forward, and old complaints against the teacher had resurfaced. The media found people who were willing to go on record. Newspaper articles started coming out, and two months later, after an inquiry, the teacher was fired. The school was beset with scandal."

So she'd won. He'd hoped for a happy conclusion to this story. He reached for her hand again. "Good. I hope the teacher got jail time."

She looked off and leaned down for another rock, although she kept his hand. "He didn't. But he didn't teach again, which was good for other girls. The principal ended up resigning, but he got a job later in Upstate New York. Not everything works out fairly, but sometimes things happen that you can live with."

The tension inside of her started to shift as she flung the rock into the sea, and this time, he thought it would be her last. In his mind, a door opened, radiating bright light, and suddenly he understood what he hadn't before.

Taylor was the one Caislcán had been waiting for.

She was the one who could bring Malcolm and Aunt Mary and their like down, once and for all.

And he was going to do everything in his power to help her.

"You did good, *a stór*. You did right."

She gave another shaky laugh as she handed him his jacket, which he only put back around her shoulders, earning a beautiful smile from her. "I don't know what that means. *A store? A stork?* I tried to look it up, but I wasn't spelling it right."

He was touched that she'd tried. But then again, she had a curious mind. "I'll tell you later. What happened after this?"

Her gaze flew to his before she turned her head toward the sea. "What do you mean?"

He had a moment of indecision before he pressed it down. In this moment, he had to trust his gifts, and they were telling him to dive deeper. "Painting that mural opened up something inside you, didn't it? I just think there's more to the story."

The tension flowed back into her like it had been carried on a rough tide. "There is. In brief, I started sneaking out to hang with the guy who'd helped me. We were painting and dating. Well, I mostly painted and he helped. Then a couple of weeks after the teacher was fired and the supposed prankster was crowned a hero, he claimed he'd done it. Said he'd heard the story from a student who'd gone slumming."

He narrowed his eyes as she flipped her hair angrily over her shoulder. "He took credit? That's ballocks."

"Yes, it was. He was suddenly a hot street artist with a whole bunch of murals to his cred, ones I'd mostly done. I mean, he'd helped fill in my designs and paint in my lines, but he didn't have my irony or vision. But he did know about the streets and the scope."

"It must have crushed you," Liam said as they started to walk again, hand in hand.

"Yeah." She kicked at a rock, sending it into the sea. "I'd thought I loved him, and he loved me. He was my hero. My first. I was young and stupid, so I'd let him be my everything."

Liam could see it so clearly. This guy had helped her in a moment of need and opened another world to her. Liam couldn't understand how a relationship like that, one that had started with such positivity, could turn into such a great betrayal. "And your parents?"

"Oh, that's another tragic story." She kicked at another rock with more force. "They figured out I'd lied about being at a friend's house one night, so they searched my room. They found my drawings that I'd hidden in my locked chest, which was where I kept my diary. A place they weren't supposed to invade, they'd promised. They figured out it was me, although they thought I was helping the guy more than doing it on my own, which pissed me off."

"Of course it did." Now he better understood her desire for privacy. His mind reading would trigger those memories of invaded privacy.

"We had a huge fight. They threatened me. Yada yada. I kept on painting murals on my own. By then, I'd figured out how to do it alone. Then I got arrested one night because some off-duty cop came across me while he was chasing his dog. Anyway, my parents threatened to cut me off if I kept doing it. Not pay for college. That sort of thing. I told them to go screw themselves, and I walked out and went to a friend's. I was eighteen by then, so I could. And when I got a scholarship for college, I wanted to rub that in their face too."

She'd told him about walking out before. Now he knew from whom. "That was the last time you spoke to them."

"Yeah. They didn't come to my graduation from NYU, even though I graduated top of my class. In journalism. Not law or medicine like they'd hoped."

How could they not have seen how perfect journalism was for her? "I wish I could have been there to see you that day, what with your cap and gown and victorious smile."

She stepped back, her mouth dropping open. "Did you *see* it? Because yeah, I felt pretty victorious that day."

What could he say? "It wasn't hard to imagine, Taylor."

"Okay, I'll accept that answer since I'm pouring my heart out to you as an apology."

He took her gently by the arms and waited until she met his eyes as the sea thundered around them. "Is that what this was? I'd hoped it was your way of sharing something important with me."

A heartbreaking flash of vulnerability shot through her eyes like a lightning spark. "I also did it so you can understand why I hate men like Malcolm Coveney and why I want to bring him down. Hard."

He reminded her of the teacher. "Well, Taylor, it just so happens that I also want Malcolm Coveney to face justice for what he's done. How about we agree to help each other do that?"

Suddenly, he had a flash of intuition. That was what the spray paint was for.

"Oh, shit." She stormed a couple of steps away. "I can see it on your face. You already know what I'm planning."

He made a helpless gesture with his hands. "*A stór*, I can't always help it. I told you it comes in out of nowhere sometimes. Like now. You matter to me. My every sense seems to be on high alert."

She crossed her arms over her chest, looking oddly protective. "Let's leave that for now. Tell me what this *a stór* means."

His heart gave a little shudder. How would she react? Well, he would have to take a chance and share with her as bravely as she'd shared with him. "It means *my treasure*."

Her mouth flickered with a thousand smiles before she leaned down and picked up a piece of red sea glass from the sand. "Like this?"

He walked over to her. "No," he said, taking her hand and putting it over his heart. "Greater. Greater than any sunken Spanish galleon off the coast of Ireland. Greater than even the fountain of youth."

Her chest rose and fell with a massive breath before she shook her head. "Liam O'Hanlon, I don't know whether you're my soulmate, but you certainly are something to me. So..."

She went all attitude suddenly, arching her dark brows, which made him start to smile.

"Are you going to kiss me after that or what?"

Yeah, he was definitely going to kiss her. He waited a beat to see if she was going to close her eyes. But she just kept watching him, her longing and vulnerability obvious. "Come here, *a stór*."

She gestured to herself. "I'm right here."

Oh, she was magnificent. "Closer, Taylor." *So close I can feel your heart next to mine.*

One step forward, and she was pressed against him. Her breath rushed out as one of his hands cupped her hip and the other cupped the side of her face. He looked deep into her eyes a beat longer. There was still vulnerability there, yes, but curiosity too. In his own eyes, he imagined she could behold the love he already felt as well as the amusement and desire.

Lowering his head, he paused right above her lips, feeling her breath rush out in anticipation. He hadn't even kissed her yet, and still, he felt her energy rising to meet his. He was smiling as his mouth finally touched hers. She rocked back from the force of it, but he was ready. His hand tightened on her hip, bringing her back to him. His feet were steady under him as he caressed her lips lightly at first, fighting the urge to go deeper. Then she grabbed the back of his head, her fingers tangling into his hair, and devoured him with her mouth.

He pressed her closer, feeling the long, lean lines of her body against his own heated frame. The connection of their mouths was bliss, but soon he wanted a deeper connection. He put his heart into that kiss and knew when she felt it reach her own heart. She gasped against his lips, but then she moaned and sought his mouth, frantically kissing him until he caressed her cheek to settle her down.

He knew what she wanted, and it wasn't just a kiss. Slowing the movement of their mouths, he concentrated on helping her feel the energy of his heart. In every angle, in every way.

When she finally pressed back and lowered her head to his chest, he hugged her to him.

"Well, that *treasure* stuff sure had its effect." Her exhalation was audible as the waves crashed against the shore. "That was one heck of a kiss."

He kissed the top of her head. "And we've only just begun."

She met his gaze then, her eyes dancing. "Now that has me thinking about sex."

Chuckling, he took her hand. "Good. You ready for that ice cream?"

She swung his hand as they walked back toward the bike. "Emotional. Intense. Comforting. Passionate. And trustworthy. I'm really starting to like you, Liam O'Hanlon."

He shot her a grin. "Being my soulmate and all, you'd have a tough time resisting me."

Snorting, she tossed him his coat and his helmet before grabbing hers. "Maybe I don't want to. Maybe I'm tired of being so careful. Maybe I want to believe it. Even if it seems crazy."

He knew it was more than that. She wanted to let him in all the way. He didn't know everything about her yet, but he did know she'd been a lone wolf, used to going about things on her own. Their bond was changing all that. Not that he was going to say so. "So how are we going to take down Malcolm?"

The grin she was giving him was one he'd remember on their fiftieth wedding anniversary. Because it told him that she'd accepted him as her true partner. "With my old playbook, of course. If you're in..."

Like he would turn around and say no. "I have ladders."

"Aren't you handy?" She batted her eyelashes at him. "I'll need a few hours to finalize my design—so my idea to have a drink and meet everyone at the pub is out—but I think we need to strike while the iron's hot. The media's interested since Ghislaine just put out a press release along with a link to the video of me on the road. Tonight?"

"As you wish." He gestured to himself. "I'm yours. Day and night."

She fanned herself. "Well, that's hot."

"Good to know," he said with a grin.

"We'll need more paint." She mimicked spraying paint. "And a wall."

He could already see the wheels turning. "I know just the place."

CHAPTER SIX

When Taylor had decided to trust Liam and allow him to help her with her mural—a huge step for her after Darren—she'd figured he would find some unassuming wall, but he'd brought her to the three-story southern wall of the Sorcha Fitzgerald Arts Center!

"Are you sure about this?" she asked, looking over at him in the dark of his work truck as they sat in the parking lot.

"It's perfect!" He unbuckled his seat belt and turned to face her, flicking his phone around so he could better see her, she imagined. "We're an arts center—a mural is right up our alley."

She licked her lips. "If you want to be public, wouldn't the Brazen Donkey or a public wall in the village be better?" Wasn't this too on the nose?

"I know Brady would be fine with it, but this wall is bigger. And a public wall could be painted over. This way we can control it. Plus, it suits our message—one you and Ghislaine—"

"Will continue to tell," she added, fingering her trusty

backpack, already packed with key supplies. "Once I officially start my job. Tomorrow."

"It's a heck of a first day when you think about it."

She could see the edges of his winning smile in the darkened cab. "Well, you're the new construction director."

"Which is why I can disable the security cameras and lights with my handy little device here," he said, picking up what looked like a remote and punching a few buttons. "I'm one of four people who can. We won't have an audience, Taylor, or the Garda driving through town, and given the time this is going to take, that felt important."

Important didn't come close to covering it. Not that she hadn't hidden in alley corners or behind dumpsters from cops and bums and late-night partiers. "Are you sure you're going to be okay with keeping this our secret? They'll know someone dismantled the security system."

He took her hand, making her suddenly very aware of him and his body. "You have my word. Taylor, this is what we've been waiting for. A big gesture like this. Something only you could pull off. I know this is our answer to dealing with Malcolm and Aunt Mary and everyone else who's tried to stop us."

His certainty pushed her over the edge. "You're a real trustworthy and persuasive kind of guy, Liam O'Hanlon. All right, let's go."

The moment she exited the cab, she smelled something stronger than woodsmoke in the air, along with the strong ordure of animals. They were lucky the sky was cloudy with the half-moon, and damn it if it wasn't one of the darkest nights she'd ever worked in. Her blood started to race, carrying adrenaline through her veins.

Her happy place.

She detoured with Liam to the back of his truck, and

they started pulling out supplies, their hands brushing at times. She liked that he didn't stop her from carrying her share, but he did step in to haul off the ladders. And boy, did he have a number of nice commercial extension ladders. But it was his top-of-the-line three-tier industrial scaffolding that made her drool—materials he'd bought to build the recent sheds at the arts center.

"You really couldn't be better prepared for what I have in mind," she told him as he hefted up a large plastic tub that held gallons of paint they'd obtained at one of the large hardware stores he used in his day job. The man in charge hadn't blinked an eye when Liam had presented his list, saying he was stocking up for some upcoming projects. He'd told Taylor he'd known Liam since he was in diapers and now he was the best painter in the area, although he was proud that Liam had taken his new job.

"If you ever want to say that in another context," Liam added, "I'm completely open, by the way."

He was off before she realized he'd meant something really fun and hot. Her belly tightened. He *would* be prepared for everything she had in mind, and her fantasies were red-hot. He was drawing her in more and more, especially after their earth-shattering kiss on the beach. She hadn't known kissing could be that good.

But that was for later. After they finished the mural. She was thinking it would take seven hours to pull her off mural, weather permitting. Liam had assured her the weather was on their side. He'd apparently *asked* for it to be so. Whatever that meant.

She grabbed another tub of spray paint and started after him. Like her, he had on a black LED hat for night painting, although his was a stocking cap style and hers was a ball cap. After they'd unloaded the truck, he parked it inside a shed. Out of sight. He'd done it before she could ask, reading her mind in that eerie way of his.

"Tell me what I can do to help you," he said in a low voice, standing tall in front of her.

His strong presence was more assuring than she wanted to admit. She'd known him for a little more than twenty-four hours, and already she was trusting him more than she had anyone since Darren. "Let's arrange the supplies, and then I'll start spraying in the design from the ladders. Early on, I figured out I liked using spray paint for the outline and details. Less trash and hustle to get another can, because you can only hold so much in your backpack. Once I get that done, I'll mark the bigger sections with the color paint we want from the gallon cans, and then you can start filling in those spaces while I work on the deets."

"Like Malcolm's and Aunt Mary's faces," he added quietly. "It's a brilliant design, Taylor. I'm proud to be here with you, making this happen."

She was glad he was here too, even if it scared her. Then she caught the scent of oranges. "Apparently Sorcha sends her love too. I just smelled oranges, dammit." But soon all she would smell was the intoxicating scent of paint and aerosol, better than any perfume to her mind.

"She's only letting you know she's adding her own protections to our site tonight. Get started, *a stór*. I'm right with you."

And he was, moving the ladders and holding them in place as she scaled them to the top, some forty feet in the air. Not once did he tell her to be careful, which she appreciated. He was simply solid throughout, working the pullies on the ladders when she needed more spray paint.

She had the outline of the mural sketched out in an hour, and she credited her record time to his assistance using the pulleys to haul more spray paint up to her and take away her discarded cans. She hadn't known she'd have a wall of this size when she'd sketched out her drawing. Usually she spent more time planning her design to fit the dimensions of the space available and make the appropriate stencils, but they'd been short on time, and she'd just gone for it. He'd laughed when she'd mentioned he might be buying too much paint, but he'd asked her to trust him. It had paid off. She'd need to remember that. He was not Darren.

Jumping to the ground from the ladder, she let a full smile break across her face. This was going to be one of her best works ever. She could always feel it. Smooth sailing. Pure joy. Which included being with him, she realized. Sharing this. Really serious thoughts...

"Okay, I'm done with the outline." She massaged her hand and the pointer finger she used to depress the spray can to keep the blood circulating.

"Your hand sore?" he asked, taking it and giving it a bone-melting massage.

She wanted to purr as her belly tightened. "I'll slink to the ground if you keep that up."

"Later," he told her with a grin and an easy final caress, her LED illuminating the handsome planes of his face.

"Deal. Let's open up the paint cans. Then I'll tag the colors for the lower shapes and you can get going while I work on the details. When I finish, I'll help you with the upper shapes. Cool?"

"Supercool."

He was already striding to the neat rows of paint they'd lined up according to the color spectrum, from white to black. The soft *pop* of paint cans being pried open by a screwdriver filled her ears. She rubbed her hands together and went to work behind him, hauling cans and the appropriate brush to start the first shapes. She'd adjusted her design to fit the wall, making the shapes bigger.

She glanced over her shoulder, watching Liam crouch from one paint can to the next, moving with the efficiency and focus of someone used to working on large house projects. Somehow, she knew he would find his own rhythm for how he wanted to do what she needed. She had only to point him in the right direction. And try not to keep admiring him while he worked.

She unloaded her bag of empty spray cans from her backpack into the portable freestanding trash bin he'd set up, wincing at the noise.

"It's fine, Taylor," he called in a low voice from a few feet away. "No one out here but us and some nearby sheep."

Still, her heart was pounding. Was his? They couldn't be caught for trespassing, but she wanted to be out of sight before anyone was the wiser.

Repacking her bag with the next batch of supplies, she headed for the left extension ladder. "Keep working," she called out in a loud whisper. "I don't need you to spot me. I've been up on ladders millions of times."

His work on the paint cans paused for a few moments, as if he was weighing the wisdom of letting her be up at those heights without him holding the ladder. The ground was damp, something he said was common in Ireland with the rain. But they worked with damp ground and ladders all the time, he'd told her, so she could trust he'd secured it well. And she did. Which was why she didn't think twice about climbing the runs of the ladder to the top and starting on Malcolm's big face.

He was going to be a grotesque cartoony figure in her depiction, with a portly body and giant gold diamond rings on his swollen fingers. His head, although close enough to reality that no one could question it was him, was proportionally smaller. He would be looming over her, of course, positioning her in the center of the painting. Her figure would be something of a Joan of Arc representation, standing tall and defiant but much smaller in size than him while his goons circled her, their faces eerie depictions of greedy malevolence, as dark water swirled around her.

Behind her figure would be other people he'd threatened. Sophie would be the immediate one, and then the remaining figures would be indistinct, becoming smaller and smaller until they were Thumbelina size. Since she was a child, she'd loved that book, and it had informed her street art.

She finished Malcolm's face, adding a touch of green spray paint to his eyes and cheekbones to symbolize the greed coming through his very pores. Yes, she thought, looking at that large, round face. She had captured the essence of him. The arrogance. The cruelty. The lust for power and dominance over others.

Descending the left ladder, she found Liam waiting for her, extending his water bottle to her. "I can't see it, but I can feel how delighted you are. I'm glad I'm here to share this with you."

She was aware of the intimacy of drinking from the same bottle, but she was more aware of him watching her. Putting her hand on his fleece jacket, she could feel his heat. Yeah, they were both keyed up, from each other as much as the work. "I am too, Liam. I'm heading up to the middle. How are you doing?"

"I've got the lower shapes done except for the scene you didn't mark in the right corner."

Right. She had a plan for that. "You're done?" She

reluctantly dropped her hand from his chest and walked over to inspect. "Wow! You work fast. And good. Nice strokes. No visible lines."

His amused snort carried. "I'm a professional, remember?"

She walked back to him and fingered the collar of his fleece, teasing the hot skin there. "So it seems. Okay, let me tag the next shapes for you."

He gave her cheek an answering stroke. "It's like paint by numbers," he joked, following her to the line of paint cans.

She could already see where he'd discarded the gallons he'd used. "One of my favorite moments is when all the paint cans I've lined up are gone."

"Mine too. You can see the progress as you toss the used ones out. Come. Show me what's next."

And so she did, tagging the shapes quickly as he set up the portable scaffolding. "I think it will be easier if it's ready for me to use."

He was right. She would glance his way from time to time as she worked on the next batch of details, starting with herself and then working down to the goons and Sophie and the smaller indistinct figures. He went from being below her to joining her in the center, working on filling in the dark water threatening to envelop her and the others.

When his light touched her, she looked over to find him some five feet away. "It looks incredible from here, Taylor. Powerful. You do as well, by the way. I'll be coming around your left side now."

Man, he was fast and seeing him like this, working beside her, made her want him even more. "Perfect. I'm almost done with this part, and then I'll be going to the right corner."

She resumed her focus and worked on painting her descending figures as time-honored carrot shapes before descending the ladder.

"There's some more bottled water to the left of the paint," he called in a loud whisper. "And coffee in the blue thermos."

When had he made coffee? When she was in the zone, she didn't register what was happening around her sometimes. "Seriously?"

"I work here, remember?"

God, she wanted to throw her arms over her head and laugh. She worked here too now. With *him*. How was it going to be running into him every day? How had she not thought about that before? Right, because she'd been battling her previous reservations about trusting him. Now she was going to have to control herself from grinning at him like a lovesick girl because she was so crushing on him now.

And when she tasted the coffee, she fell in love. "OMG! You make good coffee too?"

His soft laughter was like carnival music, the kind that had made her want to skip as a child. "You're only beginning to become aware of all my talents, *a stór*."

Treasure. He was calling her his treasure. She'd never been anyone's treasure. She'd mostly been treated as a nuisance by her parents. Her heart cracked open a bit more and she couldn't quite clear all the emotion from her throat. "Do you need anything?" she managed.

"Only one of your smiles," he called, making her sigh into his thermos as its steam wafted over her face.

She would give him a smile and more after they finished. Heck, maybe she needed to stop fighting the whole soulmate thing and go with it. Clearly being with him was working for her. Plus, she wanted him like she'd never wanted any guy. She wasn't sure whether it was the fumes from the spray paint or the magic of creating the mural together, but she was feeling like she could make the leap of a lifetime.

First, though, she needed to tackle his aunt. He hadn't needed to show her a photo. Mary Kincaid was, after all, part of the briefing book Bets had provided to her prior to coming to Caisleán. There'd been photos along with some basic information about what she'd done to undermine the center, everything from closing it down to harassing its employees and destroying some of Bets' prize roses. Taylor already hated the woman. She was a viper. Cruel. The kind of person who wouldn't stop.

Well, Taylor was going to make her stop. Fairy tales were shorthand for the kinds of archetypes people faced every day, and she'd decided Mary Kincaid would be the haggard witch from "Hansel and Gretel." The two children she was harassing would have apple-colored cheeks and wholesome faces out of a Norman Rockwell painting. But inside the oven the witch was hoping to cook the two children in would be a single red rose, dripping with blood, the kind she imagined Mary grew in her famed garden.

Taylor went to town on the images, starting with the scene in the cottage before tackling the three figures. Because she wanted people to recognize Mary, she kept her face mostly realistic in style except for a slight bulge in her eyes to show her greed and avarice. The children were a piece of cake, and she had them finished in a half hour.

When she stepped back, she had a flash of inspiration. She dug out a few cans of spray paint and painted a black cauldron in the corner with fire billowing out as the witch fed books into it, since Taylor knew Mary had been behind the attempts to censor an art book the center had wanted to use in the children's program.

Yes, that was it. Taylor could feel all her anger at people like Mary Kincaid draining out of her. Expressing her feelings in her art did that. Then she'd read the paper the next day, and the news would be filled with more villains.

Still, she would take her stand. She checked her watch. They were heading into the sixth hour. Right on schedule. They would be out of here by five, well before the first sheep farmer emerged at sunrise, which was around eight at this time of year.

She headed over to the center ladder. "I'm ready to join you on the scaffolding," she called in a loud whisper.

"Come on up," he shot back, peering over the side at her.

When she reached him, he helped her up, his touch igniting fires on her tired and aching hand. He handed her a brand-new paintbrush. They shared a conspiratorial smile, and she felt her heart roll over in her chest.

"Thanks." She wanted to kiss him but told herself to wait. "Let's finish this."

They didn't speak after that, painting together in companionable silence. She was aware of him stretching from time to time, which encouraged her to do the same, as she tried not to think about his beautiful body. Her own muscles were starting to feel the burn, as was her neck. She imagined he felt the same. When they reached the last shape, he gestured to it grandly.

"You should finish it," he said softly, his green eyes somehow even brighter in the light from her hat now.

She appreciated the gesture but shook her head. "Let's finish it together."

His mouth curved before he nodded. She imagined he would start whistling if he didn't know she was worried about the noise carrying.

"Don't think this means I'm a hundred percent sure you're my soulmate or anything," she said in what she hoped was a flirty tone. "But I'm willing to admit the idea is growing on me. Hard. But I can confess that I have a very serious crush on you. Like spray paint serious."

She caught the sweeping smile on his lips. "Progress then."

The sound of his paintbrush rushing up the wall filled her ears, making her smile. Yeah, it really was.

She made sure to do the last shape from the outside in. He did the same. They crept closer and closer to each other as the black paint covered the wall. When their shoulders touched, they exchanged a look and grinned. The final stroke of each of their brushes finished the mural. Taylor lowered her hand to her side in triumph. "Well, that's it."

"Nice working with you, Taylor McGowan." He put his arms around her, and she leaned her head against his shoulder.

"You too, Liam O'Hanlon."

They stood there for a moment, the silence wrapping around them like an embrace. The dark of the night felt far off given the lights they had illuminating each other. There was the call of a loud bird overhead, one she didn't recognize, and she laughed as the joy of their victory poured through her. It had been so easy!

"What?" he asked softly, his arm tightening around her waist.

"I was just thinking how glad I am that no birds have bugged us. If you had any idea what a pain pigeons can be when you paint like this."

"You'll have to tell me those stories, *a stór*." He faced her, his eyes bright with a soft emotion she didn't want to name yet. "I almost touched your cheek before I remembered I have paint on my hand."

Warmth spread through her chest. "Good catch. My cheek, huh? How are lips? I don't think I have any paint on mine, and yours look...normal." If gorgeous and delicious were normal, which they were *not*.

He was already smiling as he lowered his head. "Good idea. Your lips are clean as a whistle too, and all the more tempting for it. Let's see how this goes."

The first touch of his mouth was a mere caress, and then he sampled her bottom lip.

"You're going to make my knees give out if you do that again," she said, her voice a murmur. "And we're on scaffolding."

"I won't let you fall," he whispered, taking her bottom lip between his teeth ever so gently as his hands cupped her protectively to his body.

She couldn't take it. She crushed her lips to his, needing the pressure. He changed the angle to take the kiss deeper, making her moan. She lifted her hands to grip his back, both of them careless about the paint as they tasted each other with pure delight.

He pulled back this time. "Okay, we are on scaffolding, so I'm going to be the responsible one and say we need to stop that. But when we're gone from here, I'd very much like to kiss you again."

"That can be arranged, Mr. O'Hanlon."

He sent her a sexy wink as he helped her make the transfer from the scaffolding to the ladder and descend to the ground. She tossed her paintbrush into the bin and started to clean up while Liam worked on packing up the extension ladders and the scaffolding. By the time he had the heavier equipment stowed, there was one remaining paint can on the ground.

"That's the only one we didn't use," she said, kicking it because it felt good to hear the answering thud. "You rocked the supply count. I'm glad your gifts helped us there."

He laughed. "Actually, I helped Carrick paint this bitch back when he built the house. I knew what the wall would take, and then with your design... But I have to be honest. I had some backup paint in a few colors in the supply shed."

She wanted to kiss him again. "Honest, professional, and good company. I think this has all the makings of a beautiful relationship, don't you?"

His smile made her shiver in delight. "I do. Come, *a stór*. Let's get you home."

Her buoyant spirits dipped. They would be leaving each other, and she wasn't ready for that.

"Maybe you could stay over?"

He picked up the last paint bucket and met her eyes. "When you're truly ready for that, you won't ask it like a question."

If he hadn't smiled, she might have been crushed. But he did. And it was that simple gesture that had her lifting her hands to the dark sky as the heady sense of freedom shot through her while he walked to the truck to stow the can.

She gazed up at the length of the three-story mural. She would not be able to see its full effect until daylight tomorrow—like everyone else—although she'd pore over the closeup photos she'd managed to capture before going to bed. Deep inside, though, she knew it was flawless, even if she hadn't painted every shape. Liam had given his all to this mural as much as she had.

Her first mural in Ireland. She'd considered not

signing it with her tag, but who was she kidding? She *had* to sign her work. Because there was no way her fans wouldn't recognize her voice. Besides, wouldn't the attention it brought do more to help her take Malcolm down? Yeah, she didn't think it was arrogant to admit it would. Her fans were going to go bananas over it. She glanced at the corner where it would go. If she added her tag now, she'd have to tell Liam the rest of her story. He might even have heard of her. As she watched him clean up the last of their supplies, she acknowledged what her heart had already known—her secret would be safe with him. After tonight, she trusted him completely. Impossible perhaps, but still true. He had more than proved himself to her.

"I said you could trust him," she heard Sorcha say from behind her.

"You had to show up and gloat, didn't you?" Taylor joked back as the scent of oranges tickled her nose.

"Of course." She swept forward, surrounded by a white light very reminiscent of the ethereal glow Taylor had used for the Joan of Arc impression of herself in the mural. "I'm very proud to have this mural on the building with my name on it. Now your name will be on it too, a decision I'm glad you came to. You two did well."

"Thank you," she said, uncomfortable to feel the ghost's approval mattered.

"You must hold tightly to each other now." The scent of oranges intensified then. "To prepare for what comes next."

With that, she vanished.

Liam jogged over, taking her by the arms. "You all right? What did Sorcha say?"

"We need to be ready for what happens next." She gripped his paint-covered hands. "Now, I need to ask something of you. This is the last of my secrets. I think I know the answer, but can I trust you a little more?"

"Always," he said immediately in that solid voice of his. No hesitation.

She leaned down and picked up her favorite spray can, the one she used to sign her name. Veritas. It wasn't just a word to her. It was her creed. Her purpose. She was aware of Liam coming to stand behind her as she sprayed the word and added a bold line under it.

"Truth," he read.

"Yes," she said, turning around to face him while searching his face. "And my tag. Liam, I don't know if you've heard about the street artist Veritas—"

"Of course I have, *a stór*," he said, taking her hands and gripping them with a powerful brand of strength. "I love his work. Or should I say hers?"

Okay, even though she trusted him, her belly still trembled at how huge a moment this was for her. "Yeah, it's funny. Everyone thinks Veritas is a man. Even that first street artist who took credit for my first mural believes it. He said so in an article once. I couldn't believe he didn't recognize my voice."

"Clearly he was an idiot as much as he was a thief."

"Right? But no one can believe a woman would be able to make it as a street artist. That's why I know my parents haven't realized it either, although I'd love to see their faces at reveal time. The line is that it's too much work to haul paint. We women are too weak. We're not safe on the streets. Bullshit. But it's been good cover, although sometimes the gender dissing pisses me off."

His heart was beating faster, and she imagined it was because of her touch. "*Eejits*, as we say in Ireland."

"Yeah, *eejits*." But not him. Of course he wasn't. She

could never fall for an eejit, and he was supposed to be her soulmate.

"Well, it's nice to meet you, Veritas." He held out his hand and shook hers crisply when she took it. "Thanks for sharing your identity with me. It's good and safe, I can assure you."

She touched his chest, knowing his heart carried the truth of those words. "I know. That's why I told you. There's probably more I need to tell you."

"We have plenty of time, *a stór*."

As they walked away from the first mural she'd collaborated on in nearly fifteen years, she found she was ready to trust him completely.

He'd just become her partner in crime, after all.

CHAPTER SEVEN

L inc stared up at the masterpiece on the south side of
the arts center.

Malcolm's evil cartoon face was the kind of stuff that
gave children nightmares, and Mary's terrifying depiction
as the witch from "Hansel and Gretel" would put those
same kids in therapy for sure.

But it was the image of Taylor standing tall in Joan of
Arc armor that caught him by the throat. She looked so tiny
amidst the huge monster-like characters and black tides, but
Linc knew that was the point. It was one hell of a depiction,
holding everyone around him spellbound.

His Bets stood next to Donal and Ghislaine, who had
their hands on each other with their mouths open. Even
Wilt's brows were knitted as he tilted his head up to the
spectacle. Linc knew he'd gaped like a trout, but truly, he
wondered how in the hell the internationally famous street
artist Veritas had ended up in bumfuck Ireland painting on
their wall—not that he wasn't grateful for the support.

"I knew Carrick wouldn't joke about something like

this, but I still didn't completely believe it when he woke us," Bets managed to say.

"That Irish luck y'all talk up has kissed us hard," Linc responded. "We somehow managed to come to the attention of Veritas. My Ellie's going to squeal with joy."

"I'm squealing on the inside now that the shock has passed," Ghislaine said, shooting photos with her phone as Donal stalked the building's length, still gazing up at it in awe as the sunrise broke out around them in peach, rose, and blue.

"To think Veritas came all the way to our small town after Taylor's incident with Malcolm and pulled this off," Donal said, thrusting his hand at the mural. "How did he know about Mary and the rose?"

Yeah, that made Linc's gut twitch a little. It was also puzzling why Liam wasn't depicted in the mural. "The rose competition stuff would have been in the papers."

"Our local paper!" Bets exclaimed. She started pacing, something she did when she couldn't contain her energy.

"Maybe Veritas is Irish," Linc mused, caressing his unshaven jaw. "No one knows who he is, so it's not out of the realm of possibility."

Wilt appeared beside him, all business again. "Someone turned off the cameras and the security lights last night at 10:07 p.m."

Linc's gut clenched a little more.

"What?" Bets cried out. "How is that possible?"

His woman was getting all stirred up, and they hadn't even had breakfast. "Veritas had inside help, it seems, sugar. I doubt it's the first time he's reached out to someone local for assistance."

"But he's *anonymous*," Bets continued.

She was going to wear out the grass if she kept pacing

like this, so Linc pulled her to his side. "I imagine he emails anonymously to ask for help in some cases or people email him about issues. If he'd emailed me, I would have given it. Of that you can be sure."

"Me too," Ghislaine said, grinning like she'd up and won the lottery. "Our center is going to have international media attention again. Big-time. The sheep are nothing compared to this. Veritas just put our fight on the map."

Linc wanted to kick his heels together and give a *yeehaw* but he couldn't manage it. Not with that evil visage in the top corner looking down at him. "Malcolm is so not going to like this."

"Neither is Mary." Bets took off, this time heading straight to the lower right corner of the mural. "I mean, look at this! She's going to hate being the witch—even though that's exactly what she is. I'm so glad it's obvious even to people who don't live in Caisleán."

Linc turned as a car skidded to a stop in the parking lot. A squeal pierced the air. He fought a grin. Damn, his baby was such a fan girl when it came to art.

"*Oh my God!*" Ellie cried out as she came running, in her pink and black polka dot bathrobe no less. "It's true! Veritas really came to our arts center. Holy shit!"

Kathleen followed her, more grumbly and wearing faded jeans and a pullover.

"You couldn't get her dressed?" Linc asked as she reached them. Ellie had bypassed them entirely to run up to the wall.

"She didn't give me time to brush my hair," Kathleen said, pointing to her own bedhead.

Linc put his arm around her. "I wasn't going to say."

She scowled for good measure. "Wait until you see Brady. Declan was up and about to head out to work when

Carrick texted the news. Sheep farmers are Ireland's town criers, aren't they?"

"Seems so." He almost laughed when he saw his son-in-law coming forward in green wellies and a bathrobe.

"Nice of you to dress up for the outing, Brady," he called out.

Declan, who was right behind his brother, rolled his eyes dramatically. "They're a pair, these two. Ellie started screaming at us in Latin and the next thing we knew, we were being shoved out the door and into the car. Who put this crazy graffiti on our wall?"

"Oh, Declan!" Ellie cried out, her arms falling heavily to her sides as she turned back from the wall to look at him. "How can we be in the same family?"

Brady whispered conspiratorially to Linc, "I didn't know who this Veritas person was either. All I got from Ellie's jabbering was that he's some street artist. Is he pretty famous?"

Linc bit the inside of his cheek after Kathleen made a comical face behind Brady's head. "Ever heard of Banksy?"

Brady nodded solemnly, his hair mussed with cowlicks.

"He's like that," Linc supplied, watching as Ellie marched over and grabbed Kathleen and proceeded to point and squeal at the mural.

Brady stuck his hands in his pockets. "So this is big, then?"

"Yep." Linc clapped him on the back for what had to be the understatement of the century. "Son, best keep that robe closed or the women folk might faint."

The younger man fumbled with the robe's tie. "Thanks, Linc."

The arrival of more cars in the parking lot had Linc shaking his head. The circus was about to start. They needed a plan and stat. He fell back to where Wilt was standing, checking God knew what on his tablet. "You find anything yet?"

"No. Someone who had access to our systems shut them down. Only four people have that access. After tonight, I'll make sure everyone has a separate login for identification purposes."

Linc ticked them off. "You. Me. Bets. Liam. Since I know you and Bets didn't do it, that leaves Liam."

"Seems that way to me," Wilt agreed.

"He had the perfect motivation to help Veritas," Linc continued, warming to the theory. "Malcolm hurt Taylor, and Liam was there on scene. Plus, it's in the wind that Taylor is Liam's soulmate, as the Irish like to say."

"So I've heard around town and at the pub." Wilt shut down his screen and tucked it under his beefy arm. "You should also know that I have been told about Sorcha. By more people than I can count. In fact, I have a few video surveillance tapes from the arts center with her in them."

Linc took a step back, flummoxed by the news. "You do? But how is that—"

"Being new to the supernatural, I had to do some research." Wilt's mouth twisted. "Apparently spirit photography goes back to the 1860s. It turns out it's very common for a ghost to be seen in a photo or on the video from a security camera."

"Seriously? No specialized camera gear is needed?"

"No," Wilt deadpanned.

Linc suddenly had a light bulb go on. "Perfect. Do you still have those images of our lovely Sorcha?"

Wilt nodded. "In fact, she was the first thing I saw when the cameras were turned on last night. I don't know if this is significant, but she was grinning like a little kid as she danced in front of the mural."

Oh, that sweet woman. If she weren't a ghost, he'd kiss her for this. "If you're asked—by anyone—you'll say it's possible Sorcha used her supernatural powers to make sure there was no recording of last night's events."

Wilt swung his head to Linc. "Sir?"

"You heard me. Sorcha turned off our system." He clapped Wilt on the back for emphasis before heading over to Ghislaine.

He had to protect Liam as much as the center. Malcolm was going to want heads to roll for this depiction, and he wasn't getting Liam's.

"Ghislaine," Linc called in a low voice, prompting her to look up from her phone. "I want you to get a press release out ASAP and post as many pictures as you can justify putting online."

She raised her brow. "Already begun, Linc. Do you think I don't know my business? Besides, since Taylor is one of the subjects, it would be better for this to come from me. We should schedule a press conference. People are going to want to see this beauty up close and personal. I assume we're leaving it up for now."

"You thinking someone might want us to paint over it?" The look she gave him had his stomach clenching again. "Yeah, I thought so too. We'll deal with it."

"Any idea why Wilt didn't get a notice that someone was on the property?" she asked with her usual insight.

Shit. Now he was going to have to lie to his own people. Or dance around the truth. "The system went down, but the first person Wilt saw when it came back online was Sorcha."

The usually perfectly composed Frenchwoman nearly dropped her phone. *"You have a video of her?"*

Right. The press would devour that kind of story, right? "We do."

She turned into super publicist before his eyes, her eyes hungry and as crafty as the Cheshire cat's. "I want it, Linc. Bad."

"Tell Wilt to give it to you," he said, feeling a little guilty that he was making decisions like this on the fly. He'd brief Bets later.

"You should know that Veritas posted a couple of photos of the mural himself online ten minutes ago. LED lights and central images. Not the whole mural obviously. That will be our job." Ghislaine punched something into her phone and held it out to him.

She was right. The photos didn't do the work justice— LED illuminated shapes in a sea of black. Three stories in one night. The scope and logistics were unfathomable. "How many followers does Veritas have?"

"Nine million on Instagram alone," Ghislaine answered. "Linc, you think we had attention before, but we're at a whole new level now. Taylor should be called. Do you want to do it?"

He looked over to where Bets was standing. She had a crowd around her, growing every minute as more people from the village arrived after hearing the news. They were all familiar faces. Eoghan and Sandrine were gesturing to the mural with Donal while Sophie and Jamie talked to Brady with little Greta, who was dressed for school. Carrick was holding baby Emeline as Angie hustled up to Ellie and Kathleen.

Then he saw Liam approaching with Taylor beside him and inclined his head toward Ghislaine. "No need. Liam handled it. You take the lead here. Taylor's had a hell of a first few days."

"She's going to be the center of attention, Linc." Ghislaine touched his arm. "There's no getting around it."

No, there wouldn't be. "Do what you need to. I'm off to do what I do best."

He strode over quickly to where Liam and Taylor had stopped, well away from the cluster of townspeople. "Morning. Heck of a way to start your Monday, isn't it, Taylor?"

She put her hand to her throat as she gazed at the mural. "It's a lot to take in, that's for sure. I mean. Veritas."

He inclined his chin toward the mural. "Seems we have another supporter on our side. You're a reporter. You would know how big this is. Ghislaine is point since you're part of the story."

"So much for her only putting in consultant hours when needed." She nodded, looking wan. "This will be a full-time job for a while. That's probably good for the arts center, but I feel bad about not doing my job."

Linc patted her arm again. "Malcolm's fault, like most things around here. Liam, can I speak to you for a moment?"

Their eyes met at last, and the younger man nodded. They walked a few feet away until they were out of earshot. "I'll talk quickly so your mother doesn't get all worried. Sorcha appeared on the video cameras last night when the system came back on. I've asked Wilt to tell anyone who inquires that Sorcha and her supernatural powers might have shut our system down last night to help Veritas with the mural. As someone who has access to the system, I wanted you to know what we discovered."

Liam didn't blink for a moment, and before he could open his mouth, Linc said, "Malcolm and others may inquire. If anyone asks you, you'll say Sorcha must have been behind it. Ghislaine will be sharing the video of her with the press and online. Understand?"

He shifted on his feet, frowning. Linc put a hand on his shoulder.

"Son, I know the kind of man you are, but you need to trust me. Sorcha played a hand in this. That's our line here. Don't deviate from it. At least not until I speak to our lawyers, all right? There's more at stake here than either of us know, I suspect."

As if prompted by his remark, an eerie scream sliced through the air. Linc's head whipped toward it. Mary Kincaid was standing at the edge of the parking lot in a brown dress, her fists raised to the air in rage.

Linc's gut trembled at the view of her in full witch mode. He motioned for Bets to stay put. Mary was unpredictable and dangerous, and he didn't want her anywhere near his woman. Then he started toward her, waving off the others too. Wilt sidled up to him as he reached her.

"Morning, Mary," he managed over the sudden dryness in his mouth.

"You will paint over this monstrosity today, Linc Buchanan." The whites of her eyes seemed to be filled with veins of fire. "This is the worst kind of defamation. It's criminal. I'm calling the Garda. Whoever did this is going to go to jail."

Wilt shot him a look before Linc stepped in to answer. "This mural was painted on private property—ours—and we sanction it. Feel free to talk to the Garda, Mary, but I fear you're shit out of luck on this one. Or... You can deny that's you down there burning books and ready to shove little children into your oven. That's what I would do if I were you."

She stepped forward until she was an inch away from

him, a vein throbbing in her forehead. "If I can't get it taken down, you can be sure Malcolm will. And he won't stop at repainting. We'll take over your arts center, Linc Buchanan, and close it down for good. You wait and see."

Watching her storm off in her plain brown shoes, Linc rubbed the bridge of his nose. Bets arrived at a jog. "I know you were trying to protect me, so I stayed back, but what did she say?"

"Same shit, different day, Bets." He drew her to him because he needed a little comfort after that altercation. "We need to make some plans. She's right about one thing—Malcolm won't be far off."

Sure enough, Malcolm arrived only forty minutes later, under Garda escort from his town, likely to help him arrive faster. He had more goons this time. Eight in total. All in black leather, looking like they would happily break old ladies' kneecaps.

"You finally made the wrong move," the man of the hour called, his ten rings flashing as he straightened his suit jacket and ambled closer. "You need planning permission for street art, and I happen to know you don't have it. Veritas doesn't work like that. You will paint over it. Today. Or you will go to court for obstruction of justice. And I will have them close down the Sorcha Fitzgerald Arts Center once and for all."

Bets took Linc's hand and clenched it hard. "You just try, you—"

"*Bets*," he said softly, never taking his eyes off Malcolm.

Wilt leaned in and whispered, "If it's on private property, you've given permission, and it has artistic or cultural merit, it doesn't need planning permission."

Malcolm would know the law too, and Linc could feel the noose dangling in the air between them. The bastard wanted them to commit to a story. They weren't going to do it today.

"Malcolm, you go on and do what you need to do," he drawled, picking lint off his jacket as if he didn't have a care in the world. "Personally, I'd think you would love the attention you're about to get in the media. I mean, look at that depiction of you. If people weren't scared of you before, they sure as hell will be now. Won't they?"

Linc could all but hear the music swell like it would in a Western when two men faced each other down in the street for a gunfight at high noon. Malcolm spat on the ground in the direction of the mural, which only made Linc smile more broadly and rest back on his heels.

"Your little Yank does look so very small in that depiction, doesn't she?" Malcolm threw an eerie smile toward Taylor, whom Liam was standing with beside one of the sheds. "But we all know that St. Joan of Arc's life ended so tragically. I wonder what Veritas was trying to say. It's so hard to know with art, isn't it?"

Bets' audible intake, along with Malcolm's second strait-jacket smile in Taylor's direction, had Linc saying, "While you're looking into that planning permission detail, we'll be informing the Garda about the threat you just made to Ms. McGowan."

"*Threat?*" He looked around at his goons and the couple of Garda officers with him. "Did you hear me make a threat?"

They all shook their heads.

So that was how it was going to be.

"You know, Malcolm, if you stopped a stranger on the street and asked him which was worse—threatening a woman repeatedly or putting a bunch of paint on a wall—guess what the majority of people would say? You think investors want to work with someone like that? Do you think tourists will want to go to Watertown after they learn you're the one who runs it? Your businesses are the ones that will be closing, especially after we're done with you in the media."

"You'll soon see what a mistake you've made," Malcolm said as he flashed his overbleached teeth. He signaled for a goon to open his car door. "You have my word on it."

Linc watched as Malcolm and his entourage took off, the Garda sirens wailing their complicity.

"Planning permission!" Bets raved. "Are we really back to that? Linc, tell me he's bluffing."

"Sugar, I think so, but we'll want to be sure."

He needed to call their lawyers stat.

CHAPTER EIGHT

Taylor hadn't directly experienced the shock wave caused by one of her pieces since her first mural to take down the math teacher.

Every townsperson from Caisleán, it seemed, had chatted her up about the incident, introducing themselves to her as they hovered under the mural. She'd felt really weird responding to questions about how she felt about Veritas' depiction of her. Like totally weird. When people raised the question to her about why Liam wasn't in the mural, she went with the truth: she'd been the focus of Malcolm's intimidation. Having Liam in the mural would have diminished that. Of course, Kathleen and Ellie added their two cents about Taylor not needing a man to save her, which satisfied others. But the discussion about the mural continued around her as she tried to act casual.

Bets tried hard not to mother hen her, but it was obviously tough for her after Malcolm's second threat. That dude was a real douche of a human being. And then there was Linc, who'd put his hand on Taylor's shoulder and told her everything was going to be okay somehow.

Who was he kidding? The Caisleán situation was about as out of control as ever after Malcolm and Mary had shown up breathing fire and damnation.

There was one bright spot: Liam. He was a bastion of calm.

"I should never have involved you," she told him after they'd returned to her place, pacing back and forth in her living room as he sat peacefully on her couch drinking a cup of tea. "I was reckless and overly emotional. I didn't look at all the angles. I should have investigated the laws more. I put you and the center at risk. Liam—"

"*A stór*, why don't you sit down and drink the tea I made you? There's nothing to be done right now. Linc told me to take you home and sit tight, and that's what we're going to do. How can I help you find some peace here?"

She stopped short and gaped at him. How could he look so Zen and gorgeous right now? "*Peace?* They're threatening to shut down the arts center because of what I did. You could get into trouble if they figure out you were the one who helped me."

"Linc already told me that the official story is that Sorcha must have been the one who shut down the system last night. I'm not sure how I feel about that. I'm still letting it sit."

"*Sorcha?*"

"Apparently she was the first image on the surveillance video when the system turned back on," Liam informed her, raising his super sexy sandy brows.

"I told you that I had your back," the ghost said suddenly from behind her.

Taylor let out a shriek. "Oh my God! Stop doing that."

Liam rose gracefully and gently led her to the couch

next to him. "Why don't we sit and listen to what Sorcha has to say? She doesn't show up unless it's important."

"Thank you, Liam." The ghost sank onto the matching ottoman, arranging her dress as if they were having a soiree. "I always did appreciate your levelheadedness. Now, it seems to me that Taylor needs a crash course on the dark side of Ireland. I believe you're familiar with the corruption, so you'll understand what I mean when I say there are a lot of backdoor dealings. That's something Malcolm is good at."

"Plus, he has a lot of goons," Taylor added. "Did you see his posse today? He wanted us to be peeing our pants."

"Exactly! The new Garda officer, Mr. Hart, while perhaps a fair arbiter of the law in Caisleán, isn't a match for someone like Malcolm. You need something bigger to take Malcolm down than media clips and street art. If you can prove he's been swindling his friends, you're golden."

"Because money is serious business, and you don't swindle your so-called friends," Liam finished. "Linc knows who has been investing in Malcolm's hotels—"

"Can you get me that file?" she asked, perking up.

Her green-eyed pirate soulmate possibility simply gazed at her. "And what do you plan on doing with it?"

Her frown didn't change the patient, sweet way he was looking at her. "Not me. We need someone who knows how to investigate this kind of jerk and go deeper into his corruption. Like Sorcha said."

"Thank you," Sorcha said. "I believe we're finally speaking as friends."

"Friends might be pushing it," she told the ghost with a smile. "But yeah, we need someone who's got serious cred in pulling down corrupt bigwigs." The mural clearly wasn't going to be enough.

"Taylor, I have no idea who that might be in Ireland," Liam answered.

"Just wait, Liam," Sorcha cautioned, sitting back on the ottoman and resting her arms on the sides like a queen. "You're about to see why Taylor is the one who'll bring Malcolm down."

She chewed her lip, surprised. "Flattery?"

"You've had a few trying days," Sorcha said. "If I were still alive, I might have even baked you some soda bread in consolation."

Liam muffled his laughter. "I can't wait to tell Carrick that."

Taylor didn't pick up on the joke. "Were you a terrible cook?" she asked, making Sorcha snort and Liam laugh. "I need my phone. Wait! What time is it?"

"Just after eleven," Liam said after checking his watch.

She groaned. "Crap. The person I want to call is on Mountain Time in the US.. I'm going to have to wait."

Liam put his arm around her, his touch and his scent making her brain turn foggy. "How about we watch a movie then? Linc said we both have the day off."

Yeah, because she and Liam were part of a big story right now, and he wanted them protected at home. Wilt had even called the mobile home a safe house.

"*Jaws*?" they said at the same time.

"I'll leave you," Sorcha said, rising from her chair, although it was more of a float. "You might try and forget about all of the challenges right now and maybe cuddle on the couch. You two are soulmates, after all."

Taylor threw a sofa pillow at her, but Sorcha vanished before it went through her. "She's such a know-it-all."

Liam laughed. "Come on, soulmate. Let's get our minds

off things for a while. Maybe after *Jaws,* we can watch *Moby Dick?*"

"Perfect," she responded and girded herself to pass the time until she could reasonably make her call.

Cuddling with Liam would help, of course. Truthfully, he redefined cuddling. Not only did he know how to make her aware of every line of his body as his arms held her close —so totally hot—but he'd lean in from time to time to place a kiss somewhere, be it her neck or the line of her shoulder. She couldn't remember anything, not even her social security number.

Who needed meditation or mindfulness? All the world needed was Liam. He was her personal retreat with a side of smoking sensuality, and she planned to enjoy it.

The credits for the second movie were rolling when she checked the time. "You've been doing that every fifteen minutes for the past four hours, Taylor," Liam said with a low laugh. "I'd hoped the movies were going to take your mind off things, but maybe this will work."

Suddenly she was in his lap, and he was lowering his head slowly, giving her time to decide. She simply flashed him a smile, which had his mouth curving the moment before his lips covered hers. Man, he could kiss. He poured an intensity of feeling and passion into the act she'd never experienced before, all the while keeping her guessing at how he was going to kiss her next. Her bottom lip? The right corner of her mouth? The seam? Oh, he was a wily one, making her breathless with need, but she could handle it.

She curved her hand around the nape of his neck, tangling her fingers in his thick, gorgeous hair, and opened her mouth to him. He gave an answering groan, which had her mind snapping shut again as she fell into a sea of sensation. His breath touched her lips as he kissed them, softly and then urgently. She moaned, making him tuck her closer to his body. Electricity danced between them, and all she wanted to do was devour him whole.

When he pressed back, he remained poised over her. She had to fight to keep her eyes open at the glorious view as she moaned.

"Do you have any idea how beautiful you are? How perfect for me? Taylor, I know things are strange right now, but I'm so happy you're here."

"Even if you end up in trouble?" she asked softly, pushing a sandy lock of hair back from his forehead. "Because I would hate that."

"I really don't see that happening," he said, kissing her softly on the mouth, "which is why I don't want you to worry."

She pushed him straight up. "Right! You're psychic. You'd know if anything bad were going to happen."

He bit his lip to keep from laughing. "Hopefully."

Her muscles went lax with relief. "Whew!"

"But the energy can change," he said.

"I should sock you for that," she replied, but all she wanted to do was stroke the strong jaw she adored. "It's weird. I never imagined trusting anyone with my secret again, and I told you everything after knowing you for a hot second."

He kissed the corner of her mouth, making a sigh float out of her. "I have a news bulletin for you. It's because I'm your soulmate."

She wanted to glare at him. She really did. But her smile couldn't be contained. "I really am starting to like you, you know. Like big *L* like."

Another kiss, this time to her bottom lip. "I know."

AGAINST EBONY IRISH SEAS

She laughed and pushed him back further. "All right. Now I am going to make my call. If he doesn't pick up, he'll call me back."

"You know this guy from when you lived in Europe, right?"

She shivered at his mind reading. "I won't ask how you know that because you know everything. Yeah, from art circles. He's a great guy."

Liam turned off the TV. "Trust me. He'll pick up."

She gaped at him. "You can see that too? Oh, Liam. Once I get over how weird it is, I'm going to use you like a divining rod for water."

His mouth twitched. "You can use me any which way you'd like, *a stór*."

Her breath caught in her chest, and suddenly all she could see was the broad lines of his shoulders, which led to her imagining where she'd touch—

"I'll go and make us some more tea," he said with a rakish wink, interrupting the beginnings of her fantasy.

"Don't think I don't know a strategic retreat when I see it," she called, reaching for her phone and dialing the one person she thought could help them.

Liam was right. J.T. Merriam picked up on the second ring. "Taylor! I can't believe you called! I've been following your story since your live feed went viral. And Veritas painted the incident with you in it as Joan of Arc! Linc must be having a field day."

"You know Linc?" She wanted to slap her forehead. "Of course you do. Art is a small world, right?"

He laughed. "The smallest. He's even been up to our museum here. Plus, my dad knows him from boards and the like."

She winced. "Jeez. All you billionaires know each other."

"Don't throw me in that pool. I'm one of the good guys. Not the one who might blow up the moon one day with his new space rocket."

"Funny, J.T."

"You sound like you need a laugh. It must be crazy on your end."

"The craziest," she responded. "In fact, that's why I'm calling."

He laughed again. "I didn't think it was because you wanted to catch up. Although the Merriam Museum is kicking ass."

She sank back down onto the couch. "I know! I saw my old paper picked you guys as one of the best up-and-coming museums in the world. Big praise!"

"Caroline and I have been working our asses off, and it's finally paying dividends here in Dare Valley."

She'd visited them there to write an article about the Merriam Museum—and had been thoroughly charmed by the quaint small town in the Colorado mountains. "How's the baby?"

"Terrific. Raphe is ten months old and already walking fast. Being a dad is the best gig out there."

The reporter in her had to ask. "Even better than running a museum?"

"Hell yes!"

"Wow! That's..." She remembered when he'd been a jetsetter dashing off to art and fashion shows and the like. "I didn't expect that. The rest of your family good?"

"Taylor, do you really want me to catch you up on all the Merriams? Although I told my two brothers who live in Cork—you've met Trevor and Quinn—that they need to head up your way once the arts center you work for puts that museum in. I still can't believe they got Tom Sarkesian to do it. He passed on us and broke my heart."

"So Trevor and Becca are still running her bed and breakfast?"

"Yeah. And Quinn and his wife are running their merged company close by. And chasing kids. We've all got at least one now, although my little sister Michaela and her husband had twins. Michaela was always an overachiever. So now that we've caught up, why are you calling? Because I'm guessing it's not to make reservations at the Wild Irish Rose Inn."

She smiled as Liam came back in with their tea and settled beside her on the couch, putting her cup in front of her. God, he looked good doing little honey-dos like that. "You know, maybe a little getaway would be the perfect thing right now." Her mind wanted to fly off with fantasies of Liam naked in bed waiting for her, but she reined them in. "Where are they in Cork?"

"Kinsale. It's beyond picturesque, but that's Ireland for you. You're in Mayo, right? I haven't been up."

"I haven't seen much of the area yet, but the sea was ridiculous. Liam, how far is Kinsale from here?"

His brow winged up. "About five hours."

She told J.T. before continuing. "I'll let you know about a getaway. It's been an age since you, me, and Trevor used to hang out in Rome. Okay, on to my favor."

"Tell me," he said without hesitation.

"Is your uncle Arthur still doing some investigative pieces on the side?"

There was a short pause before J.T. said, "Not often. Only when it's really juicy. Usually his granddaughter,

Meredith, and her husband, Tanner, handle that kind of thing since they took over running his newspaper."

Yeah, she knew about that. Every journalism student studied the founding of *The Western Independent* and the storied career of its Pulitzer Prize-winning creator, Arthur Hale. He was the definition of a living legend. "Well, I need someone who likes to investigate corrupt king-men and then take them down in print."

"That's Uncle Arthur, all right." Another pause. "We talking about that terrifying man in the Veritas mural, right?"

"Yeah. Malcolm's big up here in this part of Ireland, but I don't know if he has his tentacles down in Cork. Liam, do you?"

He lifted a shoulder. "He might. It's a small country, run by a few men."

She conveyed that to J.T. "I was hoping your uncle might be willing to look into him. I'm not an investigative reporter, and I certainly don't have the authority he does."

J.T. snorted. "Don't let him hear you say that. He'll tease you about it being a roundabout way of saying he'd old. Not that he is. He may be eighty-five, but he's spry as ever. Heading over to Kenya twice a year with my aunt, his lovely wife, Clara, and then hopping on planes to see the rest of the family who isn't in Dare Valley now. Let me talk to him and get back to you. You'll laugh, but he's actually in Kinsale right now, visiting the Irish branch."

"You're kidding me!" Her heart rate sped up. Before Ireland, she would have chalked a piece of luck like that up to a coincidence. Not anymore. "Thanks for asking him, J.T. I can send you some info if that helps."

"Trust me. Between the video and the Veritas mural, he'll have seen the story. The man still wakes up at dawn and reads a million papers. No one knows more than Uncle Arthur. Not even my aunt Clara, but swear you won't repeat that. I'll talk to you shortly, Taylor. Take care of yourself, okay?"

The gravity of his voice rooted her in her seat. Yeah, they all needed to take care. "I will, J.T. And thanks again for talking to your uncle! You'll have a VIP pass to the opening of our museum here."

"You're a sweetheart, Taylor. Later."

"Later." She clicked off and pressed her phone to her chest. "Oh, please, please, please!"

"What are we praying for, *a stór*?" Liam asked in that deep, steady voice of his.

She took his hand, wanting to touch him. "A miracle."

His smile made her feel like she was soaring in the clouds. "I love those."

Thirty minutes later, they had their miracle.

Arthur Hale wasn't just willing to look into Malcolm Coveney.

He was coming to Caisleán to investigate.

CHAPTER NINE

L iam had never seen people juggle so many balls in
the air.

His mother was talking on the phone, gesticulating
wildly, in the corner of the arts center's newly outfitted
conference room. Linc was sitting at the table with Wilt,
Donal, and Eoghan, deep in discussion, while Ghislaine
conducted a virtual meeting on the computer in the glass-
walled media room on the opposite side.

"I should be helping with all this," Taylor said beside
him as they stood in the doorway.

"You have. Which is why we're here to tell them about
Arthur Hale coming."

Liam put his arm around her as his mother looked over.
She gave a hasty wave, the kind he well remembered from
his childhood when she had a million things on her plate.
He gave a calm answering wave. She would need some of
his calm energy as much as Taylor did right now, although
with Taylor, he had another tool at his disposal. Their
attraction and close proximity cleared her mind of all

thoughts better than any meditation practice could. Him too.

"We shouldn't interrupt. How about I give you a tour of the arts center while we wait for an opportunity to speak to them?" he suggested, taking her arm.

She shot him a look. "Really? Tour director Liam in the house right now?"

"Taylor, there's nothing we can do but stand here and wait, and since you're practically jumping out of your skin, I will endeavor to keep you distracted. Since kissing in front of everyone doesn't seem like the right option."

She agreed with a laugh, and he did his best to make the modified tour entertaining, but her attention was scrambled. Even though they didn't go outside to look at the mural, they were both aware of the locals milling beneath the windows to check it out. When they'd arrived after Taylor's call with J.T. Merriam, the parking lot had held more than three dozen cars, unusual as his mum and Linc had decided to cancel the art classes today. He'd spotted cars from other counties and known some people had driven up already to see in person what was gaining ground online.

Veritas had put them on the map, and only Liam knew Taylor was one and the same. His mum had sent out Veritas' post on Instagram to every employee of the center using the pronouns he and him. He still was having trouble adjusting to the idea the world thought Veritas was a man. Of course, he had made the same assumption himself before learning the truth.

"Liam!"

He turned at his mother's voice while Taylor froze beside him in front of the pottery kilns. "Hey, Mum." He crossed and kissed her cheek and wrapped her up in a hug.

"Taylor and I were hoping to talk with you guys. She has this great idea for another person who could help us."

His mother glanced over, and Liam could feel the tension in her muscles. "Oh, Taylor. I can't imagine how you're feeling right now."

Taylor started to squirm a little, and Liam gave his mum a warning squeeze.

"I'm trying to stay in fix-it mode to keep me occupied," Taylor answered crisply. "Can we grab a few minutes, Bets?"

She lifted her head to meet his eyes and nodded in response to his silent plea to keep things professional. "Sure thing. Let's go corral everybody together."

Fifteen minutes later, they were seated around the conference room table with Linc, Donal, Eoghan, Wilt, and Ghislaine.

"I know I'm part of the story right now," Taylor began when Bets gestured to her to start, "but I also feel guilty for not contributing as the new media director. Even though I know Ghislaine is a powerhouse, I wanted to do something. After Malcolm's threats this morning, I got to thinking about another way to bring him down. Because he needs to be brought down."

Linc folded his arms and leaned on the table. "The lawyers have some ideas about how to stop him, but this sounds different."

Taylor's mouth rose and fell on a smile. "It is. Linc, you're friends with the Merriam family, I understand."

His silver brow winged up. "Friendly, I'd say, yes."

"Well," Taylor continued, looking very comfortable at the conference room table and filling him with pride, "J.T. Merriam and I go way back in the art world. We knew each other when he used to live in Rome. I called him today and asked if his uncle is still doing investigative pieces. Arthur Hale, for those of you who don't know, founded a pretty famous newspaper in the U.S. and has won the biggest journalism prize time and time again."

"That's a big fish," Linc drawled. "I like where this is going."

She flashed a brilliant smile. "Turns out, he's down in Kinsale—five hours away—visiting his two Merriam nephews and their families. He's agreed to come up and investigate Malcolm his way. While he doesn't run the paper anymore, he still writes the occasional hard-hitting piece."

"I love this idea," Ghislaine broke in. "Hard and soft journalism to the rescue."

"You might also be interested to know Sorcha appeared," Liam decided to break in, "and made a few observations about how Ireland works. If you're corrupt, you're more likely to get in hot water if you're caught swindling your friends than if you break the law. Taylor thought this journalist might be able to find that kind of information and publish it."

"And given Arthur's reputation," Taylor picked up, touching his arm, "people might be more open to listening. Because to be really honest—I didn't feel super great seeing Malcolm show up with some Garda officers as an escort today. Which I'm sure was the whole reason he brought them along."

"On that we agree," Linc said, tapping the table decisively. "I haven't met Arthur Hale, but I've read *The Western Independent*, of course. If he wants to pop up here and look into things, I'd say *thank you kindly*. Because we're at the place where it's all hands on deck. Unfortunately, Malcolm was right about the artist needing planning permission for the mural—unless someone associated with us authorized it."

Liam's calm center shuddered before he stilled it. "Linc, about that. Do you still want to go with Sorcha bringing down the system last night?"

They shared a look. "What we say in this room doesn't go any further," Linc said, "but after talking to the lawyers, I think we might need a different story."

Taylor reached for his hand, and he squeezed it gently. "Taylor and I looked up the law as well. It seems keeping the mural will be easier if we say someone gave Veritas permission, doesn't it?"

His mum fisted her hand on the table. "Before anyone says anything, are we sure saying we granted permission will put an end to this?"

Everyone turned to Linc. The tension in the room was razor sharp. "The mural isn't for commercial purposes, which is another way they could get us, but the lawyers don't think anyone can make a case that it's against the Equal Status Acts in this country."

"The very idea is ludicrous," Donal ground out, shaking his head.

Eoghan muttered his agreement under his breath.

"That only leaves defamation, which likely couldn't be leveled at us, although Malcolm may try. The argument goes like this. We had no way of knowing what image Veritas would ultimately paint here. It's street art, for heaven's sake, and as such, artistic expression. Plus, public opinion is already on our side given the incident with Taylor. You see, there *is* evidence that Malcolm harassed Taylor, and the fact that Veritas painted something that genuinely happened, even if he gave it an artistic interpretation, keeps it from being completely damning. Make sense?"

Liam had never been a fan of legalese, but working in construction, he'd dealt with his fair share of legalities. "So the balance starts to tip more in our favor if we state that we gave permission to Veritas."

"Yes." Linc folded his arms across his chest. "And Sorcha's say-so probably wouldn't count, although our lawyers said it might be interesting to try that approach out in an Irish court of law given there've been legal cases involving ghosts before."

"I'd sell tickets to that trial if they brought on Sorcha as a star witness," Eoghan said with a chortle. "Since I'm ninety-four, I nominate myself to say that I gave Veritas permission. I dare them to come after me, especially with public opinion behind us."

Liam winced. He glanced at Taylor. Her brown eyes were narrowed, but she nodded, knowing what he had to do. They'd discussed the possibility before arriving. "Eoghan, that won't be necessary. I gave Veritas permission. I shut down the system. I—"

"That's all I want you to say right now," Linc interrupted, holding up his hands with a warning in his light blue eyes.

"I agree," his mum finally said, her fingers now gripping the table's edge. "No one is going to be hurt by this. Do you hear me? Dammit, this shouldn't even be a thing. It's our building!"

Linc pried her hands away and took them in his own. "Everyone is working on their part, sugar. It's going to be fine and dandy. I mean, hell, first Veritas, and now a Pulitzer Prize-winning journalist? We might not be out of the woods yet, but we're more than halfway through. Now, what are we going to do about Mary? She could go the defamation route, I'm told, seeing as she wasn't involved with the incident on the road on Saturday."

Liam felt Taylor's muscles tense again. "I told Veritas about the rose competition stuff."

"You met him then?" Eoghan asked. "In person like?"

"Let's not get into specifics," Linc implored, helping Liam's center remain calm. "For all our sakes. Our new Garda officer, John Hart, has already asked for a meeting. The lawyers will be there for the interviews, and we're going to see what questions he has for us. Our plan is to only respond to what we're asked without volunteering more information. We'll see how far Malcolm—and Mary— plan to take this and respond accordingly. We are not on the defensive here, folks. Malcolm is. We keep the heat on him. Ghislaine?"

"We have interview requests galore, as expected." She pulled out her phone and tapped the screen. "Taylor, no shock, but some big news anchors want to interview you. I've sent you an email just now of who I have so far and which ones I recommend you do. We're also having a press conference this Friday and hope you can speak. We can discuss everything. I know this isn't how you expected to start your new position."

She licked her lips. "No, but I'll do whatever I can to help."

"Thank you, Taylor," Liam's mum said, sending her a smile. "And if you need anything, you let us know."

"Thank you." His soulmate pushed her hair back behind her ears, her first show of nerves. "Liam has been taking care of me so far, but I'm eager to branch out a little more."

"We should head to the Brazen Donkey tonight then." Eoghan clapped his hand on the table. "We'll welcome you the Irish way. With whiskey and music and good company."

"I can't wait," she responded with one of her first easy smiles.

Linc stood. "Our coveted board of *Who's Who* will be coming in for the press conference—as much to stand with us as to see one of the largest Veritas murals to date. I didn't know for sure whether we have the record. There's other good news, folks. Hans Shumaker wants to start his painting for the museum a year earlier than expected, and Tom Sarkesian has pledged to present his plans for the new museum at our upcoming press conference—three weeks ahead of schedule."

His mum gasped. "Why didn't you say anything before?"

"Because you should always end a meeting on a positive note," Linc added with that charming grin of his. "But I like Eoghan's idea better. We really should party tonight and welcome Taylor. Liam, seeing as you're the unofficial tour guide for Ms. McGowan, do you think you can have her at the pub around six? A few of us still have some calls to make, but I think we can sneak off around then."

He glanced over at Taylor. She looked tired, but she nodded at his silent question. She'd wanted to go to the Brazen Donkey last night, but they'd decided to do the mural. Tonight would be a bigger crush, but he would help her navigate it. "As Ms. McGowan knows, I am completely at her disposal. Still, I'll let her answer."

Taylor squeezed his hand before saying, "We'll be there."

"Then the meeting is adjourned," Linc declared. "Liam, can I speak to you for a second about the party tonight?"

He knew a ruse when he heard one, but he headed over

anyway. Linc pulled him into the corner as the others filed out. "I meant what I said about keeping the details about your communication with Veritas quiet. Nothing is to be said unless it's absolutely necessary, and only then after conferring with the lawyers. Got that?"

Liam bit the inside of his cheek. God, he hated lying. Still, he had to answer in a way he could live with. "Only Veritas and I will know the details, I promise." He and Taylor would have to decide just how Veritas had contacted him.

The older man clapped him on the back. "Good. Now, go and hug your mother some. She's been a basket case, worrying about you."

"She loves me, what can I say?"

Linc gripped his shoulder. "Well, I do too, and since you're Bets' boy, that makes you mine as well. Liam, I won't let anything happen to you."

No one could make such a promise, and they both knew it, but he nodded all the same, deeply moved. "It was a blessed day when you arrived in Caisleán. And Linc, since you're my mother's, that's makes you mine too. I won't let anything happen to you either."

The older man gave him a friendly shove. "Oh, get on with you. I'm going to cry if you keep that up."

Liam walked over to his mother and did indeed wrap her up. She held on to him a bit more tightly than normal. He did his best to assure her, but he was aware that he had trouble being present with her. Unusual that. It was Taylor he was looking for when he let his mum go, his heart seeking her out as much as his eyes.

She was his soulmate, after all.

Even better—she almost believed it.

CHAPTER TEN

Never say the Irish didn't know how to party in tough times.

Taylor was surprised by what a good time she was having despite all of her concerns. Then again, it helped that she was cuddled up next to Liam at the pub at one of the packed tables. This afternoon, they'd made arrangements to cover their tracks. Liam had received an anonymous email from Veritas asking for help with the mural and had sent an answering reply with a commitment of sorts. The hacker she worked with to conceal her identity had altered the time stamps, making it look like their communication had occurred on Sunday before the actual painting had been done. While she and Liam didn't like playing that game, it was what it was. Protecting the center was a must.

The dear ninety-four-year-old artist, Eoghan O'Dwyer, had settled himself in the chair beside them, and he'd also helped her kick back and enjoy herself. He was such good company, so inspiring, finding art and love in his nineties. And he knew more jokes and stories than anyone Taylor had met. She found it easy to laugh as Brady handed her a second whiskey. On the house, which was really sweet.

The crush of people around her had her nearly sitting in Liam's lap, not a bad thing to her mind, and the sound of conversations was almost deafening. She hadn't expected the whole town to show up for the party. It was a Monday night! But no one seemed concerned about having to work the next day.

"You know," Eoghan said, brushing beer foam off his mouth, "since the arts center started, we've never had so much to talk about. Now we have a mural from the internationally famous Veritas. How I wish I could have been there last night to watch. Excuse me, Taylor, but my Sandrine is motioning me over, and when your love calls, you must go."

Liam rubbed her back. "The whole town is thrilled with the attention," he said. "We take great pride in our village, and being seen as a cultural mecca for artists is another boon. Try and look at it like that when you're thinking other thoughts."

She knew what he meant and nodded. He was right. Feeling guilty about the Veritas talk wasn't going to help anyone around her.

"Come on, *a stór*," Liam whispered in her ear, making her shiver in that heart-tripping way he had. "Let's move our seats in this crowd and watch the crazy new game Kathleen has brought us from America. It's called Hot Potato/Shot Potato. Her brother's Irish pub in Boston hosts game nights every Tuesday night to great reviews."

Once they finally found a place for prime viewing, she watched as Brady played yet another Irish song from behind the bar, prompting Ellie to throw the potato across the large circle of participants to Angie, who shrieked and then dumped it in her sister Megan's lap.

When the peppy music abruptly stopped, Declan was holding the potato, which meant he had to take a shot. In this case, the group was playing with beer so things wouldn't get out of hand too fast. But the laughter was already pretty contagious, and Taylor found herself laughing as Ellie put the potato on her head and pretended she was a debutante in finishing school trying to learn her balance.

The whole pub erupted in laughter when it bounced into her lap and rolled across the floor toward Linc's feet. He certainly wasn't playing the game, but he promptly put the potato on his large head, balancing it perfectly. Someone started to count—Donal, she noted, who was sitting beside him—and the whole pub joined in. Linc made it to thirty-seven seconds before Bets tickled his ribs, making him jerk with laughter.

Then Liam's mother picked the potato up off the floor and dragged her chair over to the ever-expanding circle to play.

"You know you want to join them," Liam cajoled huskily in her ear amidst the din.

She nearly melted in her chair as his hot breath touched her skin. "Stop that. I'm *trying* to be professional and casual here. This is my new town where I have a new job, which hasn't exactly started off normally. I can play games once people get used to me. Right now, I'm simply that chick who got waylaid by Malcolm and is now international news."

Of course, some of that was her fault for jumping in with the mural. Veritas did make waves when "he" painted something.

"They already like you, Taylor," Liam added softly. "First, they admire how you handled Malcolm. Second, you're Sophie's friend and you showed your loyalty when you did that article about her, Jamie, and the troubles at the arts center. And third—"

"I'm your soulmate." She blinked her eyes coquettishly before rolling them. "Yes, I got that when Brady hugged me as soon as we arrived at the pub and whisper-shouted to you, *She's totally brilliant, man.*"

He started to laugh. "Come on, *a stór*, you have to admit that was funny."

She wasn't going to agree too easily, although she did really like his friends and couldn't wait to get to know them better. "I seem to have fallen through a hole in the Universe and am living in some delusional dimension where ghosts appear, soulmates unite, and good and dark forces battle. I'm waiting for a Hollywood producer to show up and option Caisleán for its own reality TV special. Especially now that Ghislaine released the footage of Sorcha at the arts center, hovering around in all her illuminated eeriness."

Liam grunted. "I agree that was a little weird. But Sorcha knows what she's doing."

Again, she wanted to beat her forehead against the proverbial wall—a ghost knew what she was doing? Yeah, she'd fallen into a hole in the Universe, all right, and things were getting crazier by the minute. Tomorrow *she* had media interviews back to back, with her being the interviewee for a change, starting with a big British morning show and then moving on to the American ones.

There was even talk she might end up on Jimmy Fallon. If her current luck held, he'd probably ask her if she'd seen Sorcha herself, and there she'd be telling Jimmy Fallon on nighttime TV that yes, she had seen the ghost who smelled like oranges. More, this ghost had united her with her hot pirate soulmate.

Taylor McGowan's reputation as a serious journalist

and person would be ruined. Coming out as Veritas sounded more palatable, and *that* certainly wasn't happening. The anonymity was part of the mystique. Without it, Veritas was nothing but another punky street artist.

"You fretting again?" Liam squeezed her side. "Taylor, honestly, you should join the game because you probably have two choices tonight. That game..."

She glanced over to see Eoghan pull up a chair to join the circle, setting his beer on the hardwood floor in front of him. The moment he sat down, Declan shot the potato toward him, which he deftly caught.

"You see how boxing training stays with you," Eoghan called, "but maybe we should swap out the potato for a nice round stone."

Everyone groaned, Declan most audibly.

"I don't get it," Taylor said.

Liam plucked her up and settled her on his lap.

She did her best not to wiggle, but her breath stopped, that was for darn sure.

He made a humming sound before explaining, "Eoghan used to have Declan catch stones during his boxing training. It's an old Irish thing. Intimidates opponents and gives rise to a boxer's lore."

She took his gorgeous face between her hands. *"He trained with real stones?* Oh my God! I'm in a nuthouse, which happens to be in jolly ol' Ireland. I can't believe I'm hanging around with ghosts and people who throw stones at each other for fun. I must be crazy."

"So be crazy." He cupped her face, a dimple she hadn't noticed showing in his cheek—God, he was too cute for words! "Have fun, *a stór.* It's the Irish way. Because if you don't play Hot Potato/Shot Potato, you're probably going to have to dance later with my mother and the rest of her friends. They call themselves the Lucky Charms, and they like to perform in front of the whole bar. With feather boas. To Bon Jovi."

Her delusional universe was complete. "No. Freaking. Way."

"Would I make something like that up about my own mum?" He shuddered and then laughed. "Trust me. It's taken me a long time to realize it was a much-needed outlet for my mum and her friends. But still, I have to do some meditative breathing when she gets a little crazy with her boa."

That did it. "I'll take the potato game!"

"Good choice." He lifted her off his lap gently and then hefted both their chairs up in that manly way of his that had her knees going weak.

If he really was her soulmate, she had found herself one hot guy to be with for the rest of her life.

"Taylor!" Eoghan cried out, making space for them as the others closest to him expanded the circle. "As the newest member to join, you get to have the potato to start the next round. You know, this potato reminds me of an old Irish saying."

Liam held her chair as she sat down and took the potato from the older gentleman.

"*You must take the small potato with the big potato.*" He glanced around the circle like a professor might. "Do you youngsters know what that means?"

Ellie's hand shot up. "They both taste delicious?"

Declan barked out a laugh before Kathleen silenced him with a jab of her elbow. "Ellie loves mashed potatoes," the Bostonian told the group, fighting a smile herself.

"I do," Ellie replied eagerly, "and it doesn't matter if the potatoes are small or big. They both get mashed up."

Eoghan's shoulders were shaking with laughter. "That's a lovely answer, Ellie, but it's not exactly the meaning. Liam? We can always count on you to know the wisdom of our past."

Taylor turned her head to regard the man who could silence her crazy mind. Man, she was starting to think of him like that too. Wise with a huge side of reliable.

Liam only smiled as he said, "It means a person must accept one's lot in life."

"I don't get it," Ellie said after a moment.

"We'll draw you a picture at home later," Kathleen said. "Brady, hit the music."

Another fiery reel began, and Taylor granny-threw the spud over to Kathleen, who caught it deftly. Declan cried out and glared at her as she dumped the potato she'd palmed into his lap.

"Pay attention, Ace," she said like a siren's call.

"So that's the way of it," her husband replied and made a rapid show of throwing it over to Eoghan before shifting his aim quickly to Liam, who caught it with an audible thud.

"Foul!" Bets called, pointing at them like a ruffled mom. "Boys, it's called Hot Potato, not Misdirection Shot Put."

"Hear, hear!" Ellie called, thumping her knee with her hand. "Let's everyone be nice."

Liam gently tossed the potato to his mother, who caught it and blew him a kiss. "That's a good boy, Liam."

Taylor nearly laughed. Until Bets tossed the potato her way with a saucy grin. She hefted it over to Angie, who boggled it, making it roll across the floor. Eoghan bent down and snatched it up just as the music cut.

He grabbed his beer and held his glass out. "To all the

days here and after, may they be filled with fond memories, happiness, and laughter. *Sláinte*."

Taylor's heart filled with warmth at that toast. Man, she was a goner for good words like that. The journalist in her appreciated their directness while the artist loved their whimsy. She was going to have to learn some Irish toasts herself if this was how they partied.

She only had to drink twice, which was a victory to her mind. Liam—whose friends really did call Yoda, she discovered—didn't have to drink at all. His sixth sense applied to games like Hot Potato, it seemed. He was always one step ahead of the music. But he hadn't once dumped the potato in her lap, and that made him a nice guy. Gosh, she was so going to kiss him later as a reward for all his recent good behavior.

A chair scraped loudly, and Taylor looked up to see Ellie playfully dragging Sophie's chair into the circle. From the grin on Sophie's face, the tug-of-war was just for show. Still, when she sat down, Eoghan stopped the game.

"You're missing your drink, dear Sophie," he called as Ellie put the potato in her friend's lap.

"They don't play games like this in Provence, do they, Sophie?" Taylor called with a little snark. "Go on. Someone give that girl a beer. On me."

Her friend's cheeks went pink before she looked over her shoulder. Taylor followed her gaze. Jamie nodded to her friend with the most mysterious smile on his face. She narrowed her eyes at the subtext.

"I'm just drinking water tonight, folks," Sophie declared with a grin before coughing loudly.

She was pregnant!

Liam reached for Taylor's hand and squeezed it, and she knew his Spidey sense was onto them too.

Sophie must have seen the looks on their faces because she shot them a pleading glance. "I'm heading off the Irish flu," she added with another fake cough.

"There's a flu going around?" Ellie gasped.

"That's Irish for hangover," Declan told her, fighting laughter.

"Water?!" Eoghan wiped the silver wisps of his hair off his forehead. "You're in Ireland, girl. The water of life is whiskey."

"Eoghan..." Sophie gave him a stern but kind smile. "I'm drinking water. Now, let's play."

Bets was grinning as she yelled, "Brady, turn on the music."

The game resumed. Taylor managed to dump the potato off on Bets right before the music died. They shared a conspiratorial grin. Thank God Bets wasn't being all weird with her like she'd feared. So far, she'd mostly been cool.

Then Bets rose and declared it was time for the Lucky Charms to do their *thang*, and suddenly Taylor wanted to run and hide in the bathroom stall. Bets had gathered her older friends around her and was starting to hand out feather boas, but surely she'd ask Taylor to join them, and then—

"Feeling the need to flee?" Liam asked, putting his arm around her.

She made a face as her internal temperature spiked from his touch. "I still have nightmares of stumbling over my feet and falling on my butt at prom when I attempted the Macarena."

He chortled, his gorgeous green eyes dancing. "This story crushes me. I adore the Macarena."

"You do?"

3a

His kiss on her cheek was quick and delightful. "I was kidding, *a stór*. Come on. I'll make up your excuse."

She made a raspberry sound. "I can face Malcolm, but I'm having trouble with saying no to your mother. What does that make me?"

"Human," he replied with a devilish grin.

That she was. She was kissing him back on the cheek when she heard someone calling her name. Bets!

She went rigid instantly.

What was she going to say? That she had a muscle spasm from all the potato throwing? Jet lag?

She was turning when she heard Linc shout, "Stop everything!"

The pub went instantly silent as he rose, his face a wild mixture of shock and joy.

"Wilt Mather just called the Garda," he announced in his booming voice. "He caught Mary Kincaid trespassing on the arts center property attempting to paint over the mural. We've got her!"

A cheer erupted in the pub.

"Bon Jovi can wait!" Bets yelled after giving a wild jump of joy in the air. "Let's go, everybody. We've been waiting for Mary to get her just deserts and that dish is about to be served."

Taylor's heart rate tripled at the thought of someone trying to paint over her mural. Of course it had happened in the past, and sometimes she'd been plagued with sadness for days afterward. She knew her artwork wouldn't be permanent, of course. Street art was the antithesis of the grand masters and the formality of wooden frames and high-tech lighting. Still, when her art disappeared, it was gone for good. No photo or print could quite capture the original.

"You okay?" Liam rubbed her arms briskly, his soft gaze searching her face.

"Yes," she replied quietly as people headed to the door. "This is what we wanted. Next up, Malcolm Coveney."

Except Taylor didn't believe he'd be so easily caught.

CHAPTER ELEVEN

Bets had waited a long time for this day.

Arriving at the arts center to find Mary Kincaid being interviewed by two Garda officers as the blue lights flashed atop their vehicles would be one of her precious keepsakes. And she didn't care if that made her a bad person.

"I'm taking a photo of this moment," she told Linc as she dug her phone out of her purse.

"Ghislaine will be documenting it for the media," Linc told her as they pulled to a stop in the lot. "I still can't believe she'd make this kind of a mistake."

Bets grinned as she zoomed her phone camera in on Mary's taut, severe face. "I don't care why. All I care is that she fries."

Linc snorted. "Sugar, you might want to save those comments for later, but I love that you're rhyming now. Is haiku next at the arts center?"

She unlocked her seat belt and launched herself at him, barely noticing when her knee knocked into the gearshift. "I so want to kiss you."

The rumble in Linc's chest reverberated through her body. "Me too. But you are aware that everyone from the pub is parking around us."

She looked out Linc's window and waved as Ellie's face contorted in shock at the spectacle they were making. "I don't care." She pressed a kiss to his mouth. "This is for the first rose competition when she changed the label on my prize rose to hers after seeing mine were bigger."

"I can tell you something else that's bigger." He caged her waist to halt her. "*Bets…*"

"And this one is for—"

"Enough!" He lifted her off his lap and deposited her in her seat with another swift kiss. "You can document every slight from that witch later, without interruption. But right now, my daughter just stopped in front of my SUV and mouthed *WTF*."

Bets started laughing. "It's good for our kids to know we're still having sex at our age. Gives them hope, don't you think?"

Suddenly she couldn't stop laughing.

"Sugar, this is the kind of meltdown people have after their plane crashes and they're being handed a blanket by a flight attendant." He caressed her arm, his brows narrowing. "Just how much stress have you been holding in that hot body of yours?"

When he tickled her side, she cried out and continued to chortle. Someone knocked on the window, and Linc turned the car on so he could roll the window down.

"She's finally going to pieces, huh?"

Her son's voice. She looked over to see Liam peering into the cab at her. "I can't stop laughing, Liam. Mary's finally going down. And by painting over some graffiti. Isn't that ironic? She tried to stop us from painting, and now she's going down because *she* wanted to paint."

"She could stand being hated by the community," Liam told her in that wise way of his, "but she couldn't stand being laughed at."

Even that was funny, and his serious tone had her laughing like a hyena. "Yoda is always right. Yoda is always right."

"Oh, brother." Linc ran his hand over her nape. "Will you stay with your mother? Great, now I'm rhyming too."

Not a babysitter! Bets emitted a series of high-pitched giggles.

"Sugar, try and focus for a second."

She stared at Linc and then burst out laughing again.

"Let's start over," he said, taking her hand. "I need to talk to Wilt and be ready for John Hart to ask me if we're pressing charges. Bets, I don't think I have to ask this, but we *are* pressing charges, right?"

She was gasping for breath as she laughed. "Charges! Yes! Every charge we can level. Painting without a license. Trespassing—"

"Got it." Linc leaned over and kissed her soundly. "We're throwing the proverbial book at her. Keep laughing, sugar. Get it all out of your system. And then come join me. You don't want to miss Mary being cuffed and put in a police car."

She snorted with laughter, holding her belly, which was hurting. "Cuffed? Her witchy ways won't stand for that."

The car door chimed as he opened it, the sound like a happy circus.

"What's wrong with her?"

Donal!

"Nothing's wrong!" she called, throwing back her head

against the seat and laughing at the ceiling. "Everything's just peachy."

"Take care of your mother," she heard Linc say.

"Take care of your mother," she drawled in her best Linc imitation, which made her laugh harder. "When did my cowboy get so serious?"

"Oh, Mum, you really were stressed to the gills, weren't you?" Liam asked as he slid into the driver's seat beside her.

"Like a fish," she sputtered. "See."

She made a guppy face and started chortling with laughter when he only stared back. "Everything is so funny, Liam."

He took her arm and started soothing the skin above her wrist. "I know, Mum. Just laugh it out."

"She killed my roses, Liam, my babies," she said in a high-pitched voice as her laughter clawed at her throat. "Chopped them into pieces. Who does that?"

And suddenly she was crying—hard, angry tears that left her face hot and her chest gasping for breath.

He pulled her half onto his lap and hugged her to him, humming softly in her ear like she was a child.

"Why am I crying?" she managed through the sobs. "I'm happy this finally happened."

Her son just kept rocking her. "You're not happy, Mum. Everything with Aunt Mary has been sad and tragic since you first stepped foot in Ireland with Dad over thirty-some years ago. This is decades of disappointment and hurt coming out."

"But Liam!" She wept against his chest. "I hate her."

He squeezed her tightly. "I know, Mum. But in the beginning, I bet you didn't want to. It's not who you are."

That made her weep harder. "She's made me feel like a

bad person for all the bad things I've thought about her. Liam, I never wanted it to come to this."

"I know, Mum." He resumed his gentle rocking motion. "I know."

She cried until she couldn't breathe through her nose. "Liam, I used to think your dad was angry that we didn't get along."

"No, Mum." He kissed the top of her head. "When I was a kid one Christmas, I told him I didn't want to wish her Happy Christmas because she wasn't a nice lady, and he told me that was okay. He didn't want to either. He knew, Mum. He understood. You can let that guilt go."

"I did try hard in the beginning, dammit." She wiped her nose and finally lifted her head. "I came here not knowing anyone but your father. I wanted people to like me, especially his family. Do you remember how I gave her cuttings of her mother's roses for her own garden? She practically spat on me when she refused to accept them."

"You did what you could, Mum." He cupped her jaw in his hand. "Now, take some deep breaths with me. That's good. Keep going. You had a lot in there. It's good to finally let it out."

The breathing helped, as did the way Liam was looking at her. God, she loved him so much. She finally looked out the windshield to where the crowd had gathered. She couldn't see Mary anymore—or Linc. "I looked like an idiot in front of my friends."

"Nah, Mum. Not any more than when you dance to Bon Jovi with your boa."

She smacked him and gave a shaky laugh. "You're trying to rustle me out of my mood. Don't think I don't know."

"And it's working." Liam helped her back into her seat and wiped her face with the edge of his cotton shirt.

"You're treating me like a kid," she protested weakly before adding, "I kinda like it."

"So do I." He held out his hands to her. "Before you head over that way, I'm going to finish my Yoda moment with you and tell you that the laughing and the crying was your body's way of dealing with negative emotions. It had to happen. So don't feel guilty later or apologize to anyone. Mum, Aunt Mary has hurt a lot of people. Her choices brought her to this moment. Not you."

She traced his strong jaw, the line of it so like his father's. "I won the lottery when I got you for a son."

He smiled and tapped her nose. "I must have four-leaf clovers in my blood with a mum like you."

Gosh, that slayed her. "You're going to make me cry more. But I'm stopping now. I must look a mess. How bad is it?"

He made a face and then laughed. "Bad, but it's dark out."

Another swat had them both laughing a little more. "Okay, let's go."

She realized her body was tingling like the whole thing had gone to sleep. Needles coursed through her legs as she hit the ground. The top of her head felt like it had blown off. The heat in her cheeks was sweltering. But she kept her head high as she walked around the edge of the crowd, sensing Linc's presence. That was where she wanted to be —next to her cowboy.

Mary was still talking to Officer Hart, but he and the other officer had removed themselves to a fair distance from the crowd with Mary. Bets couldn't hear what they were saying, and Mary's back was to her. Beside the officer was an open duffel bag, and from her vantage point, she could see the tops of a couple cans of spray paint.

"You better, sugar?" Linc asked when she reached him. He put his arm around her as Liam headed over to where Taylor was standing.

"Right as rain after that unexpected meltdown." She kissed his arm. "Catch me up."

"Wilt is pulling the surveillance video for the Garda now as well as our file on Mary—which includes her 'talk' with Sophie when she arrived—"

"Where she called her a whore basically and told her to leave," Bets finished. "Good."

"I also had Wilt write up the past items—like the destruction of your roses, going back to Donal's sheep being released and driven up your drive."

God, that was back when she'd first started the arts center in a shed she'd had Liam refurbish behind her house. She'd asked a newly unemployed Angie whether she wanted to come over and teach painting classes, and that was all it had taken. The one spark to make the vision come together, even though it had morphed into something so much bigger than she could ever have imagined.

"Wilt is feeling a little torn," Linc murmured. "If he'd let her begin the vandalism, the case might be more clear cut. Right now, we have her on trespassing, dead to rights. She has an established angst with the center, so we'll push for the malicious intent under the Malicious Damage Act. Our lawyers are on top of it."

"I'm glad they're still in town." She rubbed her thighs as the needles continued to stab at her legs. "But I'm starting to think we need an on-site legal counsel for the center."

"I love it when you talk big like that." He peered down at her. "What's wrong with your legs?"

"They fell asleep. Maybe because of my hysterics and

maybe because I was stretched across the gearshift of your car. Hurts like hell."

His blue eyes suddenly seemed brighter in the harsh outdoor lights. "I could pick you up all Prince Charming like if you want. There's nothing more to do here but rubberneck."

She touched his face, swamped with the crazy love she had for him. "You'd risk that with your old bones?"

He shot her a clever grin. "You love these here old bones."

She sure did. "Maybe later then."

But truthfully, she didn't need the gesture.

She already knew she had a Prince Charming.

CHAPTER TWELVE

Taylor could never have imagined she'd spend her first week at work giving interviews to the press.

But so it began early on Tuesday with Ghislaine teaching her something new she hadn't expected—how to dress, talk, and sit on camera.

"I still can't believe I have to play these games," she told Liam, who was sitting on her couch when she emerged from her bedroom in a casual navy blue suit, one Ghislaine had selected from her wardrobe only an hour ago before telling Taylor to make herself up.

When she'd texted Liam that she needed him to inspect her "makeup"—an unnecessary ruse—he'd appeared with more of that delicious coffee he'd made the night of the mural painting along with some soda bread from Brady's mother, who had dropped a few loaves off at Summercrest, a place Taylor still needed to see.

"You're not playing games." He rose and eyed her outfit as he came closer, munching on a slice of buttered bread, looking all hunky hot in faded jeans and a forest green pullover that made his eyes a shade darker. "This isn't Hot Potato/Shot Potato."

"That *would* be more fun," she said, adjusting the seam of her skirt in front of him because they were buds and all, soulmates probably.

He took her shoulders, the gesture as sensual as a naked caress. "You look like the professional you are, ready to communicate about a very serious situation. You're going to be as brilliant at this as you are at everything else."

She leaned up and kissed him on the mouth, humming at the taste of buttered bread on his lips. From now on, she would make sure they always had butter and bread in the house—because she had to taste him like this daily. "I'm not brilliant at everything. Let's get that out in the open now. In case Sorcha's right about the two of us."

"She is," he bandied back with a rakish grin, "and I know you're not perfect."

"You do?" She rounded on him and gestured to herself, amused. "*How* am I not perfect?"

His laughter was the skin-sizzling kind. "Don't you have to get to the arts center? Because I think you're more than made up. You're shining with light and so beautiful every person who watches your interview won't be able to look away."

Aw...

"Come on, I'll drive you."

"I have my car." She narrowed her eyes. "Wait! You're escorting me, aren't you?"

He simply shrugged. "We're going the same way. Call me a little overprotective where you're concerned. After last night, anything is possible."

She studied him. They'd all gone to bed late after the Garda had finished questioning Mary Kincaid and then taken her into custody. According to Ghislaine, she'd been charged with trespassing, malicious intent to private property, and threatening and abusive behavior.

Liam's phone bleeped and he pulled it out. "That was fast. Aunt Mary's lawyer showed up first thing and posted her bail. Guess where he's from?"

Her diaphragm tightened. "Watertown."

He gripped his phone. "Malcolm isn't going to let her go down. We were wondering."

She didn't have to ask whom he meant by "we." He'd left her at her door last night with a tender kiss and said he was heading over to his mother's house with a few others to talk about the next steps. She'd weighed going, but given her early meeting with Ghislaine and complete lack of rest the night before, she'd gone with getting some sleep. Not that she'd slept like a baby. Tossing and turning seemed to be her new normal, and she'd looked longingly at her couch when she'd gone out to make herself a cup of tea at 2:05 a.m., wondering if she could sleep better there. Or if Liam was with her... Which only made her toss and turn for other reasons.

"What would you think about bunking here?" she made herself ask.

He pocketed his phone and put his hands on his hips. She could all but feel him reading her mind. This time she let him. Because yeah, she wasn't stupid. Malcolm was dangerous, and she was the cause of his new set of troubles. He was going to strike back, and she didn't want to think about how long it would take Wilt or the Garda to get to her if the alarm went off. Especially if Malcolm brought his own Garda with him like last time.

"I'd be happy to." He paused for a moment. "This is where I want to be clear. We both know what's between us, but I feel like this is more about you having someone you trust around so you can sleep better. Because I can see the fatigue around your eyes."

"It is about that," she managed, clearing her throat. "Although I'm close to being ready for the other. I'm just not sure which day it'll be yet."

His mouth twitched. "Which day, huh? I didn't expect that kind of specificity, *a stór*. It will happen when it happens. We don't need to rush anything. You trusting me like this feels like a victory."

"It should. This whole string of events is totally abnormal for me." She crossed to him and put his hand on her chest. "But since you're the mind reader here, why don't you tell me which day you see us taking this to the next level?"

"*Taylor.*"

His voice was so playfully sexy, she simply had to kiss him. Slow, sweet, and then a little more urgently.

"Maybe I want to know." She fingered the collar of his pullover. "Sometimes it's all I can think about. Especially when you have your hands on me."

His chest rose with a deep intake of breath. "It's the same for me. But I don't see a date in my head. Only images."

She touched her tongue to her teeth. "What kind?"

He fought a smile. "Are you going to make me say it?"

"Uh-huh." She kissed him again on the mouth, caressing his chest in little circles she could feel was making his heart beat faster. "Tell me about them, Liam?"

He pulled her to his body, making her belly clench with heat. "They're of us making love."

"Are they hot?" she asked, smiling into his now fiery green eyes.

"More than hot," he said, taking her bottom lip between his teeth softly and sucking it. "Cataclysmic. Mind-blowing. Earth-shattering. Like forget everything you thought you knew about sex because we're at a whole different level."

She fell back a step as her body flashed with molten heat. "Oh my God! How am I supposed to talk sensibly on camera today when I'll be thinking about *that*."

"You asked," he all but sang in his sexy Irish accent.

"You're a total flirt." She kissed him soundly on the mouth. "I love it. Never stop. Assuming we're soulmates and all. All right, now that I am totally overheated and horny, we need to go. God, I can't believe this is my first week. If you knew what I had in my head..."

"Come on." He took her hand. "We'll take your car. I can have someone drop me home later to pick something up after work. Assuming you're finished for the day."

"I'm going late with the American media tonight. West Coast and all."

"Can I make you dinner then? So you can come home and just chill?"

Her heart fluttered in her chest. "I'd love that. And I'll return the favor when you need it."

"I don't keep score, but I like the idea of things being equal between us. Relationships with balance tend to be happier."

"Yeah, imbalance breeds resentment. Been there, done that. You good with me driving?"

"Of course. Like I said, equal. You won't find me clinging to gender roles in our relationship."

He watched as she set the alarm, and then they walked out the front door. She glanced at him as she unlocked her car. "But you'll still take the garbage out, right? Because I really hate that."

He was laughing as they got in her car. "I can do that."

She started the engine. "And kill spiders. That's nonnegotiable."

His touch on her thigh was electrifying. "Anything you need, *a stór*. Always. But just so you know, I try and bring insects outside and not kill them if I can."

Of course he did. "That works for me so long as you understand I'm not as interested in coaxing pests into jars to release. Still love me?"

She meant it playfully, but he only smiled. "You know it."

Putting the car in gear, she decided it was telling that she didn't freak out after that exchange. But she did have trouble remembering to drive on the left. When they arrived at the center, he kissed her goodbye and wished her a good day. She stood by the car and touched her lips as she watched him walk over to one of the center's sheds. She could still feel his touch, his heat, and the sweet care he put into every caress.

"You're already in love with him."

Turning, she spotted Ghislaine in the doorway to the center, dressed in her black Chanel suit with her long blond hair trailing down in perfect locks. "No comment," she replied, but then she smiled.

Ghislaine smiled back. "That's perfect, but don't say it too often or people will think you have something to hide."

She reflected on that wisdom during the first interview as she answered question after question about the Veritas mural. Her favorite: *what does it feel like to be enshrined in an artistic masterpiece?*

She wished she could send that one with a photo of her mural to her old art teachers.

She'd picked a purposefully neutral answer: *I try not to think about it.*

Yeah, she really did.

Ghislaine sent her media impression sheets by email every two hours, organized with tabs demarcating the source, location the piece was published, and her overall impressions. One thing Taylor really liked were the *Noteworthy* items in response to what had happened at the center, anything from a heartfelt post from a street artist in a highly repressed country who was inspired to paint something about the current government to a mayor from a small town in the Midwest United States who'd suggested they start their own arts center.

She worked that mayor's call to action into an interview with a leading New York newspaper, and after the interview ended, Ghislaine put her arm around her and gave her the highest praise: "You're a natural."

"But I feel really guilty about not helping you more on the media side," Taylor protested despite her inner somersaults of joy. "You're being inundated with media requests and the press conference has to be work-intensive—"

"And when would you have time to help?" Ghislaine clicked on her tablet and turned it over. "Do you see any holes in this schedule?"

Taylor had to wince. "I don't have to sleep."

Ghislaine gave a very French sounding snort. "Like you don't have to spend time with your soulmate either..."

She stared at the older woman as she pushed her blond hair over her shoulder. "You believe in all of that too?"

Her wedding ring sparkled when she held out her hand. "I'm here because of Sorcha. I stayed because of Donal. Yes, I believe. Besides, when you're together, you seem like you've already been together for twenty years. Locked in. Complete. It's a powerful feeling, isn't it?"

Hearing that one of the most sought after publicists in the business had fallen into the same proverbial hole in the Universe made her feel better somehow. "The craziest."

"Which is why I'm ending all your interviews by six today and bumping the West Coast ones to tomorrow." She gave a cheeky smile. "Besides, Donal is waiting for me as well, and that is something I don't plan on missing. Are you coming?"

Taylor ran after her to their next interview in the media room.

And so it went.

Liam was cooking dinner for her when she dragged herself home. She kicked off her heels next to his work boots —loving that addition to her life—and headed toward the spicy smell. "Honey, I'm home."

"So you are," he said, looking over his shoulder from the stove and giving her a killer smile.

Just like that, her lady parts started sizzling like whatever he was frying in the pan. This was her new life? The only thing missing was the sex, which made her want to fan herself. God, it was going to be so good when they got to it.

"You're a bit pale, but my fabulous lamb curry will warm you up just right."

"Oh, don't worry," she assured him in a flirtatious tone, "I'm starting to heat up pretty good seeing you here."

"Domestic duties make you hot, I've realized." The rumble of his laughter made her knees weak. "You were practically flushed thinking about me taking out the garbage and battling insects for you. Now... Beer or wine? I asked Linc if I could filch a bottle from his wine cellar. He has the best selection in town."

"Wine, please!" She sank into a chair at the kitchen table where she could still see him. He had on the same outfit of worn jeans and a pullover that made her drool.

"I'm glad you don't mind me making myself at home," he said, tapping the wooden spoon on the side of a pan she hadn't known she had and reaching for the bottle of red wine on the counter.

"I gave you my second key at lunch, remember? I did it around lunch so it wouldn't seem like such a colossal deal."

"I know."

Of course. "Mind reader!" she accused playfully. "Also, Ghislaine is fully on the soulmates train. She nearly knocked me over when she told me she'd come to Ireland because of Sorcha and then hung around because of Donal, all the while flashing her wedding ring."

His chuckle sounded as he popped the cork.

"You do know that most people would think we're in a cult and drinking red Kool-Aid, talking like this." She rose because she wanted to be closer to him.

"They've clearly never been to Ireland then," Liam only responded, handing her a glass of wine and then pouring himself one. "You do know we have the largest match-making festival in the world, right? Lisdoonvarna is only a couple of hours away."

She sipped her wine and then lurched forward and kissed his cheek. "Thanks, and yes, I've heard of it. Only...I didn't read about it being run by a ghost."

He settled back against the counter, his mouth twitching. "I'll bet there are plenty of ghosts helping the organizers. Taylor, this is Ireland. And was that supposed to be a welcome home kiss? Because I think we can do better."

She bobbled her wine, making it almost slosh over the rim. "We can?"

He took her glass and set it down next to his. His green eyes were warm and bright as he pulled her to him. The first brush of his mouth had her moaning softly. God, she really was easy, but she didn't care. No one's arms had ever felt so right. She locked her arms around his neck and dove in to pure bliss as their mouths met and merged. Her eyes closed, her heartbeat pounded, and for the first time in her life she had the experience of her toes curling.

"If that was a welcome home kiss, sign me up," she managed, her breath coming out shakily.

"I missed you today," he answered, cupping her cheek and staring into her eyes.

God, he was going to make her mush. This confession deserved an honest response. "I missed you too. How is that possible? I kept looking out the windows of the arts center when I had a break, hoping to see you."

"Linc had me meet with the construction company we hired to build the hotel," he answered. "He wants to break ground a little faster than we'd planned since Tom has the final design for the museum ready earlier than expected. We need to find another construction firm because our number one pick can't handle two projects this big at once."

"He wants to start building fast because of Malcolm."

"It isn't because of the weather." He kissed her again. "How about we give that subject a rest? You want to talk about your interviews?"

She fiddled with the edge of his pullover and then traced the gold earring in his left ear. God, he really did look like a hot pirate. "You mean where I did my best not to coo like a turtledove whenever I got asked how I felt about Veritas immortalizing me? Liam, that part is so not fun. I don't like misleading people."

He fitted her wineglass back in her hand. "I had a

similar moment when Linc told me not to discuss my inter-actions with Veritas with anyone."

She tilted her head toward the ceiling. "Oh, God! And he's like your stepfather."

"Not officially," he answered, picking up his wine. "But my mum loves him, and yesterday he pretty much told me that because I'm hers, that makes me his."

"Ah... That's really sweet. Do you feel guilty? Because I'd hate it if I'm making you act against your values."

He cupped her nape so she'd look at him. "Taylor, I wouldn't have done it if I didn't feel it was the right thing to do. I was meant to help you. We're partners. Even if we're both in unfamiliar territory."

"Because you never keep things from friends and family, and this is the first time I've ever been the subject of my own street art." She laid her forehead against his chest. "We're a pair, but I'm glad you're my partner. Liam, I can't think of anyone I'd rather be with."

His hands massaged the tense muscles in her neck. "Glad we're on the same page. By the way, I put my stuff in the second bedroom. Unless you want me to be on the couch closest to the front door."

Electricity seemed to jolt her skin. "Maybe I want you in my bed."

"We're not ready for that yet."

She had to see his face then, so she looked up. "You still don't have the day pinned down after our talk this morning?"

His mouth curved, which made her trace his gorgeous lips. "We're ready when you know for sure you love me and I'm your soulmate. Because I don't think I can make love to you any other way. Once we make love, I'm yours. Body, soul, and spirit. I want you to be the same way. I need you to be."

Longing swamped her, catching her by the throat. "All right." She blew out a hungry breath. "That's fair. You should have what you need—we both should. Only...you see us together. In your images."

He nodded slowly.

"That means that I come to all that body, soul, and spirit stuff." The sound of her heartbeat was suddenly loud in her ears. "Any idea where they sell Kool-Aid in town so I can speed this process up?"

His laughter soothed her and she found herself grinning back at him. "I'll look for that at SuperValu when I go shopping next."

"You go shopping too?" she asked, leaning up and kissing his mouth. "You really *are* the perfect partner."

He nibbled at her mouth. "But I don't iron or hand-wash. And I really don't like to dust. Just so you know."

Wow, were they already discussing domestic duties? "What about vacuuming?"

"I can do it. But with us both working, we should probably hire someone to clean. Kathleen found a great person after she and Ellie concluded Declan and Brady were slobs. Completely true."

Right. His roommates at the haunted Summercrest Manor. "But not you?"

"With three sons and a mud-caked farmer, my mother made sure we all knew to clean up after ourselves. I'm pretty housetrained. Brady's mom is a bit of a mother hen. She'd make you a cup of tea and butter a slice of bread for you as soon as you came through her door. My mum would yell, 'Make sure and take your filthy boots off by the door.'"

Good for Bets. "I might have noticed those boots when I got home. It made me all girly on the inside."

He kissed her cheek. "Come on. Dinner is just about ready. Why don't you pick a movie?"

Right. Because Wilt had called this the safe house for the moment. "No bike rides, huh? Because I probably couldn't handle everyone's energy at the pub again tonight."

His green eyes narrowed for a moment before his face relaxed. "No, I think we stay home for the moment. One, Malcolm is going to strike back. Two, you're the kind of person who needs to recoup her energy after going at one hundred and ten percent. And three—and this is a big one for me since I love my friends and family—I want to be alone with you."

Suddenly she was worried about speaking complete gibberish, drowning in emotion at his words. "I want to be alone with you too," she answered finally. "And thanks for understanding my energy, as you say. Some people get charged by others. I get drained. But not by you."

His mouth tipped up to the right. "While we're on this subject... I like most people's energy, which is why I moved into Summercrest, although you know I love my meditation too. But with you, I'm finding I don't miss being around so many people. Taylor, your energy fills me in a way I've never known."

She swallowed thickly. "Okay. Any more gooey talk and I might start stammering. What movie do you want to watch?"

Their eyes met and held, and her heart thumped loud in her chest before he said, "Something like we watched the other night works."

"I'll be right back," she called, heading to her phone for ideas.

When she picked it up, she saw a text from J.T. Merriam and pulled it up immediately.

Hey! Uncle Arthur is already doing his thing. He wants to come up for the press conference Friday and interview you and a few others afterward if you can swing that. Trevor and Aunt Clara are going to go up with him. Becca is swamped with guests, and Quinn and Francesca can't get away from the company right now. But they all say hi!

She shot back a quick response.

Cool! Anything he needs. I can't wait to see Trev again and meet your aunt. She's a huge patron of the arts, if I recall. Thanks so much!

This time she did a little dance in place. She still couldn't believe it. Arthur Hale was going to investigate Malcolm Coveney.

"Find a movie?" Liam called from the kitchen. "You have two more minutes until my rice is ready."

She was grinning as she did an internet search for man versus nature movies. She'd seen most of them, but there had to be something out there like *Moby Dick*. After two minutes, she wanted to pull her hair out. Were there no movies before Netflix started making them? She couldn't believe what articles she was being served.

"Try *The Poseidon Adventure*."

She uttered a shriek and juggled her phone in her hands as oranges filled her nose. "Oh my God! Stop doing that!"

The ghostly woman in the white dress simply swayed in her parlor like she'd stepped out of a Jane Austen movie.

"You were hitting a wall. I figured you might like Gene Hackman the way I do. I was only being helpful."

"Helpful? Does appearing to me like this really come under the category of matchmaking?"

She gave one hell of a good smirk for a ghost. "Isn't Liam cooking you dinner?"

Taylor shot her a smirk back for good measure.

"And it's Saturday, Taylor." Then she gave her a long look. "The day you've been wondering about."

With that, she vanished. Taylor sank down on the couch's arm. *Saturday?* Like this Saturday? Five nights away Saturday! This ghost was making her totally nutso.

"You ready for dinner?"

She looked over. Liam was standing in the doorway, hot as hell with a shamrock potholder in one hand. Should she tell him what Sorcha had said? Nah. She couldn't take it if they were both counting down the days. She could almost hear a movie announcer in her head—*Only five days to go, Taylor McGowan, until you get freaky with the hottest dude on the planet. Get ready!*

Lust roared like a lion through her overheated system. Oh, she was so ready in body, but the whole spirit and soul thing? What did that even mean really? She made herself smile. "Sorcha suggested a movie. I hope we'll like it."

"How nice of her," he said, coming over and taking her hand and leading her back into the kitchen. When she took a seat at the table, she noted he'd lit a candle, set the table properly with cloth napkins, and set her wineglass beside her plate. God, she'd hit a home run with him.

"Mum says hi, by the way."

"So she's passing me messages through you already? Like a couple? And she'd been doing so well. No wobbly expressions as she watched us together."

His shoulders were shaking as he brought over the bowls of rice and curry. "Wobbly expressions, huh? I'll have to look for those."

When he started to serve her, suddenly it was too much. She put her hand over his and stopped him from dishing up her rice. "I know we've established that seeing your domestic side makes me hot, but you don't have to do all this."

He grew puzzled. "What?"

"Dish out my grub." She grabbed the spoon to the curry and started dishing herself. "I can do it."

"But I'm happy to do it." He laid his hand over hers. "Hey! What just happened?"

"I'm drowning in all the Kool-Aid." She searched his face, thinking about Sorcha's sex prophecy. "Do you not have any moments where you think this is all really weird or too fast? Liam, I just got our movie night suggestion from a ghost!"

Who'd also told her the day they were going to get it on.

"Is it a good movie?" he asked, his mouth twitching as he spooned himself up some really nice-looking jasmine rice, followed by the spicy-scented curry.

"I don't know, but it's got Gene Hackman in it. Sorcha likes him and thought we might have that in common."

He forked up a spoonful. "And do you?"

She glared at him and mixed her curry and rice together as he chewed. "Millions of people love Gene Hackman."

The agreeable sound he made after sampling the food had her lips twitching as she watched him continue to eat. "I like him too, by the way," he said as she finally tasted the meal.

She moaned before she caught herself.

"And I thought you might like curry like I do," he added

with that same devilish smile, accompanied by the sexy dimple she now knew to look for.

She tossed her napkin at him, which he caught deftly. "I have two older brothers and a legion of friends, Taylor. You're going to have to up your game to get me."

Because the company and the curry was so nice, she only let her brow arch. "Noted. But I should remind you that I have managed to stay anonymous this whole time as Veritas and draw quite a following. How's that for game?"

He laid his foot against her arch under the table and rubbed. "Not bad. But let's see how you do up close and personal."

She fought the urge to clench her thighs together. "After the movie." Heck, after dinner. She wasn't sure she could chew anything now.

"Eat your dinner, *a stór*. There's plenty of time for everything."

How did he do that? She barely had time to freak out before he calmed her down again.

"Are you versed in hypnosis?" she asked as she inhaled another delicious bite of lamb.

"No, why?"

"I keep wondering why I go from crazy to calm in moments around you." She lifted her wine and drank.

He finished chewing. "When someone gets worked up, I imagine enfolding them in peace."

"Like with your mind?" she asked, narrowing her eyes.

"It's so natural I don't know how to describe it now. My dad taught me to practice it with animals when I was little. Like wrapping them in a warm blanket out of the dryer. I was afraid of sheep at first, what with them being taller than me. Now it's just part of me."

He had a lot of parts, her Liam, ones she looked forward

to understanding better. "You know, I still haven't seen the Kindness Sheep." She glanced out the window to the dark night. "I'll be getting home after dark every day this week."

"We'll introduce you, don't worry." He reached out and rubbed the corner of her mouth. "I'm glad you like the curry."

She lurched back and pressed her hands to her face. "Oh my God! Did I have rice on my face?"

He nudged her napkin toward her. "Only a couple of grains. Don't worry. I still love you."

She slumped forward. There it was again, like in the car this morning, but more explicit. He *really* did love her. She could hear it in his voice. And yeah, she loved him too already. But was she at the capital Love or the lowercase love? She had to be at the capital Love to make love with him, right? That soul and body thing wasn't a lowercase kind of love. And Sorcha had said it wouldn't happen for five days...

"Your mind is working overtime, Taylor." He picked up his plate and stood. "Let's start the movie. You need a distraction and to recoup your energy."

He knew her too well. Sometimes all she could do when she got home from work was veg on the couch. "What do *you* need? I'm sorry I didn't ask earlier."

He smiled as he grabbed her plate as well. "Just you."

She waited until he'd left the room to press her hand to her heart. Her heart didn't feel like its normal size. It was pressing against her ribs. She was sure of it.

"Taylor," Liam called. "I found the movie."

Good. She headed for the diversion.

Only the movie couldn't possibly distract her from Liam when he had her cuddled between his legs, her back against his powerful chest. By the time the opening credits had finished, she was a line of earthy sensation who could only think about sex and count the days down.

His heartbeat pulsed against her back and the way his thighs cradled hers was more delicious than the smell of spray paint. By the time the tidal wave attacked the cruise ship and killed all but ten passengers, she was fighting the urge to whimper and turn in his arms for a kiss. A really hot, wet kiss.

But she persevered because he was still behind her, obviously enjoying the movie. His capacity to go all Zen was flat-out incredible. She knew he must think he was giving her space to recharge her energy. Talk about nice. Maybe he needed a break too.

She needed to distract herself from the allure of his warm, manly body. Like right now. The movie wasn't working. Not even Gene Hackman's urgency to save himself and the rest of the passengers could zap her out of this lusty frenzy.

Closing her eyes, she decided to count sheep, something a teacher had suggested she try when she couldn't nap as a kid. She couldn't help but wonder who'd come up with that tactic. Was the founder of the Sheep Counting technique Irish? A shepherd, maybe? Or perhaps he'd left his homeland and missed it so much that it brought him comfort to envision it. She knew she could never count sheep again without bringing up the green rolling hills of Ireland.

Her body warred with the sheep counting in the beginning. She got to three sheep before images of her and Liam hot and sweaty took over her mind. Reining them in, she made her sheep cuter and managed to count until twenty before her next fantasy stole her attention.

Trying to ignore the feel of Liam under her took every ounce of her focus. She had to get into major Veritas mode to silence her inner sexy feelings. She was very pleased with herself for having reached one hundred and fifty one sheep consecutively when Liam's breath tickled her ear. "I knew you were brilliant," he whispered against her ear, "but I've never seen anyone watch a movie with their eyes closed."

The sweet-faced sheep in her mind vanished like Sorcha. Her eyes popped open, only to see him staring at her from inches away. Her mouth went dry, and every small gain she'd made in focusing on cute and cuddly sheep evaporated. She fought the whimper at the back of her throat as he gazed at her in that deeply intense way of his, like he could see everything she was thinking. Oh, wait! He could.

"What was I thinking just now?" she asked in a flirty tone because she knew another way to silence her mind.

"I suspect you're wanting to kiss me but you're fighting with yourself like I am over it as we probably need to take things slow."

"You weren't enjoying the movie?"

"I was giving us both some time, and you seemed relaxed."

"I was trying to keep my mind off all this." She gestured to his body. "It's more distracting than an action movie, and Liam, those are my favorite."

He turned her in his arms until she was lying on him. Like the whole hot, manly length of him. The moan she'd been tamping back came out like the bleating of a sheep, and she wanted to die. Right there.

Five days, was it, Sorcha? She wasn't going to make it.

He laid his hands on the small of her back. "Let's try something else, *a stór*. For us both. We agree we want each other."

Her girly parts were starting to realize they were flush with his manly parts, and things were starting to tingle in a

Hollywood blockbuster fashion. "Want seems a tame word at the moment."

His hands slid down her sides until he cupped her hips. "What words will do?"

What was she? A walking dictionary? "Crave. Need. Yearn. Thirst. Require. Hey, that wasn't bad for spur of the moment. Oh, and hunger. We hunger for each other, Liam."

She was breathless as she gazed into his now forest green eyes. They were darkening with the same desire blazing a path through her. She'd never gotten this hot this fast before. Like *rip your clothes off right now* hot. Some part of her cried out *soulmate* as she crushed her mouth to his.

He slowed her down, cupping her cheek and gentling the kiss. She climbed a little higher up on his chest, wanting an angle that would satisfy this raging need inside her. He turned them onto their sides, keeping them on the couch, and gave their bodies some room.

She was having none of it. Her hand found its way under his pullover and searched for the edge of his shirt underneath. When she found hot bare skin, they groaned into each other's mouths. He turned them and rose over her in one splendid line of male glory. She gripped the hard side of his waist as his tongue swept into her mouth, making her cry out in an urgent melody. She felt his hand snake under her work clothes, and she tugged her shirt to give him the access they both wanted.

His fingertips trailed over her belly before reaching her breasts, cupping one and then the other through the lace of the nice bra she'd worn, thank God, in her professional-from-head-to-toe mantra.

He slowed the kiss as if he were concentrating on the shape of her, and she used the moment to suck in some much-needed oxygen. He took the opportunity to kiss down the length of her neck, making her close her eyes in bliss.

"This is getting out of hand," he whispered against her skin. "I want to keep going, but I think we should stop. I don't want to torture us both, and we haven't crossed the line into agony yet."

Agony would be around the corner, no doubt, since they wouldn't be assuaging this hunger. "You're right. If we keep going, I might tear your clothes off and forget about the whole mind, body, and soul thing."

He laid his lips over hers, so tenderly, so softly, her heart changed size in her chest again. *Why does it keep doing that?* But she didn't care. She only threaded her hands in his thick sandy hair and kissed him back for all she was worth.

When he lifted his head, his green eyes were shining with light. "Trust me. The whole body, mind, and soul thing will be a game changer."

"Ever had it?" she asked, wrapping one of his locks around her finger.

"No." He kissed her again, soundly this time. "That kind of connection is only for one person."

She drank willingly from the Kool-Aid this time. "Let me guess. Your soulmate."

"Exactly." He shifted off her and rose, not disguising the hunger he had for her. "I know you mentioned sleeping in the same bed, but I can't do it. I want to. But having you next to me. Being able to feel and smell you. Only inches away. It would drive me mad for sure."

Wasn't she trying to calm her racing heart? "I totally get it. And Liam... Thanks for staying. I liked this. Tonight."

His smile was breathtaking in its fullness. "Get used to it. Even my Summercrest friends knew I wasn't coming back."

Her mouth parted.

"This is the rest of your life, Taylor McGowan. I'll just go clean up dinner."

"Thanks," she called weakly as he walked toward the kitchen. "I'll make you breakfast in the morning."

"I'll take you to see the Kindness Sheep," he answered.

God, they were making daily plans. Next, they'd be discussing who would buy the milk. "It will have to be pretty early because my first interview is at eight."

When she didn't hear him reply, she imagined he needed a moment to gather himself. She understood. If there was a huge trough of ice cream, she'd immerse herself in it. But this feeling was more than heat. Sure, her heart was pressing against her ribs again, but all she wanted to do was smile.

She remembered her earlier words. And the final pronouncement he'd uttered before he'd excused himself —*it would drive me mad.*

It was more than true.

They *were* mad for each other.

CHAPTER THIRTEEN

Watching Bets' son be interviewed by the police was up there with munching on roadkill for lunch. It didn't help that the dark Irish sky was pouring buckets outside, the rain a thunderous overture in the tense room.

Bets had a death grip on Linc's hand under the table, and Donal, sitting on his other side, had a massive frown that was probably a lot like the one Linc felt on his own face.

Even though their lawyers had written up Liam's short four-sentence statement that he'd given Veritas approval to paint the mural, John Hart had insisted that he and another officer needed to question the young man on this fine Thursday morning. The cops and lawyers flanked Liam, who rode the guest of honor spot at the head.

Linc couldn't blame Bets for her worry—he wouldn't want Ellie involved in anything like this either—but it seemed the only way to circumvent the trouble Malcolm wanted to dish out. They could have pled guilty and paid the fine for not receiving planning permission, sure, but that would have meant they'd have to paint over the mural. No one wanted that. Plus, who knew what Malcolm might do if they pled guilty? He was still being quoted in the Irish papers about the public insult and its incitement to insurrection against him and his businesses.

Insurrection? Who did this guy think he was?

Linc spotted Taylor watching them from the other side of the glass wall separating them from the media room. She sat next to Ghislaine, who was punching information into her phone. The younger woman was pale. Her feelings for Liam were all over her face, but Linc was glad Liam had suggested she not be at the table at his side. Talking Bets into being absent had been impossible. Still, even surrounded by tension and worry, the young man's stillness was remarkable.

"So I was the one who granted permission to conduct the mural," Liam finished, his voice strong and true. "That about covers it."

John Hart rubbed the age lines around his temples, looking a few years older than he had before the trouble began. Like everyone else, he was feeling the lash from Malcolm's proverbial whip. He riffled through his handwritten notes while the more junior Garda officer kept his head down, clearly uncomfortable. "Thank you, Liam. That was brief and to the point. I have a few questions, of course. Routine."

Donal crossed his arms over his massive chest while Bets nearly cracked Linc's fingers as she tightened her grip. He gave her an encouraging look before glancing over at their three lawyers. He liked the lead counsel, Patrick O'Shaughnessy, the best, but he'd feel a whole lot better when they hired their own full-time person. The other two had their legal pads out, continuing to jot down their notes.

"The altercation with Malcolm Coveney happened on

Saturday," John reiterated. "At what time did Veritas contact you for permission?"

Even though Liam had already gone over all the responses with the lawyers, Linc's stomach still turned sour. No one wanted more questions here.

"Like I said in my statement, Veritas asked for my help on Sunday afternoon, which I granted."

"Do you have any proof of this?" John asked, making Bets straighten in her chair. "An email, a call log—"

"Officer Hart," Patrick broke in. "I don't see how this is relevant. Liam is a respected employee of the arts center and this community. If he says this is how it happened—"

"I'm only asking since this is our first experience with Veritas," John broke in, giving the lawyer a measured look. "We're trying to understand how it is that Veritas arrived so quickly after the incident and knew how to reach out to Mr. O'Hanlon."

"Please call me Liam," the young man said. "I'd assume Veritas did the research needed. I was in the video of Saturday's incident, after all, and I'm listed on the center's website as construction director. But again, I can't comment on that."

"Surely you have some impressions about Veritas," John pressed. "His general height and weight—"

"Why would you need to know that, John?" Linc asked sharply.

Bets rushed in to add, "Veritas is an anonymous street artist. Besides, Liam's statement is about the permission he granted on behalf of the center as an employee."

"Which is his right," Donal gritted out, "and one the board approves of."

The officer only looked down at his notes, riffling through them uneasily again. "As I said, this is routine."

"Officer Hart," Patrick added, "you didn't give any indication that there would be questions along these lines today."

John cleared his throat—never a good sign to Linc's mind. "The Irish government has expressed some concerns about Veritas coming to Ireland like this and would like more information. Mr. O'Hanlon is the only one with such information."

"I don't see the relevancy here, Officer Hart," Patrick continued.

Linc glanced over at Donal and fought a curse. He could smell Malcolm's whole "inciting insurrection" crap in this line of testimony. "Hold on a second. You haven't been tasked with leading some crazy manhunt to go after Veritas, have you, John?" Linc drawled.

Liam was suddenly leaning forward in his chair. "Why would you want to go after Veritas when I gave permission for the mural?"

Because Malcolm didn't like his johnson being pulled. He wanted blood. "I'm sure Officer Hart is planning on telling us that."

The Garda officer tapped his pen to his notes. "It's struck a few of my supervisors and others that Mr. O'Hanlon is not represented in the mural."

"What?" Bets asked sharply, glancing around the room in shock. "Why would that stand out to anyone?"

Linc had noticed it as well, and he'd heard the talk about it amongst people in the village and some of the conjecture about why. But he didn't think the Garda were interested in discussing different artistic interpretations.

"Mr. O'Hanlon was on the scene with Taylor McGowan, which is what the mural was based on." John laid his hands over his notes. "Why wouldn't Veritas depict him as well?"

"Maybe because it's art." Bets' hands were now gripping the table's edge. "And Malcolm was on that road to threaten Taylor. Not my son. Although he threatened him too the moment Liam arrived. Why aren't you pressing any charges against that man?"

John picked up a pen and gripped it tightly. "That isn't my jurisdiction, but I've been told the Garda in the area have spoken to Mr. Coveney."

"And?" Bets pressed, prompting Linc to put his hand on her rigid back in solidarity.

"I think you should ask that question of the appropriate Garda," he hedged.

"Please, Officer Hart," Patrick implored. "You're in the same Garda. Surely you can provide some enlightenment. My calls have gone unanswered so far."

"Malcolm claims they had car trouble," John said, "and he has witnesses to back up his statement."

"And what about Denis following her from the airport?" Donal pressed.

"The airport hasn't been able to locate the appropriate security tape so far," John answered, his face a blank wall.

"Convenient," Donal muttered.

"I would like to return to what Mr. O'Hanlon can tell us about Veritas," John reiterated.

"I don't think so." Linc shook his head. "If the Irish government has some beef with Veritas, they can take it up with Veritas themselves."

"Mr. O'Hanlon is a material witness—"

"In what?" Patrick asked sharply.

Everyone sat up a bit straighter at that, including Liam.

"I thought I was clear," the young man reiterated. "I approved the mural, which makes it legal."

"Yes," John said, fighting to keep a poker face. "I've been instructed to ask some more questions—"

"Why don't you send those over to Patrick here since Liam and I have a meeting about the museum," Linc announced, standing and checking his watch for show. "John, our thanks to you and your fellow officer for coming. Y'all have a good rest of your day."

After a round of handshakes, Patrick and the other lawyers escorted John and the other officer out, and they were back to being a confidential quorum.

"That went fine until they wanted Liam to dish about Veritas," Linc said, kicking back in his chair and crossing his ankles. "If the Irish government wants to waste resources trying to find Veritas because Malcolm's knickers are in a knot, then more power to them."

"It's all for show." Patrick smoothed his blue silk tie. "Malcolm's government friends are placating his ego by offering to have Irish resources look into finding Veritas."

"Good luck with that," Donal ground out. "He'll be long gone from here."

"I still don't understand what they would charge Veritas with if I gave permission," Liam said, resting his elbows on the table, his face showing unusual worry. "We agreed I would only show the email if pressed, but I don't want to answer any questions about Veritas that involve some sort of manhunt."

"The whole thing is ludicrous." Linc waved his hand. "Don't give it another thought."

"We'll see what kinds of questions Officer Hart sends us." Patrick gave Liam a measuring look before turning to Linc.

"Don't worry. This line of questioning is only a bunch of official idiots running around trying to make it look like they're doing something. It happens all the time in this country."

"Yes, it does," Bets said, tapping the table, "but I don't like them questioning my son any further."

"Mum—"

"No, Liam, this is just more harassment from Malcolm via proxy," she snarled, her cheeks turning bright red. "Dammit, I thought John was supposed to be different."

Bets' voice must have reached Taylor and Ghislaine through the glass because they both looked over with concern. Linc shot them a smile of encouragement, something he didn't feel right now.

"John Hart is removed from personal influence and the like here in Caisleán," Donal said, "but that doesn't mean other people won't try and pull his strings. Including his superiors and those above them. Malcolm has ties all the way to Dublin. Don't forget that. Any further word on Mary Kincaid?"

"Other than that she was released and someone paid her trespassing fine?" Patrick gathered together his notes and put them in his briefcase. "The lowest fine possible— one hundred and forty euros."

"That's all?" Bets' outrage carried across the room. "I thought trespassing was a serious crime in this country. Every farmer posts signs for their fields—"

"All show," Donal growled. "Nothing ever gets done if you find someone in your field harassing your animals."

"I have worse news," Patrick continued.

"Great!" Linc scratched his chin. "Just lay it all out."

"They decided against charging Mrs. Kincaid for malicious intent." His mouth twisted. "She's an old woman—"

"She's a *dangerous* woman," Bets emphasized. "One who keeps striking at us."

"So we'll keep vigilant." Linc took her hand under the table, knowing they all needed to settle down. "Wilt's increased security procedures are in effect, and with the news of her arrest spreading around the village, I feel a lot better. We should keep reminding people around here to keep the morale up."

He glanced at Liam and inclined his chin toward Taylor, whom Ghislaine was doing her best to distract with some spreadsheet. It made Linc sleep easier at night knowing Liam was with her. Even with the alarm and the procedures, everyone should have a partner right now.

"Liam, we do have a meeting about the museum," Linc said, "but before we get to it, do you have any other concerns you want to express? I'm sorry they surprised us like that."

"It won't happen again," Patrick reiterated, frowning savagely. "I'll talk with some sources in the Irish government. I want to see how serious this Veritas thing is."

"That's what I want to know too." Liam looked around the room, the old soul that he was clear in his serious gaze. "I don't plan on giving them any information about Veritas. The mural was a gift from an artist whose whole nature is anonymous, and we should respect that. Not cooperate with the Irish government on a wild goose chase."

"Agreed!" Bets cried out. "Next time we'll tell them what they can do with their questions."

Linc snorted out a laugh. How he loved it when she talked like that. "If Malcolm thinks catching and unmasking Veritas is going to help him look like some big bad man, then he's delusional. Public opinion around the world is on *our* side, and we'll use the press conference tomorrow to drive that home. I hear Ghislaine's even agreed to give Keegan O'Malley's sheep some face time to do their thing for the press, since they're so beloved."

"Who knew sheep could become famous?" Donal groaned like only a long-suffering sheep farmer could. "I still can't believe it."

"We also have Arthur Hale coming to do research for his story tomorrow," Linc reminded everyone. "I know these little bumps are a pain, but Malcolm is on the defensive. So is Mary."

"I'll believe it when I see it," Bets said harshly. "Twenty bucks says the fire under her cauldron is all the bigger after her arrest and humiliation."

"I wouldn't take that bet," Linc told her with a smile, "and I've been known to gamble. Everyone stick to the program. We're in the home stretch." God, he sure as hell hoped so.

Donal stood and clapped him on the back. "You're a good cheerleader, Linc Buchanan. Too bad you didn't wear the cute little skirt."

Bets gestured heavenward as she winced. "Thanks for putting that image in my head, Donal. Liam, are you really okay?"

If there was one thing Linc admired about Bets, it was her mother henning. She'd been calling and texting the boy more than usual. Linc figured Liam would tell her when he'd had enough.

"I'm fine, Mum." He stood up and smiled, although it didn't reach its usual wattage. "Now, I should probably go and assure Taylor. See you in five minutes, Linc?"

"That would be great," he responded, already calling up his bullet points for the meeting.

Bets hit him a little stronger than her usual playful

socks. "Is there anything we need to ask Patrick and our legal guys before they leave?" she whispered.

He shrugged as he watched their lawyers pack up their briefcases and shuffle into their wool coats. "I figure he'd tell us if there were."

"Something still doesn't feel right."

Turning in his seat, he spun her chair to face him. "Sugar, we're in unknown territory, but we have the best people and the best plans we can in place. Don't borrow trouble."

Because he knew from past experience that trouble had no problem finding you.

CHAPTER FOURTEEN

L iam had never been much for walking tightropes, but there were moments when he couldn't dismiss the fact that he was walking one now.

First, with his own body when it came to wanting Taylor. To keep control of himself, he'd limited their evenings to some fun flirting, dinner, a movie, and some increasingly hot interactions on her couch—never her bed.

Second, with his mum, who had surged into overprotective mode, checking in on him and his well-being way more than usual.

Third, with his friends, whom he had seen little of since devoting all of his free time to Taylor.

But he knew all about the seasons in life. He'd waited years for his soulmate, and now that she was here, being with her and building their relationship was his number one priority. Even after only living together for three days, more or less, they were establishing a rhythm, and he'd never been happier in his life despite the looming press conference this morning and a whole host of moronic power games he had no interest in participating in.

"Liam, have you seen my gray heels?" Taylor called out. "I swore I put them by the front door."

She swept into the kitchen in a rush like usual, looking professional but breathtaking in a charcoal suit with a white silk blouse. He'd learned Taylor was so not a morning person. By the time she woke up, he'd usually completed his yoga, meditation, and morning check of emails.

He walked over and kissed her slowly on the mouth until she sighed, caressing the crease from her pillow still on her newly powdered cheek. "Morning. I believe you carried them into the kitchen and put them on a chair yesterday when you got home, thinking you'd stow them in your closet later."

"You mean when I dropped them to kiss you hello after another hard day of interviews? Dammit, I forgot about that."

He leaned in and kissed her bottom lip, a lip God had designed to drive him mad. "I'll have to do a better job of kissing you tonight if you've already forgotten about it."

"I *meant* your kisses made me forget." Her hand trailed down his chest, igniting fire. "You look hot, and you smell even hotter. You don't normally wear a suit and put on aftershave."

He gestured to his clothes and ordered his body to calm. "I usually only wear this kind of outfit to weddings and funerals. I thought I should match your style. Plus, Ghislaine sent me a memo about dressing up."

She laughed heartily. "The truth comes out. She picked my outfit too."

He let his eyes scan the lines of her body while his fingers traced the edge of her blouse, teasing the bare skin peeking above the silk. "You look beautiful as always, and if it's any assurance, I plan to be by your side whenever you need me."

Her smile bloomed slowly before she rested her cheek against his chest. The simple gesture was like the ease with which they were "playing house," as she liked to call it, and it gave him the kind of joy mentioned in his favorite books about sacred partnerships.

"By my side, huh? You have been since the beginning. I'm pretty happy about that, you know."

"Me too. It's been the best part of this whole week. Eggs? Oatmeal?"

She lifted her head, a fierce grimace on her face. "I might puke if I eat. You know, I've been to a million press conferences, but I've never been the main act. Yesterday, Sophie told me not to sweat it."

"You got to talk to Sophie?"

"Only for two minutes. We ran into each other in the bathroom."

Ghislaine ran a tight ship, but Taylor said it was all about the media cycle. Liam personally couldn't wait for that cycle to be done. He imagined she felt the same way.

"What else did Sophie tell you?" Liam asked, sensing there was more when her mouth quirked in humor.

"She also said not to imagine everyone in the audience naked like people tell you to because it doesn't work. Not. At. All."

He couldn't help but laugh. "Naked, huh? I can't imagine why someone would suggest that."

"It's supposed to distract you from your nerves." She slid her finger inside the top of his shirt, looser than it might be because he'd forsaken wearing a tie. "But if I imagined you naked—which I do at least six times a day when I need a mood lift—I'd definitely be distracted. Of course, I'd also moan a little on the podium, which would be awkward. Liam, I tossed and turned all night, wanting you."

He'd had to pull away after she'd tugged his shirt off last night during a movie neither one of them had managed to watch. They'd both thought *Dante's Peak* would deliver. It hadn't. "Me too, *a stór*. And talking about it is not helpful when we need to go soon. Come. At least have some fruit."

She kissed him before reaching under the table for her shoes and prying them onto her cute little feet. "I didn't expect you to take care of me like this. I really like it."

"You went all domestic on me too." He tossed her an apple, which she caught deftly. "I really enjoyed watching you mutter to yourself while you cooked spaghetti and meatballs last night."

"I got tomato sauce on my work clothes, and I hear from Ghislaine that she hasn't yet found a dry cleaner that she trusts."

Yeah, there was that—they were in the boonies, after all, something she was so not used to. "Despite our lack of modern conveniences like you had in the city, you have to admit this is really working."

She bit into the apple with the kind of passion with which she did everything. "You mean you and me, right? It really is. Minus the sex we're not having. But I have it on good authority that the time for that is almost upon us."

That paused him from biting into his own apple. His mouth went dry as other parts of him roared to life.

She smirked. "Are you thinking *thank God* like I am? Because I'm close to losing my mind. But I think it's probably better we didn't do it before today because I probably would have blanked out while I was giving my statement, thinking about your six-pack and those sexy green eyes of yours as you hovered above me, doing what I can only imagine right now."

He wasn't going to ask who the authority was. Sorcha was the only one who fit that bill.

"You want to tell me a little more about those hot visions of us?"

"Not at the moment," he said with a laugh as she fanned herself.

"Wait! I'm imagining it."

His phone rang—making her slap her hand over her mouth to cut off her moan. He headed to the counter to see who it was. Mum. He decided not to pick up, as he didn't feel any urgency to it. She'd been calling before work, saying she wasn't sure if they'd run into each other at the center. He and Linc were meeting with Tom Sarkesian for the museum after the architect had flown in Wednesday. But they both knew the truth: she was being a bit more mother hen-like lately. Not smother mother crazy, though, thank God.

"Your mom again?" Taylor called, tossing the apple core in the garbage. "How does she feel about us practically living together already?"

He picked up her purse and walked over to her, holding it out. "She hasn't said anything about it beyond being glad you're not alone. So far..."

Taylor rolled her eyes. "Whew! I've felt a little bad waving to her from the media room. My life has been Ghislaine and whatever media person I'm talking to. Then I collapse in your arms."

She made a show of leaning back like he'd catch her, so he walked over and enjoyed the feel of her playfully slumping against him. "We're on a roller coaster right now. It will settle down."

He took the opportunity to kiss her thoroughly, knowing she'd be putting her lipstick on shortly. Her sigh feathered his lips when he released her mouth, but she kept her arms around him. "When you do that, I forget about feeling a little guilty we haven't spent time with anyone else. I haven't even seen much of Sophie."

"She understands." He kissed her again softly as he set her on her feet. "Everyone does."

She nodded and walked over to her purse and took out a lipstick, doing her lips without a mirror, a sight he was surprised turned him on. "Time to get serious. We have a big day ahead with some big fish in town. Including Arthur Hale, all of our illustrious board members, and some other major artists coming to support the center."

"Yeah, when I ran into Ellie yesterday, she jumped up and down and babbled about someone named Dinara Zalensky coming. I had to look her up."

"She's been imprisoned for her anti-government art in Russia. I interviewed her a couple of years ago, before her last prison sentence. Six months for a watercolor. She inspired me to sneak into Moscow and paint a mural about her. It was one of my scariest trips ever. Man, the police are everywhere."

His sternum tensed. Until this week, he'd been a fairly calm person, but he'd had to increase his yoga and meditations in the morning to counter the surges of anxiety he'd been experiencing. "We're still learning each other's stories, I know, but how many trips have been like that?"

She lifted a shoulder. "I don't know. A fair number, I suppose. You didn't look Veritas up? Not once?"

He'd warred with himself a little about that, he had to admit, an unusual reaction for him. "No, I told you. I want you to tell me who you are."

"If I didn't have lipstick on, you'd so be getting another kiss." She swiped his cheek playfully with her hand. "Come on, we're expected. Ghislaine wanted us to arrive ten minutes before everything started, the better to build anticipation."

That kind of anticipation was new to Liam, but it was clear from the moment he parked her car in the packed lot. The reporters lingering outside for a smoke or a scoop all turned to see why Wilt was walking in their direction.

"Linc wanted me to see you both inside and run interference with the reporters milling about who aren't gaping at the mural." He had his tablet tucked under his arm and looked all business. "Taylor, some meet and greets have been arranged for you. Liam, I assume you're joining her."

He nodded and touched her hand as they walked, giving her the chance to decide whether she wanted to hold it. She took it without hesitation, making his heart expand. With that, they headed into the sea of reporters fanned out in front of the building. Cameras flashed and people shouted questions at both of them. Somehow, he hadn't been prepared for the barrage directed at him.

Did you see Veritas?
What was it like to help him?
What did he look like?
How did he contact you?
Did he tell you why you weren't in the mural?

His calm demeanor wavered momentarily as Taylor's grip tightened, and she whispered, "We should have gone in the back."

Only they didn't really have a back entrance, he thought as someone called his name. He turned to the source and was blinded momentarily as the flash caught him in the eyes. Right. He was part of the story too now that he'd made a statement about having given Veritas permission.

Wilt cleared the path with the brisk efficiency of a professional bouncer, although Liam was already doing his best to shield Taylor himself. He was oddly protective of her, but he supposed that would be his new normal.

When they reached the main doors to the center, Ghislaine was there in a bold red suit, holding her tablet, her blond hair swept up in a twist, a frown on her beautiful face. "I'm sorry about that." Her French accent was more evident when she was irritated. "Apparently my directive about waiting until the press conference to ask questions wasn't strong enough with the Irish reporters, whom I don't know as well yet. That will be remedied, I promise. Go on to the stage. I'll be right behind you after I talk to those *eejits*, as Donal would call them."

Liam was glad he wouldn't be staying for that lecture.

They made their way onto the stage. The VIP seats were off to the left of the podium, but he wanted a little time with her before settling in. He became aware of the sound of people talking which fell when the seated reporters spotted them.

"This is going to be fun," Taylor whispered to him. "I'm concentrating on Arthur Hale being here. He's the older man in the front row, seated between the elegant silver-haired woman, Clara, and the handsome dark-haired man in the navy suit. That's his nephew, Trevor."

"The one who runs the inn in Kinsale," he said, nodding to the group as they smiled their way. "I like the look of them."

"It's a dream to meet Arthur Hale. That's what's keeping me going. I can't vomit in front of my idol."

Maybe he was picking up on her vibes, because his stomach suddenly felt seasick as well. "You're going to do great."

Moments later, Ghislaine strode onto the stage and introduced Taylor. Liam squeezed her hand and left her to it, taking a seat beside his mother, who sent him an encouraging smile after he kissed her cheek.

"Hi, I'm Taylor McGowan, and we really should stop meeting like this," she began, flashing a conspiratorial, droll smile. "After the last press conference where the Kindness Sheep got harassed, you'd think the arts center would be sailing in easy waters. But no, here we are. Still dealing with factions who are using intimidation and harassment to try and shut us down. Let me catch you up on why a Veritas mural has come to grace the south wall of the arts center."

She breezed through her statement, a pro at using humor to punctuate some very nasty details about Malcolm stopping her on the road and Mary Kincaid being arrested for attempting to paint over her visage.

Her references to Veritas were much like Liam's: emotionally neutral without the use of gender-revealing pronouns. Taylor couldn't bring herself to go there, and oddly, neither could he. When she was finished, he took a quieter breath than his mother beside him. Then the questions started coming as she opened the floor.

All of them were pretty standard to his ear, save one from one of the pesky Irish reporters who'd flocked them. "Ms. McGowan, I noticed you holding hands with Liam O'Hanlon, who came to your rescue on the day of the incident. Have you two begun a relationship because of recent events?"

That had Liam sitting up a little straighter in his folding

chair. His mum, true to form, chuckled under her breath and whispered, "If only that idiot knew…"

Taylor paused and looked over at him, a full smile gracing her rosy lips, before turning back to the audience. "Well, it *was* pretty romantic, wasn't it? Liam appeared on his black Triumph out of nowhere and put himself between me and Malcolm. Next question."

His muscles relaxed again as he thought about her response. She'd avoided going into details, which was clever, although he knew any canny reporter could find out he was staying at her house. Soon they would need to address that. There would be talk, and he wanted the wider community to know it was more than a fling based on sharing an emotionally charged moment together. She was his, and he hers.

When Ghislaine stepped in to cut off questions and thank everyone for coming, a couple of reporters shouted out requests for Liam to make a statement about Veritas. He did his best to relax as Ghislaine leaned forward to the microphone and answered, "We hadn't planned on Mr. O'Hanlon speaking today."

More protestations came from the crowd, prompting Taylor to put her hand over the microphone and whisper something to Ghislaine, who nodded. When they both swung their gazes in his direction, that seasick feeling in his stomach returned.

Taylor cocked her brow, and he could all but feel her letting him decide. He rose fluidly, reaching for his calm as he stepped up next to her at the podium. She touched his back supportively before speaking into the microphone. "Be nice to Mr. O'Hanlon, folks. He's had as weird of a week as I have. But first, let me ask Liam the question on everyone's minds. Can you describe the man everyone seems to think is Veritas?"

He had to give her credit for the wording. "I can't actually. I didn't see the man."

Taylor shrugged to the crowd. "I've been to other press conferences after a Veritas mural popped up, and the MO here is the same, I'm afraid. I'm sorry to say we won't be unmasking Veritas today."

"Only Veritas received permission from Mr. O'Hanlon," a reporter shouted out. "That *is* different."

Taylor smiled at him before answering, "Actually, it's been done before. Always through an anonymous email account. Same here. Right, Liam?"

He nodded with a short smile, greatly aware of how much he felt like a fish out of water while she looked radiant in her power. Then again, she would need nerves of steel to be Veritas.

"What can we say? Veritas is really good at covering their tracks. Now, I think we're a little late with the Kindness Sheep segment, and from what I've heard, those sheep don't like to wait. So if you'll head to the windows..."

She was already leading Liam away from the podium, much to his relief. "You did great," she assured him in a low voice.

He touched her arm. "You were the showstopper. I'm only romantic eye candy."

"Yes, you are," she replied with a laugh, kissing his cheek. "Got any ideas for a quiet place to watch the sheep and talk to Arthur and company? I don't want to be overheard or seen to be playing favorites among reporters. They can be a sensitive lot about exclusives."

All the things he was learning...

"I recommend the second floor from one of the classrooms. Do you want me to get them and meet you there? Ghislaine is waving you over, it seems."

She looked over, the red highlights in her hair flashing under the lights. "She's with the artist Ellie was going crazy about. I'll only be a minute. Thanks, babe."

"Sure thing, *a stór*."

She caught his hand before he could step away. "Thanks for trusting me to help you up there. With the Veritas thing."

His smile was easy at last. "I'll always trust you. See you shortly."

He managed to catch their party as they were walking down the long aisle of chairs toward the windows. "Hi, I'm Liam O'Hanlon. Taylor wanted to invite you to a better view upstairs if you have a moment."

The older man held out his age-spotted hand and gave him a hearty handshake. "I'm Arthur Hale, and I'm old as dirt and don't have too many moments left, so a better view would be great."

Arthur's beautiful wife clucked her tongue. "I'm Clara Merriam Hale, Liam, and my advice is not to take anything this cranky old man has to say seriously. If I did, he'd still be walking with a cane."

The older man waggled silver brows over light blue eyes filled with humor and wisdom. "She took it away from me when we started dating. I fell down for days."

He had to fight the urge to laugh at their banter. They had the gift for gab, as they'd say in Ireland.

"I'm Trevor Merriam, Liam," said the tall, dark-haired man. He shook Liam's hand with a firm grip. "I agree with my aunt. You can't take Uncle Arthur seriously, but he is one hell of a reporter."

"Which is why you're here," Liam managed, "something we all appreciate. If you'll come this way."

Taylor was waiting at the top of the stairs with a huge smile on her face. "I snuck away faster than expected. Hey, Trev! Nice of you to swing up this way. Been an age since the last time we hung out in Rome."

The camaraderie between them was obvious, and Liam liked the chance to see more of the Taylor he was madly in love with.

"You mean the night you and J.T. decided we needed gelato at three in the morning and dragged me into the streets to find a place that was still open?" He stopped in front of her and put his hands on her shoulders, smiling broadly. "Good to see you, Taylor. J.T. said to kiss you Rome style for him, but I'm too Irish now for that. So you get a hug."

"I'll take it." She squeezed him tightly enough to make him grunt, then nudged him in the ribs. "Now, introduce me."

Liam had to smile at the playful demand, and so did the man Taylor had described as her hero. A heady thing, meeting one's hero...

He swept out his hand grandly, earning a harumph from Arthur. "My aunt and uncle, whose names you already know. Beware. Your life will never be the same after you meet these two. I'm hitched and running a bed and breakfast in Ireland with llamas in my yard. Llamas, *plural*."

Liam fought a chuckle. An odd animal to be raising in Ireland. He sensed a story.

"They're alpacas," his aunt corrected with a snort, "and you agreed Buttercup needed someone else to love after you married Becca."

"Buttercup wanted to set up house with Trevor the

moment they met." Arthur laughed heartily. "You've never seen a grown man run so fast."

"See, a laugh a minute," Trevor responded with a grin that belied his tone. "You should come visit when things calm down. I think Buttercup might take a shine to Liam here."

"I completely agree," Clara said, giving him a wink, which he returned.

Taylor laughed. "It's hard not to, with that sexy, soulful pirate look and all."

"I love the earring, dear," Clara added. "Very Tyrone Power of you."

"Land sakes, Clara," Arthur barked out, "he probably doesn't even know who that is."

"I do, actually, from *The Black Swan*," Liam responded. "We Irish take Maureen O'Hara's films pretty seriously—or my dad did. And that was one of her first. Speaking of other things Irish, come and see those sheep."

Trevor groaned. "Becca has a whole troublesome herd for wool, and you should know she's taken to letting our children spray-paint words on them like your Kindness Sheep. Although I'm mostly the artist since the kids are young."

Liam thought that was a nice point of connection, and he found himself eager to visit their inn with Taylor when they had a break.

"How old are your kids now?" Taylor asked as they reached the windows in one of the painting studios.

"Roarke is three and Brenna is one, which is why I'm only allowed up here for the day," he joked. "Seriously, though, they're angels. Take after me, of course."

"I doubt that," Taylor responded, punching him in the arm.

Liam fought a smile. He could already see her punching Brady or Declan in the arm like that. He knew she was going to get along great with his friends once everything settled down and they all had time to hang out.

Arthur put his arm around his wife as they stood in front of the window. "Taylor, be warned. Trevor gets what he thinks is his cleverness from his aunt. This woman runs me ragged with all the trouble she gets into. Ah, here are the sheep now. A wonderful idea, I must say. The world could use more kindness."

"But not more sheep, if you ask me," Trevor grumbled. "Liam, you aren't in sheep, are you?"

"My dad had them, which cured me young," he responded as everyone turned their attention to Keegan O'Malley leading his herd up to the arts center, accompanied by Carrick, Jamie, and Kade and their sheep dogs.

"Smart decision, Liam," Trevor said with a wry smile.

"Oh, aren't they simply adorable?" Clara pressed her face to the glass like a little child. "Arthur, I might need a couple at home."

"No way," he answered gruffly. "Absolutely not. We have enough of a menagerie of babies and young children around to constitute a zoo. You can buy a T-shirt. Less mess and baaing that way. Right, Trev?"

"I'd agree but Aunt Clara might sock me, and she packs a good punch."

She gave him a gentle sock anyway, making Liam laugh. She was a firecracker, much like his Taylor. "You'll have to meet our oldest artist here at the center, Clara. Eoghan O'Dwyer is ninety-four."

"I read about him when Arthur started his research about your arts center. He's my new hero. I told Arthur I might take up painting nudes like your man Eoghan."

The older man groaned while Trevor muttered and closed his eyes, "Nudes? Kill me now."

"I live to terrify them," Clara said with an adorable chortle. "You can bet I plan to do a little shopping here. I love art, and if possible, I'd like to make a donation to the center."

Liam gestured for Taylor to reply to that one. "That would be very kind of you, Mrs. Hale—"

"Clara," she corrected. "Wonderful. Oh, look! How clever. Those sheep make a sentence."

Liam peered down, noting the string tied between the cluster of sheep to form a longer message. *We. Stand. Against. Malcolm.* "Not exactly under the formerly kind rubric." His friends wouldn't have gone for this. Keegan must have wanted to spit in Malcolm's eye publicly.

"But a heartfelt one nonetheless." Taylor pointed to the left. "I like *Stop. Harassing. Our. Center.* Brief and to the point."

"Bullies don't care to be called out," Arthur mused, taking off his glasses and polishing them before repositioning them on his nose. "I imagine Mr. O'Malley knew that. Besides, that message will go viral, I imagine. Better than newspaper headlines, those sheep."

Liam thought over how that would play out. Arthur was right—Malcolm wouldn't like it. Then again, Malcolm didn't like anything they did. "I'm sure Keegan meant it to raise more awareness."

"But I'm here because awareness isn't enough, aren't I?" Arthur asked boldly, looking over at both him and Taylor with his serious intellect showing. "To take down a giant, you have to make good shots, and sometimes you only get one. This is a strong hit. It will poke at his vanity and embarrass him publicly. That's what Veritas intended too."

Liam kept his face neutral, but when Arthur turned toward him, he was shocked to see that the man's easygoing, joking demeanor was gone. He had the look of a dog who planned to go after the bone.

"Are you sure you don't know more about Veritas than you've said, Liam?" he asked, lowering his head and peering at him over his glasses. "Because I've got black ink running through these old veins, and my instincts are screaming that you do. In fact, I'd say you have the goods on something that could blow this whole story open."

Liam froze like a shocked hare, pinned by the man's intense blue stare. He didn't dare look over at Taylor.

"Care to tell an old reporter what you're hiding?"

CHAPTER FIFTEEN

Taylor had never imagined that Arthur Hale's great reporting skills would be turned on them.

Her, specifically.

She locked her knees and held her breath as Liam continued to stand silently under the older man's scrutiny.

"Even if I did," Liam finally answered, "I wouldn't be able to tell you anything. You're a reporter. You know what confidential means."

"I know exactly what that word means," Arthur continued, "even to the point of going to jail if it came to it. Are you telling me you'd go that far to keep Veritas' identity secret?"

"Yes," he answered without hesitation. "Some secrets are worth preserving, and Veritas' identity is one of them."

She wanted to kiss him. So hard. Not that such a scenario would ever present itself, thank goodness. Legally, they were covered.

"Mmm," Arthur only answered, taking his glasses off once again but continuing to watch Liam.

"He can't let a good story pass," Clara said with a sigh. "Don't let him ruffle you, Liam. That's his intent, you see."

"Aren't you here to help us with Malcolm?" Liam countered, tilting his head to the side.

"Indeed, I am," Arthur agreed. "Trevor even gave me everything the family business has on him."

Taylor watched him transform into the version of a man you didn't want to tangle with, one she was glad was on their side. "Even though Malcolm Coveney hasn't really crossed us, Quinn and Francesca have a file on him. He's a dangerous man with a lot of influence and power in Ireland, which you know firsthand."

"Unfortunately," Liam agreed as Taylor nodded crisply.

"There's something else you should know." Arthur looked at them straight on. "Malcolm appears to be looking at ways to use his influence illegally to identify Veritas and charge him with a crime."

Although Taylor had already heard that, somehow Arthur's delivery turned her blood cold. "Accusations of vandalism will be tough since Liam gave permission."

Arthur shook his head. "Ever heard of Portraitgate, my dear? It happened here in Ireland in 2009, and it involved a supposedly anonymous artist hanging two objectionable comic-strip-like nudes of the then Taoiseach of Ireland, Brian Cowen, in two Dublin galleries."

"I remember that," Liam said, his mouth now tight with tension. "The artist was Conor Casby, a schoolteacher from Claremorris. Not far from here."

Taylor felt a new injection of tension in her body, like someone had given her a shot. "What happened to him?"

Arthur continued polishing his glasses. "Mr. Casby was hunted down by the Garda and brought in for questioning on potential charges of hate speech, indecency, and some others. A major media station reported the story, only to later apologize for hurting the Taoiseach's feelings. I'm paraphrasing here. Taylor, you should look it up because my early sources in Dublin are saying Malcolm is using a similar playbook. Only this time, he plans to put Veritas in jail if he can. Under the new hate speech laws."

"But how could he do that?" Taylor asked. "No one even knows where Veritas is."

Arthur shot her nerves to a new stratosphere as he slowly rubbed his lenses with a cloth. "But Ireland is an IT power now, right? The government has good tech people who are saying they can find Veritas using the email Liam received—"

"You know about that?" Taylor asked, glancing at Liam. "But the center's lawyers only sent it to our local Garda this morning."

"News travels," Arthur said, "what can I say? I actually heard about it from one of the Irish reporters milling around before we went into the arts center this morning. He was trying to impress me."

"He was a big fan," Clara said with an eye roll.

Taylor suspected it must have been one of Malcolm's guys or someone on his payroll, to know about something like that.

"Anyway, they may compel you to deliver more information, Liam. Or possibly even compel Facebook—which has a big presence here in Ireland and owns Instagram—to hand over the location of Veritas' posts about the mural. We should all fear the information Facebook has on us. Trust me. Don't ever read the user agreement."

"I'm sure Veritas is familiar with how to remain anonymous," Liam responded casually, and Taylor figured it had to be all his meditating that made him sound so at ease while she was trembling inside.

"Let's hope so," Arthur responded, returning his glasses to the bridge of his nose. "It seems the sheep parade is finished. Shall we move along? Clara, I'd better start you shopping early, or we'll never get to lunch."

Taylor managed a smile as they bantered, but her mind was spinning. Was she in trouble? Her hacker was one many street artists used, and he was well versed in creating barriers for their anonymity, complicated mazes of IP addresses and possible fake locations. But would it be enough?

Liam's hand on her arm brought her back to the present. He held her gaze, assurance in his very touch and look. "Shall we go downstairs? Maybe have a tour?"

"That sounds great," Clara said with enthusiasm.

As they were walking down the stairs, Trevor sidled up next to her. "J.T. told me we should offer Flynn's help—have you met our baby bro?"

She only shook her head.

"He can help Uncle Arthur find Malcolm's secret bank accounts and dig into finding Veritas. J.T.'s always been a big fan of Veritas. I've had to take a million pictures of that mural for him."

She had to slow her steps, her ears buzzing now. "I'm confused."

He threw back his head and laughed. "Did J.T. never tell you about that time he tried to disappear off the grid because of his ex-wife?"

She shook her head as Liam took her hand as he caught up to them.

"Flynn was the guy who found him. He's got mad tech skills."

"He really does," Clara told her with a proud smile. "He could give the Russians a run for their money."

Her stomach dropped to the floor. How had this happened?

She had invited in the very family capable of unmasking her identity.

CHAPTER SIXTEEN

T aylor's day with her journalistic hero should have been happier, but Liam could feel the strain under her smile.

He couldn't blame her. Arthur Hale was a tempest in a teapot, and Trevor's proud revelation about his brother's hacking abilities had broken Liam's shaky calm. He held Taylor's hand as they led the group on a tour of the arts center with Linc, Bets, and Eoghan, and he felt a trembling in her fingers even though they were both amused by Clara, who was more than a match for her charismatic husband and nephew.

After buying two of Angie's landscapes, three of Megan's pottery pieces, and commissioning Eoghan to paint her in whatever way inspired him—including a nude, she'd said with a gusty laugh—she'd managed to freeze even Linc's easygoing smile when she casually handed over a five-million-dollar check for their children's program as they stood in the now empty entryway of the arts center.

Her reasoning, beyond the wish to see more children learn art, had been sweet to Liam's ears. She'd said her grandnieces and nephews might want to come up for a summer session sometime. Liam wondered if the apple didn't fall far from the tree. If so, Jamie and the other teachers would have their hands full.

"Holy hell, Clara," Linc cried out, handing the check over to Liam's mum, whose mouth dropped to the floor. "You interested in joining our board?"

"I'd love to, Linc, but our trips to Kenya and the family keep me well occupied," she responded as Arthur released a clear breath of relief. "But you might ask Quinn's wife, Francesca. She loves the arts, and she and our nephew Quinn have been helping Arthur investigate Malcolm. They have some good friends in high places."

"Which you need to work in this country," Trevor said, "as you know, Linc. We've just been in the game longer."

"I told Bets we'd do better if I'd built a new windows factory here." He made a *cha-ching* sound for effect. "Jobs equal money, and that wins over art in most places."

"Sad but true," Clara agreed, linking arms with Eoghan, who was beaming beside her. "Now, my new friend promised me a good Irish lunch at a place named after a naughty donkey."

"It's a *brazen* donkey, Clara, for Pete's sake," Arthur said with a long-suffering sigh. "Where is your mind?"

"Where you like it, my dear." She blew a flirtatious kiss. "It was a pleasure to meet all of you. Taylor, you especially. J.T. is very selective about his friends."

"Trevor, not so much," Arthur joked, clapping his great-nephew on the back. "All right, let's head to the *Brazen* Donkey. Linc, I'd hoped to talk to you and whoever else you'd like to join us about Malcolm. Perhaps we can trade notes."

Liam watched as Linc and his mum traded that secret

look couples shared. He thought he and Taylor had begun their own silent form of communication. He glanced over at her doing her best to smile, but he could tell she was jittery. He couldn't wait to get her alone and calm her down. Of course, he would need five minutes of deep breathing to get there himself.

"That would be great, Arthur," Linc said, gesturing to the door. "It seems you've hit it off with Eoghan, and he and his son know this part of Ireland better than anyone."

"Wonderful," Arthur said brightly, rubbing his hands together. "I don't do too many stories anymore, but this one has my blood pumping. Especially since I have family here in Ireland who may encounter Malcolm at some point."

Liam took that as a sign to stay out of the man's journalistic ways. He didn't want to reveal anything about Veritas or be forced to lie to the older man. While it wasn't his call, Liam thought Taylor could trust the reporter with the truth —Trevor too—and he planned to tell her so as soon as they were alone. But they had agreed from the get-go to keep it between them, and he wasn't about to break that promise.

He tipped his proverbial hat. "Well, I'm off to do more work on the construction side." He walked over and kissed Clara on the cheek. "It's been a delight to meet you. I hope we see you again. Trevor. Arthur. A pleasure."

Arthur held his gaze a moment longer, making Liam's pulse race. He was racking up unusual experiences lately. He broke eye contact and gave Taylor the kind of look Linc had given his mother.

She excused herself and joined him outside, well away from the door. "You're leaving?"

"I thought it best to stay away," he told her, tucking her hair behind her ears when the wind blew it askew. "Arthur—"

"Yeah, Arthur." She threw up her hands. "How could I overlook the fact that he's going to sniff out every detail related to this story?"

He began soothing strokes on her arm to calm her. "I think you could trust him and Trevor if it came to it."

She looked up to signal they were on the video feed. Yeah, he'd forgotten about that. "I can't handle that right now. All right, I'm off to...what was it? The Naughty Donkey? I'll see you after work." After a quick, hard kiss to his mouth, she was off.

He settled into his work after clearing his mind, but it was an ongoing battle to focus. An hour later, he gave in to the urge to find out how their lunch was going and called Brady at the pub.

"Hiya," his friend answered while laughter and conversation buzzed in the background. "Where in the world are you? Taylor's friends have everyone entranced. Did you know Arthur was a huge reporter from America? And Clara a major philanthropist for the arts? Then there's their nephew. I've already booked Ellie and me a room at their lovely inn for the next bank holiday. I swear, this arts center has brought in more interesting people than this village has ever seen before."

Brady's enthusiasm could always be counted on. "It's still a workday here." He hated that it wasn't totally true.

"We all miss you at Summercrest, you know. But of course we want you to spend time with your soulmate. What a girl she is, although you can tell things are wearing on her. I can see it in her eyes when she doesn't think anyone is looking. I thought you'd want me to take care of her."

A lump formed in his throat. "You're a good friend,

Brady, and I appreciate that. Try and make her laugh for me, will you?"

"When Eoghan stops telling tall tales, you can be sure I will. He's got the whole group chortling over that time when he went fishing with Donal and caught the giant crab who fastened his claws onto Eoghan's pants."

"Which Donal made him shuck off in the cold December rain, only for them to be swept into the water by the wind," Liam finished.

They both started laughing, and the relief felt good. Liam had needed to release some of the underlying tension his breathing hadn't taken care of.

"Thanks for looking after my girl, Brady."

"She's one of us now. Talk to you later then."

He signed off, feeling more grounded, and focused back on his part in building the future of the arts center. After the sun set, he realized he should head home soon. No one had come back to the center, and it wouldn't surprise him if everyone had stayed all afternoon at the pub. It was the Irish way, after all.

The house was quiet as he let himself in, and he decided to use the time to meditate and relax himself some more. When Taylor finally arrived, he rose from his mat and headed to the kitchen. Normally they had a beer when they came home, and he'd keep to that routine unless she told him she'd had enough at the pub. Her heels crashing to the floor was now a familiar sound, one he was coming to really love as much as the way she called, "Honey, I'm home."

He was smiling easily for the first time since morning as he walked to the front door and handed her a beer. Her auburn hair held a bit of frizz from the soft drizzle outside, and her big brown eyes had dark circles under them. She tapped her now unpainted lips, which held a burgeoning smile, and then he was kissing her lightly on the mouth until they both sighed.

"Sorry about leaving you earlier," he said softly as he continued to nibble. "I'm not used to subterfuge, so it seemed the best course."

"Surely you have some Irish saying about keeping secrets?" she asked, cuddling close. "I swear I took my first class in Irish education today, with Eoghan as the teacher. Your history is riddled with pirates and intrigue. I didn't realize Irish pirates often fought off the bad guys, the ones like Malcolm. Arthur and Clara loved it."

He was happy to hear the couple had enjoyed themselves, Arthur especially, but he winced as one of the most famous Irish sayings came to mind. "We do have one. *Three people can keep a secret if two of them are dead.*"

"Better sleep with an eye open then," she joked, kissing him again as she rubbed her bare heel to the back of his calf. "I'm kidding. It must be Eoghan's influence. Man, can he tell a joke and thread a story. Master class."

He put his arm around her waist. "I know. Your journalistic guest is gone then?"

"Yep. They're likely boarding the family's private jet as we speak." She linked her arms around his neck, cooling his neck with the beer. "What. A. Day."

"Do you want to run through the highlights of what happened after I left?"

"I'd rather make out with you for a while until my stomach settles and my mind stops spinning." She blew out a savage breath. "There were a couple of moments there when I thought I was going to get sick. You being asked about Veritas at the podium. Later, hearing Malcolm is going after Veritas hard with a playbook I didn't know about. When Ghislaine and I looked up Portraitgate online at the pub. In that moment, we both questioned our decision to move here. The whole story is insane!"

"As you know, big power brokers don't like to be made fun of." Liam led her to the couch. "I wasn't joking about what I said. I'd go to jail to keep your identity secret."

She laid her head on his shoulder after setting her beer down on the coffee table. "I don't want to *think* about that. I would never let that happen."

He stroked the rigid line of her back. "Then let's do what we can to keep positive and make sure it doesn't. Taylor, there are a lot of people working to neutralize Malcolm, if not take him down."

"Ghislaine says you've gone viral as my hot rescuer," she said, lifting her head. "What with the whole romance we seem to be having after you swept in on your motorcycle and saved me from the big, bad wolf."

He frowned. "Which you didn't refute at the press conference. I noticed you didn't tell them you had it all under control when I arrived. You're no damsel in distress."

She traced his frown with her fingertips. "People love that kind of stuff. Besides, neither of us can be sure what might have happened if you hadn't come."

Yeah, he'd had some bad thoughts on that score, ones he'd had to work hard to banish in meditation.

"The Kindness Sheep have gone viral again too," she added. "Ghislaine and I think they might be the best media tool we have in our arsenal. We're thinking up ways we can do more to feature Keegan and his sheep and Caisleán's reaction to those cuddly little billboards."

"That's a good way of putting it." He traced her face. "You need to shut your mind off for a while. Me too. I realized I was too worked up to make dinner when I got home. I wasn't being present."

"Oh, no," she joked, flopping back on the couch and covering her eyes dramatically with her hand. "Not that!"

He tickled her right side, making her squeal with laughter. Covering her with his body, he propped himself on his elbows and looked down into her pale, but now grinning face. "You want to pick out the movie tonight?"

The routine they'd settled into gave her time to recharge. Sometimes at dinner, he'd catch her staring off into space, clearly exhausted. Even if safety weren't an issue, he wasn't sure he'd be suggesting they head out to a pub or take a night ride on the beach. Not with all that was going on around them. The truth was he liked cooking for her, or her for him, and talking to her at the dinner table. Sometimes they fed each other, and their awareness of each other would begin to build. The problems pressing them would start to fade, and by the time she was settled against him on the couch, he could simply fall into the joy of being with her, not needing to do anything at all.

She shook her head, the silky waves of her auburn hair calling to his fingertips. "Prepare yourself. I have something else in mind."

Her brown eyes were filled with a new warmth, and the love he had for her rose up and seized him by the throat. He knew what she was going to say.

"I'm happy to report Sorcha was wrong for once." She caressed his jaw, holding his gaze. "I love you, Liam O'Hanlon. With all my heart. And I want to be with you. Body. Mind. And soul."

When she took a deep breath, he could feel his mouth curve. "Admit it. My assertion that I would go to jail to keep your secret today did the final trick, didn't it?"

She worked her mouth before smiling grandly. "Yep! It shocked me too. But then I realized it shouldn't. I mean, anyone can give a girl dinner and a movie, but saving a girl on a road from a bad guy and then following up with a vow to go to jail to protect her... Nothing beats that."

Still, he made sure to hold her eyes, searching for her inner truths. She blandly stared back. Then he heard her chuckle.

"You think this is funny?" he asked, tickling her again. "I want to be sure."

She grabbed his face between her hands. "Look to your heart's content, Liam O'Hanlon. Here be your loony soulmate. In all her secretive, wacky wonderfulness."

Loony, his eye. "I love you too, *a stór*. Come to bed with me."

He was helping her off the couch when Sorcha appeared before them. Taylor let out a yelp, falling back onto the couch as Sorcha crossed her arms over her spectral chest.

"For the record, I wasn't wrong." She smirked. "I thought you'd be more open if I told you the wrong date. Plus, I knew you'd want to prove me wrong if you could. And I was right. Have fun, kids."

When she vanished, Taylor threw up her hands. "How does that make any sense? She was just covering her invisible behind, which is really freaky by the way. Don't you think?"

He helped her off the couch. "Do you want to debate the limits of Sorcha's spirit form or make love for the first time?"

"Good point." She stepped closer to him, running her hand seductively down his chest. "Aren't you supposed to sweep me into your arms or something? I've never had soulmate sex, and I would think it would require some pretty big rituals."

She was totally pulling his leg. Well, he was Irish. He could pull back. "I could light some incense. Chant a little. No, wait! We could meditate together. Set our intentions."

Her mouth was twitching. "You mean like how many orgasms I'd like to have? Trust me, if we go over two in one night, it's a record."

He fought a smile. "Only two? *A stór,* I'm not one to brag, but I've definitely seen you having more than two."

She started dragging him playfully toward the bedroom. "*Really?* Like how many? Because I'd like to have an idea before we start."

Because she was curious. Always curious, his Taylor. "I didn't count them when I saw the visions. I just saw you coming and coming and coming. Over and over again. Back arched. Eyes closed. Pleasure raining through your body."

Her body sagged against him, and this time he had to hold her up. "You're kidding, right? Because if you are, I need to tell you that joking about the number of possible orgasms is slime-level low."

He used his muscles to playfully assist her down the hallway as she kept her body weak. "Would I joke about your pleasure?"

That made her straighten up. "No, I don't think so. Oh, Liam, put your hands on me."

He had other things in mind. "I want you naked first."

She let out a breathy moan as she reached to unbutton her suit jacket, backing into the door of her bedroom. "If I'm naked, you're naked."

"I can live with that," he said, unbuttoning his shirt as he followed her.

He couldn't take his eyes off her as she undressed in front of him, as bold at this as she was at everything else. When he opened his pants, her gaze dropped, and she let out another breathy sound that had his body hardening even more.

"God, you are so damn hot." She swept off the last of her clothes, standing naked as he chucked off his remaining items.

"And you're so beautiful you steal my breath away," he said, taking in the slender lines of her body.

She was strong, he knew, but her curves called to him. This was his woman, his soulmate, the one perfect partner for him. "I've waited a long time for you. For this. Come, let me love you."

His mouth was on hers then, and she twined her arms around his neck as their lips found each other and retreated before seeking that connection again. He couldn't stand another moment of separation, so he pulled her against his body.

The feel of her skin was electric, and they both uttered dark groans of pleasure. She fitted herself to him, pressing as close as she could, as if she couldn't get close enough. He understood, but he also knew to let their bodies' energies follow their internal wisdom. He could feel the click between them starting at their lower bodies, traveling up to their hearts.

She pressed back, her eyes going wide as she felt the connection strengthen. He cupped her face, savoring the magnetic pull between them. The love he felt for her was like an eternal shower of delicious rain or the endless stream of sunshine.

"Is it always like this for you?" she asked softly. "This is new for me. I feel like your heartbeat is pulsing inside me. Liam, it's so weird, but it's really wonderful."

He embraced the energy as it traveled up higher, merging their minds. She would be able to read him now, in this sacred moment, and feel everything he was feeling. They would be equals in that too. "No, it's never been like this."

She swallowed thickly as her energy harmonized with his completely. "Soulmate sex is *intense*."

He kissed her softly on the lips. "And we've only just begun."

The answering press of her mouth swept them both along a tide of no return. Their urgency rose with the glorious slide of their skin together, the blissful dance of their mouths, and the urgent caresses of their fingertips.

When his mouth touched her neck, she arched into him, moaning aloud. Already he could feel the energy in her belly growing stronger. Pulsing. He knew she would be coming soon. He had only to encourage it.

Sitting on the edge of the bed, he drew her onto his lap. She twined her legs around his waist as he guided them, groaning as their bodies touched intimately for the first time.

"Oh, God!" She suddenly stopped. "I probably should tell you I got on birth control before I arrived. Just in case Sorcha was right."

He ran his hands under the backs of her thighs where she framed him with her body. "That was an act of faith."

She bowed back, resting her hands on his knees for balance, the sight of which had him growing impossibly hard. "Yeah, I thought so too. Do I get points?"

He was laughing as he cupped her breasts, tugging on her already aroused nipples. "Do you need them?"

"I don't even remember what we're talking about." She rocked against his arousal, making his jaw clench. "I usually need more warming up, but I want you inside me. Like right now."

He arranged her until he could position himself at the entrance of her body. "I'm all yours, Taylor. Take me."

She lifted her head, her brown eyes fevered with passion, and then she pressed forward, taking him slowly, inch by glorious inch. He fought to keep his gaze on her, wanting to throw his head back and surrender to the desire pulsing between them. She lowered herself, taking him all the way, making them both groan.

"Oh, God, I think I'm going to come," she breathed out, arching into him.

He locked himself in place inside her as her muscles started contracting around him. "Come for me then. Right now."

She pressed against him and exploded, her body pulsing around him. He sought his breath for control, staying still inside her as an avalanche of pleasure washed over her. He stayed that way, focusing on his breathing, until she touched his face. A fraction of his control snapped, and he took another deep cleansing breath as he finally looked at her.

Her entire being was shining, her soul radiating sunlight from her eyes. She traced his face with reverence before kissing him slowly on the lips. The slow slide of her tongue into his mouth frayed more of his control. His breathing shattered. He put his hands to the small of her back and surged forward.

She cried out and arched back. "Oh, yes. Oh, yes. Oh, yes. Do that again."

He repeated the motion, keeping himself high and tight against her core. She ignited a second time, crying out as the waves rocked her again. He let his breath go and joined her in the rush, surging deeply into her again and again and again until his orgasm took him under. He was weightless, connected to something larger and more powerful than anything he'd ever known. When he heard her cry out, he answered with his own, twining his arms around her as she locked her legs to hold him tightly as she pulsed and pulsed and pulsed around him.

He let himself lay back on the bed after unmolding her legs but kept them joined, wanting to feel her body in every aftermath of pleasure as she lay over him.

He wasn't aware of his own body, only of the sensation of her, warm and pliant against him. His heart floated until there was nothing but a heartbeat, his and hers, the sound of their love combined for all eternity. Behind his eyes, the light was a glorious gold, so beautiful and bright, he felt himself change in its presence.

There was a reason some considered sex sacred, he thought, as he descended from the clouds. In the arms of one's soulmate, nirvana was attainable, the state of perfect contentment the masters spoke of. And it was all because of this potent love...

She stirred and poked him in the ribs, which brought him back the rest of the way. When he finally opened his eyes, she had a cocky smile on her face. "You communing with the gods? Because I have to say, I feel ya."

He stretched until he had his hands under his head with his elbows out, which she tickled as well. Because she could, he imagined. "The secret to the meaning of life was in that experience."

Her eyes grew larger. "Really? We should hold another press conference."

That she would balance his deeply spiritual side with her grounded sense of humor only made him smile. They were perfectly paired. "Maybe tomorrow. I think we have more newsworthy items to pursue. Like how many orgasms you can take in one night."

"I've already lost count." She shifted on his chest and gave an earthy moan. "I mean, that was seriously like one long commuter train of orgasms. One stop and back to the rush. Another stop and—"

"You have a way with words as much as with art," he interrupted, rolling them until she was underneath him. "But, *a stór,* you are indeed lucky. Because I have a way with soulmate sex, as you call it."

He could already feel his energy rising again, kicked up by the swirling and pulsing center in her core. Her breath was already growing more rapid as her body readied for him again.

"You certainly do." She arched into him, one long gorgeous line of surrender. "This is where I say, 'Now boarding.'"

His mouth covered hers, taking her to where they both wanted to go.

CHAPTER SEVENTEEN

W aking in the arms of one's soulmate had to be the most delicious way to wake up.

Liam's arms were wrapped around her, his warm, gorgeous body fitted to her backside. She might just become a morning person. Maybe.

Her muscles were buzzing with life as her skin came alive with that crazy electricity they generated. The close contact was like the hum of a generator through her bones but with the rush of a hurricane wind. Heck, minus the violence, there had even been the report of a shotgun kind of energy between them.

They made love throughout the night, sometimes hot and urgent until she wanted to scream, and other times so soulful and slow she couldn't imagine ever unsealing herself from him. Time had stopped, and her reality was only them. Together. The whole concept of orgasms had been redefined. She'd been on one long ride, where the journey went sometimes in a rush and then in a whisper.

She'd always been amused how people talked about the skin being the biggest organ in the body. Last night, it had shown her its full power for the first time. At one point, she'd been so sensitized, she could have sworn her epidermis was dancing its heart out. Like she'd told Liam, soulmate sex was intense. She never wanted to go back to the old kind.

"You awake, *a stór*?" he whispered, kissing the line of her shoulders.

"You mean, you didn't feel my inner nuclear plant turn on when my body became aware of yours?" She turned in his arms until they were facing each other, but his eyes remained sleepily closed. "Good morning. How are you on this fine day?"

His rumble of a chuckle was as sexy as the scruff on his face, which her fingertips had to rub. "You sound more cheery than I've ever heard you this early," he observed in that always insightful way of his.

"Turns out soulmate sex is transformative." She let her fingers detour down to his hard chest. "I was thinking I might be a morning person now. I feel terrific, and even though we didn't sleep until after four, I'm supercharged. I'm starting to think world peace might be possible if everyone has this kind of sex. What do you think?"

"I think you're as talkative as ever." Those green eyes finally rested on hers, making her heart soar up like a cheery yellow kite. "You're happy. I am too. It's even better than the way I saw it."

She snuggled against him, purposely wiggling as she felt his morning arousal. "Right. We were too busy last night for details about your visions."

"We were *experiencing* the details," he said with a laugh, caging her hips with one arm.

The press of him had her body pulsing in urgent beats. "I want to experience them again. You okay with staying in bed all day? I know it's our day off, and you haven't seen your friends much this past week, but please say yes."

His mouth settled over hers, and the weightless feeling in her heart magnified. "Of course, I want to stay like this with you. As long as we can."

"Good." She fitted her leg over his hip as she took him inside her, making them both groan. "I'm probably going to have to thank Sorcha at some point."

"Later, *a stór*," he whispered as he pressed in deep.

She arched into the slow friction of their joined bodies. "Yes, later. Much later."

The entire day contained more revelations, a frequent flyer card to paradise, and when she could actually hold a thought in her head—when her body wasn't keyed into bliss mode—she wondered how she had ever lived without him. It was only a week ago that she'd arrived, but her entire life had changed.

She told him that, along with a few other suggestions for some additional spicy soulmate sex as they ate on the couch as night fell. He made a fire, wanting to see the light play over her skin. God, he knew how to get to her with words like that. Their lovemaking was as intense as it was connected. She'd never looked into anyone's eyes this much during sex before, but in Liam's eyes, she had found everything she was looking for.

They fell asleep in front of the fire, and she awoke when he jerked straight up awake, breathing hard. The suddenness pushed aside her sleep.

"Bad dream?" she whispered as she touched his face.

He nodded quickly. "Just give me a moment. I need some water."

She realized he was drenched in sweat as she rose to follow

him. Dawn's light was visible from the windows with ribbons of red, yellow, and blue hovering above the rise of the green hills. She grabbed a hand towel as he downed a glass of water and wet it in the sink before pressing it to the back of his boiling neck. His eyes were clenched tightly, focusing on his breaths. She ran a comforting hand up his back, aware he was trembling.

This was bad, whatever it was. She'd never seen him this discombobulated, not even when he'd rushed to her rescue the day she'd arrived. She waited until he finally set the glass down, his hand no longer trembling. Leaning back against the counter, he studied her, his entire body knotted with tension.

Her own muscles locked in place. "Can you tell me? I want to help."

He touched her arm as he walked past her, picking up his phone to turn on the ringer. "I figure we'll be hearing soon enough."

The phone rang in his hand, making her jump in place. He took a deep breath and answered, his face grave. When he held his hand out to her, she grabbed it and pressed herself to his now cold frame as he did nothing but listen. She could hear a woman's voice crying on the other line. The air was heavy with something dark now, and she squeezed her eyes closed, trying to fight it off.

"I'll be there in a minute, Mum." He clicked off and wrapped both arms around her. "In my dreams, I saw a fetch. It's an Irish apparition of something real. Then Mum called. Taylor—"

She looked up as he pressed his hand hard to his mouth. "Just tell me."

"Someone sheared the Kindness Sheep, and in the process, they killed two and left a message of their own."

She gasped, tightening her grip on him. "No! How could anyone do that?"

He swallowed thickly before dragging her tightly against him. "Taylor, I need to go. Mum is beside herself, and Keegan is out of his mind. The Garda is coming. The village will be showing up…"

She hugged him hard, wanting to comfort him but still in shock herself. "I'll go with you."

"It's your choice." His sigh was heartbreaking, as was the way he lowered his head to her shoulder. "I would never stop you from doing something. But it's going to be ugly, and I would spare you that."

Cupping the back of his neck, she forced herself to be strong. This was her moment to give back to him. "We're partners, remember? I go where you go. We get through this together. Plus, it's my job as media director to…"

She trailed off. She had no idea what the media director of an arts center did with news like this. But Veritas…an image formed in her mind—of sheep floating up to heaven with angel's wings. She would think about that later.

"Come on." She kissed him softly on the neck, all the love she had for him rising within her. "Let's get dressed and go."

"I have something else I have to tell you." Another firm press of his forehead into her skin before he lifted his head. "I had another vision while I was dreaming. Only this wasn't a dream either. Taylor… God—I don't want to tell you this."

The sharp tentacles of fear wrapped themselves around her. But she'd faced them down before and would again. She bit her lip to bring her back to herself. "Just say it."

His mouth worked before he managed to get the words out: "I saw myself behind bars."

The tentacles locked into place, caging her in. She could almost hear them snap shut. "We won't let it happen."

"I don't know that we can prevent it." He took her face between his hands, his green eyes shining with emotion. "The energy's changed. I first noticed it when I saw Keegan's sentence about Malcolm."

She remembered the moment. He'd been uncomfortable with the message, she recalled. "It's words. Expression. Like my mural."

"Malcolm doesn't see it that way." He inhaled shakily before exhaling a long trail of tension, the only sound in the silent kitchen. "But if it does happen, I don't want you to be scared, okay? Somehow it's going to work out. I just don't know how yet."

"Not be scared?" She gripped his shoulders, locking her gaze with his. "Liam, I love you! If you get put behind bars, I know it'll be because of *me*. Because you helped me. I know I said your willingness to go to jail for me cinched it, but I don't want that. It's one thing for it to happen to me. It's my art, but you going... I can't live with that, dammit!"

"Taylor, listen to me." He took her hands until they were linked around his neck, bringing them closer so she could feel his heart and take comfort from his strength. "If it comes to choosing between me going to jail and you, my choice is clear. I make it freely. You are not to tell anyone you are Veritas. Do you hear me? Because he could still get to you. You heard Arthur. Malcolm is still looking for Veritas through other means. Having both of us in jail solves nothing. Nothing! And if I can stop them from looking at you, I will."

She wasn't a crier, but tears filled her eyes. "Don't be crazy. You going to jail would solve nothing. It would only give Malcolm a win."

"I'll do anything to keep you safe, *a stór*." He kissed her softly, making a tear fall. "Also, being Malcolm's target is safer for me—as a man. We both know it, Taylor."

He was talking about the math teacher, and her body shuddered. Even today, she could feel his old hands grabbing her under her uniform skirt. Was Malcolm capable of the same offenses to women?

Yes, she bet he was.

"I don't like this," she said, her voice shaky. "We'll figure out another way."

"We have a lot of people supporting us," he told her urgently. "I trust in that. You should too. But promise me that you won't tell the authorities you're Veritas. Not even to get me out of jail. Please, *a stór*, it's the only thing I would ever ask of you."

She looked at him as her hands fell to her sides, weighed down by the decision before her. "I want to promise, but I just can't. Liam, I wouldn't be your partner if I let you take the fall for this. I'm not going to let this happen."

His throat worked as he regarded her. "I always told you that you had a choice. I do as well. Taylor, I told you this because I love you. Remember that. No matter what comes."

He turned and walked out, heading to their bedroom, where she'd insisted he move his clothes into yesterday. She fisted her hands, trying to fight off her urge to go after him.

"It won't work," a familiar voice said quietly.

She turned to see Sorcha standing in the kitchen, her dress billowing slightly around her legs.

"I disagree." She crossed her arms over her chest. "This whole discussion is stupid."

"I concur," the ghost replied, her oval face wrecked with sorrow. "But when you truly love someone, your natural urge is to protect them, as you both are discovering. What you both must realize—you most of all—is that there are others who want to protect you as well. When the time comes, I want you to remember that, Taylor. You must."

Her intensity rooted Taylor's feet to the floor in fear. "*I must?* Some ghost you are. Why can't you stop this? Why couldn't you stop those sheep from getting killed?"

For a moment, it looked as though tears were falling down Sorcha's cheeks. "I did what I could. Go and dress. There is much ahead."

With that, she disappeared. Taylor wanted to throw something. How did any of this make sense?

"*A stór,*" Liam called softly from the doorway, fully dressed. "I must go."

"I'll be right behind you," she said, crossing and kissing him on the cheek before walking toward the bedroom.

She heard his motorcycle moments later as she began pulling on her clothes. Gathering her courage for what was ahead, she splashed cold water on her face before heading out herself.

By the time she reached the pasture, there was a line of cars parked on the side of the road. Blue Garda lights were flashing. She parked at the end and started walking to the gate after eyeing the brush and the barbwire. The sounds of crying were audible as was the urgent, frantic baaing of sheep. Her insides started to tremble. She had to force herself forward.

When she reached the first mass of sheared wool on the ground, she paused and kneeled down. The word Keegan had lovingly sprayed was no longer visible, the harshly sheared wool a tangled mess. She wondered what the word had been as she continued walking toward the crowd clustered ahead. The scene before her had her biting the inside of her cheek. Sheared wool shot with blood and paint littered the ground. Ahead, the victimized flock stood clustered together, Donal, Carrick, Kade, and Jamie out among them. Each of the living sheep had one bare side—the positive sentiments brutally shaved off of them.

Her heart broke. All the goodness in life seemed to be gone.

She sighted Liam and had to blink back tears. He had his arm wrapped around his mother, who was standing silent as stone next to Linc as Keegan talked to John Hart and Wilt Mather took notes on his tablet. Both his mum and Keegan were crying. She made herself keep walking to where Liam stood. When she reached them, she saw two sheep lying on their sides, blood staining the ground around them.

Dear God! Those poor sheep. The words sprayed on them in harsh lines had her belly quivering in terror.

Mind. Yourself.

Her head went light. She shook it to clear it. She felt Liam watching her and looked over. Sadness ravaged his face, and his jaw was locked tight. They shared something wordless before she walked over to Ghislaine, who was photographing the scene with her phone.

When she touched the woman's back gently, she jerked. "Oh, Taylor. It's— I have no words, and I need some. Because I'm going to fry the people who did this in the media."

They both locked eyes and then had to look away as tears surged. "Let me help."

"You have your phone?" she asked, her voice hoarse.

She reached into her pocket and pulled it out, gripping it hard to control her emotions.

"That's our best tool right now." Ghislaine rolled her

shoulders back. "We want to take moving photos of this monstrosity. I'd photograph Donal and the others trying to soothe those poor sheep, but every time I get close, I want to cry. I'll never forget the look on Donal's face when we arrived. He jokes about all the troubles he's had with sheep, but he loves them."

"We all do," she said, taking Ghislaine's hand.

The woman nodded crisply. "Yes. Word is spreading far and wide, I expect. We need to finish taking pictures before the whole village and the surrounding townspeople arrive."

But Taylor thought that would make its own powerful statement. Hundreds of people coming out to pay their respects to these sheep that had given inspiration to so many. They needed to recreate these emotions for people online. Maybe they could hold a moment of silence? She would have to think on it and fast.

She fell into her razor-sharp Veritas zone. She would need to work quickly and without emotion to take the photos they needed. Liam could find her when he was ready.

The images she captured would change her. It was like that every time she painted a mural. And seeing strong, grown men wiping tears from their faces as they viewed the carnage would take a chunk out of anyone's heart. She photographed the image of Keegan's wife, Lisa Ann, kneeling on the grass, gathering sheared wool together to form a word. She had to force back her tears when she saw what it was.

Love.

Rage shot through her. Malcolm Coveney wouldn't know love or kindness or even basic decency if it bit him in his big ass. She imagined him laughing as he ate a full Irish breakfast, not at all put off his appetite by what he'd done, and she had the urge to get in her car and head over to his office to give him a piece of her mind.

Then she spotted Sorcha at the far end of the pasture, her dress billowing around her. When the woman beckoned her, she put her phone away, her gut sensing something, although she didn't know what. Her feet made impressions in the grass as she navigated the field of desecrated wool. When she reached Sorcha, the woman's eyes were shining with crystalline tears.

She pointed to the barbwire fence. For a moment, Taylor didn't understand. Then she spotted it. A ripped swatch of muddy brown cloth.

Her gaze flew to Sorcha. "You'll remember I said I tried to help. This is my offering for what happened today."

"I don't understand," she said, feeling the force of the wind grow around them.

"As Mary Kincaid was leaving, I appeared."

Taylor's eyes latched on to the cloth, recognizing it from the morning Mary had come to see the mural, raging at its injustice to her. What a liar! "She tore her dress."

"Yes, in fright." Her dark hair blew as the wind rushed around them. "I wanted to scare her, and I did. The ones who govern me will have to decide if what I did was right and just according to our rules. But I could not let her and her kind continue on in such a way. To torment the living who can fight back is a horrible enough offense. But to maliciously harm and kill animals such as these, who would never harm anyone..."

They both fought tears.

"Maybe it's because I was Carrick's wife, and I came to understand sheep like a true Irishman. But this could not be borne. You'll want John Hart and the others to see it."

Taylor nodded, and because she trusted her instincts,

she took out her phone and captured that horrible swatch of muddy cloth flapping in the breeze from where it was pinned to the barbwire. "They should burn in hell for this."

"As the Irish say, from your lips to God's ears." Sorcha looked off and gave the slightest motion of a wave.

Taylor glanced back to see Carrick striding toward them, his powerful legs moving quickly across the grass. The rest of the men were right behind him.

"I let them see me." Her smile was sad. "Someday, I hope you can tell Carrick the full story of what I did over a pint as his children run around him. But not for a while yet. When you tell him, I want him to be able to smile and think, 'That's my Sorcha.'"

Fighting more tears, she managed to say, "You have my word."

Her ephemeral hand brushed Taylor's face. "And I know how strong your word is. My final thoughts for you—as I am unclear whether we will see each other again—is to remember what I said about other people being here to support you and Liam. You might feel as if you two are alone, fighting against ebony Irish seas, but there are others who would help you. You must reach deep into your heart to decide on your next steps. For the challenges ahead are great. I wish you God's speed, Taylor. You *are* the one Caisleán has been waiting for to finish this."

She disappeared in a flash of light. A hand touched her shoulder and swung her around. Carrick's face was lined with sorrow. "What did she say?"

Taylor pointed to the torn cloth as the rest of the men arrived behind him, a wall of giants.

"Sorcha said it's Mary Kincaid's."

CHAPTER EIGHTEEN

B ets watched as the two sheep were lowered into the freshly dug ground under Sorcha's favorite tree.

Carrick had suggested the idea to a distraught Keegan while Donal had locked his jaw and shaved the warning from their freshly killed bodies with brisk efficiency, burning the wool with a lighter on the spot.

She'd lived in Ireland a long time, and the term *Mind yourself* was a strong one. Delivered like this, it was a chilling warning and one that had made her feel real terror for the first time in her life. If they could kill harmless sheep, what would they do next?

"In all my days, Bets," Linc murmured beside her, the lines around his mouth as stark as cracks in dry earth. "In all my days."

She leaned her head against his strong shoulder as Liam rubbed her back in comfort. Taylor stood at her son's side, her face white and strained. What must she be thinking? Bets wouldn't blame her for wanting to be on the first flight home. Only the young woman didn't strike her as someone who could be frightened off. She'd taken photos and worked with Ghislaine in the background after the explosive evidence from Mary's dress had been bagged by John Hart himself.

Her whole body flushed with rage again as she thought about Mary being involved in such a travesty. Of course, she'd had help, and judging by the irregular cuts and erratic tufts of wool on the surviving sheep's bodies, this crime hadn't been done by professional sheep shearers. It had been a hack job by Malcolm's goons, they all suspected. Not that they had proof, although Wilt had walked the field with John Hart, looking for more evidence.

"We didn't protect the sheep," she whispered to Linc. "We had a plan for everything else—"

He leaned down to her ear. "Bets, no one in their right mind would have thought we *needed* to protect sheep."

Still, she couldn't stop beating herself up. It felt like more should have been done. That this could have been prevented.

Keegan stepped forward, his large hands clenched in front of his stomach as he surveyed the crowd. "I usually say a prayer when I lose a sheep."

His voice broke, and Bets had to fight back tears as Lisa Ann rushed forward to hold his hand.

"Maybe Psalm 23," Lisa Ann said, her voice gruff, as Keegan covered his eyes to hide his grief.

Someone started it: *The Lord is my shepherd; I shall not want.*

The crowd joined in in quiet unity. *He maketh me to lie down in green pastures. He leadeth me beside the still waters. He restoreth my soul.*

Bets had heard this psalm read a million times at funerals but being outside in a green pasture like this, strewn with cruelly shaved wool, she found no peace.

Malcolm and Mary wanted to make them lie down, and she'd be damned if she'd do it.

When the moment of observation was over, she marched over to John Hart at the edge of the massive crowd. Bets numbered it close to three hundred people.

"What do you plan on doing about Mary?" she called loudly.

Officer Hart tucked his hands in his uniform pants and strode over. Wilt looked up, his usually professional face grim. Bets felt Linc's hand on her back as others gathered behind her.

"The torn cloth is not conclusive evidence," he began. A few people called out their disagreement, and he held up a hand in acknowledgment. "I have requested a search warrant of Mary Kincaid's premises based on the number of people here swearing the cloth is from a brown dress they've seen her wear."

"One she always wears," Bets told him.

He gave a long-suffering sigh. "Should it match a dress we find in her home, she will be charged under the Protection of Animals Act and questioned accordingly."

When he paused and looked at his feet, Bets lurched forward until she was in front of him. "And what does that mean?"

He cleared his throat before looking up, although he didn't meet her eyes. "It means she will be fined—"

"*Another fine?*" She could feel a rage coming on. "First, trespassing and now this. How much?"

He worried his mouth before responding. "It can range from twenty pounds to twenty-five hundred."

She fisted her hands at her sides as Linc cursed softly beside her. "That's it? They killed two sheep and sawed the

wool off over thirty other sheep today, meaning to intimidate Keegan and this community. How is that just?"

"It's the law, Bets," John Hart answered, shaking his
head as more people swore harshly around them. "I'm
sorry."

"And what about the men who worked with Mary?" she
pressed. "What are you going to do there? Because you can be
sure Malcolm hired them. Mary's cruel, but she doesn't have
muscle to have pulled this off on her own. Do you have any
idea the kind of strength it takes to shear a sheep, even badly?"
Her Bruce had taught her that on her first summer in Ireland.

"When I interview Mrs. Kincaid, I plan to ask her about
any associates—assuming we find the torn dress." He put his
hand on her shoulder, and she held back the urge to shove it
away. "But we may not, Bets."

Because Mary had her cauldron up and would burn it.
Her spirit plummeted. That bitch was going to slip through
their grasp again. She swung around and marched through
the crowd. "It's never going to end," she whispered harshly.

Liam caught up with her. "Mum, you need to take a
breath."

She stopped, fearing she was going to lose her grip on
her emotions. She needed to stay mad, or she'd never get
through this. "Did you hear what he said? A fine, Liam!
That's all. They must have known nothing would happen to
them."

"Yes, they knew," Linc said, arriving with his long
strides along with Donal. "Easier to intimidate us this way
and circumvent harsher crimes."

"It's ballocks," Donal ground out. "But it is the law, if
you can believe it. Men have lost an entire herd to dogs in
this country and all the dog owner receives is a piddly fine.

Rarely any compensation to the farmer for the loss of the sheep. It's a disgrace. Sheep put bread on people's tables."

Ghislaine arrived with Taylor. "The law might not work in our favor, but public outrage is going to be red-hot by the time we're done. That I promise."

"We'll have more photos for you to take," Liam broke in as Taylor came to his side.

Bets could see how much of a unit they had become in the way they instantly wrapped their arms around each other's waists. She was glad for that.

"A bunch of us are going to head over to Carrick's sheep and start spray-painting," he told them, "and then we'll move on to whoever else wants their sheep marked. The Kindness Sheep aren't gone. And we'll make sure Malcolm and Aunt Mary and everyone working with them knows it."

She fought tears as her pride in her son rose up. He was such a good, strong man. Bruce would be so proud.

Donal raised his fist. "Count me in. We'll spray-paint every sheep in Ireland if we have to, and with Malcolm's face on the sheep's arse if it comes to it."

"That would be a sight," Linc drawled, rubbing his jaw. "But we should stick to the high road. The lawyers are looking into what we can do, and Wilt will be drawing up a new security plan for everything we didn't think was at risk before."

Bets picked up a handful of wool and let the wind take it. "You should include sheep this time."

"We plan to. We'll install cameras like we did for your roses after Mary hacked them to bits," Linc assured her, rubbing her arm.

"To what end?" Bets pointed to where John Hart was talking to his other Garda officers. "The laws suck. Mary can hack up my roses and work with Malcolm to saw the words off sheep and nothing will be done. Even if she's found guilty, all she'll have to do is pay a measly fine. And I bet Malcolm will pay it for her—just like he did with the one she got for trespassing. They're kicking our asses, Linc!"

"We need to contact Arthur Hale and give him an update," Taylor said in a flat voice. "A man like Malcolm with all that power has to be brought down by corruption and side dealing. I'm betting there's plenty of dirt to be found if we manage to dig deep enough. Public outrage isn't going to cut it, although we should still keep up the pressure there."

"She's right," Liam said, looking around the circle. "We're playing amongst the trees while Malcolm is burning the forest. Now, I'm off with the other men to make a statement. Taylor, you call Arthur and get him doing what he does best while you and Ghislaine pepper the media with what happened on this land. Linc?"

"I'm talking to our lawyers," her cowboy said, taking her hand and squeezing it. "Bets?"

She thought about the best way she could contribute. "I'll show Wilt the pastures where we'll want to add cameras."

"It might be a good idea to add them to a few other spots in town," Donal suggested. "Places we all frequent whose business owners are agreeable. The Brazen Donkey comes to mind."

"It's a plan," she said, nodding, hoping it would make her feel better.

By the time Wilt was hanging the last camera over the sheep fields, in Sorcha's trees no less, her spirits weren't as raw. Carrick had brought the newly sprayed sheep over to the green pastures around the arts center. He'd done it to make a statement, she knew. She watched as three sheep

233

walked past, reading the words on their large cream-colored bodies.

Love. Always. Triumphs.

Looking around, she hoped to see Sorcha. But didn't. Except someone had to be responsible for that sign surely. "Dammit, that's going to make me cry."

Her phone rang. When she pulled it out of her jacket, her breath stopped. Her screen said it was an unknown number, but she just had a sense.

"I think Malcolm is calling," she shouted to Wilt, who hastily climbed down the tree and ran over to her. She showed him the screen. "I figured I shouldn't answer it alone."

He took out his phone and pressed a button. "We'll record him if your instincts are right. Go ahead."

Tapping the screen to answer the call on speaker, she answered. "Hello?"

"Bets, love, it's Malcolm Coveney. I hear you've had some trouble down there. I was calling to pay my condolences."

She went for her meanest voice. "You have some gall to call me after what you did to those poor sheep."

"Bets, you shouldn't accuse people randomly," Malcolm answered in a gratingly arrogant voice. "Defamation is a terrible offense in this country with fines of up to €75,000."

"More than killing innocent sheep, you bastard. How perfect for you."

"Must I caution you again, Bets?" Malcolm shot back. "I would have thought that today's events would have you and the others minding yourselves."

It was no accident that he'd used the same words that had been sprayed on the dead sheep. Wilt's mouth tightened, and she wondered if his grip might shatter his phone. "Mary may give you up, Malcolm."

"Again, you should be careful with such groundless accusations, Bets, especially when a flimsy piece of cloth amounts to no conclusive evidence."

He already knew about that?

"Especially when no one can discover who it belongs to," he continued, "as I've heard from my close government friends. It seems Officer Hart concluded that only a short while ago after a short interview with Mrs. Kincaid."

Bets wanted to scream. "You must be spinning all ten of those gold rings you have on your fat fingers you're so happy."

"The rings signify power," he bit out, his tone harsh and frightening. "A power I have. One others would be wise to remember. Veritas, for example."

"Veritas kicked your butt and stuck the truth of you on a wall for all to see. Public outrage proves how little regard people have for men like you."

"And yet, people like me are the ones who make people like *you* run around chasing your tails."

Bets thought back to Liam's earlier comment. *We're playing amongst the trees while Malcolm is burning the forest.* "You should just stick a crown on your head and declare yourself king. Only, the last time I looked, this was a free country."

"But the old kings would be proud of me and the way I handle things," Malcolm replied savagely. "This land began because of men like me—my forefathers go back to the kings of Tara—"

"And my people come from the Easter Bunny," she spat back. "Guess who people like better?"

"Bets," he said in an eerily singsong voice, "it's not about people liking you. It's about people respecting you. Ask me why."

Her guts gripped, and she had to slowly breathe out the fear he'd created. "Tell me, Malcolm. I know you're dying to."

"Yes, I'm practically salivating to see what you'll choose." He paused, for effect, she imagined. "You see, I've learned that a special investigation led by the government of Ireland has uncovered the real identity of Veritas."

Bets held her breath as Wilt's mouth twisted. "I doubt that, Malcolm. According to everything I know, Veritas has managed to evade detection since the beginning."

"Ah, but this time, he was too cute," Malcolm responded, his delight evident. "He left himself out of the mural he'd depicted."

Bets looked at Wilt in confusion, only to watch as his face changed, his brow line sharpening in anger. "Oh, spit it out, Malcolm. I don't have all day."

His dark laughter could have made the devil himself pee his pants. "You don't know, Bets? I thought for sure you would, seeing as you're so close. As close as mother and son."

She almost dropped her phone as comprehension hit. "You're headed for the loony bin if you think my son is Veritas, Malcolm."

Another monstrous chuckle sounded on the line. "But it's not what I think that matters, Bets. It's what this special Garda unit thinks."

"This is bullshit, Malcolm!" She wanted to punch his stupid face. "Our lawyers are going to have a field day with this. There's no way you can prove Liam is Veritas. He lives here in Ireland while Veritas travels the world."

"And yet your son has traveled to some of the same

places where Veritas murals appeared. New Delhi. New York. London. Paris. Of course, it will take some time for all the *T*s to be crossed and his travel logs to be cross-referenced, but the story will be a big one, don't you think? And the penalty for hate speech in this country is a harsh one. Unlike the unfortunate incident in your backyard today, crimes falling under the Prohibition of Incite to Hatred Act actually carry prison time. Up to five years. Even before a trial can occur."

Her breath stopped, and Wilt looked off, his jaw locked.

She searched her mind for what she knew. "But that law is supposed to stop people from using hateful speech around age, ethnicity, religion, nationality, sexual orientation, or gender. Nothing more. This ain't it, as Linc would say."

"But it's wider than that definition, Bets." His voice carried a terrifying delight. "The act covers any offenses that communicate threatening, abusive, or insulting material that stirs up hatred. And Bets, that is exactly what that damn mural has done. You and your arts center have continued to post and speak about the mural. You are, in fact, communicating such material. About me. And now it will stop."

She wasn't even aware she was shaking until Wilt put a grounding hand on her arm. "You won't get away with this."

"Again, Bets, it's not me who is investigating. However, a close friend in the government said they might withdraw the forthcoming charges against Veritas—your son—if you volunteer to close down the arts center. Permanently. You seemed like the right person to ask, being the one who started it."

She fought for breath. "And here I thought you wanted

us to move it to Watertown—under your direction, of course. Make up your mind, Malcolm."

"I no longer have any interest in dealing with any of you," he gritted out. "I want you and your arts center gone. So what will it be?"

Was he out of his mind? How was this even a choice? "You're asking whether I will shut down the arts center or let my son be charged under this bogus act?"

A sudden wind surrounded her, and for a moment, all she could smell was oranges. She trusted in the sign. Tears filled her eyes. She let them fall. "That's no decision at all. The Sorcha Fitzgerald Arts Center will stay open and continue to serve Caisleán and the greater community."

Wilt gave her a thumbs-up.

"Ah, you disappoint me, Bets, but you do not surprise me. From our first meeting in my office, I knew you were a spirited woman. Now we will see how much spirit you have once your son is in custody. Which is about to happen right now..."

The phone went dead.

She sucked in her breath. "I need to call Liam."

Her hands were shaking so badly Wilt took her phone from her. "I'll call him."

He put it on speaker, and she listened to the rings—one, two, three, four. She heard Liam's cheery recorded greeting before Wilt clicked it off.

"Call Carrick," she told Wilt as she grabbed her phone back. "I'll call Donal. Someone will pick up."

But no one did. She called everyone she could think of who would be with Liam, but their phones only rang and rang and rang. She shot off a frantic text to Linc before sinking onto the ground under Sorcha's tree, the powerful orange scent making more tears pour down her face as she kept dialing and dialing and dialing.

When Linc called her, she gripped the phone. "Do you know where Liam is? No one is answering—"

"Bets, sugar, I don't know how to tell you this."

She lowered her head to her knees, her spirit finally broken. "They came for him," she whispered, starting to cry again.

"Yes! Bets, they're saying he's Veritas. Some special Garda unit came as he was out with the others spraying sheep. Eight men, Bets. You'd think he was a fugitive. There was press with them too, taking pictures and videoing it all. The men tried to stop them, but Liam told them to save our energy for the bigger fight. I'm so sorry, sugar. Bets, we are going to get him back. I'm working with the lawyers right now."

Usually Linc's voice was a comfort, but all her mind could focus on was Liam talking about the bigger fight. She didn't even know what that was anymore.

Her precious son was in jail.

CHAPTER NINETEEN

V eritas Finally Unmasked.

Sitting in Bets' living room, Taylor stared at the special evening news report on an Irish TV station. Images of Liam being led in handcuffs out of the pasture and into a Garda vehicle like he was a criminal made her sick.

It was a nightmare.

She shoved off Bets' couch, needing to move, needing space, and Liam's family and friends did their best to move out of her way. His Summercrest roommates were clustered against the wall holding hands while the other artists from the center and their spouses sat on chairs brought in from other parts of the house. Linc and Donal were both on their phones, sitting with Ghislaine, also on her device, in front of Bets' fireplace as they tried to figure out a solution. Meanwhile, Bets prowled like a tiger in front of them.

If Bets found out her precious son was in jail because of her... She put a hand to her mouth, trying to hold it together.

Weaving through the maze of chairs took some doing,

but Taylor was determined, even when Eoghan reached out to graze her arm in comfort. When she got to the window, she stared into the black as pitch night. Muted conversations buzzed behind her. There were too many people around, too many emotions pinging around the room. She needed to fight through the distractions to focus on a solution. Because if she let herself think about what Liam must be going through—because of her—she would crumble like a sandcastle from a giant wave.

"Malcolm and friends certainly had a media plan for this travesty," Ghislaine commented in a raised voice, her French accent stronger than usual. "They'd hoped to eclipse the story about the Kindness Sheep being shorn and a couple of them killed, and guess what? The Irish government supposedly catching Veritas *is* bigger news. Even if it's fake."

When she'd first heard the news and realized why Liam had been arrested, Taylor had thought it would be easy to get him released. It had almost been a *relief*. She'd posted on Veritas' social media that Liam O'Hanlon *wasn't* Veritas the moment she'd heard the news. Other people had claimed it in the past and been refuted. Slam dunk.

Only... Malcolm's people had been ready for that. The special beady-eyed Garda investigator who'd "caught" Liam said someone with access to Veritas' social media accounts was attempting to cover up the truth. Linc had worked with the lawyers to show Liam couldn't be Veritas with his passport stamps, but they didn't seem interested in the evidence. This was a setup, plain and simple.

Now she had another plan: She would have to paint another mural while Liam was in jail.

She was tempted to do it in Malcolm's hometown, but it

would be painted over quickly, reducing its local impact. Also, Watertown's Garda might be patrolling more heavily, anticipating the move.

She needed time and space to think, but she didn't feel like she could slip away from this depressing soiree. Wouldn't everyone think it was weird if she didn't want to stay to discuss what to do to get Liam out or increase public outrage, both as his girlfriend and the media director for the center?

"The lawyers still haven't been told where this special Garda unit is keeping Liam," Linc announced loudly, clicking off his phone.

Her stomach dropped to the floor. Every conversation stopped.

"But how it that legal?" Bets cried out.

Taylor looked over as Linc rubbed the back of his neck. The poor man had been on the phone nonstop with Bets stalking around him, her face going from an angry red to crestfallen white as her mood vacillated.

Taylor could only feel rage. She'd thought back to Liam asking her to promise not to tell them she was Veritas. She'd gone back and forth on it before the "breaking news" report about her social media post hit, only thirty minutes after she'd posted as Veritas. Now she suspected that even if she came forward and said she was Veritas, this special unit wouldn't believe her.

They *wanted* Veritas to be someone directly associated with the founding members of the arts center. Malcolm's blackmail call to Bets had made that crystal clear, and Taylor's respect for the woman had gone through the roof when they'd all listened to the taped conversation. Of course, the lawyers had sent it to the Garda along with copies of Liam's passport pages, but clearly the beady-eyed head of the Veritas unit was Malcolm's pawn. They didn't think it would go anywhere. Malcolm had every base covered.

"Nothing about this is particularly legal," Linc nearly spat after a moment, looking about as unhinged as she expected was possible. "What hard evidence do they think they have? The charge is asinine with a capital *A*! And all we're doing is sitting on our butts as that boy is in jail."

His voice broke then, and Bets pressed her hand to her mouth, tears filling her eyes. Taylor bit her lip as emotion flooded the room, the observers' faces overcome with a crestfallen pain she was afraid showed on her own.

"I'll never forgive myself for this," Linc said at last. "Bets, I'm sorry. I promised you Liam would be safe and I've failed you both."

"*Never.*"

She had to look away as they hugged each other fiercely, their anguish touching a chord inside her. She couldn't give in to the emotion—she needed to focus. Doing a new mural had to work. It had to.

"None of my friends know anything." Donal broke the silence, pocketing his phone and putting an arm around Ghislaine's waist. "I've called every person I know who might know something or someone to call. Malcolm has this locked down to a circle we don't have access to."

"We'll just have to keep upping our media reach," Ghislaine said, patting his massive chest. "Bets, I think we put you on every major morning show we can."

"And have me say what?" Bets faced her, looking as small and helpless as Taylor felt. "I'm supposed to cry on TV while I tell people my son isn't Veritas. That this big bad guy named Malcolm Coveney is behind it?"

Taylor thought that was a great way to lead off.

"He'll have you in jail next for defamation," Linc ground out.

"I don't care!" she practically shouted, shocking the group. "Put me in jail. I couldn't close the arts center down to save Liam, but I can speak for him. I'll yell from the rafters to anyone who'll listen to get him out."

Donal crossed to Linc, and the way he laid his hand on the man's shoulder conveyed a deep friendship. "We all want to protect Bets, Linc, but there's merit to what Ghislaine is thinking. Of course, it makes sense to talk to the lawyers first. We need to be clear about what we can say."

"It won't matter," Taylor said softly, drawing everyone's gaze. "Malcolm has been ready for everything so far. We need to take him down a different way. I'm going to call Arthur again."

She'd called him with an update after the sheep were found, knowing he'd like an update, but now she wanted to dive forward with his article to take Malcolm down.

"What did he say after you called him with news of the sheep?" Bets asked, crossing to her in a charged line of tension.

"He said it was reprehensible." But his gruff tone had conveyed a deeper grief, one felt by a man who'd seen too much cruelty. "Then he told me he was working as fast as possible but uncovering this kind of wrongdoing didn't happen overnight."

She'd finally stared down the fact that a story like this could take months to research and write. It wasn't like Malcolm was stupid. He'd have covered his tracks well. They needed to speed things up now that Liam was in custody, though—that was a must—and it would require resources. More manpower.

Then it hit her! "I should go down to Kinsale and help

Arthur on-site. I'm a good reporter, and under his guidance, I can follow threads quickly. We can't just leave Liam in jail!"

Bets touched her arm, her blue eyes swimming with tears.

Taylor took a breath as everyone stared at her. She could all but feel their pity and concern. Her soulmate was in jail. She was a complete mess, and they obviously knew. "I'm okay," she told everyone.

"No, you're not," Bets said, her voice breaking. "You love my son, and he loves you."

She stared at the woman in whom she could now see traces of Liam—the curve of his brows and the shape of his ears. "Yes, I do... But please, Bets. Don't bring that up right now."

The older woman nodded, her orange hair a mess from combing her fingers through it in frustration. "I want to go with you. I can't just sit around doing nothing while my son sits in jail."

Linc was suddenly beside them, moving swiftly for a large man. "You won't be sitting. Ghislaine, we'll talk to the lawyers, and once you're clear on the legal guidelines, call the reporters you know you can trust and put Bets on every major show you can."

"Linc, what if it doesn't do any good?" Bets asked, tugging at his white shirt.

He wrapped her up. "We have to believe it will, sugar. The rest of us will keep working this from different angles, doing what we can."

"Which is what, exactly?" Brady asked suddenly in a loud voice. "I can't even think about opening the pub and pouring the village drinks right now."

A few shocked gasps told Taylor this had to be the worst kind of admission in Ireland.

Eoghan finally stood up from one of the many chairs in the room. "You'll open the Brazen Donkey and pour this community drinks because people are in mourning right now, and the pub is a place of comfort and community."

"I'll pour them with you, since I can't punch the people who are behind this," Declan announced, holding up his fists.

Taylor wanted to yell, *hear, hear.*

"I'll pour too," Kathleen announced, "because Eoghan is right. My family pub in Boston always opened after a funeral so people could come and grieve or lend an understanding shoulder."

"We'll all pour," Ellie said as tears rolled down her face. Looking up at Brady, she added, "And if any of us need a break for comfort, we'll give that too. Liam would want that."

Taylor had to look away as tears sprang into people's eyes at the mention of Liam's name. She was going to lose it if she stayed any longer. "I have to call Arthur."

Declan's boxing allusion crystalized her plan. They needed a one-two punch. If she was able to get away for a few days, she could do two things: hasten Arthur's investigation and paint a mural somewhere down that way to prove Veritas was definitely not in jail right now. Her voice as an artist was undeniable.

"Taylor, wait up," Kathleen called as she was leaving the room.

She waited until she was a distance from the doorway of Bets' parlor before turning. Kathleen scratched the back of her short black cut before wincing.

"I know we don't know each other well yet, although God knows I sense a fellow tough girl in you, but everyone at Summercrest wants to invite you to come and stay with us. In Liam's room."

Suddenly she could smell him, and the control she was trying to hold on to so hard snapped for a moment before she fastened it back in place with her inner staple gun. There was no way she could sleep in his bed without him and be among his possessions when he wasn't there. It would crush her. She focused better when she was alone, and with Liam in jail, the stakes had never been higher. Trying to connect with people and take comfort from them would only split her time and energy right now. Worse, she didn't want to have to evade talk of Veritas or lie to her friends, because Ellie was a huge fan and Veritas was very much the "man" of honor in current conversations.

She made sure to soften her answer with a smile. "I appreciate it, really, but I'll probably be going down to Kinsale—"

"Only tonight then." She weakly gestured in the air. "I know I'm feeling awkward when I don't know where to put my hands. I work with my hands..."

"It's okay. We're all in horrible new territory."

"To say the least," Sophie said, appearing in the large entry hall. "I was going to offer to have you stay with Jamie and me and Greta too, but I know the cottage is a bit small."

"Bets and Linc already asked me to stay with them too," she told both women. "Really, I just...I need to be alone. To focus. Keep my mind clear."

"We have a meditation room at Summercrest," Kathleen told her with a small smile. "Liam turned the old dungeon into one."

The fact that Taylor didn't know that story had her heart rending in her chest. They hadn't had enough time together. She wanted that time with him, dammit. She wanted all those stories. "That sounds like Liam."

Sophie came over and touched her back, compassion shining brightly in her eyes. "I remember being so upset when Jamie and I were going through a tough time only a short while ago, and I understand the need for space. But if there's anything we can do to make a moment a little easier, we're here."

"I appreciate it." She blew out a loud breath and hugged her friend. "Keeping moving is my way of holding it together. Because if I don't, then Malcolm has won, and I won't let that son of a bitch win. I can't."

The other women both nodded.

"I'm going to talk to Arthur," she said with as much of a smile as she could muster and then walked to Bets' kitchen for some privacy.

"I'm sorry that I'm calling again," she began when he answered.

"I was expecting it after seeing the evening news about Veritas being caught. Complete horseshit! Anyone with a brain would know Liam can't be Veritas. It's a trumped-up charge, but it's backed by people with a lot of power."

She finally allowed herself to lean against the table as there were no chairs to sit in. "We can't find out where they're keeping him, Arthur," she admitted hoarsely.

"That's very bad news. I'm sorry, Taylor."

Her nose dripped, making her sniff. Dammit, she could not cry. "That's not why I was calling. I thought I might help you with the Malcolm investigation. On-site. If there's a room at the inn I could register for, great; otherwise, I'll find somewhere else to stay."

"I don't own the inn, but I have it on good authority that you would always be welcome. It's low season, so no one's here. Now, as for the idea of you helping... A man's life is at stake, which makes the urgency all the greater."

She was so relieved he understood that.

"I'm only used to working with the people at my newspaper," he told her, "and while I've tapped Meredith and Tanner and a few others to help out with key tasks, they have their hands full with the entire news cycle. Extra hands might be just the thing."

She wanted to cheer. "Great! I'm there."

"I also have a few other people I'm going to call who I think will volunteer. They have sound minds. More or less. I'll tap Trevor, J.T., and Flynn. Maybe I can even snag a little of Quinn and Connor's time. We need some big finance geeks involved to sift through the company and bank account side of things."

Relief crashed through her. It also occurred to her that if she was with them she'd be able to steer the focus toward Malcolm, and away from any interest Flynn or the others might have in Veritas. "Thank you for helping!"

"Of course! My dear, consider yourself a member of the Merriam Investigative Taskforce. We're going to kick that dirty Garda unit to kingdom come, along with Malcolm Coveney, or my name isn't Arthur Hale."

"I'll be there as soon as I can," she replied in a scratchy voice.

"Bring Eoghan with you," Arthur declared, sounding more robust with every order. "We'll need someone with a long memory and a good understanding of that part of Ireland."

A companion hadn't been in her plans, but she could see the merit of Eoghan's inclusion. His help could be invaluable. She would figure out how to evade Eoghan's watchfulness so she could do her mural. "I'll ask him along."

"Good," Arthur declared. "We have a plan."

Taylor only hoped it would be enough to combat whatever Malcolm had in store for them next.

CHAPTER TWENTY

L iam wasn't sure where he was.
In life and his travels, he hadn't always needed to know, going with the rightness and flow of things. But the not-knowing bothered him in this case. He knew he wasn't in Caisleán, that was for sure. They'd put a hood over his head after they'd left city limits, but he'd judged his ride in the back of the Garda vehicle to be about ninety minutes or so. Not Watertown then. Too obvious a choice.

The concrete floor was cold under him as he sat in his meditative cross-legged stance. The room was constructed with whitewashed cinderblocks. The light bulb hanging precariously from the ceiling emitted dim light due to the dust and spiderwebs surrounding it, and the yellow farm bucket in the corner was mottled from use. Somehow, he hadn't expected the lack of bars and a bare-bones cot and toilet.

Clearly Malcolm intended to make his point, and Liam was to be the nail in the proverbial coffin.

At least he wasn't in chains.

While he'd had a vision of being behind bars, he hadn't expected to be named Veritas. He'd tried to sense what Taylor had felt at the news. Outrage? Shock? He'd felt both when he'd done his best to connect to her in spirit. Something else that had come through: she hadn't compared it to the time when the other street artist had claimed credit for her early work. That was something he was glad of because it showed how deep their trust ran. He had to believe she would trust him to do this and not come forward, although he imagined it would cost her.

The very charge of him being Veritas was ludicrous, but then again, Malcolm cared nothing about the truth. This monumental misuse of power was supposed to drive home a lesson to everyone in Caisleán, including his mother. She would be coming out of her skin, and since he knew her, she would feel guilty. When he got out, he would need to help her let that go.

But right now, he had to focus on letting go of his own anger. Because it wouldn't help matters, and he sensed Malcolm was planning to visit him. He could feel the man— and the darkness he danced with—in the building.

He didn't have to wait long. Liam was deep in meditation when the metal door opened and the large man strolled in.

"I see you aren't missing a chair," he commented as a Garda officer brought one in for him and set it down in front of Liam, who remained on the floor.

"And *I* see that you aren't going to hide behind the Garda as the perpetrator of this injustice," he shot back, remembering how it had thrown Malcolm when Taylor had gone on the offensive on the public road.

"Direct, eh?" Malcolm rested his swollen fingers on his knees, his ten gold rings shot with diamonds shining even in the low light. "I expected that of your mother, but you? I'd heard you were something of a free spirit, the kind who liked yoga and probably ate tofu."

Liam knew the mention of his mother was meant to be a trigger. He only smiled in response. "Tofu isn't that bad, but that's not why you're here."

Malcolm leaned forward, peering at him through narrowed eyes. "No, it's not. I thought you might cooperate for your release. By confessing to all the bad things the arts center is secretly up to."

Liam forced his muscles to relax again. "The arts center is one of the strongest and most forward-thinking community projects in the west of Ireland. It serves Caisleán—"

"But it has all that money," Malcolm said, rubbing his hands swiftly together. "And I do so love money. I can't have enough of it, especially after growing up in near poverty."

"As another human, I have compassion for the child you were, but you're an adult now. Only a weak man continues to use childhood experiences as an excuse for making the wrong choices. That's talking like a victim, and Malcolm, I fear my impression of you is as wrong as yours is of me, if that's what you're trying to say."

The man's face went mottled red. "You little prick. No one speaks to me like that."

Liam fell into his breathing, keeping his face neutral. The stare-off commenced, and Liam knew it was one Malcolm would lose. No one could beat him in such things after all his training in meditation and mindfulness. He could sit for hours at a time without moving. His Summercrest roommates had discovered that in a playful challenge one night.

"You seem to think you're smart, Liam O'Hanlon,"

Malcolm said, rising slowly as he took a couple of steps forward.

Liam only tipped his head back and looked at him, aware it would infuriate Malcolm that he wasn't intimidated.

"It appears we're not going to get anywhere." He spat on the ground inches from Liam's knee. "You're just like your mother. How does it feel to know she could have gotten you out of this whole mess if only she'd agreed to close the arts center? What kind of mother sacrifices her own son for something so stupid? She clearly doesn't love you."

Liam shook his head in pity. "I believe you're speaking of your own mother now, Malcolm. Not mine."

The man had his hand wrapped around Liam's neck in a heartbeat, and Liam dropped into his heart to find calm after the initial shock. The man's grip tightened, restricting the flow of blood in his neck. Liam struggled for breath, refusing to look away from Malcolm's wild eyes.

The man released him, his own breath whooshing out as Liam dragged in oxygen. "You're a cool one, aren't you? I could use someone like you on the payroll. But fine. You want to rot in here longer, it's your choice. Only you might be interested in another visitor, one I thought might ruffle your feathers. Guards!"

The door opened. His aunt Mary walked in, dressed in an old black dress Liam recognized. She'd had it for twenty years, he figured, going back to when her husband had died. He'd never been one to judge other people's clothes, but the color, he now understood, only vibrated with the darkness inside her.

"Hello, Aunt Mary."

She took the chair when Malcolm pointed to it, her

black serviceable shoes crossed at the ankle. "Your father would be disgraced to find you here."

So that was her play. "My father—your good and kind brother—would have been outraged at this injustice. But surely he would have been disgraced by his own sister being a party to killing sheep and sawing their wool off so badly they left their bodies bleeding and scraped. You do know that more might die from the cold with the near-winter nights upon us, don't you? As a woman whose family was in sheep—"

"I've hated them all my life," she gritted out, her eyes as dark as her dress now. "Putting words on them was ridiculous, something Carrick did in the madness of his grief. When Keegan O'Malley took up the torch, everyone in Caisleán groaned. Now they're famous. Sheep! Because people want to hear about *kindness*. The world is full of poor, pathetic fools. And you're one of them, Liam O'Hanlon. Your mother raised you wrong, and my brother let her."

He simply looked at her. Whatever blood tie or physical resemblance they might have, he was not related to this woman in spirit. "The mural showed you for what you are. The children in the fable symbolize lambs being led to slaughter. Innocents. From now on, people are going to call you a sheep killer as you walk by them on the streets or in a store. I personally can't imagine anything more humiliating than that."

"You little shite!" She flew to her feet, and for a moment, he thought she was going to slap him. She'd done that to his older brother Rhys once. It had happened at Christmas dinner—he'd called her a mean lady for making their mum cry. That was the last Christmas they'd spent with her in attendance.

Malcolm clapped his hands slowly. "You forgot to tell

me how entertaining your family is. I can't wait to meet your son, Mary. Liam, you should know I'm working on his release while you remain imprisoned. Unless you've decided to change your mind."

A nod wouldn't suffice. "I haven't and I won't."

His aunt pointed at him. "See! A fool."

"Liam," Malcolm said, sinking to his haunches, "we have a number of Irish laws we plan to use to keep you under lock and key without anyone's knowledge for a long time. Hate crimes are taken very seriously in this country, and we don't want you or anyone associated with you to incite more hatred. Enjoy your stay. Come, Mary."

He rose and walked to the door. Liam's aunt leveled him another hateful look, one he had to repel due to the punch of dark energy that came with it.

"One last thing," his aunt said as Malcolm knocked on the metal door for it to be opened. "You tell Sorcha she had better stay away from me. Her little stunt by the fence so I'd tear my dress was pathetic."

"And yet the Garda has a piece of your dress as evidence—"

"Which I burned in the stove when I got home because I'm not the stupid one here." She walked over until she was directly over him and leaned down so close he could smell the offensive hair spray she used to keep her gray curls in place. "You and yours would be wise not to underestimate me. And you tell Sorcha...I know the old ways. I can make sure she never appears again."

He fought a shudder as an unnatural cold entered the room. He could feel its fingertips touching him as a wraith-like form swirled around his aunt. He closed his eyes and brought in the light. He heard her gasp as the cold vanished.

"You forget, Aunt Mary," he said, meeting her hard

gaze. "That power runs in my blood too, a blood you can't curse without cursing yourself. Only I use the good, and believe me, there is more on our side than Sorcha alone."

He was aware of Malcolm watching. His aunt only smiled, a feral smile, the kind he imagined a fox gave before it killed a sheep. "We'll see."

She turned and strode past Malcolm, who turned one of his rings contemplatively. "I've always heard that prisoners reveal the most incredible information under duress. I'm delighted to see it's true. I was right to bring your aunt. This visit was most enlightening. We'll talk again."

The door slammed shut, and overhead, the lone light bulb shook. Liam cleared the space with more light, and then spent a few minutes breathing deeply to center himself. He was human. There were a few moments when he'd felt shaken toward the end, especially when his aunt had threatened Sorcha.

Anyone who knew the old ways would know how to bind a ghost—whether to a tree or a rock or even the earth itself. Liam didn't like that kind of power, although Ireland was riddled with its use—had been since the beginning of time. He could feel the dark energy when he came upon it. Sometimes he could even hear the bound ghost crying out as he went by, especially in the bogs, the most cursed of lands. But without knowing why it had been bound, he didn't interfere. He didn't dabble in the dark. If he had to banish a ghost or a being full of malice, as he had with his aunt's wraith, he did so with light.

Now he would need to bring in more light than ever before.

"Sorcha," he called, wanting to warn her. So far she hadn't appeared.

He waited for a time, breathing in through his nose and

out through his mouth in meditative sets, doing his best to clear the negative energy remaining from Malcolm's grip around his neck. When Sorcha didn't appear, he grew concerned, and he did the one thing he hadn't done since three months after they'd buried him.

He called his father to him.

Unlike their last encounter, he wasn't wearing the last outfit he'd been wearing when his heart had given out—his well-washed navy pants and green waterproof jacket along with his black wellies whose heels were caked in mud. Liam studied his father's new garments. They were silver, so bright they blended with his thick hair. His whole being glowed, and it gave Liam happiness to see him as such. His father's light had grown stronger since they'd last met like this, and he looked more at peace than he'd ever been while alive.

"Hi, Dad," he said, allowing his full emotion to rise at last. He didn't grieve his father anymore. He'd gone the distance on that—the journey the hardest he'd known. But he still missed him.

"Hello, Liam." He cocked his head the way he used to do when he was ready to listen. "I hoped you would call me."

Liam lifted his shoulder ruefully. "That's nice to know. I stopped trying, knowing I needed to let you go."

"And you have... Which is why I can return to you now."

That made sense somehow. "You have a new look, I see."

His father gestured to the close-fitting shirt, pants, and boots. "I do indeed. These are the garments of a guardian. We don't call it that among ourselves, but it's the easiest way to explain it. Now, how about I help your neck? It's bruising fast."

His father had taught him how to hold his hand over hurt things, whether it be a plant, an animal, or a person. Later, Liam had traveled to Bali and learned how to use his mind simply to heal, a ladder up of sorts. "Thank you. Your touch is stronger. Dad, I need your help. I can't feel Sorcha, and usually she comes to me when I call."

"True," his father said with a nod, "but the powers that govern us have decided she's made her work with you all a little too personal at the moment. She'll be sitting out for a time."

He wouldn't ask how long. Time worked differently on the other side. All the Irish myths said so. It was also probably for the best, given what Aunt Mary had said. Liam sensed they already knew of his aunt's threat, and he wondered if that was the other reason Sorcha could not come to him. "Then I need you to look after someone for me."

"Since I always look after you, your mum, and your brothers—in my own way—this must be about Taylor." The light from him grew brighter. "Oh, you've picked the best apple in the barrel with that one, son."

His heart expanded with love as he thought of her, his bold, direct warrior. "Yes, I have. I want to add her to the family, as she's mine."

A flash of light appeared around his father as he said, "It is done."

"Thank you. I'm glad to hear you're looking after all of us, of course, although I've always felt it. Mum, especially. She must be wrecked by me being in here."

He gestured grandly. "Of course she is, but she has the

heart of a lion. You should know. I'm glad she's found love again. Lincoln Buchanan is a good man, a true partner in a way I wasn't, something I've done my best to make amends for. He sees the truth of her better than I did, and he encourages what she holds in the deepest sanctuary of her heart. She had a lot to give, and it gives me joy she's finally expressing it all."

"It's a wonder to behold." He found himself not wanting this moment to end, and he smiled sadly as the old vulnerability of longing caught him. "I still miss you, you know."

"As I do you," his father said, his green eyes filled with love, "but despite current circumstances, you're doing rather fine for yourself. I'm proud of the man you've become, Liam."

Suddenly, he couldn't swallow over the emotion in his throat. "That's good to hear. Because, you know...prison."

They both laughed for a moment as he gestured to the bare room.

"You know," his father said, "you told my sister the right of it. There are more forces on your side than just Sorcha. You have me and more angels and spirits and other Irish beings than you can know. The light is strong with your Taylor and so many others in our beloved village of Caisleán. Remember that when your spirits fall. And call on me if you need a friendly visit."

He couldn't keep the tears from falling and didn't try. He gazed up at his father, wishing they could embrace. Then he remembered all he needed was to share his heart. He focused on doing so then, and he could feel the change in himself, the warmth and peace that came through him, along with the purest surge of love as his father returned it to him.

"I know you feel it, but words are important too, as your mother always told you." His smile was radiant then. "I love you, son."

"I love you too, Dad," he said as his father disappeared.

CHAPTER TWENTY-ONE

With its two-story structure punctuated by dramatic towers on either end, the Wild Irish Rose Inn would be a marvelous getaway for her and Liam at some point.

But today she was arriving without him, to wage war against their enemy. And when she could slip away from Eoghan and the others, she would enact her plan to ensure Liam was vindicated of being Veritas. She'd stayed up all night researching possible cities and walls before settling on one and then designing the most perfect mural she'd ever painted. One she hoped to execute tonight. She'd had to downscale her design after Linc had insisted on having his private plane take them to Cork as opposed to them driving the six hours by car. If they'd taken the car, she could have stocked some supplies in the trunk.

"It's a lovely sight," Eoghan commented, patting his heart, as Trevor unloaded their suitcases in the front of the inn. "Even dormant, the wild roses call to my Irish heart, as does the sea. You have a beautiful place here, Trevor Merriam."

He touched the older man on the arm gently. "You can tell my wife. Oh, here she is. Eoghan and Taylor, this is Becca, along with my other favorite people, Brenna and Roarke, who is holding our cat, Hatshep. The Irish setter is Boru, and the lovely couple coming around the side are Cian and Aileen, who are like Becca's own family and run the inn with us."

Taylor heard a loud animal cry and turned at the pounding of feet on the ground. My God, that alpaca was grinning. She took a step back and hit the car Trevor had picked them up with from the Cork airport.

The animal dove at Trevor, pressing its fuzzy cheek to his as he cringed and playfully pushed it away. "Buttercup, I told you. Roarke is the one who wants your kisses, not me."

The little boy giggled as he set the cat down and rushed over. The alpaca did indeed give him her version of kisses, which had Taylor smiling. Trevor swung the boy up in the air and then hugged him before setting him down and turning to hug the little girl, whom he set on his hip. Then he planted a healthy kiss on his wife.

"Welcome," Becca said as she crossed swiftly, her shoulder-length dark brown hair swaying in the sea's cold breeze. "I'm sorry to meet you under such horrible circumstances. Even as an Irishwoman, I'm shocked by it all. I hope you enjoy your stay, even though I know you have serious business. Please let us know if there's anything we can do to make things easier."

"You're very kind," Taylor responded, glancing over as another man stepped out of the cottage. "You came! I can't believe it."

J.T. opened his arms as he strode out. "Aren't we lucky it's low tourist season and we can take over the inn?

Welcome to the Merriam Investigative Unit's HQ. You're looking at its smartest member."

Becca and Trevor snorted at the same time. "He's addled," Becca said, and Trevor nodded and grinned. "Delusional. Like always."

"*I'm* the best of the MIU," another man said as he stepped out after J.T. The Merriam in him was very evident in his handsome jaw. "Flynn Merriam. It's a pleasure to meet you. I think we met at a museum party in Stockholm twelve years ago, but I didn't stay long."

"He was probably with a model," Becca laughed and murmured to Taylor. "He used to love them."

"All in the past now, and happily, being a family man and all," he answered. "I believe you've met my brother Quinn at a gallery showing in London. Or so he thought."

A third man emerged from the inn's doorway, and she caught sight of Arthur and Clara standing inside, along with a Merriam she was sure she hadn't met. That meant it had to be Connor, the Big Bad Wolf, or so he'd been called by his younger brothers in the past.

"Hi, Quinn," Taylor said as Flynn started talking excitedly to Eoghan, leading him to the inn. "Thank you for your help. Arthur said you've been using the sources you and your wife have cultivated since moving your company here to look into matters. Please give her my thanks."

He inclined his very impressive chin, one all of the Merriam men shared. "You're actually helping us out. Malcolm is the kind of guy we'd probably knock heads with at some point, having a company in Ireland. Better to knock him out of the way before he darkens our door. I'm very sorry for your troubles, but we're going to fix them. Right, Con?"

He stepped out, a quieter man than his brothers, with gray at his temples. "Absolutely. I'm Connor Merriam."

"Quinn and Connor compete for the Best Fixer Award in the family," J.T. explained, "while the rest of us loaf around eating bonbons."

"I thought it was biscotti, J.T., given your Rome fetish," Quinn shot back. "Let's get you inside before you freeze. The sea air is a bitch today. I told Uncle Arthur and Aunt Clara we don't have time for frostbite."

She shot Arthur Hale a smile. "I'll bet they loved that. I see Flynn has already managed to draw Eoghan inside."

"Aileen probably has him beside the fire in the front hall with a cup of tea in his hand," Trevor told her with a laugh. "I asked her to give you some space, but I predict she's going to shower you with the inn's famous scones. She can't help herself, between strong motherly impulses and Irish hospitality."

"It's all right," she answered as he picked their luggage up before Taylor could grab her carry-on. "I just can't thank you all enough for helping. When I asked J.T. to contact your uncle—"

"You didn't know you'd be getting all the Merriam men?" J.T. asked, making a sweeping gesture at his brothers. "Even if you weren't a good friend, most of us admire and respect Veritas. Some of Arthur's kin in Dare Valley would have given their right arm to join us, but he drew the line, saying we had more cooks in the kitchen than he'd ever had on a story. Come on. Let's head on in."

She smelled baked goods the moment she entered the inn and the cozy setup around the fireplace. "I'll never be able to repay you for the kindness. All of you. But most especially you, Arthur. Hello, Clara."

"Come and warm my cheek up with a kiss," Arthur

called, pointing to his craggy visage. "These idiots worried I'd get frostbite if I put a toe out of the inn today. Which is ridiculous since we're not even staying in the inn. My lovely wife and I always stay at the Honeymoon Cottage, where we began our journey here. It's outside the main building."

"They were saving me from knitting you another hat you won't wear," Clara said, wrapping Taylor up in a hug. "My dear, I can't imagine what you must be feeling with your boyfriend in jail. And those poor sheep…"

"Aunt Clara, we said we wouldn't talk about it," Trevor murmured in a low voice. "Roarke and Brenna would cry for days if they heard about that."

"Fine." She mimed zipping her lips. "We'll have tea instead, and then we can get to work."

"We?" Arthur scoffed.

Her sock was practically tender, but he playfully grabbed his arm as if she'd injured him. "Stop being a baby. Now…I happen to have a sound mind. I plan to have a role on this unit as well. Men like Malcolm should not wield power."

Her husband kissed her cheek. "We'll find you a task. Gads, I hope I can manage this big of a team. I haven't done a story like this since the bail bonds scandal in the 1980s."

"Which is why I asked someone with impeccable management skills to come and help," Quinn announced, checking his phone. "She's arriving shortly."

Taylor had a cup of dark tea in her hands with a plate of scones to her right when a gorgeous dark-haired woman sauntered into the inn. Francesca Maroun walked over to her husband and kissed him soundly on the mouth before saying, "Hello! I'm Francesca, and I hear we need to take down a very bad man. I'll be setting up the storyboard for you under Arthur's direction."

The force of the woman was woven into every aspect of her, from her tailored clothes to the power of her subtly accented voice, a hint of French and Arabic from her Lebanese background. Taylor liked the look of her immediately.

Francesca made for Arthur, and the older man groaned theatrically as he pushed himself out of his chair. "I suppose I can handle you being involved too. Did you bring the munchkin?"

She nodded as she kissed both his cheeks. "Yes, I let Becca steal Devlin up to their tower to play with his cousins, although Brenna insists on pointing her chubby little finger at him and grunting when he doesn't crawl fast enough. Shall we? We have work to do."

"I've already been replaced by the task master," Arthur joked as they followed her and gathered in the inn's large dining room. Four dry erase boards had already been set up at the front beside the kitchen, along with a buffet of more scones, bread, and other treats—none of which could tempt Taylor.

"Aileen and Cian work fast like always." Francesca uncapped a blue marker and faced the room as everyone sat down at the tables closest to the front. "Arthur, lay out what you have already, and I'll start writing."

Arthur's recitation of what he had found so far captivated Taylor so much that she had to force herself to focus on jotting notes on the legal pad on which she'd compiled her own research on the short plane ride up. Eoghan was munching on a scone, listening carefully along with the rest of them.

"So, his empire stretches from Dublin to Watertown with inroads in Castlebar, Galway, Shannon, and Limerick," Francesca summed up when Arthur finished, pointing to the first board where she'd drawn a rough map of the holdings Arthur had outlined.

"Eoghan, would you say that's about right?" Arthur asked, turning to the older man beside him.

He nodded, wiping his mouth of crumbs. "I'd only say yes given the fact that Caisleán's new Garda officer came from Sligo, so Malcolm clearly doesn't have an iron fist up north. I can't say about the other towns. But everyone knows he made his original money with his construction company, which built many of the public roads in the west with hefty contracts from the government, most of which needed repaving immediately because of the shoddy materials and cut corners."

"Correct," Arthur said, "which added to his influence. He was the go-to man for foreign manufacturers who wanted factories built too, everything from American steel to Chinese windmills."

"And last but not least," Eoghan said with a frown, "the hotels and golf courses he not only builds but raises private investments for."

Arthur pushed his tea aside, setting his hands on the table. "He's had primary investors from America, China, and Russia. That's where we need to look. Thankfully, Quinn and Francesca run these kinds of business profiles regularly."

Quinn opened a briefcase on his table and passed a bound copy to Arthur. "Everything our folks could dig up on Malcolm's official holdings."

Arthur pretended the weight was too much for him, wincing as his arm lowered weakly. Clara only socked him again. "I knew you would come through," he said with a harumph. "Now, we sift through the hard stuff. Everyone will receive a list of companies Malcolm has done business with. Flynn, remind us of what we're looking for."

He choked on the scone he was chewing before swallowing rapidly. "I didn't know there would be a quiz. Lucky for you, I'm the smartest of my brothers so I know the answer. Shell companies."

"He's a megalomaniac," J.T. whispered. "We can't believe we're related to him."

"Shh—" Clara turned and pinned him with a stare.

"Thank you for playing teacher, Clara," Arthur declared after giving J.T. his own hard look. "That's correct, and in the usual countries of Panama, the Cayman Islands, the British Virgin Islands, Cyprus, Hong Kong, Singapore, Isle of Man, Seychelles, and— Flynn?"

"Me again?" He smoothed the lapel of his suit, puffing his chest out. "Star student here. Belize, Uncle."

"Exactly!" Arthur handed the report to Francesca. "Start writing, my dear. But that's only one part of the equation. Taylor is right in thinking we need to find instances of Malcolm swindling his own so-called friends."

"Ones in the Irish government to start," she broke in. "People at this level don't turn on one another unless the betrayal either embarrasses or hurts them. I'm not feeling very nice right now, so I'd love to find both."

J.T. put a comforting hand on her arm. "We'll do our best."

"That means sorting through photos of Malcolm in the media with various government officials—and anyone else we can find. Eoghan, would you be willing to work with my lovely wife on that front since you know many of the Irish politicians?"

"It would be a pleasure," Eoghan said, flashing Clara a

smile, "and if I don't recognize someone, I'll have my son look at him. He's on standby to help."

Taylor had figured as much, but Linc had thought they needed to keep Donal in Caisleán so he could continue to take in-person meetings with the local officials he knew while Linc worked with the lawyers to make further inroads with people in Dublin, something that was proving difficult since no one seemed to know who had authorized the special investigative Garda unit that had arrested Liam in the first place.

Taylor thought there might be some who didn't want to say. Malcolm would be even more feared after Liam's arrest. People would wonder if speaking against him would ensure they were the next target. He could turn anything that was said against him into hate speech, couldn't he?

That jogged her mind. She needed to work that idea into her design.

Her plan was to do the mural tonight. The time frame would be tight, and it would involve some sneaking around—especially since she'd have to walk to the village in the dark to pick up the car she'd had the rental company drop off—but she would manage it. Once she had the car, she would come back for her suitcases, packed with spray paint only this time. Her clothes were all in her carry-on.

Arthur picked up a scone and tapped it on the table, considering the boards. "After we have the companies and the photos sorted, we'll need to cross-reference the names. Our best way to take Malcolm down will be there. We find where he's in business with someone in the government, and then we look into the financing."

"Hoping the numbers don't match," Connor added, steepling his fingers. "Most government people are too filled with the hubris of their power to check to make sure no one's skimming from their investment."

"Aren't those investments a conflict of interest?" Flynn asked.

Quinn, Connor, and even Trevor shook their heads and groaned. J.T. only threw a scone at him. "Star student? This is why we put you in tech and not a head office job."

Flynn flipped them the finger. "You'll be eating those words when I use my hacking skills to find the evidence we need. Anyone want to bet against me?"

The hacking comment had Taylor's pulse skittering, but she was glad he was using it to help Liam and not look into Veritas. She would make sure it stayed that way.

"Enough playing around," Clara announced, standing up. Eoghan stood with her and took her arm. "We all have our assignments. Eoghan and I are going to do ours in the library where there's a fire. Arthur, where do we find these photos?"

He sputtered, "Wife, you need a couple of laptops and then some good internet searching. I would start by typing in Malcolm Coveney and see what hits. When you both finish about a hundred articles apiece, we'll start on the next search, like Malcolm Coveney business investors—"

"Fine." She cast him a baleful glance, which he returned with a bark of laughter. "You've made your point. Trevor, can you find us laptops?"

"Sure thing," the man said, rising from the adjoining table. "Anyone else need one? Con? I know you don't use one much anymore."

His brother cracked his knuckles. "Ten grand says I come in before Flynn here in finding the evidence we need."

"Ouch, Con." Flynn made a show of creating—and then

271

breaking—a heart with his widespread hands before he opened his laptop. "I thought you knew no one can beat me."

"You're about to go down, baby brother," Connor said, "only don't tell Louisa I said that."

Everyone laughed, including Clara as she and Eoghan left the room with Trevor.

"I don't understand," she whispered to J.T.

"His wife Louisa runs a homeless shelter and puts up an inspirational note every day," J.T. answered, powering up his own machine. "She's the soul of positivity, and she'd probably fry him for baiting Flynn and betting against him like that. But we're brothers. It's how we are."

Liam had probably had interactions like this with two older brothers, right? Except he wasn't a fighter. A warrior, sure, of sorts, the kind who would come to her rescue.

Her mind was suddenly filled with him, and she swore she could even smell him. It wasn't the first time it had happened since he was taken—there'd been a couple of moments when she could have sworn he was touching her. A cool peace would come over her, and she'd *feel* him telling her he was all right. Maybe she'd drunk the Kool-Aid, but she was happy for it. God, she missed him. She took a deep breath and told her mind to clear as she pulled out her laptop. Thinking about him would only be a distraction.

"You okay?"

She looked over to see J.T. watching her with compassion. "Yes. Focusing. Arthur, I need my names. Maybe I'll be the one to kick Flynn's butt."

The Merriam men and Arthur looked over at her while Francesca whistled softly. "Oh, I like you! Taylor, you can sit at my table. We'll show these boys who runs the world."

"What about me?" Quinn asked, waggling his brows.

"You think you can beat me, babe? How about a private bet to make things interesting?"

She walked over and plopped the thick report in his lap with a laugh. "Maybe. Get cracking, *babe*."

They hunkered down, punching keys as Aileen served them dinner—one Taylor wished she could taste as the venison, roasted carrots, and mashed potatoes looked delicious. Arthur took a break a few times after offering everyone his favorite red hot candy, his hip clearly bothering him from sitting too long. Taylor rolled her aching shoulders, fighting off fatigue, with the taste of cinnamon fire in her mouth.

The companies were a maze of names and locations, but she looked a little deeper into ones whose parent companies were in the most notorious countries. She was clicking on a company in Malta that had her gut twitching when someone tapped her on the shoulder.

"I'm calling it," Arthur said, the wrinkles around his face more stark than usual, although he had a large smile on his face. "A good reporter knows when to call it a night. I know you want to argue with me, my dear, but I promise you. Fatigue makes you miss things, and we can't afford that. We'll do a roundup in the morning. Come on, you can walk this old man to the back door. Clara told me she was leaving when I took my last break."

She stood, taking his arm as J.T. rose with them, saying, "It's frigid as hell outside, Uncle. You should put a coat on."

"The wind will wake me up enough to say good night to my beautiful bride. At my age, you don't take such a moment for granted. Good night, Taylor." He kissed her on the cheek and then touched her arm. "We're making good headway. The black ink in these here veins is vibrating with promise. Remember that and try and sleep tonight. You look like you could use some Zs."

His concern as much as the comfort in his weathered hand brought her emotions to the surface. She couldn't sleep. Tonight, she had to steal away and paint her mural. His insistence that they all go off to bed was a boon, however. Her computer clock had told her it was only ten thirty when she'd glanced at it before rising from the table.

"Thank you, Arthur. I can't tell you what it means to me to have your help."

"It's a pleasure, dear Taylor." He opened the door and cursed. "I didn't need to be *that* awake. Oh, to hell with it."

He charged out as J.T. called over his shoulder, "I'll be right back," and followed him.

She caught a blast of the wind as they shut the door behind them. Jesus, it was cold! Maybe it would help her wake up. If not, Red Bull always worked, and she had four in the suitcases she'd packed with her supplies.

But now, she feared the wind. Would it be as bad in Waterford? She'd chosen it because it was far enough away from Kinsale, and it suited her new theme. She was going to use only four shades of paint—black, white, silver, and gold —to depict a mural very much in keeping with what Waterford was famous for: crystal. Malcolm would be a grotesque black silhouette with his ten rings in gold paint. His giant foot would be ready to step on a magical crystal-like depiction of Ireland and Liam's form—the gold depicting his very noticeable earring—behind prison bars. Several other figures would be waiting in line to be jailed as well. Two sheep with angel wings would be ascending to heaven on the side, with a few others crying below.

She'd never done anything like it, and she thought Liam would appreciate the idea. Didn't all yoga and meditation fanatics like the idea of crystals, even of the man-made variety? His face swam before her again—that pirate earring she liked to play with, his sexy smile, and those green eyes filled with more love and understanding than any other human being had ever shown her.

Grief welled up inside her. What must he be feeling, trapped in an undisclosed prison? Had they beaten him? Had they fed him? She bit her lip as the door opened again. She welcomed the rush of wind.

"Hey," J.T. called. "We have something to ask you."

She looked over. Trevor was back, it seemed, and his face was really serious. Too serious. Like all of the other Merriam boys standing next to him.

"Taylor, you know we're friends, right?" J.T. asked, putting his hand on her shoulder.

Her nod was slow, given the weird buzz in the room.

"And I know you only know me and Trev well," he continued, "but the rest of my brothers all came here to help, so they seem like pretty great guys too, right? Well, except for Flynn maybe. We still don't know why Mom didn't leave him in the forest with the fairies."

"Hey!" He shoved his brother.

J.T. pushed him right back before turning to her. "Taylor, do you remember what we said about Flynn rivaling Russian hackers?"

Her skin tingled with a frisson of alarm. "Yes," she said cautiously.

"Well, there's no easy way to say this, but I got to thinking—"

"So did I," Trevor volunteered.

She wanted to run out of the room suddenly. "What did you do?"

J.T.'s mouth tightened. "We thought we'd make sure the real Veritas had everything buttoned up on the back end—"

Oh, God!

"And while it was a *really* impressive setup," J.T. continued as her head started buzzing, "Flynn found some things."

"Some things," she managed to repeat despite her dry mouth.

Trevor came over and swung his arm around J.T. "What my bro here is trying to say is this: do you need any help with the mural you're planning? Because it's obvious you are with how heavy your suitcase was, and we'd all really like to help if we can."

Maybe it was her lack of food and fatigue, but that offer did what Sorcha had only managed once.

Taylor fainted dead away.

CHAPTER TWENTY-TWO

V eritas had struck again.

Linc couldn't believe their luck as he put his arm around Bets. She gripped his shirt, watching the morning news report Ghislaine had flicked on after running in with the good news.

"God bless him!" Bets cried, hugging him fiercely. "Liam should be released now. Oh, thank God. My other two boys were planning on jumping on a plane and heading here if their little brother wasn't released soon."

Donal came over and slapped him on the back, his relief as clear as Linc's. "It's a hell of a mural, and what an incredible place to put it up. It honors their famous crystal, so there's even a chance it gets to stay permanently. Veritas is one smart fellow."

He sure as hell was, Linc thought, hugging Bets harder, aware she was fighting tears. She'd been on a constant teeter-totter of emotion, going from rage to tears in a heartbeat. Linc had stayed strong for her and everyone else in the midst of the legal impediments against them. "I want to shake Veritas' hand and invite him to dinner, but since that's impossible, I'll call our lawyers and get them on Liam's release."

Ghislaine tapped her heeled foot on Bets' hardwood floor. "Veritas tweaked Malcolm's nose but good in his social media post announcing the mural. Listen to this. *The unlawful incarceration of Liam O'Hanlon on bogus hate speech laws for being Veritas—which he most certainly is not —and the fact that his own lawyers do not know the location of where he is being held only highlights the monstrosity of the power Malcolm Coveney wields in Ireland. Ireland should stop him before he steps on the entire country. Because anyone could be next.* It's absolutely chilling when paired with the visual. The depiction of the sheep alone made me want to cry, and I'm supposedly a hard-nosed publicist."

"Like hell she is," Linc muttered to Donal.

"I want to kiss Veritas and thank him too," Bets said, wiping tears from her cheeks. "Invite him for Christmas. Anything."

Ghislaine held up her phone. "Why don't you record a short message thanking him? We'll post it on your social media accounts."

"Go on," Linc said, kissing her wet cheek. "You'll feel better once you do."

"Has anyone contacted Taylor to tell her?" Bets asked softly.

"I texted her the minute the story broke," Ghislaine said with a short smile. "As you might expect, she'd just seen it and was beside herself with relief. She said to tell everyone the Merriam investigation is going well."

"Those two young lovers deserve a reunion," Linc mused.

"They deserve a *vacation*," Ghislaine emphasized.

"Taylor's been fighting nonstop since she arrived, and Liam can't have enjoyed his incarceration. Come on, Bets. Let's share your thanks and joy with the world that he's coming home."

Linc watched as Ghislaine smoothed back Bets' hair and instructed his ladylove to lift her chin in the direction of the light coming in through the window. He was glad he hadn't had to do any interviews. He hated being trussed up like a turkey. "I'll call the lawyers and get cracking," he told Donal.

"I'll call everyone about having an impromptu celebration when Liam returns to Caisleán," his good friend responded. "You might ask Taylor if she wants to come back for it. My dad will."

"Already thought of it," Linc told him before pulling out his phone and calling Patrick. Their lawyer spouted off a bunch of legalese per usual but said he was contacting the proper authorities to secure Liam's immediate release. Although he didn't give a timetable for that, he did express gratitude that Veritas had provided hard evidence that Liam wasn't Veritas.

Yeah, a man couldn't be in two places at once. Even an idiot knew that. He took a moment to enjoy Malcolm's rage at being thwarted. He probably hadn't expected a follow-up mural. Veritas had never done two on the same subject. Would he twist off one of his showy gold rings and hurl it across his office? Would his face turn red and splotchy in his rage? Linc certainly hoped so, although he knew it wouldn't be the end of Malcolm's attacks.

Perhaps Veritas' frightening image of Malcolm stepping on the whole of Ireland would wake people up. God, they could use some allies.

When he called Taylor, he counted four rings until she

answered quietly. "Give me a minute to find somewhere to talk. We're in the war room."

War room, eh? He rather liked that name. He almost wished *he* could be in two places at once, but he understood that he was needed most here in Caisleán, at Bets' side.

"Okay, I can talk now. I have a gorgeous cat twining around my feet but otherwise it's quiet. So you saw the news."

"Yes, thank God! Relief doesn't cut it. I just wanted you to know the lawyers are working on Liam's release as we speak. They don't have a timetable yet, but I expect it'll be soon. Do you want me to fly you and Eoghan back to Caisleán so you can be here to greet him?"

"Quinn already offered us the Merriam plane since it's closer than yours. We discussed a remote plan so we can continue working on bringing Malcolm down. Eoghan and Clara are identifying government people with public associations with Malcolm while the rest of us are digging into the business side. Shell companies. Cross-referencing names. Looking for discrepancies in public contracts and end payments."

"So, looking for a needle in a haystack," Linc concluded. "I can ask Wilt to help in his spare time. Please tell everyone we're rooting for them and as grateful as two geese spared for Christmas dinner."

"Text me when you hear from the lawyers about the timing for Liam's release. Eoghan and I will hop on a plane and be there in under an hour, weather permitting. We have a nice storyboard going up here. Being able to see it is a help. It won't work quite as effectively for me remotely, but I'll manage. Seeing Liam is everything."

Her voice turned hoarse as she cleared it. Emotion vibrated on the line. Linc fought with his own riot of feelings. He really loved that kid, and Taylor was proving to be a worthy partner and one hell of a new member of their community. "You managing, sugar? Anything you need?"

"Just Liam out of jail," she answered gruffly. "I'm fine so long as I keep working."

"I hear you. I'll let you know the minute we know about his release. Tell the Merriams they have my eternal thanks."

He would have to think of something he could do for them. Maybe Taylor would have an idea.

"I'll look forward to your call," she said, her voice strong again. "Talk to you later."

"Be sure of it. Happy hunting!"

When he hung up, he filled his chest with air. He'd never had high blood pressure, but he'd wondered about the stress these last few days. Sleeping had been difficult and moving around was like walking through water. Bets was the same. They all needed Malcolm to go down. Hard.

He checked on Bets. She was wiping tears and talking into Ghislaine's camera phone. Her natural beauty caught him by the throat. Her laugh lines were more pronounced around her eyes and lips, but her blue eyes shone brightly with a mother's love as she said, "Veritas, I know you probably don't take gifts, but I'd really love to make you some of my special gooseberry jam or even send you a dozen of my prize roses next summer."

She *would* think of that, and he touched his chest as his heart swelled madly. God, he was so lucky to have her.

"You can't know how much it means that you returned to Ireland to do another mural to help my son, Liam," she continued, wiping more tears, "and to show how dangerous Malcolm Coveney is. Not only to my son but to the Sorcha Fitzgerald Arts Center and the rest of Ireland. Thank you, thank you, thank you."

Since Wilt had recorded the conversation with Malcolm's threats and the lawyers had submitted it as evidence, they could publicly speak about his intimidation. *Way to go, Bets*, he thought. Then she went from loving mother to fierce warrior. "And to all of you working with Malcolm Coveney and protecting him, wake the hell up. You're next."

"That was terrific, Bets!" Ghislaine said, already typing on her phone after stopping the video. "I already have media requests pouring in based on this new development, so let's talk through a plan for today until Liam comes home. Be a nice chance to remind people of what we're facing here. Maybe people will pay more attention to the sheep incident now."

"Give me a second to talk to Linc," Bets said, walking over to him.

She put her hands in her pockets and rocked back on her heels, looking vulnerable and overwhelmed. They each knew what the other was thinking, and for a moment, the look that passed between them said it all. Then she smiled.

"You go on and do your thing, sugar," he said, taking her into his arms and kissing her softly on the mouth, feeling his heart lift.

"What are you going to do, cowboy?" she asked, caressing his jaw.

"Find a hammock and shut my eyes for a bit." He gave a full-fledged laugh and slapped his knee. "No, wait! That's what I'll do after we take Malcolm down. Taylor sounded positive about their work down there."

"Good!" She rubbed his chest, making him aware of how tense he'd been. "You should take some time. I know you've been acting all strong for me—"

"We take turns when we need to." He tipped up her chin. "Partners, remember?"

She swallowed thickly. "The best imaginable. I love you so much!"

"I love you too." He kissed her soundly again. "Go kick butt."

"What are you really going to do while I'm off with the media?"

He scratched his jaw, which he hadn't shaved. "I'm going to do my part to raise some spirits around here. This village has been hit hard. We need to come together and find some happiness again. Liam coming home will be a big part of that."

Her eyes swam with tears. "Go on before I completely lose it."

Blowing her a kiss, he headed for the door.

"Linc?" she called.

He spun around. "Missing me already?"

"Yeah." She pressed her hand to her heart. "Thanks for coming to Ireland too. You're like Veritas, you know. You came when we needed you. Me especially."

Well, shit, now he was going to bawl like a baby. "You started it all, Bets, with your big vision. I was only too happy to help. Besides, I couldn't resist you from the moment I saw you standing in the porch light with sadness on your face. Even though I was sad myself, I wanted to wipe yours away and make you laugh."

"Which you do. Always. I'll see you later."

"Count on it."

He thought about that first night—how he'd invited her out to dinner, wanting to turn her sadness to joy. She hadn't known he'd meant in Paris. They'd had one hell of a time.

He should take her to Paris for a few days once this was over. They could both use a break.

The idea of a Paris weekend lifted his spirits. Hell, they'd bring Liam and Taylor. Shoot, he should probably take over an island or something and fly the whole village out to a resort for some time off and as a way of showing gratitude.

Because, other than a few bad apples, the people of Caisleán stuck together through thick and thin.

He'd been looking for a community and people like this all his life, and God, was he happy he'd found them. When he left their own war room, the first person he visited was his daughter—the one who'd brought him to Ireland. Being an overprotective father had worked in his favor. His whole world had opened up here—because of Ellie—and he made sure to tell her, reducing them both to a few tears before he moved on to continue spreading good cheer.

He found Angie painting in her studio with baby Emeline napping in a bassinet beside the easel. Later, he came upon Megan with her hands covered with clay as she shaped a vase while she told him about Ollie's recent attempt to ride his horse bareback. He pledged to teach the boy how to lasso before heading outside to Kathleen's shed.

The sound of her pounding metal was stronger on his eardrums than usual because of his fatigue, but it stopped as she and her workers all halted what they were doing upon seeing him. They had a cup of coffee as the rain blew in and traded their favorite stories about the woman they both loved to pieces: Ellie. Laughter *was* the best kind of medicine, and he realized he hadn't done much of it lately, no surprise.

After that, he knocked on Sophie's shed and waited to be admitted. Since her work was glass, she'd put up a sign about not barging in, something the Irish did frequently, being they were against door knocking and all. He still hadn't gotten used to it. She showed him the orange glass she'd just blown into a flower while they conversed about everything that had happened since Taylor had arrived in Caisleán.

As he left, he remarked how upbeat everyone's spirits were now that Liam was coming home. The sheep incident had been devastating enough, but to have one of their own taken away unlawfully and held in an undisclosed location was terrifying.

Veritas was right. Anyone could be next, and Linc knew it could be someone else from Caisleán. He made a call to Wilt to reassure himself everything was locked down security wise, then headed into town.

When he arrived at the pub, he sat beside Donal, who was already doing his part to raise spirits with the men of the town. Linc checked his phone—even though he'd already made sure it was turned on to receive calls—and pocketed it with growing worry. Was he crazy for thinking the lawyers should already have news?

When the five o'clock regulars poured in at the end of the day, Carrick strode over to him alongside Declan, Jamie, and Keegan. Linc sensed the change in the air and stood as the entire pub went silent.

"What's the status on Liam's release?" Carrick demanded. "Shouldn't he have been out by now?"

Linc gestured to Brady to give the new arrivals a round on him before saying, "Maybe Malcolm is drawing it out to fuck with us."

"Well, it's working," Declan responded, a muscle ticking in his jaw.

"Come on now," Linc said, clapping Keegan on the back

as Brady brought the drinks. "Let's take our comfort the Irish way. We should hear from the lawyers soon."

Only Donal was the one whose phone rang over an hour later. "It's Ghislaine," he announced, smiling—and then immediately went white as he listened.

Everyone set their drinks down and leaned forward as Linc's gut trembled. The bad news was evident. Only how bad?

"Brady!" shouted Donal, who pocketed his phone. "Turn on the national news."

They all turned toward the TV in the corner as the screen came on. Liam's picture flashed onscreen, along with the header: *Authorities Keeping O'Hanlon in Custody after Determining Veritas Copycat in Waterford.*

"No," he heard a chorus of male voices utter in sharp tones.

"That's ballocks!" Declan cried out. "It's Veritas' work. Plain as day."

"They can't distinguish their arse from their face," Keegan nearly shouted. "It's just like Mary Kincaid getting away with hurting and killing my sheep. They'll get away with everything. Even murder, I'll bet."

Linc glanced over at Donal. They shared a long look and rose, clapping backs in comfort as they made their way out of the stunned pub and into the parking lot. The wind was harsh in the darkness, the light rain like cold needles on exposed skin.

"The lawyers didn't know about this development," Linc began, "or they would have called me. Malcolm and his friends went straight to the news outlets."

"It's outrageous!" Donal fumed. "How can anyone with half a brain claim Veritas didn't do it?"

"This isn't about the truth," Linc gritted out. "We both

know that. Even if Veritas does another mural, they'll still brand it a copycat."

"But Veritas is claiming it himself!" Donal spat on the ground. "It's ballocks, it is. Dammit, the man posted photos of himself painting the mural last night in Waterford. On his own social media channels! Disguised, sure, but it was him doing the work, plain as day."

"We're in the scary age of fake news," Linc concluded. "I imagine this will light even more of a fire under Taylor and our Merriam helpers, especially Arthur Hale. As an honest-to-goodness journalist, he must be off to high heaven."

Donal hung his head. "First the sheep thing and then Liam being taken. Now this. Linc, some days I don't know what's happening in the world. Before I could say it was happening in some other place—not in Caisleán—but that's not true anymore. It's happening here, and to good people, people I care about. What are we going to do?"

He shook his head and put his hand on his friend's shoulder. "I don't know at the moment, and that's hard to say out loud."

The wind whipped around them as silence reigned. They were both men of action, men who always knew what to do.

Until now.

"I need to go home to Bets," Linc said, his heart filling with pain. "She's going to be inconsolable."

"You give her my best. I'll talk to Ghislaine. She's a pit bull about things like this. I'll bet she'll be up all night contacting people and getting the word out. It's how she releases her outrage."

Outrage, yes, but how did one release heartbreak?

Especially since Liam was still in jail somewhere and

they didn't know how to get him out. What must it be like for that poor kid?

"Are we at the Alamo then at last?" Donal asked, hoisting up his collar against the stinging rain.

The first time Bets had made an allusion to the famous battle, weeks after his arrival in Ireland, Linc had protested vehemently.

His heart broke because he wasn't so sure anymore.

"Nah," he managed, his throat hurting from his weak retort. "We'll figure something out. We always do."

As he walked to his car, he acknowledged to himself that he didn't believe it, and to a man like him, that made it feel like Malcolm had all but won.

CHAPTER TWENTY-THREE

H er plan hadn't worked.
    Taylor scanned the headlines as J.T. and her other accomplices hovered around her, as incredulous as she. They had been on an after-dinner break when she'd received Ghislaine's text. Arthur hadn't returned yet from taking a walk with Clara, and Eoghan was talking with Cian out in the front hall. All of the brothers lifted their eyes to her, and she could see a reflection of her own shock and rage.

Last night, after they'd brought her around from her faint, she'd done the impossible and trusted them like she had Liam. Ironically, after she'd run them through her plan, they'd improved upon it—which had involved raiding the paint in the inn's storage room so she could enlarge her work. God, she'd been so hopeful, and she could have sworn she felt Liam's joy at her trusting more people to help them. She'd even found enough of an appetite to eat a couple of scones after they'd arrived back at the inn early this morning. But now...

Hope had more than left the building. It had been

thrown over the cliffs outside the inn and into the dark sea below.

"We are dealing with an absolute bastard," Trev said, breaking the silence. "With powerful backers. It's outrageous that news stations would run that story."

"And what investigation?" Flynn shot back. "Who determined it was a copycat?"

"They're sons of bitches," Quinn ground out, his fist pressing into the table. "And dangerous ones. I'm sorry your boyfriend won't be released, Taylor. I know you have lawyers on this, and I respect Linc and the way he does things. But do you want our lawyers to see if there's anything they can do?"

She rubbed under her nose, fighting the mudslide of failure trying to tear her down. What kind of soulmate was she? Liam was in an undisclosed jail protecting her, and she wasn't holding up her end. She never, in a million years, would have imagined they'd refute the mural. Her style, her voice was so recognizable.

Plus, she'd posted it on her social media channels in real time. But no, the government was suggesting someone had hacked into her account and posted it. They were trying to steal her identity—as Veritas—like that douche who'd betrayed her when she was a teenager. That was so not going to work, but dammit, she was out of ideas.

"I want to know what proof they have that Veritas' accounts were hacked, dammit!" she raged.

Flynn winced. "Be careful what you wish for, Taylor. If they *do* look deeper, they might find something. You're well covered, and I added a few more layers, but you don't want your cover to get poked by a bunch of IT geeks who answer to Malcolm. I'll bet he's the kind of boss who'd take a bat to an employee's kneecaps if they disappointed him."

Her mind immediately went to Liam, and she rose on shaky legs. More than once she'd wondered if he'd been hurt. Surely, they could do anything to him. Malcolm enjoyed complete impunity.

"What's going on?" Arthur asked, holding a fresh cup of coffee. "Looks like a funeral in here."

Taylor couldn't force the words out suddenly.

"Liam's being kept in jail," J.T. answered at last, patting her back companionably. "They're saying the Waterford Veritas from last night was a copycat."

"I saw the earlier press coverage of the mural." He held out his hand. "It's a dead ringer for his work. Show me the top stories."

Taylor handed him her tablet as her mind spun.

There was only one thing to do, wasn't there? She had to come forward and confess she was Veritas.

"I know what you're thinking," J.T. said quietly to her, "but let me suggest why that would be a bad idea."

"What's a bad idea?" Arthur didn't look up from reading the news, only proving how sharp his ears and mind were. "A prison break?"

"That *might* be a better idea," Flynn agreed, his mouth twisting.

Arthur pinned them with his pale blue eyes. "Then what exactly?"

Taylor and the Merriam boys had agreed not to involve anyone else in what they'd done. After all, if Arthur ended up writing an exposé on Malcolm, which they very much wanted, who knew if the Irish authorities would want to bring him in for questioning.

Suddenly Taylor couldn't take it anymore.

"I don't think you should publish a story, Arthur," she announced. "I need to find another way. I can't live with you being charged under the hate speech laws too and ending up in jail."

Her voice broke, making the Merriam men sit up straighter in their chairs. Arthur only sipped his coffee.

She blew out a tortured breath. "I'm very sorry for that outburst. I know it's not helpful. I just think we'd do better to find out who Malcolm screwed over, and how, and leak it anonymously online."

"To what end?" Arthur asked gruffly. "And have them say it's fake news too? Malcolm and his goons will do it. You know that as well as I do. No, Taylor, we stick with the plan."

She glanced over as Clara and Eoghan walked into the library. "Eoghan just heard the news from his son," she said, her blue eyes shining with tears. "I can't imagine what you must be feeling."

"Taylor, I'm so very sorry." Eoghan crossed and took her hands, the lines of his face severe with sorrow. "Everyone in Caisleán shares your outrage. I told Clara this makes our work that much more important."

"But Malcolm could hurt Arthur—and any of you." She was losing her battle to remain emotionless. "We can't risk that. I brought you in, hoping to expose Malcolm. Right now, I don't see a way to do that publicly. He's holding all the cards. We have to leak it and hope someone in the government might wake—"

"My dear," Arthur interrupted, "this isn't the first time in my life where I've faced great odds with a story. Sit down for a moment. You're strung out, and no one here can blame you."

J.T. pulled out her chair again, and she sank into it.

Arthur extended his hand to Clara, who came over and took it. "We've faced plenty of challenges together, even in

292

these last few happy years. But we persevere and stick together and keep plugging away at our goal. We know what that is: to take Malcolm Coveney and the rest of his rotten crew down. With a story, by a man like me. Because I have street cred, as the youngsters say."

The other Merriam men were all nodding, but she couldn't agree. Veritas had street cred and that hadn't mattered. "I don't think I can live with another person I care about being in jail because of this."

Because of me.

He took his glasses off and began polishing then. "Taylor, I'm a journalist, first and foremost. To betray that would be to betray my very self."

On that they could agree. She was nodding when she caught his smile.

"I have a feeling you understand," he added softly. "Being Veritas and all."

Her head went light, her heart rate jumping, and God help her, another faint was coming on. "I—"

"Please, give me some credit." He pinned the men around her with a pointed look. "I know when something's up. And last night when you thought I was sleeping, I watched you all pile into Cian's old van after putting supplies in the trunk and removing the license plate—nice touch, by the way."

They'd been found out? She sank back in her chair, grateful that J.T.'s hand patting her back was making the black spots at the edges of her vision go away. "But how did you see us from your cottage? We were at the far shed—"

"The cottage is stocked with binoculars, my dear," Arthur said, putting his glasses back on and staring down his nose at them. "I almost joined you."

"Why didn't you wake me?" Clara protested, socking him on the arm. "I most certainly would have gone."

A few of the Merriams groaned. Arthur only laughed. *This was funny?* She had the urge to run out of the room. How was she supposed to keep Veritas anonymous when a flock of people knew it was her? Maybe she should come forward...

"Is it really true?" Eoghan asked, practically dancing forward and grabbing her hands to shake them with uncharacteristic enthusiasm. "Taylor, you had me good and fooled this whole time. Now I understand why you seem to keep your own company and didn't want me to come on this trip. You thought I might pull you down. Or find out the truth."

Truth. That was her name. Veritas. And yet she'd spent so many years lying about it. The irony was beyond her right now. She had never felt more exposed.

"Only three people know about me—or did—my hacker, my lawyer in New York, and Liam. Now I have a whole plethora of people who know, which seriously freaks me out. Not only because my fame and anonymity are based on secrecy but also because your association with me could get you thrown in jail should they discover I'm Veritas. Which might be the only way I can get Liam out of jail."

"Don't even think of coming forward," Arthur declared, pointing his finger her way. "Malcolm has proven that hard legal and journalistic facts are irrelevant in his use of power. You don't know what might happen if you reveal yourself. But I can assure you of this. Malcolm has shown he will contort the truth and hurt good people. Unmasking yourself will only cause more harm. They'd probably refute your story and find some slim pretense to throw you in the clink too. I expect Liam was the one who helped you with the mural at the arts center, correct?"

She nodded. "I wouldn't name him. I'd—"

"You're tired now, Taylor, so listen to an older man. Malcolm has it out for you after you faced him down on the road. How happy would it make him to have you as the person he can throw the book at?"

"Plus, Liam wouldn't want you in jail," Eoghan cried out, the harsh wrinkles around his face lightening as he smiled. "He loves you."

"And I love him, dammit," she said, "which is why I can't let him stay in jail for me. I hear what you're saying, but it's not right."

"No, it's not," Arthur agreed. "And you should keep posting as Veritas online, declaring your independence and discounting the charge that Liam O'Hanlon is you. Embarrass Malcolm while we keep up our investigation."

"We're going to find something, Taylor," Connor said after being quiet the whole time. "I always get this feeling close to a breakthrough in business."

"Me too," Quinn admitted.

She'd felt it too while they were working today, putting more shell companies up on the board, but how much longer would it take? How long would Liam remain in jail? "It makes me sick to say this, but we're betting a lot on Malcolm going down after you publish his wrongdoings, Arthur. Maybe he'll sidestep this too. I know it was my plan, but even if he *does* go down, am I being naïve to think other people won't step froward and take his place? They could keep Liam in jail to make a point."

"We can't think that way right now," Eoghan said, patting her arm. "We have to believe we can win."

"Or we might as well never get out of bed in the morning," Arthur added, pushing his glasses up his nose. "And trust me, there might be a lot about life that sucks, but there's a whole hell of a lot more good when you look for it. Veritas does a great service in the world. Clearly, *she* understands that."

Taylor bit her lip to keep her emotions in check. "She might be having a slight existential crisis right now."

"It happens to all of us." Arthur came over, pulled her out of her seat, and put his arm around her. "Standing for truth and decency shouldn't be hard, but by God, there are a lot of bastards out there who make it so."

"I called them bastards too, Uncle." Flynn held out his fist for a fist bump. "I feel like we're having a moment."

Arthur snorted but gave him a hearty fist bump, which Flynn playfully pretended hurt his hand. The move did what he'd intended, and the mood lightened a fraction.

She took a deep breath, finally able to fill her lungs. "I'm away from the cliff now."

"Good," Arthur said, squeezing her once for good measure, "because I don't think I need to tell you that Veritas' identity is safe with us."

That was why she had trusted the Merriams and let them help her. "With the Irish government proclaiming it's Liam, while I disagree online as the real Veritas," she said wryly. "Sometimes it feels like a single voice in the wind can't be heard."

"Sometimes a single voice is all it takes to inspire others to join in," Arthur said, kissing her cheek. "The power of numbers has changed the winds of fortune time and time again."

A single voice...

The power of numbers...

A movie scene flashed into her mind, that of man after man coming forward to say he was Spartacus, the leader of a group of slaves, after the Roman general announced he would crucify them all unless they identified Kirk Douglas' famous character.

"My love of old movies just paid off." She glanced around the room. "We need a *Spartacus* moment."

Arthur gave a chortle. "Because Malcolm can't put everyone in jail. I see where you're going with this. An *I am Veritas!* campaign."

Eoghan let out a lyrical whoop. "I know that film. We'll do it at Malcolm's very door, in Watertown, with the press looking on. Oh, what a spectacle!" He rubbed his hands together in delight. "Taylor, it so happens my specialty is bringing people forward for a cause. If you don't mind me helping..."

She remembered what Sorcha had said about trusting Eoghan. She hadn't listened before. That stopped now. "I'd love your help."

"You might also gather your millions of fans online and ask them to show up at certain locations in major cities," J.T. added, arching his brow.

"Certainly in front of government buildings in Dublin," Quinn broke in with a wolfish grin. "No reason not to remind supposedly elected officials and members of law enforcement to properly do their jobs for we, the people."

"Louisa would be happy to organize something in Chicago, I imagine," Connor said with a quiet smile. "Make it global. There are a lot of people who share your feelings about the misuse of power and don't know what to do. My beautiful wife always says something like this gives them a voice too. Let them stand up with you, Taylor."

Hope burst through her. Already it was coming together —and because she'd finally trusted people. Liam would be so proud of her.

J.T. slapped her phone in her hand. "Get started on the

plan while the rest of us fit in another marathon investigative session before bedtime. Because I'm tired. I didn't get much sleep last night."

Flynn playfully yawned. "Yeah, but it was pretty great, wasn't it? I'm buying a whole bunch of spray paint when I get home and covering our garage walls with positive words with the kids."

"Just don't let Amelia spray-paint Carrot, her poor pony," Arthur said with a grimace. "But I digress. Well, I think we have a plan. We Merriams will continue to unravel the secrets of Malcolm's empire while you run your campaign to free Liam from unlawful incarceration."

"It does sound like a good plan," she admitted, glancing around and finally smiling. "So let me be the first to say..."

Her blood sang as she prepared to do something she'd avoided for years.

"*I am Veritas,*" she said loud and clear, smiling as her delightful helpers applauded.

CHAPTER TWENTY-FOUR

The door to his prison squeaked as it opened.

Liam kept his eyes closed, unwilling to give Malcolm the satisfaction he sought. On the man's last visit, the one he'd paid with Aunt Mary, Liam had given away too much by challenging her and her powers. He wasn't going to make the same mistake again.

A chair scraped across the concrete, and Liam felt the air shift as Malcolm's large form came forward and landed heavily in front of him. "The guards say you're quite adept at sitting in absolute silence for hours. It's really quite impressive. But I thought you deserved to know that poor Veritas simply couldn't stand for you to assume his identity."

Liam opened his eyes at that. He'd tuned in to Taylor's energy as much as possible, so he'd known she was up to something. He'd seen an image of her with a spray can in one hand, surrounded by a shrouded group of tall, dark men, all of whom felt like giant protectors. He'd assumed she was making another mural, but he had no idea who the men were, only that she trusted them, which was something rare and special. "Since I'm not Veritas, that isn't a surprise really. I wouldn't want someone else claiming my work."

"The mural went up in Waterford."

Waterford? An interesting choice, not that he'd thought Taylor would paint another in Caisleán. Malcolm thrust out a tablet, which Liam took casually. He schooled his face before looking at the photo. My, how he wanted to smile as he took in the story it told. She'd done a brilliant job rendering Malcolm as a malevolent figure in ebony paint while the rest of Ireland and Liam and some sheep all were depicted as the kind of crystal figures Waterford was known for. "Thank you," he said, handing back the tablet.

"That's all you're going to say?" Malcolm tapped the screen against his thighs. "Don't you want to know what happened afterward?"

He closed his eyes again. "I figure you're here to tell me. Why ask the obvious?"

Malcolm's foot nudged him, but Liam kept himself still. He was aware of Malcolm's rapid breathing. He was growing angry. Hopefully not enough to put his hands around Liam's neck again.

"The Irish government has deemed the Waterford mural the work of a copycat," Malcolm practically sneered. "That means you're staying here. Unless you cooperate."

So they were back to blackmail...

"I told you the center serves the greater community, and I am proud to not only serve as an employee but a resident of Caisleán. Malcolm, you won't get me to work against my people. Not even if you keep me here for years."

He'd been releasing his fear about the amount of time Malcolm could hold him. Taylor and he had just come together, and he wanted to be reunited with her and continue with their lives together. More than anything. He also wanted to be back amongst his family and friends. That worm of dread stole his peace, and he needed all of it to face the silence and long hours. So far, he'd looked on this time as a retreat. Forced, of course, but everything in life was about perspective. He meditated on his beautiful future with Taylor and all the construction projects the center planned along with meetings at the pub with friends and family. Those visions kept his spirits up and his heart whole. They kept Malcolm from winning.

"You have proven a more worthy adversary in many ways than Linc and your mother. I've rendered Linc's fancy Dublin lawyers useless and neutralized all of your mum's weepy pleas for your release on social media and her heart-felt gratitude to Veritas for the Waterford mural."

The chair scraped again, and Liam could feel Malcolm's breath on the top of his head. He was looming over him in that chair, his dark energy pressing in against the light-filled bubble Liam had created around himself.

There was a hard tap on something, and then Liam heard his mum's emotion-clogged voice. His heart tightened, feeling her pain, but he opened his eyes and watched as she bravely battled her feelings to speak her truth. Her face was lined with fatigue, but he focused on the love she radiated. When it finished, Malcolm was practically salivating at having won this round.

Liam only smiled again. "I'm a lucky man to have a mum like that. Thank you for visiting me, Malcolm. It was most enlightening."

He wasn't sure how the man would greet his echo of the words from their last exchange. Malcolm's face tightened with fury as he shoved out of the chair hard enough for it to topple onto its side. "You think you can best me? I have more power than you could ever imagine, enough to wreck you and your whole village. We'll see how you feel when I transfer you to a place no one in the government knows about and throw away the key."

He could see the place suddenly. It was in an old abandoned building on the sea. Miles away from civilization. If Malcolm followed through, Liam wasn't certain anyone would be able to find him. He forced his eyes closed. He would deal with it if it came to pass. In the meantime, he would focus on his family and his friends. And Taylor...

She'd gone and painted a mural on the fly in another part of Ireland, hoping to secure his release, and let others help her. Talk about love.

"I bid you a good evening, Malcolm," he said, turning his attention to his breath.

"You don't even know what time it is. Who's the poor lad now?"

The door slammed shut, and Liam kept his focus on his practice until he smelled oranges. When he opened his eyes again, Sorcha was kneeling in front of him.

"I'm sorry it's come to this," she said softly, a vision of light in her white dress and long, cascading hair.

"I said prayers for you," Liam told her, "when I heard you might be in trouble for what you'd done with Mary. You need to be careful with her."

"I know it well, but it was your prayers and a few others that led to me being able to choose who I would visit, as you're still in my charge." She sank to the ground in front of him. "You seemed to need it more. Taylor continues to land on her feet. You should see the men she's working with in Kinsale. If they weren't already happily married, I would sign up to be their matchmaker."

Kinsale. Now he understood. She'd gone to Arthur Hale and his nephews. Watertown was a reasonable drive from there. And she'd trusted them with her secret. He was so proud of her. "I'm glad she has support," he answered. "And I know my mum does as well."

Sorcha folded her arms in her lap. "Even now, you're thinking about others. It's why you're so pure of heart and wiser than the rest. Even Kade in some things. And look at you, sparring with Malcolm and coming out on top. I wanted to tell you to keep the faith. There are things in the works, ones we hope will see all wrongs righted."

He touched her energy by laying his hand over hers. "I'll keep sending up prayers on your behalf. I don't purport to understand the powers that govern you, but I do know the love you have brought on this plane...and the love with which you did it. Not every wife, even from the grave, would wish to help her husband find another soulmate to spend his life with. That makes you special. I hope they know that."

She had to work hard to smile. "When you love someone, you wish them happiness in life—and part of that happiness is a good partner to share it with. I'm grateful they gave me the chance. For all of you."

He could feel their light growing, and he let it wash away his remaining fears about the future. "I wish you could give Taylor a message for me, but I understand that you cannot. Thank you for coming to visit me. But if you do have another chance, go and see my soulmate and tell her I miss her and love her and can't wait to see her beautiful face in the morning and as I close my eyes to sleep."

Sorcha's face brightened. "Love does change us, and when we allow more in, it can change everything around us. Bring more love in, dear Liam, while the rest of us do the same on your behalf. I hope that when we next meet, you are in the sunshine."

He enfolded her in love, making her smile widely. "And I hope you will find joy and peace in whatever is next for you."

She made a comical face, one he recognized from their old days in the pub before her passing. "Yes, you and Taylor are the end of my matchmaking contract. It's been a grand time. All of it. I don't have any regrets. If for some reason I can't return, you'll tell everyone how much I love them, won't you?"

A wave of sadness crashed over him. This was like losing her again somehow, the grief sharp and powerful and unexpected. He breathed through it as they gazed at each other with tears. "I'll tell them."

"Thank you," she said in a rare, quiet tone.

An old Irish blessing for the dead came to mind and he laid his hand in the air over hers as he said it: *May God level the road for your soul.*

She let out a gusty laugh. "What a perfect send-off. As any Irishman knows, a level road is the rarest of the rare with all our hills and potholes around. *Dia duit*, Liam."

He held her gaze. "*Dia duit*, Sorcha."

She vanished in a brilliant flash of light. The scent of oranges lingered.

He began to meditate again, wondering if he'd seen her for the last time.

CHAPTER TWENTY-FIVE

Timing and precision were everything when it came to trespassing.

No one knew that better than Veritas—and today Taylor was sharing its artform with the people of Caisleán.

She'd posted to her millions of fans in an ongoing three-day cycle about their participation in today's campaign, something the media had picked up as if it were the hottest binge-worthy series on Netflix. The real Veritas was staging a social protest for the release of the *un-Veritas*? Brilliant, the major newspapers and news programs proclaimed.

No one knew how many people would show up around the world, but artists and other community actors were organizing protests in dozens of cities with T-shirts made from her special design for the event.

God, it had all made her rather proud. She'd taken this job at the arts center to do meaningful work, and while this was nothing like she'd expected, it damn well fit the bill.

As she surveyed the hundreds of people who'd shown up at the arts center for the protest, Carrick and Kade hoisted Eoghan up on their massive shoulders with a megaphone. "What a lovely day we have for our protest," he began, grinning from ear to ear. "Thank you for coming. One of our own, Liam O'Hanlon, is being held unjustly on the trumped-up charge that he is the real Veritas. Which, of course, he is not. We are here to proclaim *we* are the real Veritas. Each and every one of us."

He glanced over at Taylor before signaling to the Veritas mural on the wall of the arts center.

"Take a good look at why we're here, and who and what we're fighting for."

"He's in his element as a community organizer," Ghislaine murmured beside her. "The photos of that little old man on the shoulders of the men in this community, *Liam's friends*—a brilliant idea, by the way—are going to bring tears to people's eyes. Taylor, I have to say. I've worked with a lot of publicists in my time, but this campaign might be one of the best I've ever come across. You're going to rock the media director job once we get past all this *merde*."

She nodded and caught Bets' smile as the woman turned to look at her. Liam's mom had cried in her arms after she'd outlined the plan to her and the rest of their core circle. Then she'd framed Taylor's face with her hands and told her Liam was the luckiest man in the world to have her, after which Linc had given her a crushing hug, lifting her off her feet.

Such affection, especially where her professional career was involved, was so new, but that moment had reached the inner fortress of her heart. This job couldn't be strictly professional. These people were Liam's family, and that made them hers as well. She needed to adjust and trust them—like she had the Merriams—so she'd opened the door more than a crack. She couldn't wait to tell Liam when he was released.

When, not if.

"Now, we have a few more items to cover," Eoghan continued on his megaphone. "First, there are T-shirts we'd like you to wear. The design made by the real Veritas. On the front they say, *I am Veritas*. On the back, *Free Liam O'Hanlon*. Now for item number two."

He paused and pointed toward the road. The buses Linc had rented were arriving just on time.

"We Irish have subterfuge in our veins, so we played a little trick. We're taking this protest to Watertown—to right outside Malcolm Coveney's office—although our behavior will be strictly within the bounds of legality. We're going to stand in his parking lot at the marina and make our voices heard. If you're with the press, be sure to follow us. If you're nervous about coming, we'll see you at the Brazen Donkey after. All right, let's head out and free our friend, Liam O'Hanlon."

The volunteers in charge of handing out the T-shirts in front of the buses took their places as everyone queued up. Taylor and Ghislaine took photos to capture the scene. Later, they would release a short documentary on recent events, narrated by one of the arts center's newest board members, a popular Irish actor.

"I'm still hoping Bono shows up at the Dublin protest," Ghislaine whispered to Taylor. "I reached out to his publicist."

Taylor fought doing a dance at the thought of Bono saying *I am Veritas*. Maybe he'd even wear the T-shirt. Hard to get any cooler than that. "Fingers crossed. Come on, let's go."

They rode in the buses for the nearly hour-long trip to downtown Watertown, where they encountered newly constructed roadblocks manned by Garda officers. *That bastard*, Taylor thought. They'd thought he'd be prepared for them, but it wasn't going to make them back down. She turned back to look at Linc in the row behind her and Ghislaine. He was already conferring with their lawyers, who'd accompanied their group.

"Driver!" Linc called, rising swiftly and heading to the front. "Find a tourist bus drop-off. We're going to have to walk. People, the lawyers have assured me we can't be arrested for arriving in a public parking lot with T-shirts on. There's more of us than them, and we have the press here. But if you're worried about being arrested, please stay on the bus."

A few people looked nervous, but everyone stood and filed off the bus.

"Stick together," Taylor called, giving them encouraging smiles.

Linc and the lawyers led the charge, and she stayed in the back of the group since Ghislaine was taking photos from the front.

"It's a stupid decision to try and stop us," Carrick ground out as he dropped back to walk with her. "He's going to look even more like a bully and tyrant than he already does."

"I think he lives for that image in the mirror each morning." She watched as he matched her stride. "Are you keeping an eye on me, Carrick?"

"I am at that, you being Liam's and all," he replied in that solid way of his.

Suddenly she swore she could smell oranges. She looked around, but Sorcha was nowhere to be found. Taylor couldn't believe she actually missed the ghost. If she'd gotten in trouble for trying to help with Mary, they would need to do something for her. Only...who did you petition to ask leniency for a ghost? Taylor was banking on Liam knowing.

Liam. Her heart sped up. *This* had to work. She couldn't contemplate how she'd feel if it didn't.

The people in front of her stopped, and she sidled to the edge of their group to see Linc and the lawyers speaking with a Garda official. The camera crews Ghislaine had invited were circling the altercation as other reporters took photos. After a few minutes, they were walking again.

"Makes you wonder what they said," Carrick offered as they walked together through the quaint Irish streets. The sound of seagulls crying overhead and the smell of the sea hinted they were closing in on the marina, and after turning right, they reached the parking lot.

Watertown's much-visited bay was filled with luxury boats and the odd fishing trawler. On a sweeping green inlet to the right was the golf course on Malcolm's new five-star resort. Only a fraction of his kingdom, but every king liked to see some portion of what he owned from his window.

They all spread out in front of the building. Malcolm would be able to see them from his office, presuming he was there, which she imagined he would be.

This time, Donal and Keegan O'Malley lifted Eoghan onto their shoulders so the crowd could see him. "All right, everyone. We know what we came to say. *I am Veritas. Free Liam O'Hanlon.*"

Saying the words herself made her light-headed in the best of ways. To admit it out loud was mind-blowing, like diving into the most delicious body of water imaginable and then floating in it as it rocked you gently in place. She let go and savored the sensation.

The crowd kept chanting with Eoghan, and Taylor watched as the large silhouette of Malcolm appeared in a window on one of the upper floors. He was smoking a cigar from the looks of it, the end glowing like caged fire.

Garda officers from Watertown appeared in front of the building, making Eoghan hold up his hand to silence the crowd. "Look at our officers of law and order standing in front of Malcolm Coveney's office as if we are something to be feared. But that is not the case. What is to be feared is what is inside. Come on, everyone. Let them hear us."

Eoghan began chanting again. The crowd joined in.

Taylor looked at her watch. The lawyers had agreed they should keep the protest to less than ten minutes. Any more and the Garda might be able to break them up on some crazy charge.

Eoghan must have gotten the signal because he lifted his hand again, making the crowd go silent. "Now turn around and show him your backs."

Donal had explained it was a serious slight, and along with the message they were sending about Liam's release, Taylor imagined it would paint a powerful picture for Malcolm.

"We expect Liam O'Hanlon released!" Eoghan shouted into the megaphone, the power of his voice scattering seagulls along the waterfront. "Today!"

With that, they lowered Eoghan to the ground. Taylor motioned for the crowd to follow her back to the buses. As she turned the corner, she nearly broke her rhythm. The original goons from her incident with Malcolm on the first day of her arrival were smoking against the brick building, Denis Walsh, the former head of the Caisleán Garda, among them.

"That's a statement if I've ever seen it," Carrick ground out. "They're trying to intimidate you."

She motioned to her fierce expression. "This is me

looking intimidated." Deciding not to poke the bear, she refrained from waving and calling out a snarky greeting. Everyone had agreed to stick to the plan to avoid any issues with the Garda or Malcolm's goons.

By the time they reached the buses, Taylor was feeling relieved. Going to Watertown had been a gamble, and they hadn't known how Malcolm would react even though they'd done their best to keep their plan under wraps. She stayed by the bus door and smiled at people as they reboarded, wondering if Irish people did high fives.

God, there were so many things she wanted to ask Liam. Oh, to spend time with him again... She loved him so much, her heart wanted to explode.

When Bets and Linc arrived, Taylor had to bite her lip not to laugh at how cute they both looked in the blue T-shirts with white lettering proclaiming *I am Veritas*. She snapped a quick photo for Liam before the woman moved in for a powerful hug. "We did it! Ghislaine says the news cycle is already running wild. Taylor, I can't thank you enough for this idea."

"Only doing my job," she joked.

Linc chuckled softly. "Let's go home then and wait for our boy."

Taylor battled to keep her hope strong. They had done what they could. Now they would have to wait. Again.

Bets glanced up at the man she called cowboy and gave a blinding smile before turning and taking Taylor's hand. "You'll wait with us, won't you?"

She nearly winced at the plea in the woman's blue eyes. "Actually, I have more research to cram in for my special project with Arthur. But I'll be over. The minute we hear news."

The drive back to Caisleán was filled with raised

voices and even higher spirits. Eoghan started a song at one point, and the whole bus joined in. The tale was about a man coming home from a long time away, traveling dark seas to return to those he loved. Taylor had to look out the window at the passing scenery to conceal her emotion. When they arrived in the arts center, she wanted to take off; otherwise, she'd be there for hours. Man, the Irish could talk, a total contrast to the clipped New Yorkers she was used to.

But she couldn't leave without first thanking Eoghan. Finding him in the crowd standing beside his beautiful wife, Sandrine, and his son, Donal, she waited a short distance away until he spotted her. She gave him a wave, and he hurried over, a sudden gust of wind blowing the short wisps of gray hair covering his head straight up in the air before they fell back in place. He was a sight in his oversized T-shirt, and her heart melted as he took her hand and kissed it sweetly.

"This village owes you a lot, Taylor McGowan," he said softly. "More than anyone can know."

He'd sworn to her that he would never reveal her true secret to another person unless she gave him her leave. Not even his wife. He'd said he was old and didn't have too many years to carry it, making her heart catch when he said he now understood what it must be to keep such a secret from those she knew. He did admit to rather liking being one of only a few who knew something so special. Like a secret brotherhood, he'd told her, making her laugh alongside the Merriams and Arthur and Clara, who had also sworn to keep her secret safe.

She believed them.

"We all do the part we must," she told him, leaning over and kissing his cold, weathered cheek. "You did wonderful as well. I'm grateful to you. For more than anyone can know."

He gave her a conspiratorial wink. "Will you come have a celebratory drink with us then?"

She fidgeted in place. "I was going to get back to our special research project."

"Of course." He looked down at his feet, his disappointment evident.

Her throat caught as she wrestled with herself. This community had come through for Liam—and her, although they didn't know it. She should honor that, shouldn't she? But it was more than that. These were Liam's people, and since he was hers, that made them her people too. She needed to let them in more and trust them as he did. "Okay, one drink."

His head shot up, a grin spreading on his wrinkled face. "Of course. Just one."

The phrase *Of course* in this situation turned out to be Irish for *yeah, you cute, shorty* because she was still at the Brazen Donkey two hours later, wedged between Eoghan and Bets, who simply couldn't stop touching her arm as the group regaled her with stories about Liam. They talked about everything from how he'd been known to heal injured animals when he was a kid to how he'd once held a headstand for twenty minutes when Brady and Declan had asked him how long he could manage it. They'd finally thrown an empty water bottle at him to stop the madness because, as Declan said, "We would have been there all night."

She was laughing at another story from Ellie when a loud honking sounded outside the pub. Her skin frizzled with tension as the pub fell silent.

And then Liam was bursting through the front door, his

green eyes shining with a brilliant light, the most beautiful smile on his gorgeous face. He found her immediately. Their eyes met, and she grinned, her heart exploding with love. He started for her, the crowd parting, and when he reached her, he looked over and gave his mother a smile before grabbing her to his chest.

Before she closed her eyes, she saw the momentary shock on Bets' face. Before Liam would have sought out his mother first—now he sought out his soulmate.

"God, I missed you," he whispered fiercely in her ear. "And what you did! I'm so proud to call you mine."

She gripped him as hard as she could before he reared back and kissed her, pressing his lips to hers as if they might never kiss again. All the longing of the last few days surged up in her, and she grabbed the back of his hair and kissed him with all the love inside her. The sound of whistling reached her ears, and she pulled back, patting his chest and scanning his features. "You're not hurt?" Only then did she note the fading bruises on his neck. Gasping, she brushed her fingers lightly over them.

He shook his head, catching her gaze. "No, *a stór*. You have nothing to worry about on that account. We'll speak later."

They could both feel Bets waiting patiently, and Taylor had to respect how hard that must have been for her. She nodded but leaned in to kiss him swiftly once again, wanting to wrap her arms around him and never let go.

"I'm so glad you're home," she whispered fiercely.

"Me too." One final rakish smile and then he was hugging his mother.

Linc looked over at her, tears swimming in his eyes. She felt some water run down her face and realized she was finally crying. She swiped at her tears and picked up her whiskey, taking a fortifying sip.

Someone took her hand, and she turned to see Eoghan holding out a wrinkled handkerchief to her, his own eyes wet. "I am Veritas," he whispered and then signaled to her.

She'd taken her T-shirt off already, but the words were etched in her soul. She closed her eyes as she let the joy skyrocket through her. Her plan had worked.

"I am Veritas," she repeated before Eoghan clinked their whiskey glasses together as the party kicked into full swing.

CHAPTER TWENTY-SIX

L iam had never been so desperate to leave a pub filled with friends and family, but the truth was he needed to be alone with someone.

Namely, his soulmate.

He also needed a shower for sure, though certainly no one seemed to mind. They practically hugged and squeezed him to death as he made his way through the pub, thanking everyone and getting caught up on news.

Taylor was always in his sight, filling his relieved and grateful heart, sitting next to Eoghan, whom he was happy to see was her new friend, and Ghislaine, of course, who continued to post live segments from his release party.

When Ghislaine suddenly cried out, *"Mon dieu!* Bono came to the Dublin protest," everyone turned as she and Taylor jumped up and did a little dance, one that had him grinning from ear to ear along with the rest.

"You might ask Bono to join the arts center board now, Linc," Donal called out from the bar where he was standing and talking to Brady's dad, who had joined his son to keep the drinks flowing.

The whole town had shown up at the pub after hearing about his release. It was going to take a power outage to shut this party down. Actually, that wouldn't do it either. Brady and the others would only light candles and bring in portable lights. He smiled slowly as Taylor looked over at him, giving him an enthusiastic thumbs-up. Then her brown eyes went all soft and dreamy, and he felt his heart clutch as the thought rolled through him that she was well and truly his.

"She's one hell of a girl," Linc said, slapping him on the back, "and she's worked tirelessly to bring you home and make Malcolm pay."

He turned to face the man and gripped his shoulder in return. "You all have. Thank you."

"I'm sorry it happened in the first place," he said, scowling. "I figure you have some stories to share with us—like those bruises no one wants to ask about—but let's hold off until tomorrow. I expect you have other things on your mind."

He pressed something into Liam's hand then, and Liam's fingers curved around a car fob.

"I'm going to take you to the back for a private conversation—or so we'll tell anyone who asks us as we step behind the bar. Those are my keys. Ghislaine will take Taylor outside on some ruse, and you two can get out of here. I've already arranged everything with her."

Emotion clogged his throat. He was lucky to have another good man looking out for him in addition to his father's efforts from the other side. "Didn't Taylor bring her car?"

Linc laughed gustily. "Son, this here is Ireland, as you know. I figured you two might not be missed for a while if her car's still in the lot."

"You're starting to get the way of things around here. Mum will be upset though."

He'd seen the way she'd looked when he'd gone to Taylor first. He hoped she could understand.

"Don't you know that old phrase? A son is a son until he takes a wife? That's why I'm glad I have a daughter. I'm pardoned for worrying about her forever." He rubbed the back of his neck. "Liam, Bets might need time to adjust, but she will. Moreover, she's happy for you. I figure it was no different for you when she started to date."

His mouth twitched as memories flooded him. "I stopped walking in unannounced, that's for sure."

"Same consideration goes for us." He guided Liam to the side of the bar, and they stepped into Brady's storage room leading to the back door. "Show up at the house whenever you feel up to it. Don't feel rushed."

Still, he felt guilty about leaving. Especially when his mum darted into the back to join them. "What are you doing?"

Linc's mouth pursed before he said, "I was taking this boy out here to ask him a few private questions. Sugar, you go on back in and keep my seat warm."

"Like hell." She fisted her hands at her side. "I want to hear what happened to him too, Linc. He's my son."

And there it was. "Mum," he said gently, "I'll tell you everything you need to know, but I'd like a little time. Taylor and I are going to make a getaway. Linc and Ghislaine are helping."

"But you just got here!" She rushed forward and gripped his arm. "You were in prison for days. I was so worried."

"Bets, honey." Linc took her hand. "He's been through

an ordeal and all he wants to do is be alone with the woman he loves. He'll come over tomorrow. Don't you worry none."

Her lip trembled, and Liam's heart trembled along with it. He went with honesty because it was his default—and all he could think to do to assuage her hurt. "Linc was just talking about adjustments. The kind I had to make when you started dating again. We're going through something similar right now. Mum, I love you, and I always will, but Taylor is my Linc, and I want to be with her right now more than I want to breathe, honestly."

She sniffed and nodded. "You're right. I'm sorry. I was only..."

"Bets, the kid said he wants it more than breathing," Linc continued, helping him out. "That's a powerful lot of wanting because if you aren't breathing—"

"I said I get it," she said, frustration still lacing her voice. "I'll see you tomorrow, Liam."

When she left in a blur, he knew she was probably fighting tears. He almost went after her, but Linc's hand kept him in place.

"Rome wasn't built in a day, son. Adjustments take time. She's barely slept, and her emotions are on a short fuse. Don't take it personally. I'll help her out as much as she'll let me."

"She's lucky to have you." He grabbed the handle of the back door and stopped. "I wasn't sure if I was going to say anything—or when—but this seems like a good time. My dad visited me while I was in jail."

Shock rippled over Linc's face. "Like Sorcha does?"

"Yes. Exactly. I just wanted you to know he's really happy you're with my mum. In fact, he said you see her better than he did and you encourage what she holds inside her heart. I thought you might like hearing that."

His throat worked as Linc rubbed his jaw. "Well, hell, I'm on a short fuse too because that moves me quite mightily, I must say. I'm glad to hear that, son. Now get on with you."

Liam gave in to the urge and walked over and embraced the man. He hugged him as he would a father and welcomed another level of love and respect between them.

When they separated, Linc laid his hand on his shoulder. "Yeah. Me too."

Liam was smiling as he walked toward the door. When he reached for the handle, the knob turned and the door cracked open.

"What are you doing?" Taylor asked, her face a mixture of joy and consternation. "I've been standing out here in the cold trying to look inconspicuous. Are we leaving or what?"

Liam almost laughed, but he was so happy to see her. Linc crossed and opened the door wide, pushing him out into the back. "You're leaving. Have fun, kids."

They faced each other in the quiet of the alley after he slammed the door.

She reached for him, only to yank her hands back. "If you kiss me now or I touch you, I'll be done. You might as well drag me to the ground and have me right here. Even though it's freezing out, I don't think I'll notice. I just want to hold you and never let go."

God, how smiling felt good after the last few days. "So we wait until we're home?"

She grabbed his hand and led him toward a side street.

"Taylor, love, you're going the wrong way."

"No, I'm not. I hear we're taking Linc's car to confound people, and you have the keys. Gimme."

He kissed her hand as he placed them in her palm. Her

answering grin could have lit the Universe. Just like that, they were partners again.

"Stay here. I'll pick you up in this alley. If someone sees you outside the pub…"

"We're done for," he said with a laugh.

"You think this is funny?" she asked.

"After the last several days, yeah."

Her face fell. "Right. You'll have to tell me about that. Be back in a jiffy."

He spotted Linc's Range Rover a minute later. The car door swung open, and he jumped in. She hit the gas, which had them both laughing, and sped out of town.

The sight of the new Kindness Sheep in the surrounding pastures—Carrick's and other farmers' and the ones of Keegan O'Malley that hadn't been shorn—had him breathing deeply to control his rising emotion. The words that shone out in the swarm of puffy bodies were more than apt—they were signs.

Love.

Blessings.

Happy.

Thanks.

Freedom.

Peace.

He had all of that and more. When Taylor rested her hand on his leg, he took it tightly and held on as they sped to her house. Pulling to a stop, she practically jumped out.

"You need a shower," she said, reaching in for her keys to unlock the door. "Are you hungry? You didn't eat much of the sandwich Brady put in front of you—"

"Taylor," he called to bring her back as he followed her inside. "*A stór,* I only hunger for you. But I do need a shower. Join me."

She gulped and threw her purse down on the couch. "You scared the hell out of me, and I missed you so much. Dammit, there's no doubt in my mind that you're mine, so you'd better get used to it because I am *never* letting you out of my sight again."

His heart pulsed loudly with his answer as he walked toward her. "I love you too. Even where time doesn't exist and back. Come here."

She laid a tentative hand on his chest. "Wait! I know what a shower can mean, Liam. It's about more than getting clean. Sometimes you need to wash a bad experience off."

He traced her cheek. "Not everyone would understand that."

She pursed her mouth as her eyes brimmed with tears. "Lucky for you, I understand everything when it comes to you. You even get a head massage in the shower."

Then she was pulling him to her bedroom and her en suite bathroom. He started pulling off his clothes—which he would burn in a fire ceremony, he'd decided—as she turned on the water in the shower. He nearly laughed when she raised a brow, hitting the button for the immersion heater, which would ensure they had plenty of hot water. She checked it for temperature with her hand before standing aside. "It's ready."

He caught her eyes on his body, already hard and aching for her. Leaving the door open, he stepped under the spray, savoring the rush of hot water over his body as he watched her undress. Their gazes locked as she drew off each piece of clothing, and then she was stepping into the spray with him, reaching for the shampoo. Her body was as beautiful and tantalizing as he remembered. He itched to lay his hands on her, but he knew she was right. The moment he did, the moment they really touched, there would be no turning back, so he turned around and let her work the shampoo into a thick lather. Her fingers pressing on his nape and the soft spot on top of his head were magic, releasing tension and cleaning the past days away along with the water.

When she lowered her hands to his shoulders and rubbed the overtired muscles there, he groaned, laying his forehead against the tiles at last. His body had sat nonstop in meditation save the few hours he'd spent trying to sleep on the cold cement floor. Soon he would need to tell her those things, because there would never be secrets between them.

He rinsed his hair as she lathered the rest of his body, igniting his raging desire as she ran her hands over him. He could tell she didn't mean for it to be sexual, but their connection meant her touch could never be impersonal. When she massaged the tops of his feet, on the floor before him, he had to raise her up.

"I'm clean enough," he said, cupping her face in his hands. "Let's wash away the rest. From us both."

Her eyes swam with all the emotions he'd known she must be fighting—the fear, the worry, the helplessness. He knew her too well not to sense them.

The first meeting of their lips had them both groaning. He could feel the urge to take her swamp him, but this was a sacred moment, and he would not rush. He gentled his mouth, sipping slowly at her lips, pouring his love into her as if he were the water rushing over her.

She fisted her hands in his hair and gave back, pressing her silken wet body against him, filling him with her love, her courage, and her undeniable power. He kissed his way down her neck, finding her breasts. She arched into him, moaning, and he caged her waist with his hands, going

323

lower until he could take her breasts into his mouth, one at a time, her nipples hard and straining.

Lowering himself to his knees in front of her, he locked eyes with her. "Let me," he whispered, touching her thighs.

She widened her stance and braced herself against the tile. He sought redemption in that moment, wanting to give to her, needing to share all the love filling his being. What she had done for him... Who she was to him... Words could not encapsulate it, only actions that brought bliss, a bliss neither of them had known until they'd come together.

Her cries and urgent presses against his mouth made him soar. He was a man. Her man. Her *soulmate*. And she was surrendering to the knowledge as much as he, as they had from the first time they'd given themselves to each other.

When she lowered onto his lap, he guided himself inside her. They both gasped, and it took a moment for them to fight past the agony of longing created by their connection.

She held his shoulders as she met his eyes. "I love you," she whispered, tracing the jaw the Garda had insisted he shave before being released.

He murmured the Gaelic to her. *I love you.* And then he began to move inside her.

They rocked together, their sounds, their breathing, their hearts—all of it coming together and finding a rhythm and beat unique to them. He could feel her tightening again, could feel the rush of his own release at the small of his back. He pressed deep and held her there, suspended over him as she cried out and began to pulse, triggering his own earth-shattering release. She gripped his hips with her thighs and arched back, taking him higher until there was no water, there was no shower, there was no sound.

Only a floating feeling of endless love.

He held her to him as she laid her head on his shoulder. The water grew cold, and that reality brought him out of those higher dimensions. He picked her up and walked her to the towels, where he dried her off and then himself.

She finger-combed her hair before taking his hand and leading him to her bed. It was unmade, the signs of a sleepless night written all over it. He lay down on the side he'd claimed, the one closest to the door, the one he'd have for all their days together.

"So..." She rolled over until she could wrap her leg over him. "After-prison sex is even more intense than soulmate sex. Not that I ever want to have after-prison sex again, to be clear. This was our one and only time."

Humor would be the way she'd get through this. He pushed back wet hair from her cheek, taking in the changes. Her fatigue was obvious in the slight strain around her eyes as much as the wanness of her color. She looked as if she had lost weight too. Both of them had, at that. "You are the most beautiful woman in the world."

She posed playfully. "Thank you. I work hard to look this beautiful. Now you. Let's get it all out straightaway. You said they didn't hurt you, but I see the bruises."

Her intensity was palpable. "I decided to tell you *everything* that happened. I don't plan to do the same with Linc and my mum. It would only hurt them and make them feel guilty. But you and I have a different pact, and I'll never keep anything from you."

Her anguished exhalation was harsh in the quiet of the bedroom. "Good, because I really couldn't talk myself into pestering it out of you. All right. Give it to me straight."

He searched for the best words to share his ordeal, and after he began, the story poured out of him naturally. Her face changed as she listened to him—her eyes shifting from fiery anger, upon hearing about Malcolm and Mary's taunts, to tears as he told her of his meetings with his father and Sorcha.

She traced his throat after he shared how Malcolm had put his hands around it, the most dangerous moment he'd had in jail, and wiped more tears as he told her that his father and Sorcha had both done their best to heal it. He finished with the news of how a Garda officer had entered his cell in silence, put a hood over him, and then driven him to Caisleán, pausing outside town to take off the hood. She expressed her shock that he had no more information about his release. All Liam cared about was that he was free and that Malcolm hadn't paid him a final visit. Then she wrapped her body around him as if she were trying to absorb him into her very skin and keep him safe.

"Now you..." he said softly, inhaling the clean scent of her, feeling the warm press of her body against him.

She began with her frustration over her Waterford mural not working, and then she backtracked to how she'd mostly invited herself down to Kinsale to help Arthur Hale, only to discover the Merriam men and Clara waiting to help. Eoghan's involvement made him smile, and he leaned in to kiss her after she told him about bringing the man into her confidence. Trusting him. Something she'd been forced to do with the Merriam men too. From there, she filled in the pieces of how the people in the pub had come to be wearing *I Am Veritas* T-shirts with his name on the back and a plea for his release.

"You know..." He had to clear his throat to free the emotion there. "This *Spartacus.* I've never seen that movie."

"How is that even possible?" She rose up on her elbow, her cheeks pinkening from happy outrage. "*Spartacus* broke the Hollywood blacklist, some of the darkest days in movies when people accused of alleged communist or subversive ties for having 'radical ideas' were denied work. Dalton Trumbo was finally listed in the credits—whereas before his screenwriting was done in secret."

He tapped her nose. "Sounds like someone else I know."

She laughed. "Yes, and now I have a T-shirt I can wear with the truth on it, because people will just think it's cool. Edgy even. Oh my God, I am so going to need to watch that clip of Bono at the Dublin protest again."

"Go get your phone." He leaned over and kissed her tenderly on the lips, overwhelmed with love and gratitude and the pure joy of being with her again. "We'll watch it together."

She narrowed her brown eyes as she flipped her hair over her shoulder. "Seriously? Like right now?"

"It makes you happy," he told her softly, "which makes me happy."

Her enthusiastic kiss rocked him back as she straddled him. "God, this *is* a big moment. I'd rather make love to you again than watch Bono at the Dublin protest. How huge is that?"

"Pretty huge," he said, nudging her with his erection.

She snorted as she fitted him to her and lowered herself. They both groaned, and his hands came up to play with her breasts.

"Speaking of all that blessing stuff, which I can feel you getting to," she said as she began to move slowly. "We need to do something for Sorcha, because it sucks if she's in trouble for what she did with Mary. Who do you petition for leniency on a ghost? Because I might never unsee the suggestions the internet gave me when I typed in *how to free a ghost.* Do you have any idea the kinds of things that are out there? Liam, I know you have gifts, but it's called woo-woo for a reason."

He fought laughter as she took him deep and then stopped, arching into him again. God, she was close, and he was going to come undone under her. "I've been thinking about it. I have some ideas."

"Good," she moaned, taking his hand and bringing it to where they were joined. "Then I really need to check in with the MIU."

He dug his head into the pillow as she picked up her pace. *"A stór,* I have no idea what you're talking about."

"I told you...about the Merriam Investigative Unit." Another moan from her split the room, making him fight for control. "We still need to bring Malcolm down. You being released is only step one."

He fell into his breathing, for it was the only thing that was going to help him enjoy their rhythm longer. "I'll help you after."

Her hands landed on his chest as she leaned forward, taking their position deeper yet. She was panting, sweat dotting her face and between her breasts. But it was the fierce love in her eyes that undid him in the best way.

"Then we need to figure out what to do about your aunt Mary because that bitch is so going down. When I think about her visiting you in jail like that and threatening you..."

He rose then, rolling her to her back. "No talk like that when we're making love, *a stór.*"

"Sorry." She lifted her hand and caressed his jaw tenderly. "Did I tell you how much I missed you when I was doing the Waterford mural? I mean, the others were great to volunteer, but only Trevor knew how to paint. Flynn was a complete disaster. I had to stick him on garbage duty. And

Connor was really precise, but he took forever. And Quinn—"

"*Taylor.*" Liam raised her leg and pressed in deep. "Try and focus on us, love. Then you can talk yourself out."

She twined her hands around his neck as he began an easy thrust and withdrawal. "It's my version of meditative breathing, which you still do way too much. I mean, only moments ago you had your eyes closed and you were sucking in wind like there was no tomorrow."

His rhythm broke then, and he started laughing. "You aren't what I expected. At all. I thought the Universe would send me a female version of myself. Instead, I got the bravest, most brilliant, and funniest woman imaginable, who won't stop talking while we're making love."

She pushed him back and rolled on top of him again, her eyes dancing with love and humor. "Aren't you the lucky guy? Because we'd *never* work if I were like you. I mean, Yoda and Yoda is like white bread and white bread kissing, whereas bread and jam are much more delicious together. I think I'm the jam in this relationship, being I'm so sweet and all—"

He set aside his breathing and let the force of their laughter bring in their pleasure.

CHAPTER TWENTY-SEVEN

B ets did some of her best thinking standing in front of a window.

She had a problem, and she knew it. Although she was thrilled that Liam had found his soulmate, seeing him go to Taylor first in the pub had driven home a fact that hadn't sunk in before. Nothing was ever going to be the same between them, and she was now second in his life. She was a little jealous of Taylor's hold over Liam. Which was ridiculous! She wanted her son to be happy, and judging from the way he'd hung on to Taylor's hand when they'd finally arrived at her house, he *was* happy. Both of them had been glowing, in fact, from the only thing Bets knew put that look on a person's face. She needed that look more, personally. All this junk with Malcolm and Mary was affecting her sex life.

"You still fretting about the green-eyed monster, sugar?" Linc asked as he strolled in after talking to their lawyers yet again. "How many times do I have to tell you that you're just going to need some time to get used to Liam having a woman in his life? Didn't I go through this when Ellie hooked up with Brady?"

She watched him plumping up her couch pillows before he sat down. He always managed to squash them by virtue of his size. "You looked like a sad puppy then, cowboy. What do I look like?"

"A basset hound," he answered, making her frown. "Fortunately, I think they're adorable. Hey! Do you want to get a dog? I'm finally over losing mine. Might be nice to have one padding around the house as we get older. Maybe it could fetch us things so we won't have to use our walkers. What do you think?"

She eyed the downpour outside, wishing it would stop so she could take a power walk and burn off her bad mood. Shouldn't she be turning cartwheels because her son was free and safe? What was wrong with her? "I think you're trying to distract me with jokes about aging and it's not amusing."

"What else might work?" he shot back, crossing his ankles. "Sex? We've both been too tired and worried for much of that, but I'm game to try and give it a go. You know I've missed you."

Hadn't she just been thinking that? She'd missed him too! Life had sucked recently, and all because of Malcolm and Mary. Liam would probably caution her against victim-perpetrator language—even after telling them in broad strokes what had happened while he was in jail—but she didn't feel like taking the high road today. What was wrong with some people? Why couldn't they just live their own miserable lives without bothering anyone?

"Well, that didn't hit," Linc mused, "which won't hurt my feelings, seeing as I know you find me irresistible. How about a movie? I could probably watch *Jaws* again."

Taylor liked *Jaws* too, which made her Liam's perfect partner.

Bets made an aggrieved sound. "I am in a terrible mood, Linc Buchanan. You might just need to knock me out."

He gave a comical full-body shudder, and with his large body, it was one hell of a show. "That I will never do. I know! You want to put on Bon Jovi and dance for me with that sexy feather boa of yours?"

That sparked a burst of laughter from her. "Who's that supposed to help? Me or you?"

His shit-kicking grin was back in the building suddenly, and it was like the sun had come out after three weeks of bad weather. "I figure we both get something out of the spectacle. Me especially when you—"

The bell from the front gate interrupted him. Sighing, he rose. "Company, and just as I was making progress. I'll go see who's darkening our door."

She fingered the curtains as he picked up his phone for their call box app. "Could be someone who wants to talk about Liam's release. Not that there's much to tell with him not even knowing where he'd been—"

"What you said," Linc responded, holding up his screen. "Sugar, it's Mary Kincaid. If we had a dog, we could sic it on her. Want me to call the police instead?"

"Not yet!" She stormed to the front door, hearing Linc hurrying after her in his cowboy boots. "That bitch has some gall coming here."

"Bets," Linc called as she jogged down the driveway, "I don't think this is a good plan. First, it's raining—"

"I don't care!" She wiped at the rain soaking her face. "Is the video at the gate on?"

"Twenty-four seven," he said, breathing hard as he

caught up to her. "This is only going to pour more salt into what hurts."

The hurt was already spreading, and this time she wasn't going to let it bowl her over. "Mary Kincaid," she yelled as she opened the gate with the button on the wall, "what the hell are you doing at my house?"

The woman stood in her ugly black raincoat with a stupid clear rainhat to show off the corkscrew curls she was so proud of, her dark eyes filled with rage. She held up an official-looking letter with the seal of Ireland on it. "You had my benefits taken away. I just had a special courier from the Irish government at my door. I know you're behind this! Damn you, Bets O'Hanlon. That's my money. The money that I live on. You had no right to take that away."

Linc whistled shrilly. "We had nothing to do with that, Mary, but it sounds like just deserts to me."

"How dare you!" Mary heaved the letter onto the ground and crushed it into the wet gravel with her heel. "You will reverse this or you will pay."

Bets snapped. "I am so tired of your threats. When Liam told me you'd taunted him while he was in jail—that you'd laughed with Malcolm—it made me sick. If the Irish government has finally wised up and stopped your benefits, good for them. I had nothing to do with it."

Mary's hands slammed through the air. "Malcolm refuses to give me money, so I'm here, begging you to give it to me. As family. You and me might have our feelings about each other, but Bruce would want you to help me."

"*Help you?* After all you've done?"

Linc put his hand on her arm, sensing she was ready to fly off the handle. He wasn't far off. She shot him a look, but she wasn't going to be quiet.

"Family? You think us being related gives you the right

to ask me to pay for you to continue to live in this town and wreak cruelty on me and the people of Caisleán? You are completely out of your mind. Mary, I wouldn't give you a scrap of bread if you were starving. Before I might have felt really bad about that, but I don't anymore. Ask me why."

The witch only screwed up her rigid mouth. "Well, go on, Bets. You want to tell me."

She curled her fingers into her palms. "I wouldn't, because in helping you survive that extra day, I'd be enabling you to visit more hurt or even death on others. On the people I care about, in particular. You knew where my son was—in jail unjustly—and you did nothing. You are a cruel and miserable person, and now I know you for a sheep killer like the rest of the people in our village. Mary, I'm glad you're out of luck, because maybe this time we'll be rid of you at last."

The woman stared at her as the rain poured, her chest heaving. "And you say I'm cruel, as you speak such words to your own kin while living in the very house I was born and raised in. You give me no choice then. Linc Buchanan, you once offered to buy my house. I accept your offer."

His brows hit his wet forehead. "Lady, that deal is dead and buried. I wouldn't buy your house if it were the last shack on the planet."

Bets wanted to kiss him, but Mary suddenly stepped forward and pulled something from her pocket. Danger filled the air, and Linc pushed Bets behind him.

"Your son didn't think I had it in me to curse you and all of your kin, Betsy O'Hanlon, because in doing so, I would curse myself."

Bets inhaled sharply as she looked around Linc's big body. There was a dead rose with a long cane in Mary's hand, the thorns dark with malevolence. One of her Black

Magic variety. The kind she'd used in her chicanery to beat Bets out of the annual rose competition.

The whisper of something slick and dark touched her skin, like insects crawling on her. "Stop this, Mary! Stop this right now."

"Mary, I'm calling the police," Linc warned, pulling out his phone.

Fear had her breath halting in her lungs. She'd lived in Ireland too long to discount the old ways. "Don't you dare."

Mary pricked her finger with the thorn and smiled as water and blood flowed. "I curse you, Betsy O'Hanlon. I curse you and your kin and all of Caisleán."

The wind gusted and rushed over the land. Bets heard a scream, and then she saw black ribbonlike forms streak by. Wraiths, she thought, the kind Bruce used to describe to her. "You take that curse back."

Mary laughed eerily as she threw the rose to the ground, the rain carrying the blood into the soil. "Never! Not even if you beg me to."

Bets watched as Mary turned with a triumphant smile and disappeared through the veil of rain. Looking down at the dead rose at her feet, Bets was aware of a bone-chilling cold spreading through her body. Linc caught her in his arms and grabbed her to his chest.

"For the record, that's one thing I hate about Ireland," he said, breathing harshly. "The Garda are coming—and Wilt— Sugar, I don't know what to do here. My balls are still plumb shrunk, and I'm terrified to touch that dead rose on the ground. And I'm a rational man... Should we call Liam? Mary mentioned him, right? If anyone knows about this stuff, it's Liam, isn't it?"

She didn't want Liam anywhere near this! She drew back and froze as Linc continued to rub her arms. Standing a little behind and to the left of Linc was Bruce. Her Bruce! The silver of his clothes appeared shot with white light, a light that also radiated from his familiar green eyes. He might still have the gray hair she remembered so well, but it was shiny and lustrous. He had never looked more handsome or content. This was the Bruce she had fallen in love with and followed across an ocean.

"Hello, Bets," he simply said.

Linc turned his head at the sound and jerked in shock. "What the—"

"No, it's all right," she assured him as the cold left her, followed by a gentle peace she recognized. Liam could bring the same peace, because his father had taught him. The rain slowed to a halt, and a shaft of sunlight broke through the gray clouds, turning the lingering raindrops on the trees and plants to diamonds. The light grew until the gray completely disappeared, changing the skies and igniting a double rainbow.

"Holy—" Linc managed before trailing off in awe.

Bets could feel a slow smile beginning on her mouth, one Bruce returned before walking over to the dead rose and kneeling down. Holding his hand atop it, he whispered something in Gaelic. She remembered he'd done something similar for her ailing rosebushes on occasion—working his magic to bring the plants back, stronger and better than ever. She'd won with roses from the bushes he'd helped cultivate.

"I never gave you roses for romance," he said, looking up. "I should have. Just as I should have pressed you to pursue what was truly in your heart. I'm sorry for that and more, Bets, as much as I am for never handling Mary properly. She's my sister, true, but I will not give her leave to curse our family."

AGAINST EBONY IRISH SEAS

Tears swamped her, and their eyes met once before he said the words, "It is undone. Never to be done again."

White light flashed over the rose, blinding her. When she opened her eyes, Bruce was gone. The dead rose had turned from black to beautiful deep red with shades of chocolate, on a green cane with healthy thorns—as though it were freshly cut.

"Did you see that?" she rasped, sinking against Linc, who let out a shaky breath.

"You mean that man?" he asked, his drawl more pronounced than usual. "What he did to that rose was insane enough, but was that really your Bruce? In ghost form? I know Liam said he'd seen him, but the reality is way different. Whoa! I need to sit down."

She pressed her hand to her mouth. An avalanche of feelings was thundering through her. She'd never thought to see her husband again. "Yes, that was Bruce."

"Heavens to Betsy!" Linc leaned against her, his weight really heavy now. "God, that saying might be a funny choice seeing as that's your name. Holy heaven, another ghost."

He sounded like he was going to hyperventilate. That snapped her into focus. She turned and tugged on his collar. "Take a breath, Linc."

"I can't." He made a helpless gesture at the rose and then the sky. "My chest is all tight. Bets, I don't think I can handle having your ghost husband around here, not even if Liam says he approves of me."

That little stinker. Liam hadn't told her Bruce had said he approved of Linc. Or that his father had any regrets about her. That had deeply touched her. "That's good, isn't it?"

"Sure, I guess, but land sakes, I hope he won't pop in like Sorcha during a tender moment between us. I mean, if I

337

thought he would, I could never put my hands on you without looking over my shoulder."

Laughter tickled her throat. "You're on the verge of becoming hysterical like I did when I had my meltdown. Seriously, cowboy. Breathe."

All he managed was a sniff. "Can't seem to suck in any oxygen while that rose is sparkling on the ground like the one in *Beauty and the Beast*. Ellie loved that movie as a kid, so I watched it plenty. It darn near looks like something we should stick under glass and hide away in a tower."

"Oh, Linc..."

"Don't 'oh, Linc' me," he heaved out. "That man—your ghost husband—just turned something dead into something living. How is it you can breathe right now? I can take a lot of Irish magic, but that might be too much for me. God, I must be tired or something because I suddenly feel light-headed. Oh, dear Lord, I'm seeing spots."

She tried to catch him, but he slumped gracefully to the ground in a faint.

Bets made sure he was okay before picking up the rose. She held it to her nose and inhaled. The variety wasn't known for its fragrance, but she wasn't surprised to discover it held the most glorious perfume.

After all...Bruce had finally given her a rose.

Then she leaned down to where Linc lay and kissed him awake—like a good heroine did in the fairy tales.

CHAPTER TWENTY-EIGHT

The bell to Taylor's gate call box was going haywire, as if a child were pressing it for fun.

Liam looked up from his laptop where he sat working across from her on the couch, helping her with company cross-referencing. After returning from Bets and Linc's house for more marathon post-prison sex—she was going to ride that particular train as long as possible—she'd called Arthur for an update and negotiated a couple hours of work for the MIU with Liam. A productivity break before they went back to making love, her new favorite preoccupation.

She peered at him over her laptop, marveling at her work view. "You don't think it's your mother, do you, with another loaf of freshly made bread?"

He gave a quiet chuckle. "It would be chocolate chip cookies this time since she'd know we haven't had time to finish the bread. But it's probably Brady, popping over to make sure I'm okay. He'd try and keep himself away—"

"But he loves you too much—like everyone does. Me included. All right, I'll go check. But let's make it a quick visit, okay? I have plans for you."

He caressed her arch deliciously. "Words I hope to hear all our life."

"Duh." She tucked her laptop away and untangled herself from Liam's legs on the couch.

"Someone *is* really persistent," Liam observed as she reached the gate's intercom.

Eoghan's face was huge in the camera, grinning like a prize bass. "It's Eoghan." She buzzed him in. "Do I need to make tea or something?"

He rose and grabbed his shirt, depriving her of his calendar-worthy chest and abs. She pouted as he pointed to her outfit. "You might want to put pants on. Not that I don't love seeing you in your *I Am Veritas* shirt and nothing else."

She shot him a knowing smile as she lifted it to showcase her bare hip. He'd made her happy when he'd tugged it on her in bed that morning, saying she should wear it because she really *was* Veritas. He was right. It did feel fun. Plus, with nothing on underneath, they'd *both* had fun. Always a boon.

A knock sounded on the door, and she winced. Something landed at her feet. Her cream drawstring pants. Making herself presentable, she opened the door.

"I wouldn't have interrupted you unless it was an emergency," he announced, holding up a burlap grocery bag.

Had he thought they'd need sustenance after all that sex? That was kinda sweet. And weird. "You were a dear to shop for us—"

He squeaked with laughter as he stepped inside. "It's not food, Taylor, it's information. The kind to take Malcolm down for good."

That drew her up short. She peered into the bag as he opened it. Inside were files. Serious-looking files, like she'd seen in those suspenseful FBI movies. "Where did you get these?"

"It's an incredible tale! A woman called me at home this very afternoon and told me she had the means to help us keep our village and our arts center safe." He took her arm as she led him into the kitchen. "She asked me to meet her in Castlebar at the cemetery, beside the grave of a man you won't know. He was a good man and died some twenty years ago, but— He's not important. Anyway, she wouldn't tell me more over the phone, and she said I couldn't tell anyone about our meeting—or she wouldn't come. Otherwise, I would have called you earlier."

"Don't think my feelings are hurt! This is extraordinary, Eoghan."

Liam pulled out a chair for each of them and helped them sit. "So you went?" he prompted.

"Yes, I hated lying to my Sandrine, but I told her I was going to the pub." He wiped his forehead as she sat enthralled beside him. "A tale she wouldn't see through, of course."

"Of course," Taylor agreed. "Then what?"

His eyes were nearly feverish with excitement. "My blood is still racing from it all. I drove all the way there, praying to the angels to keep me safe, and when I reached the cemetery, I found this lovely silver-haired woman in a green rain jacket standing beside the grave she'd mentioned. Her smile was the thing that made me trust her straight-away, as much as the fact that her hands were shaking as she handed me a shopping bag. She said she'd been Malcolm's secretary for over fifteen years before he'd set her aside for a younger, prettier girl. Now she lives on state benefits."

Figures he'd go with a younger model, Taylor thought, pushing the tea Liam deposited on the table closer to

Eoghan as Liam took the seat next to her. The dear man picked up the tea and swore as he scorched his lips before laying the bag on the table like it was a historic find from an archeological site.

"She didn't give me her name—to protect us both—but she said she'd seen our problems and sympathized. She took note of me leading the protest in Watertown and thought I seemed like a trustworthy man, one she could count on to keep her involvement secret. I won't give you her name, but I know her participation is safe with you, Taylor."

She touched his arm and smiled. "You and I are both good at keeping each other's secrets."

"That's the way of it." He tapped the bag. "I figured you'd have a better go of looking through what she gave us. Or we might want to fire up Linc's plane and take ourselves off to Kinsale. Arthur and the Merriams will know what to do with it for sure."

She drew out the files as Liam's hand touched her back. "She was a brave woman, stepping forward to help."

"She'd always known he was doing some things on the side—many Irishmen in her association do—but it sounds like he grew greedier as he accumulated more power. In the beginning, she ignored it because she was divorced and raising four children on her own after her husband ran out on her. Malcolm had paid well. But putting Liam in jail like he did frightened her. She has a son your age, Liam, and she feared Veritas was right—anyone could be next. Taylor, I couldn't wait to tell you that last bit."

She kissed his cheek loudly. "It warms my heart like a stove. Now, let's see what we have here."

The first file held copies from a ledger. The headings at the top had her dancing in her seat. "Do you see these titles? One is for actual payment while the other is for recorded payment. The numbers don't match, and they're itemized. I recognize some of the companies from the MIU."

Eoghan peered closer. "Do you see this entry? It's for Gerry Campbell. He was in the Parliament and a corrupt bastard. They say it's a campaign contribution."

"But the numbers don't match, so the extra could be a payoff," Taylor said. Lifting her gaze to him, she cried out, "Oh, Eoghan! This looks like a treasure trove."

Heart tripping, she grabbed the next file. Squinting, she said, "Why would there be two figures listed for a horse?"

Eoghan laughed and Liam joined in. "My boy, we have a lot to teach this one. Taylor, people cut deals under the table like this to keep the VAT down. This way you don't pay as much to the taxman."

"So fraud," she breathed out, sweeping her finger down the page and turning to the next one. "A whole bunch of fraud."

"Petty stuff in a single instance," Eoghan said with a wink, "but with this much discrepancy, we're talking about a lot of money people didn't receive. In the government and beyond."

"Bingo! This is exactly what we were looking for." She examined the last file and inhaled sharply. "We have a list of public contracts and what Malcolm's companies were paid. With names."

"Clara and I had some of these bastards at the top of our list!" Eoghan sat back and raised his arms to the sky. "Thank the heavens. We're saved."

She turned to find Liam smiling softly. He'd been quieter than usual after they'd returned home and started working on the Malcolm files. She could all but feel his ordeal seeping back into his mood. It would take some time for him to heal from it, he'd told her. Leaning over, she pressed her cheek to his, love swamping her. "We've got him."

He cupped her nape gently. "So it seems. You'll want to call Arthur."

Eoghan clapped his hands and wiggled in his chair. "They're going to be thrilled when they hear the news and see the evidence."

Taylor laughed. "They sure are. We need to send this information to our MIU right away. Anyone up for a drive to the arts center? I can call them from the media center. That way we can put them up on the big screen and see their faces as you tell them the news, Eoghan. After this, I think you need your own code name."

He pointed at himself and then let out a happy shriek. "Like you. It'll be between the two of us then. How about something like the Crow? There's no bird that's cannier than him."

"The Crow it is," she said, holding out her hand to him. "Nice to meet you. I'm Veritas."

"A pleasure," he said, lifting her hand and kissing it lightly. "Shall we head over to the arts center then?"

"I'd be delighted, sir." She rose and turned to Liam. "Do you want a code name?"

"He already has one, girl." Eoghan gave a full-fledged laugh. "It's Yoda, remember?"

She pressed her hand to her mouth, really trying not to join in. "Right. But do you like it?"

Liam shook his head ruefully. "The only thing that matters is what you call yourself, *a stór*, and I'm fine with Liam. It means helmet of will or resolute protector."

He had been her protector from the very beginning, from her physical well-being to her secret life as Veritas. Later, she would make love to him and show him how much she appreciated who he was deep down. Right now, there was Eoghan, who appreciated a good joke. "Well, you do have a helmet of will with all your meditation and breathing practices, don't you?"

Eoghan let out a trill of a laughter, and this time she joined in noisily as Liam grinned. "You two are hilarious," her soulmate commented. "I'll be in the car. Join me when you're finished. I'm not sure you can walk and laugh at the same time."

He was right. She and Eoghan were holding on to each other and snorting with laughter as they stumbled out of the house. The rain had started up again—a commonality, she was learning—so they ran to the car through puddles. Inside, she nearly sighed. Liam had turned the heat on high to warm it up for them. He got a kiss for that one.

She set the shopping bag on her lap as they sped out of the gate and onto the road. The night was dark, the kind of intense ebony that absorbed every other color around it. She couldn't even make out the newly painted Kindness Sheep in the pastures as they drove by. Which was why the orange glow above the horizon at two o'clock caught her attention.

"What is that?" she asked, pointing toward the windshield.

"Fire," Liam said after a moment. "A nasty one."

"In this rain?" Eoghan's hand was suddenly on her seat as he leaned forward. "Hard to imagine anything burning."

Also, weren't most of the houses made of concrete?

"We should call emergency." Taylor pulled out her phone, only to realize she didn't know what address to give them.

Her stomach did a flip-flop. God, it wouldn't be the arts center on fire, would it?

She wanted to think Malcolm couldn't be that cruel, but

she knew otherwise. The car was silent with their harsh breathing until Liam passed the arts center. The buildings were fine, thank God. She slumped in her seat as Liam increased his speed. The orange light looked like a tower of fire the closer they sped.

"It's my aunt Mary's house," Liam uttered quietly.

Taylor turned to look at him. His face in profile was a heartbreaking study in anger and agony. She put her hand on his thigh as he punched the gas. The flames were flickering in the rain, tongues of orange and yellow and red as he turned into a driveway.

Taylor gasped at the sight. Violent flames were licking up the concrete walls of the cottage and sweeping across the roof. She heard the sound of glass breaking and watched as a blast of fire blew through the front windows like a cannon shot.

Liam parked the car at the far end of the lane on the grass and sat there, breathing heavily next to her.

"Jesus, Mary, and Joseph," Eoghan breathed out, touching her shoulder. "Do you think she's in it?"

"No, she's gone," Liam said, taking out his phone. "I don't feel her. Plus, her car isn't in the driveway like usual. Hello, this is Liam O'Hanlon, and we've just come across a fire at Mary Kincaid's house. Yes, thank you."

"Should we get out?" Taylor asked after he hung up as the cacophony of destruction outside intensified.

"I wouldn't," Liam answered. "I'm going to text my mum."

She grew aware of the heat as the fire strengthened its hold. Reaching out, she touched the windshield and sucked in a breath. Even with the cold rain falling, the glass was hot.

"Her prized rose garden is blazing with fire," Eoghan observed from the back. "Nothing will be left."

"I imagine that was what she wanted," Liam answered cryptically.

Taylor couldn't take it anymore. She was a reporter, and she'd never been to a fire. Plus, wouldn't it be wise to take photos of this event in case someone needed them? "I'm going to get out."

Liam put his hand on her shoulder. "I won't stop you from being who you are, but keep well away from the house, *a stór*. There's more to this fire than is obvious to the eyes."

She nodded, his statement giving her chills. Exiting the car, she sucked her breath in at the blast of heat. Deciding it might be wise to cover her hair, she pulled up the hood of her jacket. The smell of smoke assaulted her, but she detected something else as Liam and Eoghan stepped out beside her.

"Do you smell gasoline?" she asked.

"It's diesel." Liam put his hand to her back protectively. "Slower to put out once it takes. I also smell peat—the kind she used to stockpile for her woodstove. She did this. I can feel her rage in the flames. I can even see her pouring diesel on her rosebushes."

"But why would she do that?" Taylor asked in shock. "It's her home. She's done everything to stay here."

"I don't know," Liam only answered sadly. "I just don't know."

She took his hand as they waited for the fire unit to arrive. The first responders began their battle, but with the diesel as an additive, they made little progress. Even with the heavy rain falling.

When Linc's Range Rover rolled up, Bets was jumping

out before it came to a stop. "Is she in there? Please, Liam, tell me she isn't in there!"

He caught her to him. "No, Mum, she's gone. Her car too."

"Oh, thank God!" Bets covered her mouth. "After what happened earlier... I wouldn't wish her well, but I don't wish her dead."

"Mum, what are you talking about?" Liam asked, taking her shoulders.

"She came by the house earlier," Bets said as Linc joined them at a brisk jog. "The Irish government canceled her benefits. She wanted us to give her money. When that didn't happen, she cursed us, Liam. Our whole family."

He went rigid at that. Taylor sucked in her breath while Eoghan made the sign of the cross over himself. She had half a mind to mime his actions.

"Can you stop a curse like this?" Taylor asked, grabbing Liam's hand. "It doesn't seem fair—"

"Don't worry." Bets turned to face Liam. "Your dad appeared, and he said some things. You'll understand better than I do, but he undid the curse. Mary set the curse with one of her dead roses, but your dad brought it back to life. He finally gave me roses, Liam. I've been a total wreck since, or I would have called you. But Linc fainted—"

"Well, shit, Bets," the man drawled with a wince.

"And now this!" Bets flung her hand out toward the burning house. "How could this happen?"

"Sugar, don't you smell it?" Linc pointed to his nose. "That's diesel in the air. No fire catches like this in a downpour. She meant to do it. Maybe to get insurance money on the house."

Taylor's mouth parted. "That's arson for sure."

"Yes," Eoghan said, "although who knows if they'll find

her. There's an old Irish saying from the great migration to America during the Famine—abandon your roses and you abandon your life."

Another chill rolled over her skin. God, these Irish sayings! "Well, that's cheery. Does that mean she's finally left our quaint little town? Because I'm new here, and I really need a vacation."

"Maybe we can manage that," Liam said, putting his arm around her waist. "Or a honeymoon."

She put her hand on his chest and met his open gaze. "You had better not be thinking about proposing to me right now, Liam O'Hanlon."

Bets socked him gently. "Hey! I raised you better than that."

He held up his hands, grinning. "I was just commenting on possibilities. Give me some credit."

Eoghan gave a hearty laugh and nudged Taylor in the ribs. "He is Yoda, after all, remember?"

Maybe the stress of everything had gotten to her, but she started to laugh along with Eoghan. They were a pair when it came to the giggles, it seemed.

"By the way..." she managed. "Linc. Bets. You should know. We think we have the evidence we need to take Malcolm down. We were on our way to the arts center when we made this pit stop."

"That's incredible news!" Bets wrapped her in a fierce hug, rocking her back a step. "Oh, God, I'm so glad you're going to be my daughter-in-law."

"*Mum.*"

"No, this is nice," she said, realizing what a crucial moment this was. Before, Bets had been jealous. Now she was embracing her like family. Taylor hugged her hard, feeling emotion clog her throat as Liam looked on, his green eyes shiny. She'd never had a mother who cared about her really, so maybe this would be nice. The woman *had* baked them bread before and cookies were around the corner, after all.

When Bets let her go, she touched her cheek softly and Taylor nodded. "We're going to have to work together to keep Yoda in line."

She gave a strangled laugh. "He's such trouble, our Yoda."

"All right, I'm butting in, because this news deserves a little more than a hug." Linc pulled Taylor into his arms and lifted her off the ground with a *yeehaw* before planting her back down and doing the same to Bets.

"Are you planning on doing the same to me, Linc Buchanan?" Eoghan called, opening his arms. "I might let you today."

Linc gave a full-wattage grin. "Might as well," he said, lifting the little man up in the air as they all laughed. "Well, friends, let's get over to our beloved arts center and take that bastard Malcolm Coveney down. So far, this has been what we call a red-letter day."

"Yeah, you *did* faint," Bets said with a cheeky grin. "I should have taken a photo."

"I'm never going to live that down." He slapped his hands together. "Taylor, wait until you see Bets' new rose. I have a hundred bucks that says it stays alive like that rose in *Beauty and the Beast*."

"You and that movie," Bets mused.

"I adore that movie," Taylor said, doing a twirl like a proper Disney princess. "I'd love to see a real magic rose."

"Actually," Bets said, "I'm betting Linc I'm going to be able to bare root it and win the rose competition with it someday."

Liam put his arm around his mother's shoulders. "I think that's what Dad intended."

They both shared a long look before she nudged him. "Why didn't you tell me your father said he approved of Linc?" she asked.

"I'll tell you on the way to the car," Liam said as he took her arm.

Linc and Eoghan both gestured for Taylor to precede them, every bit the old-world gentlemen this evening, before joining her. She took one last look over her shoulder. The tower of fire was losing its strength, rather like the two people they'd been fighting.

"So if you have the evidence on Malcolm, what's next?" Linc asked.

"Arthur writes an exposé and then hands the evidence over to the proper authorities," she answered. "Between Liam being released and someone in the government cutting Mary's benefits off, I'm starting to think we have a guardian angel."

"So long as it's not someone in ghost form." Linc shuddered. "I told Bets I couldn't take another ghost. Sorcha is enough."

That made Taylor remember how she and Liam hadn't discussed the solution to that problem yet. "I wasn't so sure what to make of her at first, but I've become a fan."

"Haven't we all?" Linc mused, his smile ticking up to the right. "I'll see you at the center."

She nodded. Eoghan touched her hand as he got into the vehicle. Liam was still speaking quietly with his mother, his hand on her cheek. She was glad they were having a moment too. Liam had sensed his mother was feeling a little out of sorts about his change in relationship status. That had upset him some, but looking at them now, they were going to sail through it just fine. They were both crying, but they were smiling too. Although she would totally ask him later about his dad showing up again. Did that mean he was going to be around too? She let out a breath. One step at a time.

She gave the fire one last look. The whole event seemed a statement about the kind of devastation some people could lay on themselves and those around them. But Liam had told her fire was cleansing, and as she gazed on it, she hoped that would be so. She also hoped they'd seen the last of Mary Kincaid.

Then she smelled oranges and smiled.

Somehow, she knew Sorcha was trying to tell her Mary Kincaid was gone but good.

CHAPTER TWENTY-NINE

L iam had never been one to pay much attention to the news.

A person could become dispirited from reading so much negativity. But once Arthur Hale's exposé was published in the newspaper he'd founded, major newspapers around the world picked it up for its tie-in with the recent news about internationally famous and beloved Veritas.

Schadenfreude was a peculiar aspect of humans, Liam thought—the pleasure one experienced from another person's troubles. Even he'd had to guard against sinking into it as the national news showed Malcolm being put into a Garda car at his Watertown office and taken to Dublin on multiple charges of corruption, fraud, money laundering, and the like. The list was endless, as were the people involved—government officials, business leaders, and even a celebrity or two.

Ireland hadn't seen such a massive story on corruption in over thirty years, and public trust had fallen to its lowest level. How many apples could be rotten in the proverbial barrel?

All of them, it seemed, and while few were surprised, no one was happy about it.

Well, no one but Arthur Hale, who arrived at the special arts center party to commemorate the story wearing an *I Am Veritas* T-shirt along with his lovely wife, who had on a thick pale green sweater she'd knitted herself.

He and Taylor were currently gathered in Kathleen's shed with the honored guests along with Trevor, Quinn, and J.T. Merriam, mostly because Clara had wanted to see the pirate ship's progress so far.

She beamed at it, and then at Taylor. "Arthur has been all rosy-cheeked and walking around with a spring in his step since this started. Thank you, Taylor. It's just the juice I needed to get him to make another trip to the village we work with in Kenya. It will be at the tail end of the migration season. Have you ever seen it? You two must come and visit!"

"It's really something else," J.T. added, standing between Trevor and Quinn. "If you can stand the flies."

Liam glanced at Taylor, who smiled and shrugged. He didn't have to read her mind to know she was game. "We'd love to," he answered.

"Wonderful!" Clara declared. "We'll make a date."

"You're also welcome to the Wild Irish Rose Inn anytime. For fun." Trevor glanced at Liam. "I still think Buttercup might set her eyes on your guy, Taylor."

The joke was lost on him as everyone around him laughed. "Who's Buttercup?"

"Their lovesick alpaca," Taylor told him, pinching his cheek. "Totally adorable. Like you. Now, Arthur, are you ready? The whole town is inside and can't wait to thank you."

The older man made an embarrassed *bah* of a sound before Clara shushed him and said, "Keep going, dear."

"Sure thing," Taylor said with a beautiful smile. "As we've discussed, no one should know that Eoghan and I made a visit to the inn or had any involvement in the article. We've covered our tracks with the small circle who knew."

"We are agreed," Arthur said solemnly. "Shall we?"

Clara took his arm and started walking to the main center. "Don't speak too long, Arthur. Public speaking is about leaving people hanging. Plus, we all want to get to the partying."

"*Hanging?*" J.T. whispered as they all followed behind the couple. "Where does she get this stuff?"

"Years with Hargreaves, maybe?" Quinn offered with a shrug. "Liam, that's my aunt's former butler—he's a year older than she is."

"Sounds like he'd fit in well at our arts center," Liam commented.

"He would," Quinn said with a laugh. "His artistry is incredible. Taylor, have you been to his chocolate shop outside of Manhattan?"

"Of course! He and Alice had the best treats outside France, if you ask me. And his chocolate sculptures are works of art."

She liked chocolate, did she? Liam filed that away for the future.

"Before everything gets crazy," she said as they stopped outside the door, "please thank Connor and Flynn for their help. I know they had to head back to their families in the States."

"Ouch," J.T. said, clutching his heart. "You make me sound like a bad guy for staying. Actually, Caroline and I are meeting up in Paris since I'm over here. Michaela and Boyd agreed to babysit. Connor did want me to tell you something, though. Your donation to the homeless center totally choked him up—which still gets me right here. He wasn't expecting that."

She hadn't told Liam about that yet. Ah, his soulmate. He watched as she ducked her head and said, "Please! It's for a great cause. Besides, Louisa helped organize an *I Am Veritas* protest. I wanted to do something. Also, Trevor, here..."

Liam watched as she handed him an envelope. Looking puzzled, Trevor slit it open and looked inside, then threw his head back and laughed before hugging her. "You're the best! Becca will love it."

"Let me see," J.T. said, grabbing the envelope and holding it out so the others could see it too.

Liam felt his throat catch as he read it. She'd gotten him a gift certificate to a major paint store. To refill the supply they'd used on her Waterford mural.

"God, that's a good one," J.T. said, giving her a high five. "Hey! You should start your own paint line, Taylor, as—"

"Watch it!" Trev said, smacking him on the shoulder.

"Ouch. Just saying. Quinn, couldn't the new Merriam Enterprises set her up with an anonymous line or something?"

Quinn rubbed his jaw. "I could talk to Francesca about it if you want... She apologized for being MIA today. Big construction meeting."

Taylor was clearly mulling through the possibility of a Veritas paint line, so Liam took the opportunity to ask Quinn, "You guys build things? How big?"

"As big as you need it," Quinn deadpanned. "Old joke. Why?"

He thought it over. "Well, I'd need to do more research and talk to Linc and the board, but the truth is, we have a lot of building to do here. We have a major Irish contractor involved for the hotel—our priority since there's nowhere close to stay—but they don't think they can handle the museum at the same time. We haven't been happy with the groups we've met with so far. How did we not know about you?"

"We're new to Ireland," Quinn said. "Our portfolio has been abroad, but we're making inroads. Check us out. We'd be happy to talk about what you have in mind."

Liam could already feel the energy pulsing in the air. Suddenly the very ground beneath him was vibrating with power. Yeah, this was going to work. But he would follow procedure by researching and interviewing them. Taylor must have sensed what he was feeling because she raised her eyebrow in his direction and said, "Well, isn't that a nice possibility? Umm... As for the other, I'm not sure. I'll need to think about it."

J.T. lifted his finger. "One more sales pitch. Think of all the good you could do with the money. Philanthropy is a beautiful thing. I know you have a great job here, but you'd be terrific at it."

She would be, Liam thought, as more aligned energy swirled around them. Well, another thing for them to talk about when they got home.

"I'll get back to you," she said, "but you make a good argument. Now, we really should go inside. Arthur is probably already finished."

Only he hadn't even made it to his seat beside the podium, they discovered, since he was being cheered and praised by the entire town of Caisleán. Ghislaine finally took matters into her own hands, calling him up to the podium with a joke about hearing the pub was closing soon, which had everyone rushing for their seats.

Liam cast a glance at Donal, who was grinning and nudging Linc as they sat down in their chairs on the stage. Liam could almost hear Donal praising his wife for all the hard work she'd done. Taylor was excited to start taking up more of the reins as she went from being the lead story to writing up the stories.

Sorcha had done good there as well, he thought, seeing as both women had come to Ireland to help the arts center and meet their soulmates. He tucked his hand in his pocket to finger the piece of paper with one of Sorcha's poems on it. He and Taylor had agreed they were going to take care of the last of things after they listened to Arthur's speech.

They were going to make their plea on Sorcha's behalf.

Arthur was laughing as he took the podium, the lights catching his clear spectacles as he surveyed the crowd. "You're all too much. I'm just an old man—although not at old as your Eoghan O'Dwyer over there." He pointed and the two shared a colossal grin. "Now, I should probably get serious as my beautiful wife told me to keep it short. I'm also a journalist, and I don't have to tell you that I cut my teeth in a different age of journalism. It's depressing as hell to watch people call themselves serious journalists and report outright lies and falsehoods in the sacred thing we call the news."

Liam could see the light around Arthur expand as he talked, and he was aware of a great swell of gratitude rising inside him. He was witnessing a speech given by a great man, one who had done a lot of good in the world. Liam sent up a blessing that he would live many more years, and in his heart, he felt it would be granted. He and Clara would live long, full lives, doing more good wherever they went.

"We had a great victory," Arthur continued, pointing his finger at the crowd, "and it all started here with you good people. I'm from a small town in the States, only a little bigger than yours, but I had a dream to build something that mattered, something that would help the community and the world. My contribution was a newspaper, and what you have here is an arts center. Both are important institutions of truth, and for that, we share a pact to fight off the darkness of censorship, falsehood, and a curtailing of our very expression. I can't wait to see all that you do here, and I'm glad it's easy to pop up from Kinsale to Caisleán when my wife and I come to Ireland. The truth is, we plan to visit often, but we also welcome you to come and see us in our Irish hood, as Clara likes to call it. I'm going to make sure Trevor puts up a sign that says *Fáilte*."

Cheers rose to a high decibel as Arthur finished. To Liam's mind, he couldn't have ended it better than with the Gaelic callout for Welcome. Taylor was clapping and hollering at the top of her lungs when Liam caught Ghislaine's nod as the Frenchwoman stepped to the podium.

He touched Taylor's arm, and she turned to him with a beaming smile before saying, "Break a leg, babe."

He felt full of love, for her and for the village, as he made his way onto the stage. The crowd quieted, and he gave them a smile as he leaned toward the microphone. "Hiya, everyone. I'm the last on this program of sorts before the party starts and the whiskey flows."

Laughter crested through the crowd.

"We all were touched by the life of Sorcha Fitzgerald, who was taken from us too soon, and after whom this very arts center is named."

He glanced over at Carrick, who was smiling softly as he held his new baby next to his wife. Sorcha had begun her matchmaking duties to bring them together. Now her calling would end with Liam and Taylor, and the circle would be complete.

"We all know she's stayed around in true Irish form after her passing, matchmaking and helping as she could. And since we are honoring our good fortune as an arts center and town today, me and a few others thought it fitting to honor Sorcha. So if you'd follow me outside to her favorite tree, we'd like to do a little something along those lines."

He and the other men Sorcha had helped in her match-making duties headed back to the room where they'd stored the offering that had come to Liam in meditation. No one said anything as they picked the baskets up. Somehow it was understood that nothing *should* be said to interrupt the solemnness of what they were doing.

The crowd was standing in a fan shape before Sorcha's favorite oak tree, and Liam took his position in front as he felt its roots spread love and happiness. "Sorcha used to write her poetry here when the weather allowed—as it so kindly did today. I wanted to read one I thought was perfect for today after everything we have faced together."

What will you do to bring me joy when I am sad?
What beauty will you offer me when my soul is hungry?
What word will you give me when the ebony Irish seas are against us?

I may not know, the wind answered, but I will try.
And if you need light, I will speak to fire to brighten your path.

Should you desire love, I will bring you a companion to fill your days.

For our roads should never be walked alone.
We have each other.
And in having each other, we have everything.

He had to clear his throat at the end. They *did* have everything, and he was grateful for it. "She was wise, our Sorcha, and she was quick with a kind word when one of us needed it, almost as much as she was quick with a pot of cold soup when one of us stepped out of line. Right, Carrick?"

His friend had tears in his eyes as he gave a shaky laugh along with others in the crowd.

"I know I am deeply thankful to Sorcha for many things —ones I never told her. I figured many of you felt the same. Everyone knows her favorite scent was oranges, and even today, we still smell her signature scent around the village. I thought it fitting that everyone take a stem of orange blossoms, which Linc was kind enough to send off for, and lay it at the foot of her favorite tree as a tribute to her. Whatever words are in your heart will be heard. Of that I am sure. Carrick? Would you like to be the first, seeing as how she held your name?"

His friend shared a loving smile with Angie, who was crying beautiful tears, before he walked forward with baby Emeline and picked up a stem filled with delicate white blossoms. Carrick laid the branch at the base of the tree and then touched a hand to its trunk, his head bowed. Tears ran down the faces of many he knew before the little baby girl lurched forward in his arms and touched the tree with him, making a few in the crowd gasp. Seeing that, Liam thought, was good and right. Another circle complete. He could see the little girl singing and running around the tree with other children. Sorcha would wish it so. She had loved this spot, and now the whole village would share it to honor her.

When Carrick was done, Angie came forward next and did the same, brushing at tears, and after that the whole village stepped forward and paid their respects. The perfume of the orange blossoms wrapped around them, the scent one of the most beautiful Liam had ever smelled, save Taylor when she woke in his arms.

When everyone was finished, he spotted Taylor waiting for him with a branch in her hands. They'd agreed to go last, sealing this moment for themselves alone, being the final couple Sorcha had helped. He picked up a branch himself and met her halfway to the tree. When he took her hand, something sparked between them. He felt a glorious rumble under his feet, and as they laid their branches on the pile arranged as a tribute made to their beloved friend, a flash of white light arced out of the base of the tree and then lit the sky.

He heard Taylor's exclamation before she turned to him and gripped his coat. "Wow, that's got to be a sign, right?"

His heart was pulsing in time with the earth's heartbeat now, and that seemed fitting too as he lowered to a knee before her, taking her hand.

Her brown eyes widened, and then she smiled like a well-satisfied cat. "Of course you'd do it here and now."

He was chuckling as he used his free hand to bring out the ring he'd selected with Linc's help only days before on a quick day trip to Paris. The small diamonds swirled like stars in the silver band, something he'd thought she would like. But it was what he'd inscribed that still made his heart fill with light.

"Taylor McGowan, I love you with all my heart, and I want to spend the rest of my days with you, sharing our very souls with each other. Will you marry me?"

She knelt until she was in front of him and took his hand, her gaze soft and direct. "Yes, Liam O'Hanlon. I will marry you. Happily."

They leaned forward and kissed softly, and in the background he heard a shower of applause from bystanders on the hill.

"Even though I *barely* know you," she joked, "and we're still working out our morning bathroom routine."

"I have a plan for that," he bandied back, kissing her again. "You're going to shower with me to start things."

She made a humming sound, kissing the corner of his mouth. "Good plan, Yoda."

He raised his brow.

"*What?* I happen to like it, and since you didn't pick another code name, you're stuck with it. Now, what about our honeymoon? Please tell me we're not going to Bali."

He fought a laugh. "I seriously considered it."

She gave him a playful cross look. "But you knew I'd smack you, right, being the mind reader you are?"

"Exactly!" He waited a beat, loving the playful light in her beautiful brown eyes. "How about Paris? I saw myself with you there."

"I love Paris!" she said enthusiastically. "But I have this great idea..."

He bit his lip to keep from smiling as he'd already seen it in meditation. "Yes..."

"I think we take the opportunity to create a diversion. Eoghan—the Crow—thought it would be smart to have Veritas show up somewhere else and soon. Plus, I really loved painting with you, and what better way to lay a trail that doesn't lead to us than doing a mural on our honeymoon? I mean, no one in their right minds would think of something that fantastical. Plus, there's this falsely incarcerated artist in Mali who—"

"We can talk about it," he said, because he knew she wanted the opportunity to persuade him. Deliciously, of course, as she liked to say. He loved that she was so eager to share another mural with him after all the years she'd gone it alone. He knew it was an honor, one that cemented their partnership.

"You should really look at the inscription inside the ring," he told her, sitting back on his heels. "I saved the best for last."

Her look was puzzled, but she turned the ring to the light. He watched as her lips mouthed *You are my truth.* Then launched herself at him before pressing back. "Are you kidding me? God, that's so going to make me cry, and I never cry. *I'm your truth?*"

He watched as she fought those precious tears she loathed shedding. "You're that and more," he said simply, touching her thigh.

She nodded, wiping one away as it fell. "That's the sweetest thing *anyone* has ever said to me."

The reverence with which she slipped the ring on her finger was a moment he knew he'd remember forever. Suddenly a dozen little robins flew around them, almost as if in delight. She laughed as she pointed to the birds, her expression comical, and then she cupped his jaw and kissed him soundly on the mouth. "You're my truth too."

He wrapped his arms around her. "And I have the T-shirt to prove it," he joked, wanting to hear her laugh, which she did, falling against him as his mouth sought and found hers again.

The scent of orange blossoms intensified then, and he heard in the background another wonderful sound—Sorcha's laughter—and knew their tribute had done its job.

EPILOGUE
THREE YEARS LATER...

F inally—after all the struggles and setbacks, after all the heartache, Bets took a deep breath and cut the red ribbon across the doors of the Sorcha Fitzgerald Museum.

Cheers erupted from the crowd who'd come for the opening ceremony. She turned to Linc, and they grinned at each other like little children.

"We did it!" she cried out, launching herself at him as the press greedily snapped up photos.

"Whoa, watch those scissors, sugar." He kissed her sweetly on the mouth, holding her gaze in the brilliant sunlit day, surely a gift from the art gods. "*You* did it. We all just jumped on board and helped you push this baby where you wanted her to go."

"Revisionist history, but I can't argue with anything today," she said with a laugh. "We *all* did it."

Ghislaine handed her a microphone, satisfaction dancing around her. "But you laid it down. Great work, Bets! Now, do your thing."

"The Sorcha Fitzgerald Museum is hereby open!" The mike gave feedback over the loudspeaker, making her and probably everyone else wince. "Sorry, folks. I got carried away. I know you guys want to get to touring the museum and starting the party, but I wanted to thank a few people who've made today possible. I'm Bets O'Hanlon, by the way."

Laughter spilled through the crowd.

"You are?" some upstart called. "I thought you looked like my cousin Patricia from County Kerry."

She groaned along with a few others. "Reporters—and most especially people in my village, the beautiful Caisleán, like to call me the founder of what you see here. Truly, when I first had the idea to start an arts center in the wilds of Ireland to serve our community and bring in new people and ideas, I only thought to ask my family for help. My son, Liam, didn't roll his eyes at his crazy ol' mum when I asked him to remodel one of the sheds at my house. Thanks for that, Liam."

Taylor nudged him with her elbow, prompting him to give her a thumbs-up.

Bets grinned as her other two boys jostled their younger brother. Rhys and Wyatt had come up from South Africa for the opener, and seeing all three of them together filled her heart with joy.

She had to pull her gaze away from them to continue her speech. "Then I called my cousin, Angie Newcastle, who'd just lost her job heading up an arts center in the U.S. I thought maybe I could help a girl out while kick-starting my arts center with some painting classes. That worked out pretty well, didn't it, Angie?"

Her cousin juggled her newborn and pointed at Carrick. "I got more than I bargained for."

Didn't we all? she thought, as she gestured to the rolling hills around them. "That's Ireland for you. Well, for those

AVA MILES

of you who don't know, we secured our second artist at the same time because she tagged along with Angie. They're sisters, in case you can't see the resemblance. Megan Bennet went back to teaching ceramics, much to the delight of our own Keegan O'Malley, best known for the Kindness Sheep, who connected with his wife in one of her classes."

A few people let out a whistle as Keegan turned to Lisa Ann and kissed her enthusiastically on the mouth.

"That's love and art in action," she called, stopping to applaud as people joined in.

"Where are the sheep?" someone shouted.

Bets shielded her eyes and pointed off toward the left fields. "That way. Watch the muck if you take the now famous Kindness Sheep tour. Yes, in case you didn't know, we have one. And it's free to the public—just like our museum. Moving on..."

She took a moment to gather herself, reaching out a hand to Linc, her love, her cowboy. "This next part gets even more personal for me. Angie sent out a want ad of sorts for artists to come to our center, and that's when we got Ellie Buchanan. She blew in with a ton of passion and a burgeoning cred in stained glass. Make sure you see her incredible work in our arts center, okay?"

Her most emotional moment was here at last, and she took a deep breath before saying, "Ellie brought one of the best gifts of my life—this man right here. Linc Buchanan wasn't part of my plan, which only goes to show how you never know who might show up and what they can do to enrich your life."

He muttered, "Aw, shucks," and she met his gaze as her heart thundered in her chest.

She saw in those sparkly baby blues not only the passion they'd shared last night but what they were going to share every day for the rest of their lives—love, commitment, fun, partnership, and purpose. God, she was so lucky!

She cleared her throat and turned back to her speech. "Linc's been by my side ever since, and his incredible skills and resources have helped us take this place to where we are today. He started in windows, and now he's helping with everything at the arts center. A round of applause for my cowboy, Linc Buchanan."

He ducked his head like usual and waved off the cacophony of praise from the crowd before gesturing for her to continue.

She pointed next to Kathleen, who was holding hands with Declan. "There's no mistaking the historic metal sculpture we're also unveiling today. Kathleen O'Connor's gigantic pirate ship can be seen for miles across Ireland. It's taken three years to build, but it's going to wow people for decades and more—like everything else our arts center builds. Which includes another work of art, also three years in the making, by Sophie Giombetti. Once we clear the path to the museum, her gorgeous goddess glass installation with the Celtic tree is going to be the first thing you see. Let me give you a hint. It will leave your jaw hanging open."

She made a show of dropping said jaw and then rolling it back up, wanting to keep the crowd entertained. "Inside the museum, you're also going to see the work of other artists such as Hans Shumaker. I'm going to stop there so I don't spoil any more surprises. But one work I *do* want to mention upfront is the masterpiece by our beloved resident artist, Eoghan O'Dwyer. Eoghan, hold up your hand."

The little man was grinning and blushing as he waved to the crowd with one hand, holding Sandrine's hand with the other.

"Ask anyone, but Eoghan is one of our local heroes.

Actually, he's more than that. He's what the center means to this community: a fresh start, a way to continue to be vital, and a means to share and give to others."

She had to pause as huge tears rolled down his face, choking her up. "He started taking a painting class with Angie in the beginning and then continued to broaden into ceramics and stained glass. Only last month, he celebrated his ninety-seventh birthday, and he's still going strong, traveling around Europe for gallery shows for his acclaimed art in painting and ceramics, his favorites now. His painting inside this museum is of his dear brother—an artist who died decades ago—watching Eoghan paint in his studio from his heavenly perch with a whiskey in hand. It shouldn't be missed. It's the kind of painting that tells a story we all hope for: that when we lose the people we love, they still watch over us. Help us keep on with this thing we call life."

She thought about Bruce—and, of course, Sorcha. Surely, the powers that governed the other side would let her appear today. No one had seen her in the three years since they'd won their battle of good versus evil and the last of her matchmaking charges had come together, and while Liam had told her they'd sent Sorcha off well with the tribute of orange blossoms, Bets still wanted another moment, which was funny when she thought about all those early times when she didn't want to see her pop in. My, how things had changed. Surely this victory belonged to Sorcha too.

Linc's hand tightening around her own helped bring her back. "I also want to thank Donal O'Dwyer—you know why." They traded a smile before Bets looked over to find his wife. "And Ghislaine—the dynamo publicist we couldn't have done without before Taylor McGowan came in with guns blazing. She's my daughter-in-law, folks, so forgive me if I get a little choked up talking about how much joy she's brought into my life, both personally and professionally."

Taylor gave a playful curtsy before linking her arm through Liam's.

"I'll finish by thanking our incredible contractors. The Togalai Group, who made the beautiful hotel many of you are staying at. And thank you to Quinn Merriam and Francesca Maroun's company for building this beautiful museum designed by the one and only Tom Sarkesian. Pretty soon we'll be dedicating our children's museum, so we'll have to come back and do this again."

The whistling and the cheering grew as Linc popped a bottle of champagne he'd grabbed from the nearby table and shook it, showering the spray over the sidewalk leading up to the museum, making people snort with laughter around them. Thankfully, Brady was more responsible. He popped another bottle of champagne, shooting the cork into the blue sky as if it were a firecracker before pouring bubbly into the glasses they'd set aside for the champagne toast in the VIP section.

Bets was so ready for some bubbly. "Linc clearly has a secret wish to be an Indy car racer or something. Anyway, everyone, the museum is open for touring. Now, let's start the party. We have a band coming to play and a whole host of food and beverages for you to enjoy on this fine August day."

Linc pressed a glass of champagne into her hand with a naughty wink, and suddenly everyone in their VIP circle was lifting their glasses to each other, saying, "Sláinte!"

The crisp champagne was a delight to her taste buds, and she took another sip as she studied the dear people who'd been on this crazy journey with her. Liam and Taylor stood beside her along with her other two boys while the rest of their VIP artists, employees, and employee guests fanned out to the right of the museum's front. "Can you believe it? We did it!"

A chorus of cheers went up, and Brady made everyone laugh as he began asking who wanted more champagne when it was clear no one had finished their first glass yet.

"He just can't leave the pub," Ellie joked to the Merriam contingent beside her. J.T. and his wife Caroline had come all the way from Dare Valley for the museum's opening, along with Trevor and Becca, up from Kinsale. But it was Arthur Hale and Clara Merriam Hale who made Bets smile the brightest.

"I still say, Linc," she said, leaning over to her cowboy and kissing his jaw, "we have our *live it up into our eighties* model with Arthur and Clara there. They just got back from another harrowing trip to Kenya. Arthur told me he had to paddle past a huge crocodile that had appeared alongside their boat."

Linc gave her a disgruntled look. "Sugar, I love you, but Ireland is wild enough for me. I've got no interest in crossing paths with crocs or any other man-eaters. And I certainly don't want to paddle anything in treacherous waters."

Neither did she really. "Trip to Paris then?"

"Right after this here hoopla cools down," he told her, tapping their glasses together. "We have a lot to celebrate. I mean all this arts center fun and your recent rose competition win..."

She gave in to wiggling her hips, nearly spilling her champagne. "That *is* one of my best wins, and you know why."

Linc had been a little freaked out in the beginning

when she'd gotten Mary's formerly dead rose, resurrected by Bruce, to bare root. Three years later, only last week, she'd presented the rose judges with her largest rose ever, topping out at twenty-eight inches. The rose wasn't scary black or frighteningly thorny like the dead blossom Mary Kincaid had thrown at her feet. No, Bets' plant had vibrant green canes with delicate thorns leading to a deep burgundy rose the color of Linc's favorite French Bordeaux.

The smell was somewhere shy of heaven and always reminded her of Bruce in the best of ways. She no longer resented the limits of their marriage. His help on that day had allowed her to forgive herself and him all the way and freed up space in her heart for more in her life. Which definitely included trips to Paris and long nights of passionate sex with her cowboy.

"We're leaving the minute Rhys and Wyatt take off," she told Linc, caressing his back.

He waggled his brows playfully. "Consider it booked. I might ask Liam to pack for you again. All you're going to need is a toothbrush, sugar."

Her blood heated at that idea, but she gave him a good sock like Clara would Arthur, which had him clutching his arm playfully.

"Speaking of your baby boy," he drawled. "Liam! You want to give your mama her thank-you gift now?"

She swung to look at her son. "You didn't have to do that! I should have gotten you guys something."

Taylor gave an indelicate snort of laughter. "Remember you said that, Bets."

Liam took the red gift bag Ellie handed him from the VIP table beside the museum doors decked out in flowers and French champagne chilling in buckets. "Here you go,

Mum. I hope you'll always remember how much we love you when you look at this."

"Curious statement…" Bets muttered, noticing from the corner of her eye that everyone leaned closer expectantly as she opened the bag and peered inside. "It's a— Plastic duck."

Her daughter-in-law was the queen of wacky gifts. Sure, it was a happy one in sunshine yellow with playful eyelashes, and it was life size. She drew it out and did her best to give Liam and Taylor a big smile. "I love it."

Taylor grinned. "It's for your rose garden."

Because her roses needed the company of a giant plastic duck who could bat her eyelashes? It might terrify her babies and make them drop their petals. She would put it in Linc's bath as a joke.

"Look inside, Mum," Liam suggested.

Her brow knit. "Huh?"

"Gimme." Taylor grabbed the duck and split it open at the seam, handing it back to Bets. "It's child-proofed, obviously."

"Obviously," she said, eyeing the pink fabric inside. "What's this? A T-shirt?"

"We thought you needed something else to wear today," Taylor said brightly, linking her arm through Liam's. Both of them were grinning at her along with her other boys.

She unfolded the shirt and saw the words PROUD GRANDMA. She screamed. Jumping up and down, she clutched the shirt to her chest. "Oh, you two!"

"Land sakes, Bets," Linc drawled, taking the shirt from her clutches. "What's got you all—"

He let out a whoop when he saw the message before kissing her soundly on the mouth and then sneaking over to pluck Taylor off the ground.

Taylor cried out in delight as Linc spun her around. "We got you a T-shirt too, Grandpa!"

Bets turned to Liam. Radiant love shone on his face. "We're expecting, Mum."

She rushed him. "I didn't think I could take waiting much longer for a grandbaby."

"You're not the one having the baby," Taylor said dryly as Linc set her back down. "Now seemed like a good time with the museum finished and—"

"Isn't it wonderful?" Liam squeezed her tight. "We needed to do it in our own time, Mum, but now it's here."

"Takes the pressure off me and Wyatt," Rhys joked, wiping his forehead in relief.

She shot him a look as she let go of her son to give another happy wiggle, pulling her T-shirt on over her head. "You young people, planning a baby around buildings. But I forgive you. Come here, Mama."

Taylor was beaming after they hugged. "Congrats, Grandma."

God, how she loved the sound of that. "Congrats to you too. Both of you! Wait! Why isn't anyone else going crazy?"

The whole group of friends was grinning knowingly.

Brady wiped his brow. "Keeping this news a secret tested everyone. The whole village was in on it. When Taylor got served a drink, for cover purposes only, someone else would switch it out with theirs when you weren't looking."

"We thought it might be the kind of triple-decker of news days for you, being on the date of the museum opening." Liam righted her shirt, pulling it down over her navy pants until the hem was even. "Heck, Mum, today might be one of the best of your life."

Her heart was suddenly in her throat, and she cast a

glance over to the original Lucky Charms—Nicola, Siobhan, and Brigid. They had known her highs and lows and been with her through it all, and her three friends lifted their glasses to her, because they understood what this day meant. "My cup overflows, as they say."

"About time, don't you think?" Linc bandied back with a grin.

She had a new rose trophy, a museum, and a grandbaby on the way. "Oh, I'm just thrilled. I'm—" Tears welled up and she uttered a wild squeak. "I-I'm having a grandbaby."

Linc was right there to put his arm around her, tipping up her chin. "Oh, sugar. Don't cry. This is a time for celebration. A big one."

The back of her neck was on fire, which was spreading to her face. Emotion clawed at her throat. "I know. It's just—"

She was starting a complete meltdown. Right in front of the museum, and she wasn't supposed to be a sideshow on the tour.

"I'm going to—"

Since her voice had stopped working, she pointed desperately to Sorcha's tree on the lower end of the pasture.

Linc kissed her softly. "Yeah, you go on and take a moment."

She was unsteady on her feet as she walked off, hearing Linc call, "Now, where's my T-shirt?"

When she reached Sorcha's tree, she wanted to put her head against the trunk and go to pieces. She looked down at PROUD GRANDMA, hoping it would knock her back into her happy place, but she continued to utter hiccup sobs. She was going to have a grandbaby. A little person she could play with and make cookies with and chase around. They could make cool stuff together. God, if it was a girl, they could make stuff with glitter. And glue. She sucked in more breaths as she cried. *Why glitter?* She didn't know. She only knew it had to be a deep pink.

"You're having a proper meltdown, aren't you, Bets?"

She uttered a loud shriek as Sorcha appeared beside her, her long brown hair blowing in the wind while her bright green eyes glittered with happiness.

"I'd hoped you'd come!" She gave another sob. "You look different. Your dress—"

"I got an upgrade," Sorcha said, gesturing to her formfitting silver clothes. "I had to make some amends for what I did, but the village's tribute helped. Your Bruce also put in a good word for me, and since we last met, I've more or less been on the guardian track."

Bets scrubbed her wet face, sucking in breaths to calm herself. "Your clothes are like Bruce's too! That means... God, I'm talking like I know what it means, and I don't. Care to enlighten me?"

Sorcha touched the trunk of her favorite tree, and Bets swore she saw the bark shift momentarily into a grandmotherly face. "We protect the land and the people who respect it. We right wrongs. Battle along with those who would bring more love, kindness, and goodness into the world. It started out for me as matchmaking, but my duties expanded. Largely because of you, Bets. I'm here to thank you."

This was all too much. She wiped at more tears. "But *you* helped bring us all the best gift. Our soulmates. Sorcha, I have Linc because of you, and Liam has Taylor, and—"

"Yes," she said proudly, "I'm more than satisfied with our dear couples. It's going to be my privilege to watch over their lives. There will be so many good things to behold."

Maybe it was wearing a PROUD GRANDMA T-shirt,

but Bets wanted a preview of coming attractions. "Tell me what I can expect."

Sorcha only raised a brow before laughing heartily. The tree branches whispered then, and she smiled as if it had spoken something special to her. "It seems I have special dispensation to tell you, Bets O'Hanlon, in thanks for all you have done for this land and the people of Caisleán, although your work will extend far beyond this village. Who should I start with?"

"Angie and Carrick!" She was suddenly breathless. "They were the first couple, after all."

Sorcha glanced off, and Bets wondered if she was looking in the direction where they stood. "They already have two beautiful children, and they will have two more. Three girls and one boy. Two of the girls will continue in their parents' professions while the other two will go their own way."

An artist and someone in sheep. "Wonderful. Next?"

"Kade and Megan already love Ollie and their other two children to pieces, but they will also have twenty-six more horses and thirty-nine dogs—"

"*Sorcha!*"

The ghost—ahem guardian—laughed. "You don't want to know about the animals? Bets, I think you'd love hearing that the Kindness Sheep tradition will continue in Ireland for another three hundred years. You know how we Irish love our traditions."

That was one of the things she most loved about them. "Tell me about Ellie and Brady."

Tapping a finger to her smiling lips, she leaned forward conspiratorially. "Three girls. All publicans. Although only one will stay at the Brazen Donkey... Because this pub is one for generations."

"I'm glad for that. The whole village loves it."

"Yes, it does. Moving on to Kathleen and Declan. They will also have three children. All boys. One will go back to Boston to work in Kathleen's family pub. But the best news, perhaps, given my former duties, is that one of Brady and Ellie's girls will marry one of Declan and Kathleen's sons. It's going to be fun to watch."

"I can't wait!" She went to clutch Sorcha's hand in excitement, only to touch air. "Forget I tried that. We're on Sophie and Jamie."

"We are." Sorcha somehow managed to lean against the tree despite not having a solid form. "They already have Greta and their lovely little boy. They will have another girl, and she will outrival her mother in glass. One day, her work will be seen in the museum you and this community have built. Shall we go on to your Liam and Taylor, Grandma?"

She gave an indelicate sniff. "Yes..."

"They will have three children as well, the girl Taylor is carrying now and two boys to come. Twins. The girl will have Liam's green eyes and ever-calm demeanor while the boys will want to decorate every wall in your home with paint and pink glitter." Her brow furrowed. "Bets, there is a lot of pink glitter in your future."

"The boys like the glitter?" She bent over laughing. "And here I thought—"

"Never make assumptions, Bets," Sorcha said, her lips twitching as she straightened. "The boys call it fairy sparkles—a turn of phrase from Eoghan before he passes—at the ripe age of one hundred and seven, I might add."

She gave a big sniff at that. "I'm glad we'll have him for so long."

"Sandrine as well." Sorcha drew a heart in the air.

"Love keeps the mind, heart, and body young, but back to the glitter. A plus for you is... Linc is going to love it. He's even going to glue those fairy sparkles on their cowboy boots one Christmas and teach them how to lasso Kindness Sheep."

That got her. She blew out a breath. "So Linc is good, huh? Healthy—"

"You two are going to cruise into your hundreds—like Eoghan and Sandrine and Arthur and Clara for that matter. Like I said before, love is the most powerful force on earth. But so is purpose, and you finally have what you've always wanted. This arts center and the museum will have sister centers in the United States, France, the United Kingdom— even Australia. My name will grace buildings in countries I never visited, and while people will not know me or my story always, they will know my name stands for art and creative expression. For that I thank you as well."

She was dazed by the news. Sister centers? In all those places? "Oh my God! I'm in shock."

Sorcha's signature scent suddenly saturated the air, making Bets cough.

"There, that will help knock you back into your senses," she said in a delighted voice. "I might also mention Donal and Ghislaine will be your friends into your hundreds. They also have a long life ahead, and they will be instrumental in leading the opening of the sister centers I mentioned. Donal has a new purpose too, Bets, one the two of you helped each other find. You may not have been soulmates, but you will remark in your later years that Donal is one of your best friends. Not that he ever dances to Bon Jovi with you like the Lucky Charms do. They will be well too, in case you're wondering."

She was glad to hear the news. Her vision was a little

blurry, but a smile had set sail on her mouth. "Donal would look ridiculous wearing a boa and wiggling his butt."

Sorcha's shoulders shook with laughter. "Perhaps, but I'd still come back to watch."

"I hope you do." She stared at the woman, her heart brimming with feeling. "Will you? Can you?"

Her smile was a touch of the old Sorcha—absolutely mischievous. "Perhaps. The scent of oranges will always be here in Caisleán when it's needed to lift a mood or comfort a soul. As for the other, we will see."

"I hope so." Bets clutched her hands together. "I wish I could hug you or something."

"Close your eyes," Sorcha commanded gently.

Bets squeezed her eyes shut. The wind rose up and gently wrapped around her, its warm breeze ruffling her clothes and hair. The fresh orange scent of it cleared away the last of her tears. Love overflowed in her heart like a champagne fountain.

"There. That's the best I can do."

She opened her eyes. Sorcha's own were even more brilliant now, and her silver garments were shot through with so much light it should have been blinding. Only...it was captivating, the kind of light you never wanted to look away from. It reminded her of Bruce and suddenly she had to ask.

"Will I see Bruce again?"

Sorcha drew a circle on her palm. "He will come back around, like the seasons, when the time is right. He's asked to matchmake the next generation, proposing a break from his guardian duties. But that is far off."

Bruce would be the new Sorcha for her grandchildren and the others? "Oh, I love that. I'll...lay roses at this tree and ask for it to happen. Our tribute worked with you, didn't it?"

"It did indeed." She nodded decisively. "I didn't understand it when I walked among you before, but my last piece of advice is simple. Ask for what you want. You are loved. The powers who give wish for you to be happy. Open your arms to receive all the goodness available to you. It will come."

She heard cheering then, up on the hill. "It already has and then some."

"I will leave you to the party." She looked up, her oval face in profile. "I always loved a good party. Have a glass of champagne, Bets, and party on."

They shared a smile. "I'll lift my glass to you with everyone and toast, 'She was one hell of a ghost, our Sorcha.'"

Her laughter was as light as air. "Apt. I like it. Enjoy your life, Betsy O'Hanlon. You deserve it!"

She vanished, taking the gentle breeze with her. Bets drew in a deep breath and then raced back up the hill. She found Linc and her loved ones chatting together while standing in the front row of the outdoor concert area. The last preparations for the band Linc had hired looked to be coming together as the setup crew had vacated the stage.

"Hi, I'm back," she announced as she cozied up to Linc's side in the middle of the row, where he was conversing with Ellie and Taylor while Liam and Brady chatted about something Brady was pointing to in the distance. Oh, it was the Kindness Sheep, corralled by rope and guarded by Keegan, Carrick, and...

Was that her Bruce?

It was! With a smile on his radiant face.

Linc took her chin and turned her face side to side, his blue eyes warm with love. "Your mascara didn't run too much...Grandma."

She scrubbed under her eyes, smiling at hearing her new moniker. "This grandma has news..." she whispered so only he would hear. "For later. I saw Sorcha."

His brows flew to his forehead. "I was hoping we'd see that girl. Hold tight to the news, sugar. I'll want a full account later."

She took Linc's hand, tangling her fingers with his. A sudden thought struck her. Sorcha had told her she and Linc were going to be together another... She did the math. Holy moly, another forty-some years! Were they ever going to get married? Sorcha hadn't said. Did they need to? Then she stopped getting riled up. If she and Linc wanted to get married, they would. But only if it would make them happy. Right now, she couldn't imagine being happier, and that was all that was important.

"Earth to Bets." Linc shook her hand. "Wait for this announcement, sugar. Everyone! I have something to tell you all."

The conversations ground to a halt with a bark of Brady's laughter being the final sound, making him wince at those around him.

"Well, I know y'all thought you did real good keeping the secret about Taylor and Liam having a baby from me and Bets, but if we were voting on who had the hardest secret to keep, I'd win hands down."

Over a grandbaby?

"Linc Buchanan, you have totally lost your marbles."

"Yeah, Daddy," Ellie said with an eye roll. "Everyone knows a baby trumps everything."

His shit-eating grin was in full glory. "You think so? We're about to find out. You see, I arranged for some music tonight, as you know. But I told a little fib about who'd be performing. It's not some piddly little band."

Bets and a few others gasped.

"It's actually one of the biggest bands in the world," Linc added with a cocky wink.

Ellie and Taylor turned to each other and started jumping up and down, scream-crying in unison, "Oh my God! U2!"

Bets' mouth dropped. Okay, she could feel a scream catching in her throat too.

Linc winced and held up a hand. "Calm on down. It's not U2. Although Bono volunteered. They just didn't seem right for this event."

Bets gaped in shock as everyone's faces fell.

Ellie's lip started to wobble. "You turned Bono down? Dad...I thought you loved me."

"Yeah, Dad," Taylor added.

Taylor had started calling Linc some version of father after her wedding to Liam. It had touched her deeply when he'd walked her down the aisle, and she'd said she liked the idea of having a sister in Ellie and father in Linc, since her blood family sucked. Linc had loved it, and so had Ellie, who'd promptly grabbed Kathleen and introduced Taylor to sister number two. Linc sometimes called them the Froot Loops, the next gen of Lucky Charms, since they were always raising a ruckus in the village like Bets and her friends had. They had the honorary boas to prove it now that Taylor had gotten over her dance phobia.

"I'm sure you had a good reason for turning U2 down," Bets said to turn the tide of the mutinous crowd. "I mean, I still love you."

"Yeah, of course, we love you, Daddy, but WTF," Ellie said emphatically as Taylor and Kathleen and a few others nodded.

Linc reached down for a gift bag and held it out to Bets. "For you."

"Another gift?" She sounded petulant, so she shot him a smile. "Thank you."

Her smile faded into confusion when she looked inside.

He leaned in so he could meet her eyes, which were dancing. "Recognize it?"

"I'm not the one who's lost her marbles enough to turn down U2." She drew out her precious Lucky Charms boa in Irish green. "You repurposing gifts or something? I'm totally confused."

He slapped a hand to his forehead. "You are the smartest, most incredible woman ever— You don't understand why I've just given you a boa?"

Pacing a moment, he turned around and pointed to something on the stage. Turning back to her, he sighed and took the boa from her, draping it around her shoulders before kissing her soundly on the mouth.

Music swelled on the loudspeaker, and she started dancing immediately. She *knew* that music. Her brain scrambled.

"Oh my God!" She sucked in a breath. "*Bon Jovi!*"

Girl screams punctured her eardrum, but she didn't care. She started screaming along with them, watching as a large SUV drove up to the stage on the grass and parked beside it. The doors opened, and she went faint as Jon exited, waving to the crowd before jogging up the stairs to the stage with the rest of the band.

"I need to sit down," she said, reaching for a chair behind her, wondering how her other Lucky Charms must be feeling.

Linc pulled her upright. "No, you don't. Go get 'em, sugar."

The strength of his hands on her shoulders cleared her head. "What do you mean?"

She distantly heard Jon opening the concert over the microphone with a *Hello Caisleán* and then BETS O'HANLON boomed on the loudspeakers, followed by "Come up here for this song. It's for women of vision. Just like you."

Her favorite Bon Jovi song started playing. "It's My Life."

"He just called me up on the stage!" She grabbed Linc's hands, unleashing feathers in the air as they grinned at each other. "You're the best. The absolute best."

He caressed her cheek and turned her to the stage. "Go. It's your moment. You deserve it. When you're having a bad day, I want you to remember how a widowed woman in her so-called golden years living in the wilds of Ireland got this crazy idea and went for it. With everything she's got. You're a rock star now, Bets. This is my way of telling you I see you and to never forget it."

God, that damn burn of tears was back. "Do you have any idea how much I love you right now?"

He tugged on her boa tenderly. "Yeah, same here. We're taking a ton of pictures in case you get grandma brain or something. I've heard some people can get it psychosomatically."

"Hah!"

Then she heard someone call her name again. Jon! Holy—

"That's Jon. Gotta go." She lurched forward and kissed him square on the mouth. "You'll be right here when I get back?"

He didn't make a joke for once. Only kept his loving blue eyes fixed on hers. "Always."

She started walking toward the stage after blowing him a kiss, ensuring her pink PROUD GRANDMA T-shirt wasn't riding up. The whole village was watching her, so she put an exaggerated wiggle into her hips in time with the music as she started up the stairs. Maybe she could talk Jon into letting the Lucky Charms join her. Facing her friends, she flashed them a playful smile and started singing after catching a finger wave from Sorcha before the ghost disappeared at the back of the crowd along with her Bruce.

Her favorite verse was next, and she grabbed the ends of her boa as she joined her favorite rock stars and sang the words at the top of her lungs, dancing for all she was worth as the crowd cheered and whistled her on.

It's my life.

You're damn right it is, she thought, throwing her arms up to the sky as the beat swelled, Kindness Sheep bayed in time to the music, and a double rainbow appeared in the clear blue Irish sky.

Every time you leave a kind review, a rainbow appears in the sky.

Leave a review for Against Ebony Irish Seas and get ready for a splash of color!

Ready to take a trip to Paris? Get The Paris Roommates: Thea, the first book in Ava's new heartfelt series. Read on for a sneak peek...

THE PARIS ROOMMATES

THEA

A Mother's Wish

Food is comfort. Food is home. Food is love.

In the hardest times of my life—and there have been many—I've turned to food for succor. Is it any wonder? With the right ingredients, you can create anything. There's magic in that.

So it shouldn't be a surprise that when my dear husband died ten years ago, I turned my focus to my restaurant.

Only it wasn't enough. I could still feel the empty space my dear Bernard had left all around me. The spot in my kitchen where he'd lean against the wall, his arms folded, that gleam in his cognac-colored eyes as he watched me cook for our guests. The boxy chair where he'd sit and go over the week's paperwork, muttering as he ran his hands through his thick gray hair. His rumpled side of our bed. The corner of my heart that beat for him.

My restaurant, Nanine's, was missing its main ingredient: love.

Was it any wonder I sought something to bring some

spice back into my life? To fill the silence that echoed throughout my space and my heart, because even my magical chandelier had stopped chiming its whimsical notes, bereft as I was.

And so I contacted the Sorbonne and *Le Cordon Bleu* to place an ad: *Restaurant positions open in exchange for room and board. One-year term. Contact Nanine Laurent.*

Of all the applicants, and there were many, I chose six lovely young people from the United States. I picked them because I liked the feel of them and the complexity of their diverse characters. What I didn't know was that I was putting together one of the grandest menus I've ever created.

Because it became apparent to me very quickly that that was what they were: a feast. Each of them a course in the most delicious dinner you could imagine.

Thea: First Course, the *apéritif*, the little bites designed to set the purpose for the entire meal. She was from the middle of Nowheresville, USA, as she called it, and yet she wanted to passionately bake croissant and baguette, as if she had a French soul. In her personal life, she prefers to take small steps, but those she takes capture one's attention.

Dean: Second Course, the *entrée*, the appetizer created to be the entry point into the meal, the best of which feels like a dream when it caresses your taste buds. He has so many ideas swirling in his head that he's still mastering what he truly wants to share on the grand stage of life.

Brooke: Third Course, the *plat*, the main course invented with flourish to leave its signature in one's memory for years to come. She's always wanted to be driving the show, making a grand impression, but that makes her unable to sometimes enjoy the little things that fulfill one's heart.

Sawyer: Fourth Course, the salad, a refined tradition

few today understand or give its due, which cleanses the palate for more inspiration to come. He's a throwback to a bygone era whose complexity lies under the surface, an artist at heart afraid to unleash his own brilliance.

Madison: Fifth Course, the cheese plate, another part of the meal not everyone finds suitable or pleasing, but which can change the digestion of the meal. She embodies so many brilliant strong flavors that she often cultivates a barrier to others, not believing everyone wants her or understands her.

Kyle: Sixth Course, the dessert, which is an indulgence and a delicious treat all its own, especially when it is savored and not rushed. He's the classic golden boy, appearing too perfect at times, all the while hiding the rich layers he holds inside himself.

What I have never told them is that I was the fish course, the only course served either before the main course or becoming one itself depending on the depth of its flavor and ingredients. You see, I was adrift at sea myself, delicate in flavor, unable to hold my own place in the feast of life, the current taking me where it would.

Yet for that one magical year, we all grew more confident in what we brought to one another's lives. We all learned that people could become family even though they are not related by blood.

But then our time together ended. We went back to our respective lives, changed, yes, and while we remained in touch, the inroads we'd made in becoming the perfect feast began to slip away.

I did not realize how much of an echo of my old self I'd become, rather like the shell of a cicada, a ghost of my youth —the young woman who was brave and unstoppable even in the midst of great betrayal and challenge.

Now such betrayal and challenge has darkened my door

yet again, threatening everything I hold dear. For the second time, I have called upon my Courses. This time because they are family.

And so the Courses are coming back to help me, and we will once again create the perfect feast together.

I hope.

Chapter One

Paris was a city full of what could have beens.

What could have been if ten years ago she'd stayed instead of returning to her hometown of Nowheresville, USA? What could have been if she'd gone for it instead of playing it safe?

There was no way of knowing, but this time Thea Rogers was determined to have it all.

Even if she was a sour mixture of exhaustion, worry, and fear sitting awkwardly alone at her favorite old haunt, Café Fitzy, decked out in wrinkled travel clothes and glaringly white tennis shoes with her outdated blue suitcase jammed next to her tiny corner table.

The August sun was beating down on her, keeping her skin damp with sweat, a constant state since she'd landed at CDG airport and taken the maze-like public transportation nightmare jammed with other grumpy, rumpled passengers. After the plane from Des Moines, Iowa, to Chicago and then on to Paris, she'd had to navigate who-knew-how-many Métro transits to make it to the heart of Saint-Germain.

The hour and a half transit had been a nightmare, and dragging her suitcase while needing to pee had been agony, until she'd broken down and stopped at her old favorite café for a coffee so she could use the bathroom. If the waiter ever gave her the time of day and took her order. She didn't see Antoine, the owner, who used to be a friend, and her chest grew tight. She could have used a friendly face right now.

Maybe it was the jet lag, lack of sleep, or the worry coiled up inside of her, but she was so sensitive, she swore everyone was staring at her as she sat there. The chic Parisian women smoking gracefully as they conversed in sultry French had their eyebrows raised her way, as if they were hoping she would leave. She could all hear them thinking that she was taking up space. Totally gauche. A rutabaga in a sea of exotic fruits.

If only they knew she'd once lived in this neighborhood and thought of it as her own. Forget that she'd arrived in a purple jumper with a white shirt boasting a Peter Pan collar. Because she'd thought it was coolest thing she could arrive in Paris wearing.

For that one magical year, she'd stretched her wings, but they'd been made of spun sugar, and she'd let them dissolve after returning home, where she'd slid into a routine that was as regular as it was boring.

Then, two days ago, her best friend and former room-mate from Paris had called her. She'd been at the bakery where she worked, putting freshly proofed croissants in the oven.

Brooke hadn't wasted time with any preliminaries.

"Thea!" she'd cried, her voice charged with emotion. "Nanine was rushed to the hospital after a heart attack."

The bread pan had slipped from her hand, falling to the floor.

"The doctor called me for her. She wants all of us to come if we can and stay at the house together again. You're the first of our Paris roommates I've called. I'm leaving as soon as I can arrange it with my editor."

Her roommates' faces flashed in her mind. Brooke, the go-getter. Dean, the dreamer. Sawyer, the thinker. Madison, the rebel. And Kyle, the golden boy. From the beginning, they'd been the most unlikely of friends, so different from each other in just about every way anyone could be. But their connection was proof friendship could be found in anyone, anywhere.

"I'll take off from the bakery and leave as soon as I can."

But it hadn't been that easy.

Fate had followed through with another kick in the pants—despite her years of service, her boss had refused to grant her any of the vacation she was owed, pushing her to do something she'd never imagined: quitting her job. On the spot.

The very thought of it had her sucking in air and moaning, "Oh God," making the two Parisian women who would never find themselves in a life crisis from the looks of them give her a haughty glare.

She wasn't the kind of woman who made abrupt decisions. She dreamed of owning her own bakery someday, and quitting a successful job ran counter to pursuing that dream.

But this was family. Nanine! The mother of her heart.

After quitting, she'd jumped on the first flight to Paris she could find, draining what little savings she had. Her parents had tried to talk her out of it, of course. *Thea, but you've worked there ever since you got your fancy degree in Paris. The Snyder family has been so good to you. Everyone loves you there. Don't be rash. You're not thinking straight.*

She'd tried to explain. *The bakery hasn't been the same*

since Patty died two years ago and Fred took over. He never lets me have time off. All I do is work.

They hadn't listened, of course. Her people were farmers and had married early. They'd never traveled out of the Midwest—never wanted to, especially not to a faraway place like Paris. They hadn't understood why she'd worked every job she could find to save money to train as a baker instead of living and working on the family farm, and now they didn't understand why her long-time job wasn't enough.

Feeling a little faint from heat and dehydration, she signaled to the waiter as he swept in to refill the wineglasses of the two chic women two tables over. He didn't spare her a glance, and she wanted to slide under the table in shame. She'd bet F. Scott Fitzgerald had never had a problem getting a drink here when he was reportedly writing *The Great Gatsby* in the right corner table beside the mahogany bar.

She supposed she could leave, but that would also be gauche since she'd already used the bathroom. Rule number one of Paris: when you had to use the bathroom, you got a beverage to pay for the privilege.

He was making her wait because he didn't think she belonged, and that wasn't right. This was her old stomping ground, and Antoine's place. Old Thea might have slunk away with her tail between her legs, but the new Thea she wanted to be would stand her ground.

She dug into her carry-on for her old recipe journal. If she kept herself occupied, she might feel less awkward. The sight of the dancing breads made her run her fingers over the front cover. When she'd packed, she'd spontaneously rifled through her hope chest for the perfume Nanine had given her as a gift years before, and she'd found her old spiral-bound journal under it. She'd brought it with her to Paris ten years ago, thinking to fill it with recipes, but instead, she'd filled it with her dreams after realizing it was too corny for *Le Cordon Bleu*.

As she'd lifted it out of the chest, a scrap of paper had fallen out. The glue she'd used to adhere it to the page must have given out. Much like she had on some of her dreams. The fortune cookie slip was from one of her last meals in Paris with her roommates and its message still gave her goosebumps.

The friendships you make will last a lifetime.

She hadn't known then how true that was, but she and her roommates had stayed in touch and seen each other when they could. Of course, certain people were closer with each other, like she and Brooke, and everyone had stayed in touch with Nanine. She was the rock, the anchor, the woman who had given each of them something special.

Returning to Paris and bringing her old journal was like coming full circle. The whole book was chock-full of her dreams of running her own bakery and becoming more confident, along with memories of her roommates and their time together with Nanine. She still remembered the moment she'd tucked it and her perfume away. Her mother had called her *fancy* for wearing perfume to Sunday dinner. She'd cried when she'd gotten back to her apartment, missing Paris and her roommates and Nanine.

Well, that half-life she'd been living was over. She was back and she could resurrect her dreams like she had her old journal. She turned to the first page and read what she'd written on the note card ten years ago.

Recipe for: *A Delicious Life*
Date: August 24

Prep time: One Year

Ingredients: Studying & working hard, Patience, Confidence, Openness, Friendship, Humor

Hard-to-find ingredients: see Confidence above, Mastering the French language, New look

Notes: This is your chance. When you work hard, good things happen. This year is your ticket to better things. Getting a degree at Le Cordon Bleu will help you own your own bakery someday. Listen to your teachers. Try and put yourself out there more. Don't be weird. Maybe learn a few tips on how to dress better.

Every successful recipe starts with finding the best ingredients and following the directions.

She stared at the last part. She *hadn't* followed all the directions once she'd gotten home. She'd settled back into her old life, one where every day tasted like oatmeal. Sure, she'd gotten a great job as a baker at a renowned family-owned bakery. Sure, she'd kept her friendships with Nanine and her roommates alive. But she hadn't kept up the whole *put yourself out there* part. She still didn't fit in where she'd been born and raised, and she'd gone back to hiding in plain sight.

The truth was, the prospect of turning thirty in October had made her take out a magnifying glass to examine the state of her life. As Nanine liked to say, milestones had a way of making one examine one's journey so far. She turned to the first entry she'd written on the plane—the one she couldn't even bring herself to put in the first person because that would make it too real.

> **Recipe for: *PATHETIC***
> **Date: NOW**
> **Notes: Thea Rogers works like a dog.**
> **She rarely dates.**
> **If she has a day off, she's either at her parents' farm helping out or curled up alone on her couch bingeing shows about other people having lives.**
> **Nothing in her life is exceptional except for being a baker.**
> **Life is passing Thea Rogers by.**
> **And if she continues on this track, she's going to end up alone, with nothing but bread and croissants to keep her company, which will probably make her fat.**
> **Conclusion: Thea Rogers is sick of herself and her life.**
> **Cure: Thea Rogers needs a life makeover. Bad.**

She wanted to cover the words with her hands to make them less overwhelming, but maybe she needed the reminder. Her boring but reliable life was gone. It felt freeing but terrifying, and now that she was here in Paris, she had no idea what she was going to do with herself beyond offering some comfort to Nanine. Nausea steamrolled her, so she sucked in several slow breaths of Parisian air. The faint scent of freshly baked bread helped her straighten her spine.

Being back here with no return ticket was a curveball, no doubt. But it could also be a gift—a chance to reinvent herself and her life. In Paris, where everything had changed for her once before. It could happen again.

She grabbed a pen as a phrase came to mind and wrote it on the next blank page in her journal.

Recipe for: *Living Life to the Fullest*

That would be her new recipe, she decided, especially since Nanine's heart attack had shown her just how short life could be. She was going to use her time here to become the person she really wanted to be, the one she'd originally written about. Not the boring play-it-safe nice girl from Nowheresville she'd returned to being.

Because here was a truth that both terrified and thrilled her: she planned on staying. She had a terrific résumé, didn't she? And she'd brought her essential tools of the trade so she could give a potential employer a demo of her abilities: her sourdough starter named Doughreen (God, she was such a geek), her broken-in pastry cloth, and her well-washed pink apron with a croissant and heart on its lapel.

Once Nanine was back on her feet, Thea would find a job. Yep, absolutely, she thought, nodding to a pigeon who stopped in front of her, hoping for food. He looked a little starved like she was, so she nudged a bread crumb on the ground his way. Bread has a way of making you feel better, she wanted to tell him.

Thea heard her phone trill in her purse, prompting the pigeon to fly off. She cringed as the two Parisian women glared at her for her *faux pas*. She jumped up immediately, almost knocking the table over, and darted across the pedestrian street to take the call. Digging through her remaining snacks in her purse, she pulled out her phone. Brooke!

"Hi there! I'm at Café Fitzy's trying to get a coffee. Where are you?"

"Hey, sweetie! I'm running a little late. I had an interview with one of the hottest new fashion designers in Paris when I arrived. I set it up at the last minute because I got here before everyone else and couldn't bear the thought of sitting alone in Nanine's. I'm so glad you stopped at Fitzy's."

Thea caught a dagger-eyed look from a waiter when he came out and gestured pointedly to her luggage. "I had to pee, but I might never get a coffee. I reek of tourist."

"Typical, but you can turn that around. Look the waiter in the eye and say, 'Excuse me, sir. Is Antoine here today?'"

Then Brooke repeated it in perfect French. Thea couldn't imagine pulling that off. Her French sounded like a dying tractor engine coated in rust. "Maybe I should just leave money for a coffee on the table."

"You just arrived in Paris for the first time in eight years. Follow my directions! You'll get your coffee."

Her journal's helpful hint about following directions came to mind, and for the first time since before she'd heard the news about Nanine, she felt her mouth twitch. Brooke loved to boss people around, and Thea sometimes liked it. It felt like her friend was the rudder in her boat. She'd need Brooke's help now more than ever to become the Thea she wanted to be.

"Okay, Brooke. I'll try."

"And pump Antoine for information about Nanine. The doctor said she refuses to talk to anyone until we're all here and together. I'm scared, Thea."

Suddenly she could use that comforting bread crumb on the ground herself. "We all are."

"Yeah." Silence hung over the line for a moment before she pressed, "How are you *really*? You must be going out of your mind about quitting your job."

Her stomach quivered, but she decided to give a spunky comeback. Spunky comebacks were for girls trying to turn their lives around, weren't they? "This is the best thing that could have happened to me. Not that I wanted Nanine to ever—"

"Oh, Thea, I know that. But are you seriously telling me you haven't cried? I know you. Not once?"

She worried her lip. "Well, I did run through a pack of tissues on the plane, but then I started watching all my feel-good Paris movies. Worked like a charm." Mostly.

"How many movies are we talking?" Brooke asked suspiciously.

"I started with *French Kiss*, then went on to *Julie & Julia* before ending with the movie that kicked off my love for everything France."

"*Sabrina*." Brooke sighed heavily. "Oh, Thea. I don't want you to worry, okay? You won't have rent, staying at Nanine's. What did you do about your apartment?"

Oh, that. Her nausea rolled back like a freight train. "I told Mrs. Randall everything. She's too nice to hold me to my lease. I only have to pay rent until she finds a new tenant. I worked like a dog to pack up my personal belongings before I left. I didn't have much since I was never home. My parents agreed to store my stuff at the farm." That had gone over like a lead balloon, along with them agreeing to keep her car until she could arrange to sell it.

She'd even dropped some boxes off at the Salvation Army on her way to the airport, things she never wanted to wear again, things her mother had given her. Black old lady shoes in her giant size of eleven and ugly print dresses that made her like look she could star in *Little House on the Prairie*. Her mother had always had a fondness for the show and hoped Thea could turn out like Half-Pint. Her school photos wearing floral print flannel dresses with her hair in braids would haunt her for the rest of her life.

"Out with the old and in with the new!" Brooke's enthusiasm was a soothing balm. "Thea, I'll cover anything you need. That asshole you worked for didn't appreciate you, and I'm glad you quit. I'm so proud of you."

She couldn't blame jet lag for her tears this time. It was those words—she'd rarely heard them from her parents. "You're the best. Did you know that?"

"Tell that to my ex. Ugh. Did I tell you he's dating this hot new Brazilian model named Plumonia? My editor asked if I was going to be able to still report on what she wears during fashion week."

Brooke was a style editor for *TRENDS*, which meant it really would be part of her job. Sighing, she added, "I had to bite my tongue so I wouldn't ask, but seriously, what kind of name is Plumonia?"

"Sounds like pneumonia to me."

"She's nineteen, by the way. *Nineteen!*"

Which meant their age difference was eighteen years. Now it was Thea's turn to cheerlead. "I never liked Adam. You're better off without him."

"That's what I've told myself every day for the past four months since I changed my ringtone to Beyoncé's 'Best Thing I Never Had' to help me remember. Hey! You need a new ringtone."

She'd ignore the fact that she wouldn't be using her U.S. phone in Paris because the fees were too expensive. Going back to using an international calling card had its advantages. One of them being that she wouldn't have to call her parents for a while. When she'd first come to Paris, they'd gone six to eight weeks at a time without talking, and since they still didn't have a computer, email was out of the question. "I'll think about it."

"All right, Thea," her friend said. "I'll see you in forty. Don't get into trouble. You're not in Kansas anymore, Dorothy."

She groaned. "*Dorothea* is my name, and jokes about me being from Kansas aren't funny. Iowa is an entirely different state."

Brooke's snort had her smiling again. "Sorry, you know I love you, but we New Yorkers don't care about the middle states. I'll see you soon. The others will start rolling in shortly. Dean could beat me, in fact, but that depends on traffic. The Second is a nightmare. I've never seen so many tourists around the Louvre in August."

"Wait!" Thea cried out as a new thought struck her. "You didn't tell everyone else about me quitting, did you? Nanine should be our focus right now."

"My car is here, sweetie. Gotta go."

The call ended. Thea worried her lip. She didn't want her other roommates to know about her issues just yet. They'd always considered her a little sister, the nice small-town girl who needed looking after. Okay, some of that had been true when she'd arrived fresh-faced with only two years of high school French to carry her along.

She'd been so unprepared then, and maybe she wasn't much better off now. But she didn't want her roommates' pity, and she sure as heck didn't want anyone to think her problems were on par with Nanine's heart attack.

Thea dropped her phone back into her purse, her spirits

better after talking to Brooke. Her friend had more confidence in her little finger than Thea had in her entire body. Such confidence could be catching. That was an ingredient she desperately needed for herself.

She headed back to her table, already looking forward to her café. Brooke was right. She had to have it. A coffee in Paris was not a regular event. Sawyer used to say a single cup was filled with existential meaning, decadent pleasure, and toe-curling comfort. But that was Sawyer for you, always thinking deeper than the rest of them.

As she watched for her waiter to reappear, she opened her recipe book to the photo of her and her roommates at Christmastime ten years ago. They were all drinking champagne at Café Fitzy's after opening presents. Brooke's short bob still looked stylish even though she'd been blond back then. Dean was making a funny face for the camera. Sawyer had on his very studious-looking glasses and was trying not to laugh. Madison wasn't smiling, but her golden eyes were bright with happiness. And Kyle was as beautiful as ever, being the golden boy he was, and he had his arm wrapped around Thea. Then there was Nanine, sitting in the middle of the group, her elegant long gray hair trailing down her shoulders.

Thea's heart warmed. That was still the best Christmas she'd ever had. She touched the photo. Soon she was going to be back with them all.

Coming back here was one of the best decisions of your life, Thea Rogers.

Then Antoine stepped outside and her chest welled with nostalgia. He was here! He held a pack of cigarettes in his weathered hand and walked across the cobbled pedestrian street to where she'd just been standing, lighting one and taking a deep drag. His oblong face had a pronounced chin and an insouciant straight nose that worked with his usual tourist-directed scowl. The sun-kissed lines around his dark eyes were a stark marker of his joys and sorrows while his hair was almost pure white now, making him even more distinguished. She'd known him when it was silver, and while he had a few more age lines, he was very much the same.

"Antoine!" She broke into a smile and waved like an American before she caught her *faux pas*. The French did not wave.

He took another drag on his cigarette and stared at her with narrowed eyes. Then he blinked, as if coming out of a dream, and darted over after letting an unsteady cyclist ride by. "First Course!" he called enthusiastically in French, leaning over and kissing both her cheeks in greeting as he stubbed out the cigarette in the ashtray on the small table.

She winced. "Yes, it's me, First Course," she answered in French and wanted to crawl into a hole at how she sounded. "Thea."

"Thea! You're here to help our lovely Nanine, yes?" he asked, again in French, as his face grew shadowed. "Everyone in the neighborhood has been so worried."

"Yes, I hope to." She switched to English. "You know how she is. My other former roommates are arriving soon as well."

"All six courses back in Paris," Antoine said, his dark eyes showing a telltale wetness before pointing to the photo she had out. "You are cataloguing memories, I see. I remember the night. Nanine had given you each a special gift of fragrance, I believe. You could smell the love between all of you in the air."

Thea fought back her own tears. "It was a beautiful

night. Antoine, the news about Nanine was such a shock. She's always been so healthy."

"Maybe her heart gave so much, it finally couldn't give any more," Antoine muttered. "Always a big heart for everyone, Nanine. Especially lately."

She made a conversational sound before asking, "What happened lately, Antoine?"

He shook his head. "I would not feel right, talking about Nanine's business. She is better telling you."

If there was one thing about the French Thea appreciated, it was that they valued others' privacy. And yet Brooke would want her to push. "We are all friends, are we not?" she asked badly in French, hoping to be more persuasive. "It would help us—"

"*Oui*, but you must be thirsty, Thea." The change to English as much as the shift in subject was as good as a period at the end of a sentence. "*Café crème*? Croissant?"

She nodded vigorously. Antoine called out in rapid French to the waiter who had stopped his serving and was openly listening to their conversation. He darted inside after Antoine sent him off with a flick of his hand.

Antoine gave a Gallic shrug. "He thought you were a tourist. Welcome home, First Course. Tell Nanine her first café back at Fitzy's will be on me."

Clearly she wasn't cut out to be Sherlock. She hoped Brooke wouldn't be upset. "I will, Antoine, and thank you."

His smile was a little watery as he went inside. She dashed at her own tears and told herself to hold it together. The waiter finally arrived with her coffee and croissant with a brief smile. Progress, Thea thought, as she ripped open two brown sugars and poured them into her café, stirring slowly to maintain the light-as-air foam on top. She closed her eyes and took a sip. The sweet blend of roasted coffee and rich milk saturated her senses, and for a moment, there was peace.

Everything seemed possible. Even her own transformation.

Not that she expected her renewed recipe for a delicious life to be a cakewalk. More like making bread. She would need new ingredients to come together for herself, ones she'd have to mix and incorporate until she found the perfect dough. Then she'd have to let it all sit, rise, and take shape. Fire had a way of sealing everything together, and there *was* fire inside her—her drive, her passion. When she got the right recipe, she knew she'd come out a masterpiece.

A masterpiece, huh? The Paris air is making you delusional, Thea Rogers.

No one could call her a masterpiece right now. She fingered the baggy tan T-shirt over her wrinkled black cotton drawstring pants and eyed her giant tennis shoes. Should she change before seeing Brooke? Her friend would be dripping style like always, all the way down to her fashionable heels. Thea tucked her feet together under the table in shame. Wearing a size eleven was the bane of her existence, especially in Paris where the steps on most stairs ran more to a size seven shoe.

She glanced in the café's glass windows and caught her reflection. Her brown hair was overdue for a cut and hung in a shaggy mess down her back. Because when did she have time for a haircut? Usually she put it in a ponytail.

Back home, she looked like everyone else. The one-length plain Jane hairstyle wasn't supposed to stand out. Neither were her boring, neutral clothes.

Her mother said she was a late bloomer. That was stopping now.

She signaled to the waiter for her bill when he

appeared. As she was opening her purse for her money, her journal fell to the ground and another slip of paper danced in the air before falling to the ground. She bent down to pick it up and read the phrase she'd cut out of one of Brooke's old fashion magazines.

Your dreams are just around the corner.

Emotion rolled through her, and her eyes tracked to the end of the pedestrian street as she tucked the paper back into her journal. Her eyes latched onto a man who came around the corner wearing a navy pinstriped suit.

Her heart immediately started pounding.

Suddenly all she could feel was a rumbling throughout her entire body, as if a Métro train were passing underground. She grabbed the table's edge to steady herself as she watched him come closer.

His hair was thick, curly, and ink black. He had golden skin, which she fantasized came from sunbathing on his yacht in Saint-Tropez. Black designer sunglasses hid his eyes, but his bone structure would rival that of a Greek god.

When he flashed a dashing smile and called out a greeting to her waiter, she pressed her hand to her chest, where her pulse was galloping. He was as a local, and an affable one at that.

As he turned the next corner and disappeared from sight, she slumped in her chair. She was out of breath and trembling. She couldn't even lift her coffee cup right now. *My, oh, my...*

Mr. Pinstripes was like no other man she'd ever seen. He certainly bore no resemblance to any of the Joe Schmoes she'd dated back in Nowheresville. She tried to catch her breath as she told herself she was being stupid. She didn't have a shot with a man like him.

She gulped more oxygen, but her nerves were wired

from Mr. Pinstripes. Perhaps his pheromones had some insane effect on the opposite sex. Glancing around, she eyed other women at the café. None of *them* seemed to have noticed him. If she hadn't known any better, she would have sworn she was dreaming. Then she thought back to the message that had slipped out of her journal. It had to be a coincidence, right?

She finished her café and allowed her body to settle down. Then she checked her phone again. Nothing more from Brooke, but Dean had texted her. She couldn't wait to see him. He was like a Ferris wheel, always fun but forever turning in a circle, barely stopping.

She clicked on his text. *Hey sweetie! Heading straight to Nanine's. Probably fifteen minutes out. Can't wait to see you.*

Heartened, she decided to head over to Nanine's herself. The walk would do her pheromone-crazed body good, right? She would be the first one to welcome Dean, and Brooke would arrive soon as well. She would have loved to have had someone waiting for her. Plus, she could take care of Doughreen. Her starter needed to go into the cooler, stat.

And maybe she'd run into Mr. Pinstripes again. There was no harm in looking, was there?

When the waiter finally appeared, he said, "Antoine says it's on the house."

Her eyes grew wet again. "Tell him thank you," she said as she didn't see the older man hovering in the doorway.

He gave a little incline of his jaunty chin as she eased out of her chair and grabbed the handle of her suitcase, taking off down the sidewalk as a quartet of tourists on rented bicycles angled by.

The way to Nanine's was familiar, but her eyes took in

the new bar around the corner called Speakeasy with its crisp navy awning. She'd bet Mr. Pinstripes frequented the joint, and her heart rate spiked again at the thought.

Her luggage wheel caught on the sidewalk as her attention wavered before she dragged it along. La Maison de l'Entrecôte emitted the familiar scent of grilled steak, green pepper from its succulent sauce, and frites in the air as she passed. A new tea salon called Old Hong Kong had her wanting to cross its threshold simply because of the name. Besides loving tea, she'd never been to Hong Kong but had always been curious about it. Heck, she'd never been to anywhere but France and Canada.

More bucket list items, Thea.

Next door, The Little Black Dress Shop ironically displayed a slinky one-shoulder dress in *blue*. She stopped short. Holy moly, it was gorgeous. Something she'd wear on a date with a man like Mr. Pinstripes in her fantasy world.

She rolled her eyes at herself and kept going. Walking on Paris' golden streets was like wrapping herself up in bright, shiny wrapping paper tied up with a big red bow. Her excitement spiked as she neared Nanine's restaurant and her old home. Picking up her pace, she turned the next corner and stopped cold. *"Oh, my gosh!"*

The burgundy awning was gone, the one that had sported the simple but somehow comforting sign reading *Nanine's*. The menu placard on the wall by the double doors was missing, and the curtains were gone. The windows looked grim and dusty, as if the building had been abandoned for years.

Her stomach started to burn. What had happened? Nanine hadn't mentioned any changes when Thea had spoken to her last month.

She rushed across the street to look inside.

The restaurant was gutted, the tables gone, the walls torn open. And was that exposed wire hanging out? Had there been a fire? Her hand flew to her mouth.

Was this why Nanine had had a heart attack?

She stood breathing harshly. Brooke and Dean were going to freak when they saw this. Everyone was. "Okay," she assured herself. "We'll figure it out."

Unsteady, Thea headed to the alley. She had to get inside. Reaching the back of the restaurant, she tucked her luggage out of sight. Nanine had always kept a spare key taped below an old loose brick under the back steps. Thea found it and tore the tape back, grasping the brass key. She prayed Nanine had fixed the lock. The key was notorious for being difficult, something the older woman had intentionally not fixed as she found it a satisfying battle of wills on occasion—something to get the blood pumping.

She faced the old lock. *Here we go.* She inserted the key. It stuck like it always had. "Oh, come on," she pleaded softly. She pressed the key harder and heard the metal scrape. Then it finally turned.

As she walked inside, her knees went weak with relief. The kitchen was exactly as it had been—except covered in dust, she quickly realized as she scanned the stainless steel prep counters and let her eyes wander over to the industrial range and ovens.

Nanine's famous chandelier gave a faint jangle of its crystal, almost like a weak pulse. Thea's gaze traveled across the room to where it hung in the small hallway leading to the dining room. Nanine had kept the small chandelier in the kitchen because the former owner had said it had a personality all its own, like many unexplainable things in Paris. The crystals served as a weathervane of sorts for the restaurant's atmosphere.

She coughed as dust reached her nose, and when she inhaled, she could have sworn she smelled roast chicken. Nanine was known for her roasted chicken laced with butter and herbs de Provence. Just like that, her mind flashed back to sitting at the large wooden farm table in the kitchen with her roommates, all of them laughing and drinking wine while stealing bites of chicken and roasted potatoes as Nanine smiled from ear to ear at the head of the table.

The kitchen was eerily quiet except for the sound of the antique Horloge on the wall. Nanine had hung it there because it had a second hand that new staff could watch for time-sensitive sauces like béarnaise or hollandaise.

She knew she was putting off going to the front of the restaurant. But she couldn't make her feet move in that direction. Dean and Brooke would both be arriving soon, she assured herself, and they would all face that disaster together. She could distract herself by taking care of Doughreen. She silenced any thoughts about her being a coward as she went back for her luggage and dragged it back to Nanine's walk-in cooler.

"Doughreen, you're going to be so happy here," she told her starter after unzipping her suitcase on the floor. Her airtight plastic container was perspiring in the Ziploc bag, but Thea gave a moment of thanks that Doughreen hadn't exploded like her bottle of shampoo.

She set it aside with a grimace and then shot to her feet when she heard staccato-like footsteps in the kitchen. Dean! The crystals in Nanine's famous chandelier gave a sudden clang as she raced toward the back door.

Only to be faced with three men in police uniforms scowling at her with their feet braced, as if ready to take

412

down a dangerous intruder. It took her a second to realize who the intruder was.

Her.

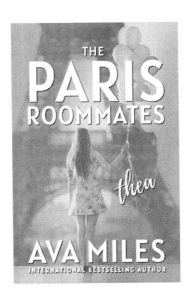

Fall in love and follow your dreams in this humorous and heartfelt new novel about the power of friendship and the bonds of your chosen family.

"Ava Miles has the gift of magic as she weaves her stories of family and community into every book she writes."

DREAM WEAVER REVIEW

Get The Paris Roommates: Thea!

Available wherever books are sold.

ABOUT THE AUTHOR

Millions of readers have discovered International Bestselling Author Ava Miles and her powerful fiction and non-fiction books about love, happiness, and transformation. Her novels have received praise and accolades from *USA Today, Publisher's Weekly,* and *Women's World Magazine* in addition to being chosen as Best Books of the Year and Top Editor's picks. Translated into multiple languages,

Ava's strongest praise comes directly from her readers, who call her books and characters unforgettable.

Ava is a former chef, worked as a long-time conflict expert rebuilding warzones to foster peaceful and prosperous communities, and has helped people live their best life as a life coach, energy healer, and self-help expert. She is never happier than when she's formulating skin care and wellness products, gardening, or creating a new work of art. Hanging with her friends and loved ones is pretty great too.

After years of residing in the States, she decided to follow her dream of living in Europe. She recently finished a magical stint in Ireland where she was inspired to write her acclaimed Unexpected Prince Charming series. Now, she's splitting her time between Paris and Provence, learning to speak French, immersing herself in cooking *à la provençal*, and planning more page-turning novels for readers to binge.

Visit Ava on social media:

facebook.com/AuthorAvaMiles

twitter.com/authoravamiles

instagram.com/avamiles

bookbub.com/authors/ava-miles

pinterest.com/authoravamiles

DON'T FORGET...
SIGN UP FOR AVA'S NEWSLETTER.

More great books? Check.
Fun facts? Check.
Recipes? Check.
General frivolity? DOUBLE CHECK.

https://avamiles.com/newsletter/